The Original Daughter

The Original Daughter

JEMIMAH WEI

WEIDENFELD & NICOLSON

First published in the United States in 2025 by Penguin Random House
First published in Great Britain in 2025 by Weidenfeld & Nicolson,
an imprint of The Orion Publishing Group Ltd
Carmelite House, 50 Victoria Embankment
London EC4Y 0DZ

An Hachette UK Company

The authorised representative in the EEA is Hachette Ireland
8 Castlecourt Centre, Dublin 15, D15 XTP3, Ireland
(email: info@hbgi.ie)

1 3 5 7 9 10 8 6 4 2

A CIP catalogue record for this book
is available from the British Library.

ISBN (Hardback) 978 1 3996 2557 9
ISBN (Export Trade Paperback) 978 1 3996 2558 6
ISBN (Ebook) 978 1 3996 2560 9
ISBN (Audio) 978 1 3996 2561 6

Printed and bound in Great Britain by Clays Ltd, Elcograf S.p.A.

www.weidenfeldandnicolson.co.uk
www.orionbooks.co.uk

For my very first readers,
Tash, Xiao Qi, & Shane,
who believed before the first word was even written,
& my family,
for whom my whole heart beats.

May 2015

Singapore

1

Arin was somewhere in Germany when my mother got sick again. She'd been sick before, but never like this, and I knew it was only a matter of time before she would change her mind and start asking for Arin. The prospect filled me with dread. My sister and I hadn't spoken for years, not since she first got famous, not even when my mother was diagnosed with aggressive breast cancer a couple of years ago. Back then, too, I'd been afraid that if things got really bad, my mother would want Arin there. But we'd had her breasts lopped off, one after the other, and it appeared to have stopped the cancer's spread. The subject of Arin never came up.

Our relationship hadn't been good for a long time, and in recent years my mother's irreverence had dampened into a more respectable muteness. But after she recovered, my mother immediately became irritating again. She'd lost so much weight from the chemotherapy, it didn't seem to matter that she had no breasts. She sheared off her fluffy black hair, wore nothing but singlets and shorts, and gleefully told everyone passing by the photocopy shop that between this and menopause, she was finally relieved of the trappings of being a woman. The word she used, one I caught her selecting carefully from the Oxford English Dictionary by our sole electric night-light, was "liberation."

Liberation? When had she ever not acted exactly as she pleased? I felt that she was baiting me; I refused to respond. Then, a few days ago, I woke to find my mother still in bed beside me, one arm thrown over her face.

"Ma," I said. "It's eight."

She was usually out of the house by six, either at the wet market or doing exercises at Bedok Reservoir Park with her tai chi group before opening the photocopy shop. To her, sleeping in was something only rich people did, a sign of weak character.

My mother peeked at me from under her arm and didn't say a word. Rare for her to forgo a chance to tease. I put my face to her wrist, her neck, sniffing. When I clambered over her body and saw the milky splatter of vomit on the floor, beside the massive potted sansevieria my mother insisted on keeping by our bedside as an air filter, she hid her face again.

"Get dressed," I said after a long moment. "I'm calling Dana."

Dana was her oncologist, one my mother had scammed into friendship. When they first met, she told Dana she'd been involved with a church deacon years ago who abandoned her when she became pregnant with me, and sweet Dana, in spite of everything one might assume about doctors and intelligence, truly believed God had called her to be the attending physician the day I brought my mother in. All lies. My mother wasn't religious, and my father was a taxi driver. But when I confronted her, she waved me off with a laugh and stayed in touch with Dana, forwarding her prayers and Bible verses on WhatsApp.

It worked. Dana loved my mother. She dropped by the photocopy shop frequently to bring her food, or just to chat, and even ordered me to bypass the hospital's call center and ring her directly if we needed anything. When the neighborhood aunties found out, they teased us relentlessly—of course Su Yang would charm the famously stuffy hospital staff, of course she would be the person to pull the wool over their eyes. Whoever heard of a doctor giving out her personal number, it was absurd, it wasn't done. But in all their ribbing there was a sense of glee, as if we had won something. Not to me. I found my mother's relationship with Dana deceitful; I swore we would never call on this favor.

Yet here we were.

It turned out to be leptomeningeal disease. Neither my mother nor I had heard the term before, but Dana was crying as she delivered the news. She knew we couldn't afford surgery; we were still paying off debt from the first one. Because of her preexisting health conditions, we didn't qualify for the experimental drug trials. Because my mother belonged to the generation too poor, and therefore too proud, for insurance, there were no secret reserves of cash that could be accessible to us via a sleight of hand in the medical paperwork. It was a terminal diagnosis. Terminal: that I understood. I wanted to know how long she had.

"Anywhere from three to six months with treatment."

"And without?"

"Four to six weeks."

I was stunned. Beside me, my mother let out a little sigh. "No treatment. I don't want to do that again."

The diagnosis invigorated her. She stood and stretched, then hopped around Dana's office, peering at confidential folders, fingering the stethoscope and green swimming goggles hanging by the door; making Dana laugh, teasing her for crying. But her voice was too bright, her eyes tired. As soon as we got home, she showered and changed into a fresh set of clothes. We stared each other down in our bedroom.

"Where are you going?"

"To work."

"They can manage without you, you should rest."

She didn't even stop. "Rest isn't going to cure me. You want me to lie at home like a useless person for the next six weeks?"

I could see her rib cage through the singlet arm holes. She'd gotten so skinny, I hadn't even realized. She watched my face twist and said quickly: "If you want to help, Genevieve, call your sister."

"She's not my sister."

"I want to see you and Arin together one last time." I kept quiet, and she pushed further. "I never ask you for anything." It was another one of her untruths; she was full of requests, both vocal and implied. "Promise me."

"No."

"Then you might as well kill me yourself."

She left.

Later that night, when she crawled into bed beside me, I didn't turn. I pretended I was asleep. But she pasted her skinny body to my back and began speaking. She repeated that she had never asked anything of me, not even when I left her back in 2010 and moved to Christchurch, New Zealand, maintaining radio silence for six months, refusing to speak to her, refusing to explain how she had offended me to warrant that kind of severance, breaking her heart, shaving years off her life from worry, forcing her to communicate only through Arin, and then when I finally returned, how I exiled Arin, refusing to bend in the last four years, despite being brought up to understand that family was the key, the heart, the cornerstone of life; that, too, broke her heart, how could I be so callous, so cruel, perhaps these rash decisions could be made as a child, but wasn't I already twenty-seven, basically thirty, wasn't it time to grow up, yes, perhaps our childhood wasn't ideal, but whose is; anyway, wasn't it kind of silly to hold on to old grudges, and more importantly, she was dying, couldn't I put aside my own selfish desires for six short weeks, might not even be six, might be four, four weeks minus one day we had just wasted on yet another petty argument, come on, how hard could it be, didn't I love her, didn't I care?

By the end of that tirade, the sun was rising. I was crying too. Wasn't she the one who insisted we would only hold Arin back, wasn't she the one who said it was better to let her go? She was reverting to her old habits of lying in order to get what she wanted, increasingly convinced by the passionate tenor of her own voice till she truly believed the stories she'd constructed. And me— kidnapped by her emotions, unable to protest. A child again.

Even in the dark she could feel me nodding; her agitation subsided.

"You'll call her?"

"Yes."

But I wasn't a good daughter and no longer claimed to be one. There was considerable freedom to be had in knowing and accepting that I was a disappointment to my mother. The minute she let me go I put her plea out of my mind. I'd spent most of my adult life trying to divorce myself from Arin and wasn't about to stop now.

The next day, as if conjured by my mother's desires, Arin appeared on the cover of *Life*! I ignored the headlines and scrutinized the picture. Once upon a time we were so inseparable, people would often get us confused. If the neighborhood aunties had to differentiate us, they'd say, Su's girls: the big one, the small one, even though I was only a year older than Arin. We looked so alike; people wouldn't believe Arin was adopted. Now, no. The picture showed Arin on a red carpet somewhere, looking straight into the camera. Her hair was coiled and resting at the top of her head like a snake, her eyebrows arched and sly, her gaze simultaneously placid and amused.

I recognized that expression, we'd practiced it together; I felt my own lips curling in response and made myself stop. I recognized, also, the dress she was wearing, a backless silvery contraption from a small Singaporean designer who had gone viral on Instagram after Arin was spotted using one of her pencil cases as a clutch. Everyone knew the story—Arin had reached out to the designer, postvirality, offering her talent a platform, connecting her to couture seamstresses in Jakarta, Indonesia. Like a modern fairy tale, the designer went from hand-sewing small leather goods to creating modern gowns, pantsuits, hairpieces; now, whenever she announced a new collection, women all over the country set alarms on their phones before bed despite their lives occasioning no gowns. But perhaps that was the true marker of her success: one doesn't buy an investment piece without also buying into a grander flight of fancy. *Dreams really do come true*, the designer had been profiled saying, *all you need is that one person who believes in you . . .*

Arin rarely gave interviews and didn't participate in the media circus around the designer, happy simply to remain the catalyst for her success, but I noticed that from then on she only wore pieces from independent Asian designers. When she turned down an offer to be dressed by Valentino, a small wave of think pieces sprouted online, opining how this signaled a turning of the tides, how these young, beautiful actresses from all corners of Southeast Asia no longer felt the need to follow the traditional Hollywood playbook— they had their own ways of doing things, how exciting, how new. The articles flooded the internet for a month before public interest moved on, but the glow of admiration endured.

The narrative was almost flawless. I was impressed. Arin had never been creative; someone in her team must have orchestrated it. But in her cool, amused gaze, I could feel the undercurrent of delight, smirking at the layers of performance she'd successfully pulled off. I folded the newspapers away.

Another day passed, then another. My mother pressed me about Arin, and I told her I'd been trying, with no luck. Arin was too famous now, it was impossible to reach her; if she didn't believe me she was free to try contacting her herself. My mother got distracted, she returned to work, she asked about Arin again. Each time she asked it was easier to fob her off with an excuse. Because I'd already given my promise, she held on to the childlike trust that it would all work out, that I'd find a way to make it happen. I don't know where her faith in me came from. It made me sick with guilt.

My mother's headaches returned, worse than before. She became even more unmoored, missing days at the photocopy shop and weeping when she realized. At her behest, I went down over the weekend and spoke to the lady boss.

It was located in a string of shops crammed in the void deck under a block of HDB flats five minutes from home, sandwiched between a value dollar store perpetually advertising a closing sale, and a barber offering ten-dollar haircuts. The void deck aunties all recognized me. As I approached, the photocopy auntie nodded and called out in Mandarin: "Su's girl. So big now."

I grimaced. "Ma asked me to apologize in person. She's not well—"

"Yes, that's obvious." The photocopy shop was full of the baby sansevieria plants my mother propagated and dispensed throughout the neighborhood, and the photocopy auntie touched a stubby, swordlike leaf as she spoke. "Tell her to take as much time as she needs."

"Ah—Auntie, can I ask for a favor? Can you let my mother come in as and when she's able? I'll return you the money, you wouldn't have to pay her."

I'd been working up to that offer all week. I wasn't sure how much exactly my mother was paid at the shop or whether I could actually afford to give the money back. I'd only just started a job marking compositions for a private tuition center, it was the kind of job that paid by the hour, a student job. The photocopy auntie waved me off. "It's been going on for a while, don't worry about it."

"A while?"

She looked surprised that I didn't know. "She misses days here and there, it's fine."

We weren't speaking loudly, but the entire cluster of void deck aunties were listening in. The value dollar auntie rang up a customer, who lingered until it became apparent the conversation wouldn't continue while she was there, then said: "Your sister hasn't been in touch?"

"No, she's on tour."

Disapproval rippled across their faces. None of the void deck aunties had seen her movies, which were too Western and modern, not their kind of thing. As a result, they were caught in between the glamour of stardom, which they did not understand and therefore were in reluctant awe of, and tradition, which they did.

In the end, tradition won out. "You should tell her to come home," the photocopy auntie said. "It's not good for Arin to forget her family when she gets a bit of success. She'll regret it later."

The rest of the aunties began murmuring in agreement. I left.

My mother was gone when I let myself back into the apartment, without even leaving a note. I wasn't worried. The parameters of her life only stretched an hour's walk either way. The older she got, the more resistant to public transportation or cars. I sat at the dining table and tried to catch up on correcting compositions.

But evening came and went with no sign of her. I started to worry. I sent her a WhatsApp, I tried to call her—nothing. When she finally walked in, it was close to 10:00 p.m. I was slumped in a corner on the floor, surrounded by unmarked papers, trying to figure out how to file a missing person's report on my phone. She looked surprised. Her phone had run out of battery, she hadn't thought to charge it. I lost my temper; how could she be so irresponsible, so unaccountable, but she found it funny.

"Life can't be lived on a leash, Gen," she said mildly. It was something I'd said to her, when I first left home at twenty-three. I ignored this, I wanted to know where she'd been.

"I went for dinner with your father." She looked at me. "You didn't tell him I was sick?"

"You two don't even talk."

"Yes, dying changes things."

She went into the kitchen, pulling her singlet off as she went, shedding her shorts, too, until she was standing only in her boxers, getting herself a glass of water. "Ma," I said, glancing at the shirtless uncle smoking out of the apartment window across from us, "the window."

She turned to face me, her chest ribbed and bare. When I averted my gaze, she laughed loudly. "Did you reach your sister?"

"Stop asking, I already told you I've tried. Anyway, she's not here, I am."

"Call her again."

"If you want to see her so badly, call her yourself."

She just smiled. "Of course I could."

Was this a game to her? Irritation surged, and I returned to my papers, ignoring her. One of her remaining six weeks had passed, but I could not imagine how my mother might go from the skinny, sarcastic person before me, still present enough to tease and make demands, to a woman on her deathbed. I had begun to doubt the doctor's diagnosis. People made mistakes; in fact, if anyone was to twist out from the grip of certain death, it would be my mother. She had no respect for rules. The thought that a medical diagnosis might be the thing to finally pin her down suddenly seemed laughable.

Dana agreed to meet me privately during her lunch break, but the warmth she exuded in my mother's presence dissipated as I explained my theory.

"For the patient to engage in magical thinking is one thing, but family members need to be realistic." We were sitting in the hospital's kopitiam. I'd offered to buy her a coffee, but she'd waved it off and paid for us both with her staff pass. She'd barely touched hers, and was speaking slowly, looking at me as if I were a child. "You need to be realistic, Genevieve," she repeated. "To be otherwise is dangerous, even detrimental." At this stage, the patient's quality of life was the priority, it did no one any good to pretend otherwise. My mother had already refused medication and surgery. Even though she seemed fine, if a little frail, we would soon reach the edge of a cliff, and the semblance of normalcy would fall off rapidly. Did I understand? It was coming, we were already approaching that point.

She downed her coffee, glanced at the wall clock, and started talking about preparations for the next stage. I nodded but couldn't bring myself to focus on her words. Dana broke off, leaving us to sit in silence as people—other medical staff, patients, families—ate, drank, fretted around us. A couple of doctors called out greetings to Dana as they returned their lunch trays; she acknowledged them with a slight nod. I braced myself for her inevitable reprimand. But when she spoke, her tone had changed. It was low, worried. Unprofessional. Just like that, my mother was with us again.

"You should probably know that a columnist from *The New Paper* has been asking around. She wants to know what kind of care Auntie Su is receiving, and if your sister has been involved at all. Obviously, hospital records are confidential, but if your mother is with a public hospital, it's not hard to put two and two together." Dana frowned. "She's persistent. She's already written to the head of radiology, and a mutual friend reached out to ask if he could connect us."

I didn't know what to say. Dana had thus far been too courteous to articulate her opinions on Arin's absence, but they hovered at the periphery of our every conversation. I was quite literally useless, but Arin? To be so successful, yet absent in person and deed, was unforgivable. "If hospital records are confidential," I said finally, "it should be fine. The reporter won't get anywhere."

Dana's lunch hour was over, she stood up. She looked at me and I felt ashamed. "Auntie Su doesn't need any additional stress now. Call your sister."

A bus arrived with Arin's blown-up portrait plastered on its side. In a fit of childish irritation I let it go by, only to be squished up against a sweaty boy in school uniform on the next one. He had his phone held horizontally and was playing an obnoxiously loud game, each electronic bleep drawing the ire of exhausted housewives and overworked students trying to take naps against the oil-stained bus window.

Then his game was interrupted by an ad. I glanced down: a trailer for Arin's new movie. It was a cheesy superhero flick, a stand-alone, Arin's character a clear Lois Lane rip-off—though no one but me seemed to have noticed. The trailer showed a transformation sequence, the protagonist leaping out of his office window in a running jump. Arin's anxious face filled the screen, her hair teased into fat waves, nose scrunching in an adorable gasp as her apparently suicidal coworker shot upward into the sky, newly wrapped in dark red spandex. The worry melted away, her eyes sparkled with admiration and mischief. A tiny X appeared in the corner of the screen, but the boy didn't notice, he was enamored. It wasn't even one of Arin's good angles, but it was easy to conflate fame with beauty. The trailer continued playing: he took a screenshot. I flinched at the sharp snap of the mechanical shutter, and the boy became aware of my presence for the first time. His body stiffened slightly; then, without ever looking at me, he relaxed into a defiant, embarrassed pride.

I got off the bus.

Dana was wrong. The tabloid writer could dig all she wanted, but Arin was unimpeachable. She was the only Singaporean in recent years to breach mainstream Hollywood, making her a national treasure—any attempt to defame her would immediately be buried by the newspaper editors, only bubbling up in gossip forums or a pathetic LiveJournal blog, if at all. But more than that: even if the writer found us, interrogated us, we wouldn't have sold Arin out for a story, no. Nor would I ever allow Arin to pay our way out of this situation, even if my mother's disease weren't terminal. Not with the success she earned by plagiarizing my life. To win by accepting her help would be no triumph at all.

But I couldn't stop thinking about Dana's expression, the way her voice had dropped as she tried to draw me into a conversation about Arin, the frustration that had flashed across her face at my dull response. In that twist of her mouth I could see what was so plainly written on the faces of everyone who interacted with me— that they had gotten the short end of the stick, that they had gotten hold of the wrong sister. I was usually able to take comfort in this; it was better they had no expectations of me. Still, on occasion, my old sense of injustice bubbled up. Like now. I went home, ignored my mother's questioning face, and thought to myself, if only people knew. The story wasn't that Arin was unfilial, abandoning the family that had taken her in all those years ago. It wasn't that she wouldn't drop everything and reappear, the shining, generous daughter, by my mother's side again.

It was that she was an impostor, a usurper. Our violent amputation took eleven years. My independence from her was hard-won, it was the most precious thing I owned. But if she came home, I wasn't certain I could leave her again.

PART I: A BEGINNING

1996

Singapore

3

Arin didn't appear the way regular sisters did. She was dropped into our lives, fully formed, at the age of seven. And she left like this, too: suddenly, decisively.

I was eight. One evening in May, right before dinner, my grandmother explained that her husband, who'd been politically "disappeared" and presumed dead when my father was a child, had actually been thriving this entire time in Kedah, Malaysia, with his other family, right up till last week, when he tripped and ripped his thigh open on a rusty nail. The wound blistered and bloomed, refusing to close up; it got infected, the fever burned through his body, shutting down his kidneys and liver, washing acid through his blood. Within two days he was dead. He'd left behind a son, daughter-in-law, and a gaggle of grandchildren, but his secret family could no longer afford to raise them all, so we would be taking in the youngest, a girl around my age. After she said this, she looked at my face, switched from Hokkien, which, like most of my generation, I could understand but not speak, to Mandarin, which I could understand *and* speak but not to her satisfaction, and in the manner of one making something absolutely clear, said, "Sepsis—blood poisoning. This is why you're not allowed to play in the longkang."

I knew better than to talk back. There is a kind of person who considers themselves superior for having endured calamity, and my grandmother never let you forget that she'd lived through the war as a little girl. Instead, I dipped my head and peeked through my eyelashes at my mother, who had turned very slightly toward my father. Her eyes were creased attentively, but in her mind a million shifting calculations flipped. She blinked once, then again, in quick succession.

My father snapped out of shock. "He's *alive?*"

My grandmother made an impatient sound. "No."

He backtracked. "Right, right. How do you know this?"

"Qiang—that's your pa's other son—wrote to me."

"Were you aware he had another family?"

"Obviously not." My grandmother drew a piece of folded yellow paper out of her pajama pants, which she wore everywhere, including to the wet market. It was full of angry Mandarin characters. My father held himself very still as he scanned the letter, clean-shaven skin drawn tight against his jawline. But I knew he was exerting himself greatly for this show of self-restraint. His cheeks blanched the way they always did when confronted with life's indignities: rising gas prices, my grandmother's tyranny, that time he accidentally drank from the cup of chicken fat my mother was saving for rice. I watched this struggle play out on his face, imagined him crushing this new information into a small, compact pill and swallowing it. I watched his Adam's apple quiver and held my breath. It seemed to me that as long as he maintained his composure, whatever threatening reality my grandmother had conjured wouldn't spill out and scald our family. His eyes ran over the paper, twice, thrice, before his lips parted.

"Even so," my father said, still in that same fantastic, careful tone. "He made his choice years ago. I don't see how this affects us."

My grandmother put her hand out. He folded the letter in half but didn't move to return it.

In Hokkien, the shrinking dialect of her authority, she snapped: "I've already agreed."

"Just like that?"

Only now did my father's voice peak. I glanced at him, alarmed. He'd forgotten to close his mouth after the outburst and his lower lip hung slightly open, revealing a pale white ring of gnawed skin. It was the first time I'd seen the inside of my father's mouth, his defeat so total that to this day the increasingly lonely sound of someone speaking Hokkien is enough to render me pliant. Calmly, my grandmother extended her wrist and plucked the letter from between his fingers.

"What's past," she said, "is past. Let's eat."

4

There was no arguing with my grandmother. The apartment was hers, she had final say over any decisions made in it. When my mother's parents disowned her for getting pregnant and dropping out of school, my grandmother took her in. For three weeks, the women shared a bed while waiting for an appointment at the Registry of Marriages, my father curled beside them on the floor. After that, my grandmother moved behind the foldable shoji screen, which demarcated her new sleeping area from the rest of the living room, disabled the lock to the only bedroom, and insisted the newlyweds take it.

We lived in a second-floor flat in one of the oldest Housing Development Board blocks located within Bedok's Fengshan Estate. My grandmother bought it dirt cheap from the government in the late 1970s with money she'd made from, among other questionable things, nursing strangers' babies in her right hand and selling contraband cigarettes out of her left, and had lorded it over us ever since. And although she could neither speak nor read English, and was in fact openly bitter about the government's decision to make English the language of administration and Mandarin the official dialect unifying the various clans of Singaporean Chinese, thereby rendering much of her Hokkien/Cantonese/Hakka/Teochew/Hainanese-speaking generation linguistically irrelevant, my grandmother would often lay open *The Straits Times* on our dining-room table and cackle at the real estate ads, mocking the newer condominium developments on the Bedok Waterfront for having one-bedroom units five times the price of our home. If I could catch her in these moments, and join her in decimating the false promises of private property by pointing out and translating the descriptions and price tags on apartments with the same square footage as our own government-subsidized flat, she'd forgive my slouching posture of perceived disrespect, my general inability to match up to the idea of who she thought I should be, and for one glorious second, look at me with pride, which on my luckiest days manifested in her giving me a dollar.

Other than that, she was mean. And unrealistic. Even I, at eight, could see this. In this home, everything was something and also something else. The living room was also my grandmother's bedroom. The dining table was also my mother's study. In the one bedroom, my parents and I were stacked. Growing up, I slept each night cocooned between both parents, their hands finding each other over my growing body and latching on so they wouldn't fall off either side of the bed. Already they had begun fretting over what they'd do when I grew too big for the bed, a point I diligently endeavored to delay for as long as possible by rationing out my meals. Which begged the question: Another child? Where would we put her?

My grandmother refused to discuss it any further. The fact that we had no money, no space—none of this mattered. She had made her decision. As my father asked increasingly agitated questions, interrogating the veracity of her account, the logistics of taking in another child, debating our obligations to relations we hadn't even known existed, she spooned small, deliberate bites of dinner into her mouth. Her papery cheeks moved only to chew the food, her throat bobbed up and down with each swallow. When her bowl was scraped clean, my grandmother unfolded herself painfully from the chair, putting one hand on the table to steady herself, and left the flat for one of her long walks, which she claimed were good for digestion.

The second her steps faded, my mother turned to him.

"Here. Let me see." She had changed into her black satin kimono right after getting home from work and, while reading the letter, toyed with the neck of the T-shirt she wore underneath for modesty. "Ming," she said, finally, "this only just arrived, Mama must have been reacting impulsively. Let her calm down, then you two can talk properly."

I let myself sink into the thick, low cadence of her Mandarin. For a moment, it seemed unfathomable that things might not play out exactly as she said.

But my father, who I had only ever seen performing loving gestures toward my mother, who still kissed her when he thought I wasn't looking and laughed at her jokes, who gave her his daily earnings at the end of each day even though the neighborhood aunties gossiped and called him pussy-whipped, surprised us both by laughing loudly.

"It's fine, Su," he said. His face smoothed out and took on an expression of amusement. "She's old, she's losing her mind. How could my father have had another family? He's been dead for years."

5

For three days, my father's good mood persisted. No one mentioned the letter or the other family, not even my grandmother. I was confused, but the memory of my father's ringing laughter scared me, and I didn't dare ask any questions.

But I couldn't relax. In the overly tender tone my father took with his mother, in the enthusiastic way he crowed out greetings when he came home for dinner each night, theatrically cracking his back as he pulled off his black polyester polo tees to reveal the sweat-soaked singlets underneath; even in the playful way he imitated the day's customers in all their affectations and ridiculous requests, I felt there was something strained in his manner, waiting to snap.

My mother watched him carefully. This happened several times in my childhood—without understanding why, or what triggered it, my father would break from his taciturn self and enter short periods where his mood became much brighter. He was older than she was—six years—but during these periods, he would adopt a boyish, rowdy excitement and imitate my mother's behavior with me: whispering conspiratorially, constantly ruffling my hair or tugging at my ear. Once or twice, he even loaded my mother and me into his taxi for what he called joyrides, racing down East Coast Parkway, which ran parallel to the coastline and had no speed cameras. He'd turn off the air-conditioning and wind all the windows down, letting sea breeze fill the taxi and blasting whatever Mandopop songs the Dongli 88.3 FM DJs were presently using to weave their web of nostalgia, garbling the lyrics as he tried to sing along, while my mother, who actually had a sense of pitch, harmonized softly to the ballads of their youth.

I loved it. Each soar and turn of his wheel filled me with pride so immense it made me queasy; if this were it, if he could continue like this, I'd be happy forever. But this uptick in energy exhausted him. He could never sustain it. Soon, his gaze would become unfocused and you'd have to repeat what you were saying several times before he responded. At night, he slept like a dead person and didn't wake refreshed.

Whenever he went into these moods, my mother would devote her attention and affections entirely to him. I used to believe you could coax anyone off the edge of a cliff with an embrace. One time, after a particularly prolonged period of strain, I walked in on them by the kitchen window, my father sitting on a stool, my mother standing beside him. My father was a short man; seated, his head came up to just under her armpits. He leaned against my mother's side, right hand cupping the back of her knee, while she gently stroked his head, reciting all the things she could see from our kitchen window. The car park. A toppled motorbike. The trash compactor. A street cat, eating from a Styrofoam container of discarded rice. The slim nail clipping of a crescent moon. It was the middle of the night, and I'd woken up to pee, but seeing them in the kitchen I backed away silently and returned to bed, my bladder a rock. Shortly after that, his mood passed without further incident, and my father returned to his familiar equilibrium of stern and bemused.

In the aftermath of my grandmother's pronouncement, I waited again. I walked to school, I came home, I completed my chores, I set the table for dinner, I labored over my times tables. The mid-year examinations were over, the June holidays nearly upon us, but the teachers still wouldn't let us slack off. Every day, lessons continued as usual despite the growing restlessness of my classmates, who were intoxicated by the scent of impending freedom. During the morning assembly's mandatory reading hour that Friday, the last of the term, as the prefects were desperately trying to shush the chittering students around me, I opened my storybook and a folded note fell out.

I recognized it immediately. It was one of my mother's personalized invitations, designed, typed, and printed at the university library where she worked. It said:

Mrs. Su Yang cordially invites her Dear Daughter
Genevieve Yang Si Qi
to a Very Special Secret Meeting
at
McDonald's, Bedok Square. 2:00 a.m.,
so Take a Nap in the Afternoon

McDonald's? The rest of the school day was useless. I hid the note in my pencil case and surreptitiously read and reread it; when my teacher caught me, I was punished by being made to stand at my desk with both hands held above my head until the undersides of each arm burned. Never before had I been publicly disciplined, and the teacher seemed personally disappointed as I joined the masses of recalcitrant students, our sweaty arms swaying in the air like a misbehaving forest of flesh. Yet the pink in my cheeks was not from shame, but pleasure, and relief that the teacher hadn't confiscated my mother's note.

At home, I stayed out of my grandmother's way, trying and failing to take a nap. Over dinner, I tried to catch my mother's eye to confirm that a secret correspondence had taken place between us, an attempt she was surely aware of, but avoided mischievously, until a single moment toward the end of the meal when her eyes met mine and lingered, sparkling, a beat longer than usual, before returning to the group conversation. After that, I could barely stay awake. I don't know how and when I drifted off to sleep, but at around two, I woke sleepily to my mother's hand tentatively cupping my cheek.

I sat up immediately. My mother was perched on the edge of the bed, smelling strongly of her post-shower Nivea cream, but her makeup was redone, and she had changed out of her kimono into a dark emerald shift she wore often to work. Glancing at my father's sleeping body, my mother put a finger to her lips and quietly slid off the bed. I followed her. We tiptoed out of the bedroom, past my grandmother's shadow on the shoji screen, locked the metal gate behind us, and slipped away into the night.

Once we left the apartment, my mother blossomed. She straightened, took my hand, and walked rapidly, crossing the empty roads without waiting for the traffic lights to turn green. Our silence became a game. I matched her pace, hopping and skipping the whole way to McDonald's. I felt her restraining her mirth, and when I looked up she was trying hard not to giggle. The actual mall was only a fifteen-minute walk and would be closed when we arrived, but McDonald's ran twenty-four hours and had its own street entrance. From afar the luminescent rectangle of those glass doors grew and grew, yet the closer we drew the more my mother slowed her walk. It took everything in me not to tug away from her and break into a run. When we finally pushed through those heavy swinging doors, we both started laughing.

Relief poured into me. I sniffed the air deeply and saw that she was doing the same.

She put a hand on my head. "Go get a seat for us."

"No, I want to queue with you."

"You're so clingy."

Even though it was two in the morning, McDonald's was busy. We were surrounded by tired college students studying overnight in groups, tipsy partygoers scarfing down crispy McNuggets, couples on late-night supper dates. We stood in line together, and when we got to the front, she put the cheeseburger on a tray and gestured for me to go ahead while she counted out notes from her pouch to pay. When she slid into the booth across from me, I saw that she had added on a side of small fries.

"Surprise," she said.

I nearly cried. We raised a fry to each other, the golden tips touching.

"Cheers."

"Cheers!"

Our booth was insulated in a private bubble of hushed joy. My mother and I drew out the bag of fries for as long as possible, and I showed her the three ways to eat a fry—straight up, biting off the ends and sucking out the potato, or licking the salt off before eating the rest of the fry. We agreed that sucking out the potato was best, but too troublesome. When we were down to the last fry, she nodded at me.

"It's yours," she said, but I bit the fry in half and offered her

the rest. She laughed and ate half of my half. We took turns split-
ting the remains of the lone fry till all that was left was its small
golden endcap, a mushed-up nub of potato, which she popped in
my mouth.

"I love McDonald's," I said, licking the salt off my fingers, watching her unwrap the cheeseburger.

"I'll tell you a secret." She glanced around the restaurant before
whispering conspiratorially: "Me too." My mother leaned forward,
holding the cheeseburger out. The first time I'd been to McDonald's was on my sixth birthday, and I'd had their hotcakes drowned
in butter; the second was when our building lost power earlier in the
year. Instead of trudging through clammy, unheated leftovers, my
father came home with a box of nuggets and wings, and the three
of us jumped around the living room and cheered. Even my grandmother, who hawked nutritious home-cooked soups in tingkat carriers to pregnant women and disapproved of junk food, cracked a
smile. This third time, I bit into the burger and flavor exploded in
my mouth, the tang of the pickle, the warmth of the thin patty, the
ketchup spreading over the back of my tongue. It was incredible.
Immediately, I decided I would work for McDonald's when I grew
up, and shared this sentiment with my mother, who looked at me
for a long time, and said, "Oh, my baby."

We stayed in that booth for over an hour. I nibbled at my half of
the burger, afraid that once it was finished she'd declare it time to
go home, but as the night went on, I relaxed. She didn't seem in a
rush to return. Her half of the burger finished, she chattered freely
about her latest plans to leap from assistant librarian to teacher—an
idea that had taken hold ever since she began tutoring me at night.
My mother had completed the first two years of university before
I interrupted, and taught herself everything else out of books. Not
only could she do complicated times tables in her head at a speed
akin to magic, under her deft manipulation my school textbooks
took on the hue of storybooks, becoming portholes into endlessly
enchanting worlds of fact and fiction. Unfettered by the guardrails
of syllabus and preening under her praise, I floated at the top of
my class constantly. Who knew better than I what an entire cohort
under my mother's guidance could do?

I nodded along as she spoke. But soon, the weight of the hour settled deep within me, and my mother's tone turned teasing. She planted both elbows on the booth table and made her hands into little talking heads.

"Look at all the times Little Gen's begged to stay up late," she squeaked, miming a yabber with her right hand. "In the end she can't even keep her eyes open."

Her left hand agreed: "Clearly she doesn't know what she's asking for."

Both hands turned toward me, tilting to the left in one synchronized movement, like two cocked heads.

I laughed, protesting: No, I was happy, I wanted to stay out all night. My mother reached out and tweaked my nose, her hands just hands again, and began tidying up, moving the wrapper and used napkins onto the tray. Then she asked, lightly, how I was adjusting to the idea of having a new sister.

Adjusting to. I sat up straight. Finally we had come to the purpose of the meeting. It didn't occur to me to lie. I said I couldn't tell if my grandmother had been serious or if, as my father suggested, this was the start of her senility. It seemed too far-fetched to be true. We all knew my grandfather had been dead since my father was a child. So it didn't make sense to spend energy adjusting to the idea, when it could be false.

My mother listened seriously, then said: "It's true."

Immediately I was filled with grief. "Can we say no?"

"Sayang, your grandmother has already decided. And besides, that family needs help. It's the right thing to do."

"Does Pa know?"

Her nose scrunched slightly, considering my question. "It may not look like it, but he does."

The thought of my father distracted me. "Is he okay?"

My mother touched my cheek gently. "It was hard for him to grow up without a father. This is a lot to swallow; we have to give him time."

According to her, when my grandfather disappeared, my grandmother's confusion and rage coalesced over time into a conviction that he'd been murdered, or he'd surely have found a way back to them. For my grandfather to resurrect like this, even posthu-mously, turned everything upside down. Still, we couldn't help any of that. What we *could* do was try our very best to welcome the little girl, who was surely as lost and confused as we were.

She had been speaking to me in the serious voice I loved, as if I were a little adult, but with those two words—upside down—a troubled levity emerged. I frowned, eager to prove myself mature enough for the conversation, tracing the outlines of her lipstick's faded imprint on the crumpled paper napkins and reasoning to myself while she spoke. It wasn't that uncommon for children to be swapped or adopted, or for families to have moving parts. I had classmates who lived not with their parents but with cousins or aunties temporarily, either because it was a better postal code for school admissions, or because their parents couldn't afford the time and energy to simultaneously work and raise children. We all knew of kids who took taxis to school every day but claimed low-income benefits by declaring only their mother's salaries while their fathers worked mysterious and untraceable jobs in China.

But us? I knew it was selfish, but I didn't want anything to change. When my mother finished, I didn't look up. Even when she inched her fingers forward on the table and touched my index finger with hers, our secret gesture for asking what the other was thinking, I didn't move. I stayed quiet until she ventured, tentatively: "Gen?"

I caved. "What do you need me to do?"

She exhaled loudly and opened her arms. I clambered over to her side of the booth, pulling my knees up on the bench, snuggling into her chest. As she pulled me into a tight hug, pressing her nose to my scalp and inhaling, I heard her murmuring softly, "Nothing, nothing. Don't you worry. We'll adapt to this the way we adapt to everything."

A week after that, Arin arrived.

6

It was the ninth of June, a little after eight. My father's last ride had ended somewhere in Sembawang, and he'd been caught in the snarl of postwork traffic on the way back, so dinner was later than usual. When he finally got home, my grandmother was more irascible than ever. She accused him of forgetting her stomach, which was old and would digest itself if starved, exacerbating her gastrointestinal issues. Complaining was one of the last pure pleasures life held for my grandmother, and she indulged in it every chance she got. She spoke as though my father alone had conspired with all the cars of Singapore to hurt her, specifically her, conveniently omitting the slice of white bread she'd eaten with sugar and butter at seven.

My father took this injustice in stride. He apologized as we settled down, not just to my grandmother, but to my mother and me as well, even though we both looked forward to our daily family dinners and would gladly have waited another hour for him. My mother began ladling soup into bowls for me to distribute, relaying some market gossip in a voice so animated it made my father smile. I set the first bowl before my grandmother, careful not to spill any of it on the table and draw her wrath.

She'd been worse recently. As far as I knew, there'd been no further conversation about my grandfather's secret family, no additional mattress purchased, no space made on our crowded bathroom sink where another plastic cup or toothbrush would go. Perhaps this was the reason for my grandmother's anger, the sense that she'd been passed over, that, despite her proclamations, something had slipped through her grasp once again. Without waiting for the rest of us to begin eating, she picked the carrots out of her soup and mashed them up on her plate with the back of her spoon, creating an orange mix that looked like baby food, her jaw stubbornly working the same bite of dinner over and over.

Then the doorbell rang.

"Leave it," my father said, after it rang a second time. He waggled his eyebrows at me and playfully shushed the door. "It's probably the Yakult auntie trying to sell more bottles. We're having dinner."

But the doorbell rang again. And again. Something shuttered in my father's face, and his good mood melted away. With his fork, he reached into his soup and pressed a floating corn cob down, but it bobbed right back up. His mouth was a straight, hard line. I turned to my mother. She'd lowered the rice paddle and was looking at him too.

My grandmother was already out of her seat. She'd leapt up at the second ring and was climbing over the stacks of paper on the floor. I twisted around to watch as she hobbled past the dining table, accidentally toppling a small heap of overdue library books supporting a corner of the shoji screen, stopping right before the front door. She straightened and touched her bun, almost unconsciously, before reaching for the knob.

Standing beyond the metal gates was a leathery man, standing ramrod straight and wearing an ill-fitting office shirt that looked like it had been borrowed or stolen. In one hand, he held a cluster of grocery store gerberas in coral and yellow, wrapped in plastic and dripping water onto the concrete corridor floor. In the other, he was gripping the arm of a small, skinny child of seven, with skin the color and texture of candle wax. Her entire body was tensed like a street cat, and when the door opened, she jerked back and turned her face up toward her father, revealing a very long, thick ponytail that extended almost to her mid back, like a tail.

My mother recovered first.

"Well," she said, turning to me. "Here she is. Your new sister."

7

The man and girl crowded into the living room, standing with their backs pressed to the shoji screen while we packed away the food. Every time my mother and I squeezed past them, the man would hold his breath defensively, as if blocking us from noticing the stale smell of his sweat. I was terribly excited. Fully aware of their eyes on me, I moved quickly, darting around the table, scooping the still-warm rice into plastic boxes, tipping the untouched stir-fry chicken into the Tupperware, not even pinching a cube of meat for myself. In our arched kitchen entryway hung a long curtain of brown beads that announced movement with a magnificent clatter; each time I ferried a dish or cloth to the kitchen a jolt ran through the man's whole body. Exhilaration made me sloppy; the wet rag I wrung halfway dripped all over the kitchen floor, something I only noticed when the girl's eyes cut to the trail of water behind me. I smiled sheepishly at her, but she looked away.

Two could play at ignoring each other: I didn't look at her again while wiping the table. I left the dirty cloth in the kitchen sink and when I returned the adults had taken their seats at the table, so I perched on the sofa arm to watch. The man had put the flowers down and was awkwardly explaining that they were to apologize for his wife's absence. Water seeped from the plastic wrapping and inched outward on the table like a tiny tide, but he didn't move to dab it with his sleeve. There was a singsong quality to his Mandarin that made me want to giggle; I bit my lip and settled for watching his caterpillar brows knit and unknit themselves. Then I couldn't resist and snuck another glance at the girl, who was still refusing to acknowledge me. As the man continued blabbering about the weather, the cross-border bus, he kept his grip on the girl's shoulder tight, as if afraid she'd bolt at any moment.

Finally, when it became clear there was nothing else to be said, he turned to the girl. Show them, he told her, and when she shook her head, he said tiredly, come on, we've been through this. Don't be difficult.

The girl didn't budge.

He yanked the backpack off her shoulder with his free hand and unzipped it. It was a dark blue bag, and when he opened it, the smell of feet wafted out. The man looked embarrassed, but continued rummaging through the bag, producing and arranging an astonishing number of things on the dining table. A toothbrush, some socks, an unsolved Rubik's Cube, a Ziploc bag with a bunch of pens, a small pink hand towel, a children's picture book, a clear folder containing official-looking documents, and so on. The girl squirmed as he did this, clearly uncomfortable, but I was transfixed.

My mother cut in.

"It's all right, thank you, we'll sort out all that later."

But he didn't stop. He let go of the girl and emptied the whole bag, until he landed on what he was looking for. "Here," he said, turning to my grandmother. In his hands was a Skippy peanut butter jar, cleaned out and filled to the halfway mark with gray sand.

My grandmother flinched, but took the jar from him, and turned it over in her hands, the dust shifting and tumbling around like in a snow globe. My father, who had been watching this exchange silently, arms folded, spoke for the first time. "What's that?" But his voice was low, angry. He wasn't really asking a question. And when nobody replied, he said: "That's it?"

The man straightened and said in a cold, proud voice: "It's the best we could do."

"A peanut butter jar?"

My grandmother interrupted. "Ming," she said, "leave it." To the man, she said, "Thank you for bringing him home."

Him? I belatedly realized what everyone else in the room already knew. The pathetic heap of speckled gray dust was my grandfather. I craned my neck to look at the jar again, fascinated, disgusted. There was so little of it. Satisfied, my grandmother tucked the jar into the crook of her arm and disappeared behind the shoji screen. She reappeared with a red packet in hand.

"As agreed," she said. "For your trouble."

A pale vein pulsed in the man's jaw; he visibly restrained himself and gave my grandmother a jerky, short nod. Then he pocketed the money and turned to my father.

"Ming? What's it short for?"

"Wei Ming."

The man nodded. Grimly, he said: "I'm Wei Qiang."

Realization rippled across both men's faces: my grandfather had given his sons the same character on which their names hinged; one choice branching into two. Almost as if the question were wrenched from him, my father asked: "You didn't know?"

"Not explicitly. Though guilt leaves its inconvenient finger-prints, as you might imagine." The man's purplish lips drew tight over his large teeth; he was attempting a smile.

I don't know if his obvious suffering softened my father; it certainly moved me. Up till this moment I had thought adults invulnerable to pain. My father's mouth fell open again, to ask another question, perhaps, but the man visibly clammed up.

Perhaps he sensed my father's quiet desperation and didn't want to relinquish any more of their father to a family he'd lived in the shadow of for so long. He glanced at the wall clock and said: "I have to get going."

The dining chair scraped against the floor painfully as he stood. Now it was the girl who was holding on to him, gripping his pant leg with both hands. The man tapped her scalp, but she didn't let go, just pressed her face into his side. He put his hand on her shoulder and pushed slightly. It didn't work.

He repeated: "Don't be difficult."

The girl clung even tighter to his leg, refusing to move, burying her face against his thigh. He looked at her, then around the house. My father had subsided back into a slump, but my mother stood, advancing a step toward him. For a short, wild moment, I thought she would invite him to stay for dinner, our Frankensteined family bloating around the table. But he ignored her. It looked as though he was going to start walking, with the girl wrapped around his leg, right out of our lives, till his gaze landed on my grandmother.

It was clear he'd ceased to exist for her the second she handed the red packet over. All her attention was on the jar; she was trying to scrape off the edge of the Skippy peanut butter label with the side of her nail. The man stared at her for a long time, but she didn't notice. Then he turned to my father, rubbed his palm on his pants, leaned over, and stuck out his hand.

That hand, large and spade-like, hung in the air between them.

Reluctantly, my father took it. The man waited until my father looked up, then gave it one big shake, staring straight into my father's eyes. They held each other's gaze for a long time, and then, unexpectedly, the man scoffed. Before anyone could react, he told the girl, his voice hard: "Let go."

Arin obeyed.

8

The man left without a backward glance. No one else moved, and the only sound after his brisk footfall faded was the slow drip of water seeping off the edge of the table and perspiring onto Arin's backpack, which had fallen off the chair and onto the floor. Even my grandmother, who hadn't acknowledged his departure, stopped scratching at the jar and now cradled it loosely in both hands.

Then she rose, and without looking at Arin, disappeared behind the shoji screen, jar and all.

I stepped forward.

"Hello," I said. Arin's head whipped around, toward me. I picked up the backpack and offered it to her. When she didn't react, I placed it on the chair. "I'm Genevieve." I thought of the words I'd rehearsed in my head, in preparation for this exact moment. "Your new Jie Jie."

I smiled to show no offense taken from our earlier standoff, but when she continued staring, I prompted: "Your turn."

"Yang Yan Mei," she whispered, finally. Her voice, though scared, emerged in a thick and wonderful alto, reminiscent of her father's melodious Mandarin. "Arin."

"That's a pretty name."

I paused, not knowing where to go from here. There were a million things I wanted to ask, but they were all too dangerous to bring up while my grandmother lay, breathing shallowly, just beyond the screen. Neither did it seem possible to take her hand and pull her into the same corridor her father had disappeared down, out of my grandmother's earshot. I sized Arin up, trying to find something to compliment, and landed on her hair. "I like your hair. Do you always keep it up like that?"

"No. My father made me."

"Can I touch it?"

She nodded. I reached for the top of her head, running my hand down the thick rope of her ponytail, letting the fine strands slip through my fingers. It was so different from my own bowl cut, which my mother trimmed every three weeks with a pair of slim, silver scissors, me perching on a low plastic stool before her, a cape of newspaper hanging around my shoulders while she squinted under the kitchen lights and called me her little mushroom. I tugged on Arin's ponytail gently and caught a whiff of her scalp, which reminded me of the night air from our joyrides, salty and tinged with petroleum. "It's so heavy, doesn't it hurt?"

Her wide, brown pupils regarded me cautiously. "Only sometimes."

"We'll cut it."

My mother snapped out of her reverie. "We can talk about that tomorrow. Let's get you washed up." She squeezed my arm gratefully, then led Arin to the kitchen, where the bathroom was. The hum of the water heater started, I turned to my father. He was still in the exact same position, but now his eyes met mine.

I walked over and wrapped my arms around his shoulders the way I'd seen my mother do many times. The night's events felt so surreal they had already begun fading, leaving only a confused sense of excitement. Surely the man was bluffing. I had the feeling he'd only come to prove a point, that he was lurking in the stairwell, and any second now, he'd pop up again to ask for Arin and the ashes back. "Isn't he going to come back for her?"

My father didn't respond. For a long time, the only sound was that of the shower. I closed my eyes, overcome by a sudden exhaustion, listening to the slow rhythm of his warm breaths. Then, a low, keening sound started—at first, very softly; I wasn't sure what it was. But the sound got louder and I realized it was coming from behind the shoji screen. My father's body tensed; I thought he would get up and go to his mother.

Instead, he said: "No, that sort of man has no moral fiber. He's abandoned his daughter, you'll never see him again."

9

Arin's shower that night seemed to go on forever, though in reality it must have lasted only ten minutes before the hot water cut off. I remember clearly the cloud of steam when she emerged, wearing one of my mother's old shirts as a nightdress, instead of the tightly rolled pajamas that had come in her backpack. The shirt devoured her; under it her legs were scrubbed tremulous and pink. A smattering of red spots had appeared right above her kneecap from the water's heat.

In the time it took for her to shower, my father had collected himself. He was right: we'd never see her birth father again. My grandmother's sobbing had faded too. I don't know if she'd drifted off to sleep or if she was lying on her side, listening intently to our every word.

"Well," he said gravely, "now we are five." Arin's cheeks were flushed, she dropped her chin to her chest and wouldn't look at any of us. My mother's eyes met mine above Arin's bowed head, brows sloped in pity. "Tonight you'll sleep in the room."

But it was clear he meant: from now on. I cried: "Pa, you won't sleep with us?"

He shook his head, watching Arin. A long moment passed, and she didn't move, not even to nod. "None of this is your fault," my father said finally, his fingers twitching in his lap. "You understand?"

But the actual work of inducting Arin into the family he left to my mother and me. The declaration had sapped all his energy; wordlessly, my father moved to the couch, even though it smelled musty and sagged in the middle. He started waking up at four instead of six, circling the airport to catch the businessmen coming in on red-eye flights who didn't yet realize or care that tipping wasn't customary in Singapore.

He'd done this before, of course, clocking dangerously long

shifts whenever household expenses spiked, spearing swirls of spinach into his mouth and flexing his imaginary biceps whenever my mother chided him to rest. But never had he appeared at the dinner table so consistently drained of spirit. Conversations became laborious, and when he realized, instead of making an effort, he sunk further into sullenness. I was frightened and tried to remedy this.

"Pa, are you tired?"

"Yes."

"Why, were passengers rude today?"

"As always."

And when I tried tipping the vegetables from my plate to his, lifting my arm to mime flexing my own muscles, he blinked blankly at me and said: "Eat your vegetables."

I felt this loss deeply. Dinners had always been a bright point of laughter and gossip, especially for my mother, who spent her day silently in the library and was bursting with stories by the time she got home. But she seemed disheartened too. Both the fact of Arin's arrival and my grandmother's evident desire to pretend she didn't exist had thickened the atmosphere of our house, weighing down everything said until it was easier to finish our food in silence.

Arin never spoke during dinner either. In fact, that first week, she barely spoke at all. This was a source of great disappointment to me. I'd worked hard prior to her arrival to put aside my personal reservations and avail myself to answer any questions my new sister might have, and could not understand how she took advantage of none of this. I'd set aside my favorite books—our house was full of library copies smuggled home by my mother—for Arin to pick from; I'd painstakingly drawn an approximately scaled map of the neighborhood on lined foolscap paper, meticulously labeling all points of interest: the bridge, the canal, the playground, the bakery, the hairdresser, marking out the best walking route to and from our primary school with a pink highlighter; I'd even gone to the bakery auntie and begged an empty tin for Arin, similar to the bright green Milo tin I kept under the bed, which would double as a locker for personal effects.

But Arin displayed no interest in any of it. I might as well have been trying to befriend a rock. When I invited her to play, she ignored me. When I gifted her the dark blue biscuit tin with a Scottish landscape on its cover, she accepted it mutely then went right back to chewing on her index finger or fiddling with the stupid Rubik's Cube that had come in her bag.

Was it possible? That I was the only one unable to sleep each night, overwhelmed by the unfamiliar smell of her wet hair suffusing the humid night air, the shuddering quality of her breath as she lay in bed with her back to my mother and me, forehead kissing the pebbled surface of the wall? Arin's natural odor was very faintly that of gasoline, which emerged when the floral scent of our drugstore shampoo dissipated, giving my dreams that week the intoxicating sensation of speeding down an unending midnight highway. In the mornings, I examined her. She'd have flipped around in her sleep, fine black hair splaying all over our pillows, eyelids parted slightly to reveal the whites of her eyeballs rolled back in concussed sleep like a drunk baby. I watched the morning sunlight glint off the fine hairs on her forehead, reluctantly admiring the slight flush of her cheeks, feeling slightly wounded. Could it be that she was completely immune to my presence, my precocious charm that caused schoolteachers and neighborhood aunties alike to turn their golden smiles upon me, the magnetic charisma that even in utero had led my mother to risk everything and pick me over her own family?

By the end of the week, I couldn't take it anymore. I followed my mother out of the house and down the stairs, complaining about how I'd wooed Arin with my best efforts, to no avail. No matter what I did, she didn't say thank you, plus she still sucked her thumb like a baby. Clearly she wasn't raised right. What more could I do, I'd already tried my best.

My mother perched on the bottom step of the stairwell so we'd be at eye level. She listened to my grievances and praised me expansively for my efforts, caressed my cheeks, reiterated that I was her pride and joy. She didn't lower her voice even when the people passing by, hurrying to the bus stop, did double takes at the sight of a woman sitting on the grimy stairs, squeezing the hands of a blushing child in pajamas.

Even though it was still early, I said: "You're going to be late for work."

"Then I'll be late."

But she stood up, and half turned to dust off the back of her dress. I nodded: it was clean. We both heard the hiss of a bus door closing, and she pulled a face, pretending to plop back down on the steps while I giggled and wrapped both hands around her arm as if to lead her toward the bus stop. Then she paused, lost in thought, and I knew our game was over.

"That poor girl has had a hard life. She must be in shock." She might as well have been talking about herself. "She'll take time to adjust, to feel comfortable here. We'll just have to be patient."

Maligned, I protested. "I *am* patient."

"You are." She laughed and took my cheeks in both hands, massaging my face into a pout, then a grin. "It's going to get better, Gen, I promise. You'll see."

That night, she came home with a stack of fuchsia flyers, which she distributed to the family over dinner.

Advertisements. On it, printed in thick, black ink were the words ENGLISH, MATH, AND SCIENCE HOME-BASED TUITION FOR AGES 7–10. ENGLISH/MANDARIN-SPEAKING TUTOR, FROM NANYANG TECHNO-LOGICAL UNIVERSITY. It took me a while to understand the tutor on the flyers referred to her.

"I'm going to need you two," she said, leaning forward and tapping first my nose, then Arin's, with her index finger, "to help me cut the bottom strips of each one to make a tear-off flyer. Here, I've already done one to show you how."

I tugged on one of the tabs and it came away easily. I held up the thin strip of paper bearing her number. "Like this?"

She chucked my cheek. "Exactly."

She'd been working on this idea all week. Arin's arrival—here she touched Arin's head briefly—had been a lightning strike of inspiration. All this time she'd been trying to figure out how to switch from the library to a teaching job, but why not have both? Wasn't she already juggling the two—with me? The going rate for home-based private tutoring at the primary level was thirty dollars an hour. If each session averaged two hours, and she accepted three students per class, that was a hundred and eighty dollars per night. Three times a week would mean five hundred and forty dollars.

That was over two thousand dollars a month. Her monthly salary doubled, just like that. She was limited only by time and energy, and as we all knew, she had boundless reserves of the latter. She spoke excitedly, gesturing toward a sweep of imaginary books on the dining table, an audience of enraptured minds.

The vision of my mother sitting at the head of our dining table, making a gift of knowledge in her low, passionate voice, enthralled me. And there I would be beside her, following her lessons with ease, refilling everyone's water glasses, the perfect assistant, looked upon with envy by her students. Turning to my mother once the last student left, a secret understanding in our eyes as she peeled the top note from each fresh stack of cash before folding the rest into her purse. The salt of a single golden fry, already on my tongue.

My father looked up from the flyer, lips pressed into a sad smile.

"I know," my mother said quickly, catching his look. "But I can do my part too."

"Me three," I chimed. "I'm old enough to work." I'd read countless books where kids babysat, walked dogs, delivered newspapers for extra cash, and identified strongly with these characters without understanding that they were teenagers, not eight-year-olds like me.

"You are old enough," my mother said, "to focus on staying at the top of your class." But she was smiling.

My grandmother interrupted. "No bringing strangers here."

"No problem," my mother said easily. "I'll go to their homes. Actually, that's even better, I can charge more." Her red lips curved upward, she beamed at my grandmother winningly. "Imagine, Mama, not having to wait anymore, we could replace the kitchen cabinet doors immediately. Get a new TV. Wouldn't you like that?"

My grandmother grunted and continued rearranging the food in her bowl. Next to it, the peanut butter jar sat, its sticky label half scratched off. She carried it everywhere with her, like some gleeful kid who'd trapped a frog in a flask.

"Eat your dinner, Ma," my father said, glancing at her bowl. "Su, if it's after dinner, you can come with me to deliver Ma's tingkats, then I can drop you wherever you need."

I brightened.

Until that moment, I hadn't realized how worried I'd been. My father couldn't seem to help being stiff and formal around Arin, limiting his interactions with her to a brusque *You okay?* then falling back into moroseness when he realized this terrified more than comforted her. Yet here he was, behaving as he used to, adjusting without hesitation to accommodate my mother's whims, the moon to her sun.

Yes, this was what we were like. In a moment, my mother would blow him a girlish kiss, my grandmother would avert her eyes in disapproval. My father wouldn't say anything out of consideration for his mother, but would gaze back at her with affection. I looked over at Arin triumphantly; I wanted her to understand the kind of family she'd been admitted to. I wanted to see her face shining with admiration and gratitude.

But she wasn't watching them. Arin was studying intently the pink flyer my mother had handed her, holding it in her lap, under the table. She wasn't reading it. With her chin dropped so low to her chest she could easily be mistaken for having dozed off, Arin folded the flyer diagonally in half, then turned the corners down. She was making a paper airplane.

10

Many years later, Arin would confess that she'd been waiting. Like me, she found it hard to believe her family had relinquished her, with such savage ease. Even though she'd sat beside her father, first on that five-hour bus to Kuala Lumpur, the Malaysian capital, then on the six-hour cross-border transfer coach to Singapore, the farthest she'd ever been from home, the journey felt unreal. The first bus had no air-conditioning, and she'd dozed in fitful, sweaty spurts. By the time they reached Kuala Lumpur, her father was dismayed to see her bangs sticking in oily clumps to her forehead. He pulled her into one of the handicapped stalls and made her rinse her hair under the sink, scrubbing her scalp with a few pumps of silky pink hand soap. He folded several squares of toilet paper and briefly wet them under the tap, gesturing at Arin to wipe her armpits and thighs, doing the same himself. Then, she was made to stand under the automated hand dryer. The recycled hot air made her head pound, yet even then, watching her father splash tap water on his stubbled neck and chin, scratching at the stubborn white fibers left behind by the damp toilet paper, she felt that at any moment, he'd change his mind, and they'd return home.

The decision to give her up felt so sudden, so arbitrary. Why her and not one of her older siblings? Was it the combination of being the youngest, and a girl? The whole journey, even while Arin's father was speaking—you better behave yourself, help out around the house, make yourself useful, don't you dare get sent back—she wasn't really listening. She was thinking about how her mother hadn't even raised her head from her washing when they'd left home. As if there were nothing extraordinary about the day. Of course there wasn't—this was just a bit of play. Once this mysterious grandmother from across the border got tired of her, Arin would come right home.

So Arin conducted a game in her head. As long as she didn't touch anything, didn't talk to anyone, didn't sink into life here, she would be able to return when her father reappeared. She was still thinking in terms of when, not if. She kept her interactions with us minimal, kept her mind separate from the physical reality of her surroundings, which wasn't too hard since the adults didn't demand anything from her. The only hiccup was me. I—and in her later retellings there was always a teasing edge—constantly badgered her, offering her presents, making space for her on the mattress, clearing out a corner in the closets that lined one wall of our bedroom, trying to start conversation, to draw her out. Leave me alone, she wanted to say. I'll be gone soon enough. None of this is real, not the situation, not this place, and not you either. But still I persisted.

How long could she sustain this game? If nothing happened, perhaps forever. Many people go their whole lives not quite believing it is theirs, feeling out of sorts in their body, convinced real life lies just beyond their grasp. Chasing a wisp of something they believe is owed to them. But I wouldn't let her be. To her, I was burdened with responsibility, my blunt bowl cut and determined manner making me seem like an angry little policewoman.

The image she painted made us both laugh. It was true, I had felt responsible. Wasn't I the one who stepped forward and broke the spell that first night, pulling Arin into our world? I thought of the little olive-backed sunbirds who built their nests in our neighbor's potted corridor bamboos, how unrestrained curiosity often doomed the newborn chicks. I remembered, as a child of five, reaching for the dark gray eggs with wonder, only to have my wrist snatched back by the neighbor, a green-thumbed geriatric who always insisted on us calling him Abang instead of Uncle. Seeing my shock, he modulated himself, returning to his usual crinkly humor, but warned me that sunbirds abandoned their eggs the second they intuited human touch. If I'd ignored Arin, if the fragile membrane separating our families had remained intact, might her father not have returned?

Regardless, things couldn't continue like this. I made up my mind to confront Arin the next day. It was still the June holidays, which meant my lone charge was keeping out of my grandmother's way while she tinkered with her assortment of herby brews. Two women in our estate were in various stages of pregnancy, which kept her usefully occupied. After lunch, she'd leave the stove, where her soups would simmer slowly for five or six hours before being ladled into the aluminum tingkat carriers, and retreat behind the shoji screen for her nap.

I waited for the afternoon heat to take her, then divided the stack of flyers and handed half to Arin, almost daring her to say no. But she accepted it, settling cross-legged on the floor under the table. All afternoon, I was lost in deep focus, moving my metal ruler meticulously in one-centimeter increments along the bottom of each flyer, creating small, even tears bearing my mother's cell number.

When my stack was nearly done, I peeked under the table to check on Arin. She'd done less than ten before becoming distracted. In her hands was a badly formed paper boat she was turning over, adjusting a fold, trying to edge her creation closer to symmetry.

Enough was enough. I slid out from my chair and plopped onto the floor. "Give me that," I said, plucking the paper boat out of her hands. Even after smoothing it out, deep creases remained. "It's spoilt now."

She didn't respond, keeping her eyes deliberately neutral. "I know you can talk," I reminded her. I'd seen her button nose twitch every time I called her name. "Stop acting like you don't understand."

Arin glanced at the undone paper boat in my hands, and I moved it farther out of reach. "You can have it back when you say something." Then, unable to resist, I cajoled: "Come on. Just two words. Two tiny words."

"Okay."

I nearly fell over. "That's only one," I said, holding up a finger. "Give me one more."

"Okay, sorry."

Unimaginable success! I gave her back the flyer. "I know how to make a paper crane," I said excitedly. "Want me to teach you?"

She shook her head.

"Why not?"

Arin sucked the inside of her right cheek and whispered: "I want to go home."

I frowned. "This *is* your home. We already bought your school uniforms."

She repeated, stubbornly: "I want to go home." Then she started, and looked over my shoulder.

I turned and found myself face-to-face with my grandmother's dusty kneecaps, knees bending slowly, until a large, milky eye descended from the table's horizon and fixed itself on us. "She's right," my grandmother said. "You are home. Come on out."

I scrambled from under the table, bumping my head against its edge, hard. Arin followed, more slowly. My grandmother had taken a few steps and was lowering herself gingerly onto the couch, setting the peanut butter jar on the coffee table. When she turned back, there was an awful smile on her face.

"Child," my grandmother said, and it occurred to me that she'd never addressed Arin directly, let alone by name. "Come here. Let me see your face."

There was nothing to be done but obey. Arin turned pliant, presenting herself to my grandmother, who took her chin between her thumb and forefinger, turning Arin's face this way and that, gaze searching. Then she let go and put her hand on Arin's head, stroking her thick black hair. The gesture, while affectionate, cost my grandmother more than she could bear. After a short while, she withdrew her hand and smiled at Arin again.

"Did you know," my grandmother said, "that I raised your grandfather? We grew up in the same kampung, he lived in the house next to mine. He was three years my junior and during Occupation he got a scar right here"—she tapped the sparse tail of her left eyebrow—"for jumping between me and a soldier. So brave." She fixed her eye on Arin. "Tell me. Does he still have that scar?"

Arin glanced at the jar. And nodded.

"Did he ever tell you how he got it? No? What *did* he tell you?"

When Arin didn't speak, my grandmother drew her thin lips back in that same smile. "You're going to deny an old woman memories of her late husband?"

A tear slid down Arin's cheek, hung on her chin, then rolled off onto the floor.

My grandmother realized she wasn't getting anywhere. "Anyway, all that's in the past. This is your home now." Her gaze wandered, then returned to alight on the jar.

Relieved, I began to reach for Arin. But before we could escape, my grandmother's voice rang out. "What did you call him?" She clarified: "How did you address him?"

"Ye Ye."

The same thing I would've called him, I noted.

"That would make me your Nai Nai." My grandmother nodded to herself. For a moment, she seemed almost benevolent. "You haven't greeted us yet. Come, child."

Arin glanced at me.

My grandmother gestured toward the jar. "Go on."

Arin's brows knit together. It was clear what my grandmother wanted her to do, yet neither of us could comprehend it. Unable to see a way out, she rotated slowly and addressed the jar. "Ye Ye," she said, then broke off uncertainly.

"And now me."

But Arin couldn't do it. Her lips formed the words, but no sound came out. I could tell my grandmother was getting angry, I could feel irritation mounting in her. She was smiling again, displaying all her gumless teeth. "Go on."

Everything in me was screaming to move, to plead injustice on Arin's behalf, but I was petrified. All I could hear, for a long time, was the whup-whup-whup of the ceiling fan as my grandmother, Arin, and I stood there, the peanut butter jar between us.

Then Arin burst into tears.

My grandmother snatched the jar back in disgust.

"Forget it," she said. Her voice was rough. "My mistake. I should have known they'd send a half-wit."

As she got up to leave, she pulled her pajama pants tight around her, so not one thread of her swishing hem would brush against Arin.

11

How long did Arin and I sit there, paralyzed? I don't know. Minutes, hours, years. Beyond the shoji screen, the woman who called herself my grandmother breathed audibly, rasping in, out, in, out, and as that tremendous white noise of my childhood crescendoed, filling the living room, buzzing incessantly in my brain, it occurred to me: I had no idea who she was. I didn't recognize her. The grandmother I grew up with could be unreasonable, she had no compunction about pinching or snapping at me for any perceived disrespect, but you could pin all that down to a kind of logic, a method of discipline. This, this was different. In her manner, in that smile, there was a hunger and humiliation that met and produced a poison that, if nothing were done, would spread, infecting her words and actions, blistering anyone it touched. I threw a fearful glance at her heaving silhouette. The sun was low in the sky, and as her outline melted into the flickering shapes cast by the paraphernalia of our lives, a shadow leaped across the shoji screen, as if to possess me. I scrambled away from it, grabbing Arin's bony arm. Our eyes met, we fled.

The neighborhood playground was deserted, emptied even of the wandering old men who sometimes napped in the green plastic slide. Panting, I turned to Arin, the only other witness, desperate for some affirmation that the horrors of the afternoon had really happened, that it wasn't a figment of my overactive imagination, but when I opened my mouth, she flinched.

This, more than anything, hurt me. I dropped her arm, taking a step back.

"I'll help you," I said, surprising myself. Tears were leaking out of my eyes, too, mixing stickily with the sweat coating my face. I mopped them away with the edge of my T-shirt. "I'll help you go home."

Arin regarded me with her wide, brown eyes, lashes clumping together from the tears.

I reached out again, more tentatively this time. Arin didn't move beyond lifting her chin, very slightly. I cupped her cheeks with both my palms, catching the fresh tears with my thumbs, the way my mother did when I cried. Her skin was warm from sun and exertion. I held her face until she stopped crying.

Then she said, "How?"

I paused. I had not thought that far. "Where do you live?"

She didn't know her address. Arin had never needed it before, the intuitive knowledge of her neighborhood with all its loose tiles and twisting pathways existing unmoored from the actuality of words, numbers. I felt a split second of dismay, followed by a surge of wild, irrational resolve. My grandmother's cruelty had eliminated the world I'd known; we had no choice but to find a different way forward. Yes, I thought, feeling comforted, how many stories had I read, of children packing bags and getting on trains, going on adventures, fulfilling missions? It might not be easy, but how hard could it really be? There was no reason we could not pull off a successful escape and return Arin to her rightful home if we tried hard enough.

As I explained all this to Arin, painting a picture of freedom and vindication, I could see her listening, skeptically at first, then testing the idea, venturing questions. Was it better for this to be a secret or were either of my parents likely to help? When would we leave? How would we get the money to go? Her questions excited me, as I answered her I became endowed with a sense of my own authority, the burgeoning thrill of saying in an adult voice: Of course, the spare key is hidden in the circuit-breaker box above the shoe rack; we'll have to forge a parental consent form to show nosy adults in case we get stopped along the way; we mustn't forget to pack Vitasoy for the bus journey, for when we get hungry. And then I saw it—the exact moment she fully bought into the idea, the widening of possibility in her eyes. She looked at me with hope so immense it was like being doused in ice water. The weight of what I'd promised suddenly terrified me.

But her face was shining.

"Are you sure?" she asked.

"Yes."

"Won't you get into trouble?"

I would. "It's the right thing to do."

But the vision of my grandmother's awful, roving eye, now fixed on me, swam before us both, and my body jerked in an involuntary shudder.

The sun was setting. The streets had gradually filled with the din of evening traffic; on the sidewalk, bodies hurried past us and toward their dinners; any second now, my parents might appear. I took Arin's hand and walked back toward our block. She let herself be led aimlessly, lost in her own thoughts. She'd seen it too: my temporary paralysis conjured by visions of punishment. No doubt she was remembering the fear that had gripped her just minutes ago, upstairs; fear I would soon face alone. With some effort I quelled the terror beginning to clamor within me, forced myself to maintain a loose, relaxed hold on Arin's hand. We came to the foot of our stairwell, and her fingers tightened around mine.

She brought my index finger to her mouth and bit down.

"Yuck," I said, surprised, pulling my hand away. The tip of my finger glistened with saliva, I made to wipe it on Arin's sleeve.

But then I saw the shape of her teeth imprinted on my finger pad. It looked uncannily like the face of a baby goblin, and when I said so, Arin gave me a tentative smile. For the first time I noticed the slight crookedness of her three front teeth, one of which sat slightly forward on her upper gum. "I'm sharing my secret friend with you."

So that's what she was doing all that time she spent with her thumb in her mouth. And here I'd thought it was a sign of mental impairment. How stupid I was; me, who received love as birthright, me for whom loneliness was foreign land. A sudden, miraculous affection poured into my chest like hot liquid. "We'll stay friends too," I said impulsively. I had only the vaguest idea of how inter-national correspondence worked, but now that we knew of each other's existence the thought that we'd ever be truly divided seemed intolerable.

Arin shook her head, clearing her mind, trying to find the right words.

In a small, determined voice, she said: "We're not friends."

And before my face could betray my hurt at this sudden shock, she continued: "Jie Jie."

Older sister. It was as much a statement as a question. I was moved, I could feel each individual finger pressing into my hand, tense with anticipation. I squeezed back.

"That's right," I said, and began climbing.

12

The following days were transformed by the illicit thrill of collaboration. I was serious about my grades, and the mere thought of falling behind in school made me want to die. Once the June holidays were over I'd be regularly clocking ten hours a day at my desk, and there'd be no time for plotting, much less fleeing. I worked out the date for the latest I could run away with Arin and be home in time for the second semester and concluded that we had to get moving immediately.

It seemed to me we barely slept in that feverish period. I distinctly remember pretending to be still asleep while my mother moved around in the shadowy light of dawn, slipping out of her black kimono, pulling off the ratty pajamas she wore underneath, changing into her work clothes and blotting her deep red lipstick with a piece of tissue. The waxy buttercream smell mixed with the scent of her moisturizer and hung densely in the bedroom even after she left for the kitchen. We'd hear the soft rattle of movement as she boiled water for her morning kopi. I'd reach for Arin's hand, and she'd already be awake, her eyes shining like coins in the reflected orange glow of the streetlights, both of us waiting for the click of the main door that would signal the start of our day.

And then we could really begin. Arin's forced pantomime with the jar of ashes had marked us all with shame, none more so than my grandmother, who now watched Arin like a hunter who'd purchased a faulty horse and was trying to figure out how to dispose of it. So while in the house with her, we kept our conversations tightly controlled. The past was dangerous, the future secret. We would mention nothing at home except the absolute present moment. We kept to this so literally it became its own game.

"This cup is dirty," I'd say, standing before the sink.

"This cup is made of a transparent material."

"You are washing it."

"Yes, and now you are drying it."

We found this unbearably funny.

It was obvious to my grandmother that something had shifted. Though what exactly had changed she couldn't figure out. She scrutinized us carefully, in the mornings as we made the bed, ate breakfast, and attended to the day's set tasks. But our conversations were so innocuous she could find no fault with them.

Only once did my grandmother confront me directly. I was coming out of the bathroom, she was waiting by the sink. Peeling an orange, biding her time. When she saw me, her arm shot out and grabbed my wrist.

"What are you up to?"

"What do you mean?"

"There's something off with that girl, and now with you too."

I explained patiently: "Ma told me to play with her, that's all I'm doing."

My grandmother let go of my hand but the sharp citrus smell trailed after me all morning.

After lunch, Arin and I roamed the neighborhood with armfuls of my mother's pink tutoring flyers, tacking them to community noticeboards, checking on old ones to see how many people had taken her number. We spoke freely then, but in low, hushed tones. Spies were everywhere. Conversations in the parking lots outside our window frequently floated up toward us, in snatches. Everyone in the hawker center across the road knew and liked my parents, occasionally the fish ball noodle seller would shout after us, telling us to say hello for her, et cetera. None of the aunties in the row of void deck shops were surprised to see Arin trotting along next to me, they already knew of her arrival, by way of gossip or eavesdropping, and no matter how sweetly they smiled at us, their loyalty was to the world of adults. I pointed them out to Arin individually, these faces that populated my neighborhood and, even then I understood, would never change: the bakery auntie who would always be the bakery auntie, the ten-dollar barber that would be razing hair until arthritis warped his wrist, the family of mee pok sellers that perpetually auditioned potential daughters-in-law for the sole purpose of ensuring the secret vinegar recipe stayed in their clan. Everyone was in everyone's business, the neighborhood running smoothly on the currency of gossip, and that wasn't a bad thing, it demonstrated interest, care, to ask after the sundry shop uncle's university-faring son, or the drink stall auntie's perpetually frozen shoulder. Yet it was crucial for Arin to understand: any one of them would tell on us and call it love.

Our plan was taking shape. The mall's travel kiosk released the week's cross-border bus schedule every Monday, with it we could figure out the exact buses to take and their corresponding ticket prices. Hiding out in the playground's green plastic slide, hunched shoulder to shoulder over our jotterbooks, Arin and I workshopped every last detail, carefully writing, in block English letters, our final plan:

NEXT WEEK

MONDAY . . . . GET UPDATED BUS TIMETABLE

TUESDAY . . . . OBTAIN ADDRESS, COLLECT MONEY
                     AND PASSPORTS (CAREFULLY)

WEDNESDAY! . . . 6 A.M. PACK BAGS DON'T FORGET
                     TOOTHBRUSH AND WATER BOTTLE,
                     LEAVE NOTE, GET ON BUS TO MALAYSIA

THURSDAY. . . . . . GEN TAKE BUS BACK TO SINGAPORE

FRIDAY . . . . PUNISHMENT

MONDAY . . . . START SCHOOL

Since Arin didn't know her home address, the key was getting ahold of the letter Arin's father had written my grandmother. I knew from composition exercises that any piece of self-respecting correspondence would have a return address on its top left corner. The bus fare presented another problem: during the school term I got fifty cents a day, during the holidays nothing at all. My Milo tin beneath the bed held seven or eight dollars. Perhaps I could enlist my mother for help—no, it was too dangerous, the idea discarded as soon as it was raised. We would simply have to locate money at home for me to repay later. My parents were both big believers in the bank and regularly deposited any spare cash they had, keeping only the bare minimum for daily transactions, but the rotation of pregnant women my grandmother boiled soups for paid her in cash, which she hoarded in a large golden Khong Guan biscuit tin by her bed. Everything came down to the small rectangle of living room behind the shoji screen. There the letter would be, and treasure too.

"Does she ever fold the screen away?"

"No, I'm not even allowed to touch it."

"Even when she's not looking?" Arin caught herself before I could correct her: "She's always looking."

I glowed. "That's right."

Yet our secrecy had its costs. My mother, unaware that Arin's time with us was limited, had decided to embark upon an intensive course of nightly tutoring to help Arin catch up before the school term began. Her grand plans to instantly double her income had not delivered. Although one or two tabs were pulled off the flyers each day, leaving the fluttering advertisement with missing teeth, no potential students had called. I could see the excruciating way my mother moved through the house, attuned to her phone, ringing, not ringing, the way she answered each time it chirped with a bright: "Hello?"

In that half second of possibility, the living room would tremble with hope, my father, Arin, and I sitting up straighter, alert—until a soft smile appeared on my mother's face and we knew it was just another routine call, from a coworker, insurance salesmen, the bank.

Disappointment didn't slow her down. Although we were already halfway into the academic year, she'd begged Arin's entry into Primary One by promising to tutor Arin herself. The principal, who was under the impression that my mother was a teacher, not an assistant librarian, tiredly waved her through, and now every night the three of us sat at the dining table after clearing the dinner dishes away, poring over verb tenses and basic addition.

Arin didn't take to study naturally. The first few days were difficult; you could see her straining hard to follow as my mother labored over the Primary One textbooks, trying to cover half a year of learning in a couple of weeks. I'd never had such trouble. In fact, I happily sunk back into the familiarity of practice, toiling over my workbooks, collecting small satisfactions as I completed each exercise, belief in my own intelligence fortified with each controlled, neat checkmark. Watching my mother reason through a question with Arin pained me. I was tempted to relieve them both by explaining that this was pointless: Arin would be gone before the term began.

But something stopped me. Perhaps I intuited that the war being fought on paper across the table encompassed something bigger than getting an equation right. It's true that my mother was brilliant, but also true that I was the only student she'd ever had. Perhaps she saw Arin as some kind of test, that if she could successfully coach Arin into academic success it would be indisputable proof of her own abilities.

And to her credit, Arin worked really hard, even though she knew none of this would be relevant in slightly over a week. Like me, she was bilingual, but far more comfortable in Mandarin, thus my mother spoke only in English to mimic the conditions of school. Arin's lips would move silently, repeating the words to herself, as if imprinting the ideas and language onto her brain, brow furrowing as she stared at the books, willing herself to understand but with limited success. The truth was, the fault didn't lie with Arin. Language aside, it simply wasn't possible to cram six months' worth of knowledge into a handful of nights. But we tried, all three of us, until the inevitable moment when Arin couldn't hold back her exhaustion any longer, button nose scrunching as she tried to swallow her yawn. The spell would break, my mother would lean back, caress both our cheeks, and announce cheerfully that we'd done wonderfully and now it was time for bed.

It was clear my mother was as disappointed as I was. All her usual techniques had failed, and the start of the school term was fast approaching. Desperate, she must have deployed the only other strategy in her arsenal. On Sunday, as Arin and I were going over our plans for the millionth time, I saw a folded notecard peeking out of her jotter book.

I recognized it immediately. Arin, following my gaze, pulled the note out and showed it to me. It was just two lines, written in English, typed up and printed on the university library's glossy white paper, letterhead and all:

> Mrs. Su Yang is cheering on her dear daughter, Arin Yang Yan Mei!
> Jia you, Jia you. Keep working, we'll get through this together!

I read the note only once, then forced myself to return it to Arin with a smile. When had my mother given her this, when had they had even a single moment alone? I felt Arin's questioning eyes on me and struggled to compose myself. Arin folded it back into her jotter book, but later that evening, when she settled at the dining table and flipped her book open, primed for a new night of learning, the note was no longer there.

I finished my vocabulary exercises early, excused myself, and, listening for the scratches of Arin's pencil against the murmurs of my mother's instruction, closed the bedroom door, feeling around under the bed until my fingertips grazed cool metal. Pulling out the Scottish biscuit tin, I eased the lid off, nerves alert to the scrape of a dining chair or any other indication of movement from the living room, and looked down.

A dirty beige hair tie. The hand-drawn map I'd created for Arin. My mother's note.

I stared at the three neatly arranged items, then, without disturbing the tin's contents, replaced the lid and pushed it back under the bed. Arin and my mother were bent over the dining table when I emerged from the bedroom, and my mother's lips curved briefly as I squeezed past them, carrying my pajamas to the kitchen. As I stepped into the shower, I puzzled. My own Milo tin was full of notes I often took out and admired, rinsing myself in my mother's love as I read and reread them. But why would Arin, whose head was turned toward her own home, bother with a scrap of paper from my mother? Did she simply want a souvenir of her time here, a keepsake with which to fondly remember this strange episode in our lives?

Or. Had I been blind to the most obvious of facts, had I willfully ignored the adoration on Arin's face whenever my mother spoke, an adoration that reflected and cannibalized my own? My vision blurred from the shampoo. I turned my face upward and forced my eyes wide open, letting the weak shower water run over my eyeballs.

13

The next morning I moved like a scythe through the day's chores. Confusion had begun uncoiling in me, and I was determined to sever it before it grew further and took up residence in my heart. It was Monday, and there were adults to outwit and bus schedules to obtain and a life waiting to return to normal. Did Arin suspect that I'd been in her tin? It didn't seem likely. I gripped her sweaty hand as we left the flat after lunch, very nearly succeeding in putting the note out of my mind, when we came face-to-face with my mother.

The three of us stared at one another in the corridor. Arin and I frozen in the doorway, my mother momentarily stunned on the top step. It was one of those disgustingly humid days where the very earth smelled like roasted rubber; my mother's forehead glimmered with perspiration. She dabbed at it, then glanced at the fuchsia flyers sticking out of my satchel and smiled. "Where are you girls going?"

Arin blurted: "Bedok Square."

I jumped in: "For air-con."

My mother sidestepped us and set her bags down inside the flat, then planted a doomed hand atop each of our heads. "Well," she twinkled, "let's go."

There was no way we could turn around or lose her without raising suspicion. She hadn't gone to work at the library; she'd spent the morning picking out herbs for my grandmother's soups at the Chinese Medicinal Hall, where she'd run into the bakery auntie, who'd surprised the neighborhood and herself by getting pregnant with her second daughter at the grand age of forty-one, and the women had thus been delayed by chitchat until now. All of this my mother cheerfully relayed as we made the fifteen-minute trudge toward the mall, oblivious to the consternation her presence was causing in us both. When we stopped at the traffic lights, my mother tipped her head back, eyes closed in pleasure as a light breeze sifted through the air. I muttered to Arin: "Distract her when we reach the mall, *I'll* get the schedule."

My mother's warm cheek appeared beside mine, pressed so close I could smell the sweaty floral scent of her face powder and feel her eyelashes bat. "What are we whispering about?"

I flushed. "Nothing."

"Hmm," she said, and straightened up again. Out of the corner of my eye I saw Arin biting down on her finger and flashing the tooth-imprinted face at me like a secret: point received, mission clear.

I nodded; we proceeded toward the mall.

Bedok Square no longer exists today, yet every heartland mall I've stepped into since reminds me of that vivid afternoon with Arin and my mother, which began with us standing in the threshold of that squat mall, stupefied by the sudden coolness of air-conditioning gushing over us, the automatic doors jerking repeatedly as they tried to close. Once inside, my mother asked playfully what we wanted to do, and laughed when she saw us speechless.

Nothing, we said finally, we just wanted to walk around.

But any hope we had that she might leave us and wander off to run her own errands dissipated with each passing second. My mother kept pace with us as we roamed aimlessly, riding the escalator up to the second floor, Arin and I reading various signs out loud; pushing our faces against the window of the optical shop before being chased off by the optician, who fervently rubbed at the glass to rid it of the smudges our noses left; riffling through the knock-off brand name snacks in the value dollar store—horribly conscious the entire time of my mother watching us, trying to engage us in play, increasingly confused by our reluctance. Was it possible that she, an adult, might have felt shut out by two children wrapped up in their own imaginative games, in their own childish secrets? The further we drew from her, the more energetically she attempted to slot herself into our conversations. Arin tried, hard, to distract her, but could not manage it: even I could tell that the questions she asked, the way she tugged on my mother's dress, was stiff, artificial; I watched all this with mounting desperation as the minutes ticked by. Any time now my mother would clap her hands and announce that we had been cooled sufficiently, that it was time to go home, and we would have no choice but to follow.

Finally I yanked on my mother's sleeve. I said: "I want to show you something, let's go to Popular," and the three of us swerved into the bookstore. Arin understood instantly. As I led them to the stationery section, demonstrating my perfect memorization of the nine times tables by carefully printing it out in my best penmanship with various pens—gel ink, roller ball, extra-fine point, ballpoint, glitter ink, metallic ink—on paper strips the bookstore had set out for this express purpose, Arin twisted into the crowd of housewives and vanished.

When I got up to twelve times tables, greatly irritating a shop assistant who had been watching me run down the ink in a cranberry-colored glitter pen, my mother leaned her elbow on the display shelf and turned her right hand into another talking head.

"Is she," the hand mimed, "the future math Olympiad champion of Singapore?"

My mother's self-serious voice, which even in the throes of anxiety pricked me with a sharp needle of pleasure, continued: "Why yes, I believe so. Though if she goes through another times table we might have to start paying for the pens."

I giggled, replaced the pen's cap, and put it back on the shelf. Then my mother realized Arin had vanished. If she was worried, it didn't show, but after calling for Arin and checking between the shelves, she took my hand. "Let's wait downstairs," she said, leading me to the escalator.

The down escalator was more exciting than the one going up—I immediately realized it was funneling us straight to the in-mall entrance of the same McDonald's where we'd had our late-night rendezvous. I glanced up at my mother in disbelief, she winked and lifted a finger to her lips. My toes curled in my sandals, gripping the rubber soles in childish delight. But she stopped right before the McDonald's entrance, waylaid by the mall's information desk, and started making conversation with the customer service officer, an otherwise bored middle-aged auntie whose mauve lipstick had smudged slightly outside her lip line.

I glanced longingly at McDonald's, squinting at the menu board, sniffing deeply. Then the four-toned chime of the mall's intercom reverberated across the floor.

"Attention all shoppers." The customer service auntie had adopted an antiquated, clipped tone, and was speaking into a desk phone. "We're looking for a young girl of seven in a blue T-shirt and beige shorts, who answers to Arin Yang. If you see her, please let her know—Arin, your mother is looking for you, at the level-one reception desk." The auntie repeated, the plastic phone pressed against her mauve lips: "Arin, your mother is looking for you."

Before her announcement was done, Arin materialized over the second-floor banister, the thick black whip of her long braid flying out behind her as she leapt, almost, down the escalator steps, taking them two at a time. At first I thought she was mortified to have been so publicly singled out. But as my mother called out: "Be careful, don't trip, it's dangerous to run on a moving escalator, calm down," I caught sight of Arin's face.

On it was an unfamiliar expression. Her brows were twisted in agony, her cheeks splotchy and pink, her eyes trained on my mother.

My mother, I realized, who had just openly claimed Arin as her own.

A half second before barreling into us, Arin stopped, checked herself. My mother let out a peal of laughter and wrapped her arms around Arin, pulling her in, rubbing the very top of her heated scalp with her thumb.

Arin heaved into my mother's stomach, panting from the run. I saw immediately that she'd succeeded: the folded bus schedule poked out from her back pocket, lifting a corner of her untucked T-shirt like a duckling's tail. As soon as we obtained Arin's address, we could each return to our rightful place. But the morning's confusion returned, rising up in me violently. In it was an unbearable possessiveness, yes, but also—an unexpected anguish. I knew I had a sister, I could not unknow it. Once Arin escaped, who else could I confide in, who else in this stupid, sad world would understand perfectly the perverted jealousy of standing to the side, mesmerized by the sight of their embrace?

I watched my mother's hand caress the top of Arin's head; I couldn't tear my gaze away, didn't want to. As if responding to my silent cry, Arin's head, still buried in my mother's torso, turned slightly toward me, waiting. I hesitated, then stepped forward, flipped her shirt down over the bus schedule, and plastered my arms around them. Arin's whole body was damp, the mall's air-conditioning raising goose bumps on her sweaty skin. I shuddered, and my mother immediately rearranged herself. I felt her hand between my shoulder blades, patting me as if burping a baby.

The customer service auntie cooed: "How guāi your kids are, what angels."

"Yes," my mother's voice floated above our heads. "How lucky I am, I know, I know."

14

We woke the next morning trapped by a surprising June shower, one of those hot, windless affairs bearing straight down from the sky, and grateful for it: if the storm had dallied by even a day we might have lost our resolve to flee. Arin and I were both shaken by my mother's unexpected appearance the day before; it revealed our ingenious escape plan to be more vulnerable than we'd imagined. To what? To circumstances, coincidences, acts of God. To failures of courage. But, I reminded myself, this was no time to waver. I'd made Arin a promise and had to see it through. As we gathered the small goldfish bags of potent chili padi drenched in soy sauce (which you could get for free in any hawker center) and carried them from our hiding place under the bed to the living room, Arin nodded at me, her determined face pale. I suppressed another confused burst of sorrow at our imminent separation and nodded back.

It was Tuesday. We had to find that letter.

My grandmother was by the sink washing the returned tingkats. The unexpected rain had put her in a bad mood. We'd closed all the windows to prevent the floor from getting wet in case she slipped and fell; as a result, the house was a furnace. All the fans were valiantly going, a weak salvation, pushing the humid air around and swaddling our bodies with sweat, yet my grandmother couldn't help but watch each rotation of the kitchen fan and tabulate our impending electricity bills to the cent. When I entered the kitchen, she transferred her scrutiny to me, tracking my movements as I climbed onto a chair and retrieved a bowl, a cup, and a dish from the drying rack above the sink, ferrying them into the living room. I arranged them on the floor and gestured for Arin to stand back behind an imaginary line.

As I made to toss a bag, my grandmother's voice rang out.

"*What* are you doing?"

As I'd hoped, she had trailed behind me and was standing in the kitchen's entryway, brown bead curtain pushed to a side.

"Nothing," I said. "Just playing."

She let go of the beads, and they crashed noisily into one another as she stepped forward. "Playing with *food*?" When I subsided into guilty silence, she said: "Go and wash your hands for lunch."

Later, at the table, the smell of salted fish wafted up as she scraped claypot rice onto each of the three plates. The triangular chili bags she confiscated from our game were arranged at the center of the table like a set of cue balls, one bag lying open and deflated on its side. She reached out with her chopsticks, pinched a cut of chili from it, and mixed it in with her rice.

Arin and I exchanged a look.

"Ah Ma," I said tentatively. My grandmother dismissed me with a flick of her wrist; I fell silent. She opened a second bag of the dark sauce, pouring it over her bowl, discarding the plastic wrapper on the table beside the peanut butter jar. For this, she would suffer. Although she adored spice, age hadn't been kind to her, sanding away her tolerance and inflaming her stomach lining with every bite, yet she refused to stop indulging till we finally found her curled on the kitchen floor one evening last year, writhing in pain from a newly opened gastric ulcer. After that, my father ruled: no more. A death sentence, she lamented, but my father wouldn't budge. It was the only time I'd ever seen them fight—my father discovering her stash of contraband sriracha, wrapped in lettuce and hidden in the vegetable compartment of our refrigerator. It was this obsession we were counting on, but she had to think it was her idea. "Ah Ma, please. I'll get in trouble for having it in the house."

She laughed, a chili seed wedged between her two front teeth. "You're already in trouble."

My grandmother was coated in a fresh layer of sweat, the delight of spice giving way to the heat eating her up from the inside out. Cursing at the weather, she retrieved some folded paper towels from the freezer after lunch, laying them on her forehead and against her collarbone.

The heat and stress of the morning had exhausted us too. Arin and I kicked around, then pulled our shirts up and lay bellyfirst on the floor, hoping the marble tiles would conduct the equatorial heat away from our bodies. We fell asleep like that, in an untidy heap.

At around five thirty the shuffle of the bathroom door being drawn shut jerked me out of my catnap. The rain had stopped, leaving behind a vacuum of still, muggy air. My ankle itched from a fresh mosquito bite. I ignored it and looked toward the kitchen archway: the beads swaying from being recently disturbed.

I shook Arin's shoulder. "She's in the bathroom. Get up."

She shot up like a cat, glancing immediately toward the kitchen, then back at me. We could both hear the faint sounds of my grandmother straining on the toilet. In an instant we were over the couch and behind the shoji screen.

I was struck by how small the area was. Yet the space felt cooler than the rest of the house, as if air moved differently there, fierce daylight dampened by the screen. My grandmother had left for the bathroom in such a hurry that the peanut butter jar was still gently rolling on its side across her thin mattress. Arin dropped into a squat beside the Khong Guan tin and started rummaging. I picked up my grandmother's fanny pack, coiled lazily by the foot of the bed, and unzipped it, looking for cash.

"The letter's not here."

I turned around. "Are you sure?"

She stood unsteadily. I handed Arin the stack of two-dollar notes I'd found, and indicated for her to move over so I could go through the tin.

But Arin didn't count the notes. She put the money back in the fanny pack and tried to arrange its straps haphazardly on the floor, the way it'd been before.

"What are you doing?" I hissed. This was our one chance.

"We were wrong, there's nothing."

"That's impossible."

But she was right. The letter wasn't in the tin—there were promotional flyers from the NTUC across the road, a half-used sheet of stamps, my grandmother's identity card and documents, a few printed photos, including one of her as a young woman, her hair cropped very short, holding a sleeping toddler, and another of a man I presumed was my grandfather, squinting into the camera, in an unfamiliar place full of skinny trees. But no letter.

I sat heavily on the edge of the mattress, mind flipping through the possibilities. Where else could it be? Arin stood before me, pulling on my arm. "Let's go."

I shifted, began to stand, then turned and sat back down again.

"What are you doing?" Arin had one hand on my sleeve, her head half turned toward the living room, desperate to leave but trapped by my indecision. "Please."

"Wait, wait. Look." I reached under the mattress and felt for the bedsheet's elastic edge, pulled it up. The mattress surface had been uneven, I'd assumed it was because I was sitting on a tangled lump of blanket.

But no. Tucked under the bedsheet, in several flat, brown bundles, were envelopes, each stack held together by a thin, red rubber band.

15

They were all from Arin's father. He had not just sent one letter, as we'd thought, but sheafs and sheafs of them. The first one was dated the day my grandfather fell. It began tersely, acknowledging the unexpectedness of the letter, the unexpectedness of their existence, apologizing insincerely for the shock. Then to real business. The fall was bad, the leg infected. It continually oozed smelly yellow pus, and the wound wouldn't close. It seemed only right to inform my grandfather's remaining family, over in Singapore. That was all.

But things continued to deteriorate. There was the issue of money. I can see it now, the slow, humiliating dance of putting pen to paper, of asking without asking, of making a disguised plea and being met with silence. First, sitting at a dining table like ours under a dim ceiling lamp, looking up and suddenly understanding how completely at the mercy of fate and strangers he was. Then, facing the stubbornly empty mailbox, roasting in the regret of sending that first letter, regretting the subsequent ones, the act of laying oneself bare, the desire to retract everything, to keep, if anything, one's pride intact. Yet since he already found himself in this deep, perhaps it seemed pointless to stop. Thus he returned to that doomed room and table, day after day, writing letter after desperate letter.

Perhaps I exaggerate, my imagination fed by the series of small, dim rooms I've found myself in so often over the course of my life. Or maybe not. Perhaps, and isn't this more likely, am I simply ripping away the gauze of courtesy to get at something no one—not my grandmother, not my mother, and certainly not my grandfather's two maligned sons—will articulate?

Imagine this. A boy born back when you'd marry whoever was

within walking distance, always raring to impress the calm, freckled girl all the kampung kids look up to as the neighborhood's Jie Jie. Imagine living through the absolute chaos of war beside an anchor such as she, imagine the natural consequence of admiration and obligation cumulating in this obvious match, not ever once suspecting there comes a time in everyone's life when they look around and understand that their youth is spent and they're now called to endure the life they've built with the bricks of expectation, imagine the lightning strike of understanding as the boy, a babe of barely twenty-two himself, stares into the face of a mottled, helpless newborn, then turns in horror toward his wife—wife! Has any word ever encapsulated so dreadfully the doomed afterimage that remains when romance fades?—and imagine, now, the casual, practiced ease with which that boy might proffer a mantle of noble, heroic ideas, begging away in answer to a nonexistent call, promising he'll be back . . . telling himself it's only temporary, this short break to steady himself. Then, imagine how easy it is to succumb to the permanent vacation from responsibility, just like stepping through a door.

What have I, in the years since, pieced together? There never was a cause he was yoked to other than his own; for most of his life, across the border, my grandfather was an assistant in a beloved shop selling songbirds in rattan cages. But the bill always comes due. Eventually, inevitably, he fell in the kind of violent love that delivered with it the delayed burden of accountability, the concrete, visceral understanding of what he'd done to his original (and now forever martyred) family, embodied in a new, second, screaming infant.

Now imagine being that second son. Living forever in the shadow of a perfect, abandoned family, marinating in his father's guilt. True that Arin would have been given away regardless, as customary of families of a certain ilk and size, yet could it not also be true that the son felt a certain pleasure in reaching across borders to deliver a cruel confirmation to that other, blissfully unaware family, depriving them of doubt, of the possibility, however slim, of the story they told themselves being true? For why else does he force that brother to look him in the eye, grip his hand, if not to say: I'm here, I exist?

And in this battle of pride, who is left?

I can still see Arin in my mind's eye, standing very still, racing through the stacks of letters. Her long untrimmed bangs fall over her eyes, obscuring her expression, which I know, even before I move to read over her shoulder, has gone blank. She cannot yet read Mandarin characters fluently, nor can I. We're skipping over every third, fourth word. But it's enough to understand the gist of it, the thoroughness of the appeal, every new letter a reinforcement of the same request. At the time, I'm still too preoccupied with our mission for the meaning of this to sink in, I'm scanning the letters for a return address, trying to memorize that unfamiliar street name, trying not to get the numbers of the postal code mixed up, adrenaline jumbling the numbers in my head. Not realizing it's a pointless endeavor. Beside me, everything has already changed.

"They didn't want me."

The seed of rage in her voice made me flinch. She had come to the end of the letters. Seventeen in total, the sheer number betrayal enough. This was no impulse decision; my grandmother had forced no one's hand. Toward the end, the tone of the letters had turned begging. I didn't know what to say. I took the letters from Arin and pushed them back into their envelopes, uselessly trying to cover our tracks. We were children; with the narcissistic myopia of the young, we'd believed so wholly in our ability to affect things, to materialize schemes contrary to the machinations of adults. And when adults uncovered our plans, we attributed it to a kind of magical omniscience, rather than understanding that we'd been operating transparently within a goldfish bowl this entire time. How many times had I gasped in delight when my mother located me without difficulty in our games of hide and seek, how often had I taken it as proof of our special connection rather than realizing nothing a child does is mysterious or unknowable to an adult? How long had my mother encouraged this belief in me?

Too long. I turned and saw my grandmother watching us. She had been standing there, perhaps for several minutes, surveying our actions. Watching us tear apart her one private corner, this forbidden square of floor, not even a room. Little gods tyrannical in the belief of our own power.

The look on her face chilled me. It wasn't triumph, as might have been expected, or fury.

It was despair.

16

My grandmother extended a hand, and I, as if pulled along on a puppet's cord, placed the letters in her outstretched palm. Behind me, Arin whimpered.

My grandmother slowly flipped through the letters, counting. A few were crumpled from being shoved too roughly back into their envelopes; she extracted and refolded them before slotting them in correctly. As she did this, she spoke. "Far be it from me to keep a child against her will." She looked at Arin, all pretense of affection drained from her face. "You want to go back to where you came from? Go."

Arin shook her head, but my grandmother continued. "I'll write them to come get you." To herself, she muttered: "Nobody can say I didn't try."

I moved to place myself more firmly between her and Arin. I would not make the same mistake I did that afternoon my grandmother demanded Arin's grotesque pantomime with the jar. "Ah Ma," I said, bravely, "it was my idea. Please let her stay."

"No."

I couldn't believe it. "Please."

She'd been blocking the entrance to the shoji screen, but now she shuffled to her left, sweeping her hand at the gap. "Go pack your bags."

Arin's hands closed around my sleeve. "Nai Nai . . ."

I winced. The words lodged deep in my grandmother's body. She shuddered, skeleton glittering under her loose coat of skin, and lost her shaky grip on the last of her precious restraint. "Wash your filthy mouth." Saliva flew from her raisined lips as she spoke. There was a kind of person, she said, who takes and takes, and feels no shame about it. How dare we sneak around behind her back, after all she'd done for Arin? At random, she peeled one of the letters from the stack and threw it on the ground between us. Enough. "I'm not your Nai Nai," she spat. "You're the daughter of a coward."

The oceanic cruelty in her words advanced in an unholy roar. If I had listened more closely, I might have heard the hurt in her voice, I might have looked around carefully at the pathetic realities of her life, contained behind the fragile privacy of the screen, with no door even to protect her dignity, a privacy sustained solely through mutual collusion. The maniacal wiping and cleaning that left her rectangle free from dust or stray strands of hair, the only space in the house not overrun by shoddy, secondhand books. But her tirade flooded everything out. I turned and saw Arin crying as I'd never seen her cry, mouth moving in half-open gasps, trying to catch her breath. I felt an unfamiliar fury rise to meet my grandmother's. The daughter of a coward?

I said: "Hand me the jar."

My grandmother's mouth snapped shut.

I repeated myself.

Arin, moving like a zombie, reacting mechanically to my instruction, turned, walked two steps, not letting go of my hand, dropped into a squat, and picked up the jar.

My grandmother spoke. "What do you think you're doing? Stop that."

Arin handed it to me.

"Put him down."

An edge of fear had entered her voice. I could hear her drawing on the authoritative manner with which she'd ruled the house, clearing her throat so the natural raspiness of her voice would give way to sharp command, her papery lips and eyes narrowing. Was this all? Her body, drawn to its full height, both hands resting against the hard, jutting fin of her hip through the faded print of her pajama pants—all to give the impression of being bigger, stronger than she was. Yes, that's all it was, an impression. I weighed the jar in my hand, turned it upside down and back again, watched the dust shift. Some of it had stuck together, and I shook the jar to dislodge the clumps. How light it was. How insubstantial. This pathetic heap of dust was what ruined my grandmother and deposited Arin here? *This?*

The clock chimed six and my grandmother took a step toward me. I lowered my head, brought the jar to my chest, and ran.

What had I been thinking in that moment? As I tore past the wooden bead curtain, sending the strands flying into knots, and slammed the bathroom door shut? No more bargains, no more trades, no more negotiations, no more allowing adults to move us around like chess pieces on the boards of their hearts. The indignation faded into a strange, tranquil calm; I twisted the jar open and ripped a finger along the inside of the rim, marveling at the coarse sand of my grandfather, bringing the medley of white-speckled gray to my nose. Salt, it smelled of, and iron. Beyond the kitchen window, the sunset shrieks of mynahs and children mixed discordantly, the hordes of evening insects shrilled post-rain, cars honked, a single amateur strain of the violin's saw floated through the neighborhood. A rush of sound: the front door opening, my father's left-leaning footfall shaking me out of my reverie.

I turned and dumped the contents of the jar into the toilet bowl. Clumps of dust immediately formed, little islands of ash clinging to the surface of the toilet water even as bits broke away and sank. I flushed once, felt, in my bones, understanding tremble through the house. Without waiting for the water tank to refill itself fully, I depressed the handle a second time, then reached for the bottle of purple hand soap wedged on our crowded bathroom sink.

By the time my father stopped outside the door, it was too late. My grandfather, all of him, was permanently scattered throughout the sewage chutes of Singapore. Irrevocably dispersed throughout the land he abandoned, the land where he belonged.

17

My father knocked. "Genevieve Yang Si Qi," he said. "Open up."

His shadow rippled across the wavy mosaic as he put his face to the bathroom's sliding door and repeated himself for the third time. His low command muffled the sound of my grandmother's panic unreeling against my mother's placating tone. I leaned my head against the door with a soft thump.

"Pa." The plea in my voice was obvious.

He flicked a switch outside. Fluorescent light flooded the tiny bathroom. "Are you apologizing from behind a locked door?"

I raised my head and lifted the white plastic latch. My father took a step back, waiting for me to slide the door open. A breeze, carrying with it the fresh smell of wet grass, drifted in through the now open kitchen window, lifting the sweat from my skin and raising tiny goose bumps down my neck. I didn't see Arin anywhere, but my grandmother wrenched herself out from beside my mother and rushed forward. She'd heard, but not believed, the sound of the toilet flush.

My father caught her, his right arm wrapping around her waist and drawing her close to his armpit. "Stop."

His gaze flicked to where the empty peanut butter jar lay drying, beside our toothbrush cups on the porcelain sink. I began to explain myself, but my grandmother's eyes found the jar and her head reared back in shock, knocking against his torso. She let out a wail, and began pounding on her chest, fist closed and making a circular motion over her heart.

"He's gone," she gasped. A flicker of recognition chased itself across my father's face. "He's gone."

In a pinched voice, he said: "He's been gone, Ma."

"He came back . . ." I closed my hand into a fist and dug my nails into my palm in order to stave off the fear. My grandmother, widow to a man who'd been returned against his will, pointed a damning finger at me. I understood, viscerally, that unless my father intervened, I would be caned.

My father closed his free hand over hers, trying to fold it back against her side. She resisted, her body wriggling under his grip, and her pajama top lifted to reveal a thin strip of crinkled pale stomach. A long white hair extended from a mole on her waist. I averted my eyes; my father said: "Leave it. She's just a child."

"An evil child. She knew what she was doing."

"No, Ma. *He* knew what he was doing when he let us believe he was running away to be a hero."

My mother came forward and put a warning hand on my father's shoulder, staring at the dangerous purple vein that had materialized on his neck. He was shaking slightly, and at my mother's touch, visibly restrained himself. The vein pulsed, subsided.

I could scarcely believe it. He had picked me after all.

My grandmother said, shocked: "You didn't know him."

He agreed—"No."

He had returned, with significant effort, to the same controlled, pleasant tone he always presented my grandmother with. But his spirit wavered. My poor, kind father, who all his life had done his best to cope—with his mother's delusions of grief, with betrayal and abandonment—had finally had enough.

And yet he still hoped. How was it she could not hear the plain appeal in his voice? She had wrenched a door open and he was begging her to pull it shut.

She murmured, glancing at the empty jar: "Give him back."

He would close the door himself. We heard it click shut as he said, again: "No."

But the single syllable drew out and splintered. He dropped his head to his chest, and suddenly, despite his wife's hand on his arm, despite his mother wrapped in his grip, despite his thirty-five years, looked like a child betrayed.

My mother raised her eyes. "Gen," she said. In her pronouncement, refuge for us all. Let us regroup, let us lick our wounds and adapt to this crisis the way we adapt to everything. But for the first time I felt the limits of her promise. Arin's forgotten figure shifted in the corner of my eye, watching from the kitchen entryway, biting down on her terrified thumb. My mother's voice: "Come."

When one door closes with force, the resulting gale must open another. Instead of running to my mother, I turned and retrieved the peanut butter jar, then slowly lifted the feather duster from where it hung by the bathroom door. With my hand wrapped around its severe cane handle, I approached the three of them: him, my grandmother, my mother, locked in a deformed triangle of despair. My grandmother didn't move, but her eyes followed me, latching on to the freshly washed jar, still shining damply, in my hands.

"Ah Ma," I said, holding both items out.

She blinked, surprised at being addressed. The multicolored feathers trembled and danced in the air. "Ah Ma, you're right to be angry." My courage was not unlimited, it was already breaking in places, weakened by terror of the punishment to come. In a doomed rush, I said: "It was wrong of me. I'm sorry."

My grandmother died the following year. We all knew it was coming. Having finally come to terms with her deferred heartbreak, all the energy went out of her. She abandoned her soups, broke off contact with her tingkat clients, and ignored the indignant husbands who showed up at our door on behalf of their malnourished wives. The furious Hokkien that had hounded my childhood vanished overnight, too, leaving her to drift silently around the house like a deflated ghost. I was, in those days, more afraid of my grandmother than I'd ever been growing up, when she'd been liberal with her shouting, pinching, caning, all in the name of discipline. I thought I'd hated her then, but now her frailness wounded me. I devoted myself to making her life comfortable. I woke earlier than ever to help with her breakfast, I offered to walk with her after meals. But she lost interest in all of it. She wouldn't change out of any given set of pajamas until they started to smell, and even then, she had to be coaxed to move. She had to be cajoled to eat, too, and when she refused, the speed with which she shrunk scared us all. When I took her shriveled arm in mine after dinners and tried to tug her toward the main door for a walk, she'd shake her head listlessly.

One night in February, weeks after she stopped taking dinner with us at the dining table, she died.

We all heard it, the little exhale from behind the shoji screen, the last sigh whistling past her lips in a tone of raspy surprise. My mother leapt from her seat, upsetting the stack of books by the feet of the dining table, causing a little avalanche. My father stood, too, more slowly. By the time he reached the edge of the shoji screen, my mother was weeping. I had been pushing around a loose incisor with my tongue for weeks; in all the commotion I bit down and warm blood filled my mouth. Only Arin saw me spit out the small, triangular tooth. She reached for my hand under the table, I laced my fingers in hers.

We cremated my grandmother: it was cheaper. My father did not cry throughout the ceremony, and it fell to my mother to sift through the sandy ashes with a pair of long metal chopsticks, to pick out the one gold tooth which had not melted in the fire. I had been punished severely, in the end, for my sacrilegious act that humid June night, though it didn't escape my notice that, in all the chaos, our other transgression—sneaking behind the shoji screen—went uncommented upon. After my apology crumpled my grandmother, my father caned me with the bamboo end of the feather duster, my mother turned her face away; my heart was swollen for weeks. Arin—and I don't blame her—hid while the confrontation with my grandmother was happening; she stayed in the living room. But when my father took my palm, smoothing it flat with his, almost gently, before raising the cane, our eyes locked. She dropped both hands, they hung loosely by her sides. No secret friend to take comfort in: in that moment it was just Arin and me. With each stroke of the cane she flinched but did not look away. The next morning, my mother hugged me and rubbed Zam-Buk on my welts. What were you thinking, she said, then when she saw the places where my skin tore, she gasped, pressed her warm lips to my palm, and said, never mind, you didn't know better, it's over now, we forgive you. But it seemed to me my punishment only truly ended the night of my grandmother's cremation.

That night, after my mother fell asleep, I reached over and felt for Arin.

She was awake, waiting. We slipped out of the bed and into the kitchen. I thought we might fold the shoji screen away, but my father had moved behind the screen immediately. We tiptoed past it, our nerves electric, attuned to any possible shift in his breathing, carefully scooping the wooden beads to the side with one hand while we passed and letting them back down gently so they wouldn't clatter. In the farthest possible corner from the kitchen doorway, by the toilet door and beside the windowsill where my disinfected tooth was air-drying on a paper towel, we faced each other. I ran my tongue over the raw gap in my gums, and asked:

"Do you have it?"

She nodded. Arin produced two pieces of blank paper, folded and tucked into the waistband of her pajama shorts. Clipped to one of them was an inky black pen. I took it from her, pinned the sheet of paper against the wall, and, squinting in the dim purple moonlight, printed, exactly, on both sheets:

CONTRACT OF SISTERHOOD
This certifies that Genevieve Yang Si Qi and Arin Yang Yan Mei
are sisters, forever and ever, till death do us part. Amen.
This contract is legally binding.

We signed our names. I retrieved the paring knife from the kitchen sink and breathed shallowly, trying to gather my courage. Then, very quickly, I slid the tip of the knife across the skin of my thumb. The skin blanched, but did not bleed. I squeezed my thumb lightly until a pearl of blood appeared, then another, then another. I smudged it under my signature on both copies.

Arin took the knife from me, her face white, and followed suit. Instead of handing the contracts back, she grasped my outstretched hand and brought both our thumbs to her face. I flinched, but rather than biting down, she blew on them until the blood began to clot. I let myself relax momentarily into the warm, truffly smell of her breath, before pulling away to wash the knife, wincing at the sting of washing detergent.

Then, holding my breath, I spun around to face Arin. Now that the contract was signed and our relationship irrevocable, I asked, in a terrified voice: "I killed her, didn't I?"

I was only nine. What did I know of my ability to exert myself in the world? But the conviction that I was, as my grandmother proclaimed, an evil child, had rooted deep inside me. I thought with time the guilt would go away, but I don't know that its grip has ever lessened.

Arin shook her head, her tiny hands squeezing mine.

"No," she said. "You saved me."

The 2000s

Singapore

18

In 2003, my mother was let go from the university library in a terribly stylish way.

I was fifteen, Arin fourteen. To us, the library and my mother were as conjoined as a rock and her barnacle. That they could be separated felt, at the time, like an unnatural violence.

To hear my mother tell it, the university must have been intimidated by the court of knowledge she held behind that checkout desk; the swirl of hushed, reverential tones as students assembled daily to pick her brain for the yet unmapped connections between the inhuman number of books she notoriously devoured and whatever assignment question they had. One of them, a graduating linguistics major, had even gone so far as to include her in his thesis acknowledgments and send her a copy—*infinite gratitude to the indomitable Su Yang for her encouragement and guidance in the darkest of academic hours*—a line nestled in a longer treatise on the value of libraries as refuge and resource. My mother highlighted the relevant portions and hung it on our wall, where it stayed for years as a favorable point in her campaign for advancement. She'd been ceaselessly applying for roles in the university as a teaching assistant, a tutor, and once, audaciously, as an adjunct professor. The university rejected her each time with the increasingly impatient explanation that without a degree she was unqualified for these roles, yet she persisted. She would come home and deliver these updates cheerfully, as if it were simply a tussle of wills between her and the university, a familial dispute between two parties who loved each other, and a matter of bringing them around to her point of view. We listened to her dispatches like they were episodes of an endless, thrilling story. Never did it occur to us that one party might break away.

You had to admire the way it was done—not by jurisdiction but

by my mother's own hand. The day she was called into the administrator's office, her blood raced with furious amazement; knowledge
that they were finally going to take a chance on her, the brittle
relief of arrival. She would smile, she decided, and be gracious and
grateful, as if she hadn't applied and been turned down every other
semester for the last eight years. When the administrator drew a
crumpled fuchsia sheet from her files, my mother gleamed with
pride. Her tutoring business hadn't taken off, though she'd continued advertising for it through the years. She inclined her long,
elegant neck to acknowledge her commitment to educating the
young, and did not at first register the administrator's voice, silky as
a blade, telling her she couldn't just go around advertising that she
was a tutor in the university. She could get into trouble.

The administrator paused, then clarified: legal trouble.

Only later did I realize it was a more merciful firing than if they'd
said the true reason, from which my mother would never recover.
She had become irrelevant. The rapid proliferation of self-checkout
booths and other technologies, along with her lack of qualifications
and tech savvy, would have rendered her obsolete in a matter of
months. Yet when my mother relayed the exchange with the administrator to us it was clear how bewildered she was. She didn't even
argue, just gathered her things and left, though on the way out she
slipped a teal-colored paper puncher into her bag.

"Look," she crowed, producing it that night over dinner. "It's
my long-service award."

How bright her voice was, how amused.

My father said: "It's good to take a break."

At fifteen I prided myself on being the top student in my year,
yet I struggled with simple comprehension. "Did they actually fire
you?" I demanded. "Or did you just leave?"

Both parents ignored me. My mother flickered. "But I did not
need a break."

Her voice was soft but we heard every word. She wouldn't
look at my father and therefore did not see that she should have
responded in private. It was the first time they'd ever presented a
less than united front; my father set his spoon aside and raised the

soup bowl to his face so his hands would have something to do. When he lowered it, his face was glistening from the soup's steam.

In the terrible silence that followed it was Arin who found the right words. Fingering the paper puncher questioningly, she asked: "Auntie, can I have this?"

My mother beamed so quick and wide her red lipstick split. "It's yours."

I couldn't wait to get Arin alone. The next day when we were walking to school, I asked: "What did you want the paper puncher for?"

We were crossing an overhead bridge. Arin stopped to examine the pink and yellow bougainvillea in the planters, looked around for nosy adults, then surreptitiously punched two holes in its crepe-like bracts, one of each color, and an additional hole in one of its waxy green leaves. She pocketed the puncher and said, grimly: "Confetti."

She meant for when my mother started a new job. In facing a crisis there were people who settled and people who celebrated. Acceptance was easier; it delineated clearly the limits one would suffer—poor Father!—but Arin and I considered ourselves part of the latter. Even so, I asked: "Aren't you getting ahead of yourself? She might still go back."

"She shouldn't. She doesn't need them."

"Mei, she loves the library."

Arin turned to me, eyes cloudy with hope. "You'll see. Give it a month and this will just be another morning in the season of success."

Season of success. The term debuted a few years prior, at the end of my first year at Grace Methodist Girls' School, when Arin was making her own decision on what secondary school to attend. It was one of the more respectable schools in the East, and on my first day I'd shown up naïvely imagining myself as one in a sea of equally eager girls ready to forge ourselves anew. But half the incoming cohort already knew one another, having gained entry through legacy, religious, or parental affiliation; perhaps that was why a new face like mine posed no threat and brokered no interest. In the first round of tests I came in a close second to a legacy girl, Chong Jia Min, who didn't even glance my way when the results were announced. It was obvious she was accustomed to winning in everything, which incensed me. I was no longer content to simply do well—I studied so hard my vision was blurry for weeks.

When I topped the cohort in the middle of the year, Jia Min burst into tears. The next morning, a woman appeared in school and rounded on me after the morning assembly.

You watch out, she said. She was wearing a lace cardigan cropped at the waist, soaked through with sweat. I had no idea who this strange woman was or how she got onto campus; I didn't know why she was leaning in so close I could smell the acid coffee on her breath and see the bubbles of spit forming between her teeth. Only when I saw Jia Min crying behind her, tugging on her sleeve, did I understand.

Later that day, Jia Min cornered me in the second-floor bathroom.

"Sorry about earlier." Her voice was casual but she'd approached me alone, her entourage of similarly prissy girls gone ahead to recess. "My mother gets really intense about my prospects."

"Your mother is crazy."

"She's not crazy, she just cares about me a lot."

"That doesn't give her the right to go around attacking people. I didn't even do anything wrong."

The pastel ligatures of her braces flashed at me. "I already said sorry. Let's be friends. Do you want to study together after school?"

If my own mother had accosted a classmate in bright daylight, I would have died of shame. Yet here Jia Min was, preening like some kind of arrogant peacock.

"With you? No thanks."

It was a mistake. The entire horde of legacy girls turned against me. After that, whenever I raised my hand in class, a snigger would ripple through the back row; in group work or presentations I was always the last to be picked; during P.E. games I was often the only remaining girl on the bench, unchosen, waiting to be off-loaded onto a team that would invariably avoid passing me the ball. At first I didn't understand what was happening. I was accustomed to being well liked, and this sudden ostracization distressed me. Was it because I was uncoordinated, clumsy? Because I shared no common interests with my peers? Or was there something more fundamental separating us, an impossible breach that rendered friendship impossible? I was miserable; if only the criterion for acceptability were explained, I believed I would have attained it to perfection.

But one day, an interfering classmate, Penelope Wong, caught me in the stairwell, and in the righteous tone of someone bestowing a favor, laid out the accusations against me. Apparently, everything about me was a problem: the lopsided way I ran during P.E., the proportions of my pinafore, how I didn't know to blot the oil on my forehead with rice paper or sip hot coffee through a straw to avoid staining my teeth. Apparently my academic success was a stroke of luck; apparently I'd be dethroned soon.

I interrupted. "Why are you telling me this?"

"Because I don't think it's right how you're being bullied."

I stared at Penelope for a long time. Then I patted her head and said: "You should spend more time studying."

I walked away from that conversation simmering with the singular desire to obliterate. Bullying? Luck? I worked even harder, and when the September Block Tests came, I stayed, through the power of pure spite, at the top of our cohort. Right before the end-of-year examinations, Jia Min approached me again. This time she'd brought a few girls with her. When I saw them I knew she'd already lost. I pretended to listen while Jia Min explained how she understood that I'd come from a neighborhood school and didn't know how things worked, but there were three more years of secondary school, and it was a pity we'd gotten off on the wrong foot.

"Friends?" she asked again. Her face the very image of charity.

"I don't think so," I said. "One day you'll be working for me." One of the pigtailed nonentities behind her laughed in shock, and I continued: "All of you."

That year end, I defended my position as top girl, Jia Min slipped to number four, and Penelope was so deep in the double digits she didn't show her face on campus for days. When I saw Mrs. Chong waiting for Jia Min by the school gates on the afternoon the results were released, I smiled brightly at her. She was wearing large, rectangular shades and clutching a baguette-shaped handbag, but even without being able to see her eyes, I could tell she remembered exactly who I was. She pretended not to see me, and it was hard for me to pretend I wasn't pleased.

I went straight from my school to Arin's. She was in the middle of the Primary School Leaving Examination, and I felt very old and wise as the swarm of twelve-year-olds thronged past me. Several threw us admiring glances as I heaved Arin's worn blue backpack onto my shoulder and adjusted her uniform's collar, which had somehow flipped up over the course of her exam.

She slipped her hand into mine and we started walking home.

"Tell me about today's paper first," I said.

"Three of the multiple-choice questions were repeats from your year. The rest weren't hard."

"Excellent."

"And you, Jie Jie?"

I gave her a beatific smile. "You should list Grace Methodist as your first choice." Her eyes widened, registering my triumph, as I said: "Welcome to the season of success."

Arin kept the teal paper puncher in her schoolbag for weeks, punching tiny holes in everything she passed—magazine covers, multicolored posters hanging from the school walls, flyers from the community notice board—assembling a massive confetti stash she was prepared to unleash over our heads the day my mother returned from her job hunt in triumph and glory.

But months went by, and nothing. My mother cycled through a ream of temporary contract positions—Fuji Xerox typist, Starhub call operator, Gramercy Music data entry officer, CAS Tech secretary—all the while relentlessly applying for academic-adjacent jobs and failing.

Then, for a brief, terrifying moment, she gave up.

One day, we came home and she was lying on the couch, fully dressed in her dark green shift, gazing at the ceiling fan, eyes flitting rapidly from right to left. When Arin and I stood above her, a directionless smile toyed at the corner of her painted red lip, and she raised a hand half-heartedly to shade her eyes, as if to block out the sun.

"Let her rest," my father said. He was spending more time at home, going straight from his cab to laboring in the kitchen, then doubling back out again after dinner for another shift. Between my parents, he was actually the better cook, having learned from his late mother the ways one might steam dory to make it taste like the more expensive seabass, how to work the claypot so the husky brown rice would emerge fragrant and buttery. He'd been careful, too, to purchase the family's groceries slightly farther away, from a wet market in Tampines, rather than Bedok, so as to avoid neighborhood speculation, and as his noble forearms, prematurely aged from years of driving in the sun, moved tenderly, running the blunt edge of a knife down a fish's scales, it occurred to me that every kite, no matter how exuberant, relied fundamentally on its patient tether to sail it safely back into harbor. I felt comforted. My father nodded at Arin and me. "Don't just stand there," he said, "set the table."

After dinner, he dropped a Ziploc bag of notes and coins into my mother's palm.

"What's this?"

"Cash," he replied proudly.

He meant an allowance. She already managed his earnings for household expenses—he must have accumulated this separately, driving all those additional overnight shifts.

It was like an infusion of electricity. My mother bolted upright and began forcefully clearing the plates. "Have I worried you all?" She touched Arin's and my cheeks, laughing loudly. "Don't be silly. It'll be fine."

Her left hand lingered on my father's shoulder as she passed. The Ziploc bag was still sitting on the table. He blinked, unsure if this gregariousness was a mirage.

Arin and I exchanged looks of alarm.

Within a week my mother was working at the photocopy shop in the string of void deck shops winding around the central market right across the street from us.

19

For a period my mother went around cheerfully, but it was the sort of unnatural effervescence that occurs after someone hits you on the head and leaves you mildly confused. It hurt to watch; I wanted to restore her old confidence but didn't know how. Until she came home one evening from the shop with copies of a study guide someone had dropped off. She must have scanned the pages, instinctively recognized their value, yet, no longer trusting her own judgment, simply duplicated the notes and handed them to Arin and me, saying: *See if anything helps.*

It did. The second we read them it was clear how different these guides were from the ones our own school distributed. I'd bulldozed my way into academic success by forcibly committing every single word in my thick textbooks to memory, even the parts I didn't fully comprehend, but these guides laid things out in a way that formed clear, concise connections between theory and application. A teacher must have gone through weighty concepts, digested them, and rewritten them in simple, easy-to-understand language, inventing examples to best illustrate each point. I could feel the pure intelligence of the invisible teacher in every line, laboring to catalyze information on her students' behalf; it reminded me of my mother, and I said so.

She smiled. "This reminds you of me? How so?"

"The quality of thinking is the same, Mama."

She read the pages again, more carefully this time. The papers' edges crinkled in her grip; I felt my heart speed up.

The photocopy auntie knew and liked my mother, and didn't mind at all when she began reproducing wholesale—to hell with copyright laws—specialized study guides from top schools like Raffles and Tao Nan, ten-year-series exam papers, and expensive reference books other parents dropped off during their lunch breaks.

She sold these additional copies on the educational black market to students who would shell out tens of dollars for access to practice papers from the top schools, and split the profit with the photocopy auntie, who was thrilled.

"Your mother," she proclaimed to Arin and me one day, "was wasting all her time trying to teach. She's a natural businesswoman."

The photocopy auntie spoke so loudly, and with such sincere admiration, that the other void deck aunties nodded and my mother blushed a girlish pink. It struck me deeply. I became convinced the pathway to happiness lay in proving, conclusively, to the rest of the neighborhood, that despite her change in fortunes, Su Yang was perfect in every way. After that, Arin and I started stopping at the photocopy shop on our daily walks home from school, presenting ourselves for examination, as if we were two glimmering fragments of my mother's character.

It worked. Before long, the void deck aunties began perking up like wilted sunflowers whenever we approached, beaming fondly at the sight of Arin pulling out a bottle of cold water, freshly filled from the school's dispensers to quench my mother's thirst; gratified by my polite greetings, by the way I attentively asked after the photocopy auntie's recovering sprained ankle, asked whether the bakery auntie's daughter passed her driving test, commiserated about how pretty the new girlfriend of the mee pok seller's son was and speculated whether this was the woman who would finally ascend to being the neighborhood's mee pok princess, worthy of their secret vinegar recipe. I could see each auntie filing away these examples and incorporating them into the gossip and nagging they carried home—Su's girls are so courteous, so thoughtful, so filial, why not you, why not you.

We were such fixtures at the shop that one afternoon, a regular customer automatically handed Arin a slim book with multiple Post-its marking which pages were to be copied. My mother started, intercepted the woman, then glanced at the clock. Weren't our exams approaching, was this really the time to waste mooning around in the company of these women, hanging on to their every word? She laughed and chased us off: Get on, go home, return to your revision. It was an idea that charmed the void deck aunties—

that they posed a thrall equal to that of study, of books. We left them, tittering, and as we traced our way back home, balancing single file on the curb along the roadside bushes, Arin and I exchanged intelligence.

"The minimart uncle's wife is suffering from sunstroke."

"The bakery auntie's husband is gambling again."

"The alteration auntie accidentally damaged some lady's leather pants. She had to compensate her—two hundred dollars."

Arin made a face: poor thing. "Ask her about it again in a week?"

I plucked a bloom from an ixora bush, pinching the thin stem and pulling lightly, then turned. Arin already had an ixora stem laid on her tongue like a bee's sting, waiting. We savored the drop of nectar, our tiny spoils, and tossed the flowers to the ground.

"Put it in the binder when we get home," I said. Our dossier on the neighborhood aunties, containing all the facts of their lives, their idiosyncrasies and tics and triggers and weak, easily flattered spots, was by that time thick as a fist.

Arin nodded and reached for another flower.

How satisfying, the feeling that Arin and I were watering the pot of my mother's confidence and watching it grow. Then one morning in April, something happened that marked the full restoration of her spirit.

I was in the habit of waking earlier than Arin on most days. So it was me who saw, first, the folded note on the dining-room table.

Mrs. Su Yang wishes her daughters,
Genevieve Yang, Arin Yang, and their Big Beautiful Brains,
a splendid and productive day ahead!

It was her first note in a long while, and the only one she had ever written in her loopy chicken scratch, rather than typed and printed at the university library where she'd worked my entire life. I could detect the subtle metallic scent rising from the blue pen ink and see the faint, ghostly movement of her hand dashing the letters off. I touched each character, the deliberate *B*s sinking into the paper, the confident exclamation point at the end, and understood that my mother had finally accepted her place at the photocopy shop. Forget the glossy white papers with their prim letterheads, forget my mother's little court of wonders: we had succeeded; she was content. Wasn't that what we'd wanted all along? So what was this grief I was feeling?

I heard Arin stirring, I folded the note away.

That day, when I went to school, the student particulars were being updated. Under my mother's occupation I listed: business-woman. I stared at the word for a long time, then at the last minute, right before the forms were due, without knowing why, canceled it out with my black pen and wrote: housewife.

I never mentioned it to anyone, not even Arin. Yet it was this my mind leapt to, the thought that my small and shameful betrayal had been somehow found out, when Penelope Wong came up to me again, right before the last O-level paper, and said she'd always known there was something interesting about my family.

20

We were not friends. Our interactions, beyond that first time Penelope intercepted me in the stairwell, consisted mainly of cordial *hi, bye, hurry up and pass the worksheet*s. I had the impression that Penelope was very nice, very rich, and very stupid: rumor had it her parents not only paid her motivation money to study, but an additional sum to stay single in hopes that, undistracted by love, she'd eventually make it to the university. Further, Penelope was one of thirty-two students who sat around doodling fruit all day as part of the Art Elective program, which nobody took seriously since Art was one of the few O-level subjects internally graded and thus impossible to fail. I, on the other hand, had deliberately chosen the most difficult subject combination so it'd be even more impressive when I inevitably received straight A's. We were of different worlds, we had no reason to talk. Yet here she was standing before me, head cocked to the side, speaking as if picking up from the middle of a conversation. All the other girls were swarming outside the examination hall, cramming as much last-minute information into their brains as possible, but a couple glanced over at her loud, inquisitive voice.

Interesting.

Caught off guard, I recoiled, as if hit, and Penelope's expression fell. The bell rang and I forced myself to refocus, turning away from her and filing toward the examination hall. We settled into our assigned seats, and though I kept my mind deliberately blank, waiting for the question paper to be handed down to me, I could feel her, three rows away, glancing over repeatedly until an invigilator told her to stop.

I completed the exam on autopilot, letting my years of rote memorization take over. But while scratching out long division sums and discerning common factorials, my heart pounded incessantly. I knew I was a target; I knew the other girls despised me for not feigning humility with my good grades. With every gesture and comment in class I made it clear that I knew I was smarter, that I delighted in inflaming jealousy and embittering hearts. Was this an act of petty psychological warfare then, a transparent attempt to topple me right before the exams? If so, Penelope had picked the wrong person to mess with. I shifted the crosshairs of my intelligence onto Penelope's face and rolled over the variety of ways Arin and I would obliterate her for daring to cast aspersions on our family, and by the time the invigilator collected the papers, I had brought the imaginary Penelope to tears.

But the real Penelope was picking her way through the crush of girls toward me. For the next two months, nothing would be demanded of us till the O-level results were released in mid-January. All around us girls were calling taxis, looking up the route to the nearest shopping mall, exchanging answers for a particularly challenging question, updating their mothers on the phone. I could see Jia Min, in the distance, bewildered by the slap of freedom, by the everlasting cord of each next test cut loose.

Penelope stopped before me. "I didn't mean to upset you," she said, distressed. "I'm not like that. Some of us are going to Swensen's for ice cream to celebrate, do you want to come? Don't worry, it's my treat." She looked at my face more closely, alarmed. "Hey, I'm sorry, okay? Don't cry. Wait, are you crying because of the exams or what I said?"

I was so worked up that tears were running down both cheeks. Mortified, I rubbed them away with the back of my hand, and said: "You. That exam was easy."

She looked put out. "Really?"

I nodded. She pulled out a handkerchief, made of soft cotton and embroidered with periwinkle thread. I hesitated, then blew my nose on it. Penelope accepted it with the face of a pariah. Then I cleared my throat and spoke. "Whatever you have to say about my mother you can say to my face."

Penelope, bless her, was too simple to lie. "Your mother?" She looked surprised. "I was talking about Arin."

. . .

Arin's classes had ended hours ago, and she was waiting for me by the school gates, leaning against the iron bars and reading from a booklet of study notes my mother had cobbled together from various top schools. She was chewing on the end of her braid, and when she looked up I could see the pearls of her saliva winking at me from between her strands of hair.

"Yay," she said quietly. "You're free."

I took her arm and started walking. I was eager to leave the knot of girls, competition, and conspiracy behind.

Once we were safely out of earshot, I said: "You're writing essays now?"

According to Penelope, Arin had won a prestigious award. It hadn't been announced yet, but Penelope's mother was on the school board and had been a guest judge.

She shook her head, perplexed. "Not me. I would have told you."

Her confusion was so genuine that I felt reassured. It was true: Arin wouldn't have drawn attention to herself in such an ostentatious way. Penelope must have been mistaken. Yet a couple of days later, a letter came inviting us all to a prize ceremony in the school hall, to be held during the first week of the December holidays. My mother slit the envelope open with a butterknife and read it aloud at the dinner table, voice quivering with pride.

"On behalf of Grace Methodist Girls' School, I am delighted to inform you that Arin Yang has been selected as a recipient of this year's CORAL award, which recognizes *one* student annually who has demonstrated exemplary character and outstanding personal qualities . . ."

I darted a look at Arin. She was horrified. As was my father, who remarked, bleakly: "Why would anyone choose to hold a ceremony at three p.m.? I suppose they think we don't have to work." Then, remembering Arin, he turned to her and said: "Good job."

She flushed mauve under her pool of hair. "Thank you, Uncle. You don't have to come, it's not important."

If it was me receiving the award, he would've nodded, relieved to be let off. But he'd never quite managed to convincingly treat Arin with anything but kid gloves. "Of course it's important."

Arin appealed to my mother. "Auntie, tell him."

But my mother had already begun discussing the logistics of taking a day off with my father, ignoring the fact that we couldn't afford to let the cab burn through a day's rental in the school's parking lot. It had been seven years since my grandmother passed—we hung her picture, the same one used at her cremation, on the living-room wall, an act that allowed us to avoid talking about her yet still feel as though we were including her memory in our lives. One grandmother lost, one daughter gained, the number of mouths to feed the same, yet somehow, thanks to either the increased demands of living or the persistent tendrils of inflation, the numbers didn't tally. Arin locked eyes with me and we slipped away at the first opportunity.

Standing under the yellow glow of a streetlamp, Arin said: "I figured it out. It was supposed to be an in-class writing exercise. Mdm Rajah didn't ask for my permission to submit it; if she had I would have said no."

Mdm Rajah was her form teacher, beloved by Arin and throughout the school for being a beacon of immense and worldly charisma. Any girl would have been glad to have been singled out by her, but Arin was painfully shy. In my pocket, my hand closed around the pinch of confetti I'd snuck from Arin's tin, intending to toss it at her in celebration, but she looked so unhappy that I dropped the confetti and reached for her instead. "It's a good thing."

"She should've asked."

I shrugged. "She's a teacher, she doesn't have to ask permission."

When the day of the ceremony came, my parents were ready first. My mother had borrowed an outfit from the alteration auntie, a pair of dark pink pants and a white pleated top. She took care to hold a cloth under her chin as she powdered her face, leaving no trace that might trigger the outfit owner's suspicion. My father had somehow obtained a tie and was struggling, by the doorway, with its loop.

Arin dawdled over everything, delaying the moment when she'd have to step onstage for as long as possible. She soaked her thick black rope of hair in shampoo, listlessly waved the hair dryer at it, took a curiously long time to iron and pull on her uniform. We were in the room together, my parents already dressed and waiting by the door, when I said: "Think about how many girls would kill to have Mdm Rajah's favor."

I was trying to encourage her, but she suddenly bent down and pulled out the binder we kept under the bed. She flipped to the last page, where a new entry had been created.

"You know how Mdm Rajah tells her classes all these stories about her good old days in America?"

I nodded.

She handed me the binder, then returned to the mirror, tugging at the navy hairband of satin my mother had procured for the occasion. My eyes scanned the page. It was a record of impressions, scribbles transcribed from Arin's memory, listing the skittish affectations of Mdm Rajah's overly charmed speech, the iron twang of her faded American accent, warped with use, like an echo of an echo, making note of her frequent references to New York, California, and Washington, D.C. Cities we recognized from movies, from the sets of TV shows and paperback novels.

"Turns out she only spent four years in America," Arin said, placing the band grimly on her head. It scraped her curtain of bangs away and exposed a forehead tender with acne. "For university. The same amount of time we spent in secondary school." When I didn't say anything, she added—"She went somewhere called Alabama."

21

For all her reluctance, when her name was announced Arin walked quickly across the stage, pale skin sickly under the fluorescent lights. But it was clear to everyone watching that she didn't want to be there. The principal had to call her back for the official photograph. As he gripped one end of the certificate, he joked— This isn't a takeout window, smile, smile. Flashes stuttered, later the pictures would show Arin staring furiously down the black hole of the camera's iris, and by some small mercy, a puzzled student writer would declare the pictures unusable and let the school newsletter go to print with only the bare facts of the ceremony.

Beside me, my mother was proud. She took a million identical pictures with her Sony Ericsson and emitted a small whine of dismay when Arin wriggled out from under the principal's grip and escaped offstage. On her other side, my father was frowning, as if he couldn't quite understand what he, a taxi driver who spent over twelve hours a day curved behind a steering wheel, was doing in this large hall sitting next to all these proud parents, instead of in front of them.

After the ceremony, while Arin was entangled with the other VIPs, I slipped away and located Mdm Rajah at the side of the school hall.

"Genevieve," she said warmly. "Sister of the hour. You must be so proud. How are you?"

I'd never taken a class with her, and in any other situation would have been thrilled she knew my name. I stuck my hand out and said quite brusquely: "Can I get an extra copy of the essay? My ma wants to get it framed."

She handed me a copy without much thought. As I crammed it into my bag and turned to leave, she started speaking again.

"My dear," she said, and although Mdm Rajah always spoke like this, leaving a flutter of fangirls in her wake, I felt the shocking cloyingness of uninvited intimacy coating her words. I braced myself. "Your sister seems very angry about the essay."

This stopped me.

"Of course not."

"I'll admit, I should have checked with her first, but really, she should be proud."

"She is."

Mdm Rajah continued, as if she were trying to convince Arin, through me. I had the awful sense that she'd deliberately looked me up before the ceremony, in anticipation of this exact moment. "It really is an extraordinary piece of writing," she was saying. "It would be a grievous sin for it not to be recognized."

"What's so good about it?"

She looked taken aback. "It's very mature."

But it was obvious she'd been thinking of something else and had caught herself in time. Her cheeks reddened slightly. Arin was right. She really did talk with a silly affectation, a layer of gloss that had just slipped, and that she was now struggling to reassert. Suddenly she seemed old and vain, surrounded by all these girls and their cheap adoration.

I wanted to get away. "Arin's not angry."

"Well," she said. "Maybe I misinterpreted. In any case, apologize to her on my behalf, will you?"

I looked around desperately. Arin was still being detained by adults, and my father had already escaped back to his cab, but my mother, standing near the stage, was deep in conversation with a group of teachers. She seemed to be taking the opportunity to talk to every single teacher she passed, as if by doing so, she could press herself closer to the lives of these young, educated women. I could tell her charm was out in full force, that the teachers standing in a circle around her were slightly dazzled by her exuberance, not yet recognizing the current of performance in her manner. I was familiar with this version of my mother, in fact I'd been enthralled and inspired by it many times. Yet now something was different. As she leaned in, lightly touching the elbow of a young female teacher, and laughed, a sharp and sudden sorrow twisted in me.

I couldn't watch her anymore. I made some excuse to Mdm Rajah and slipped out of the hall. Locking myself in one of the toilet cubicles, I snuck Arin's essay out of my bag, and began to read.

22

The essay was called "Land of Opportunity." It was short, only a page and a half, and the handwriting on it was dense, letters crammed together in the loopy penmanship Arin and I had practiced for years, in ink that was originally blue but had turned black in the photocopying process. As I scanned the paper, I could see that it followed no discernible structure, the punctuation scattered, the entirety of the essay one long, unbroken paragraph, giving off the naked impression that these frenetic scribbles you held in your hand were a direct transcript of Arin's consciousness. Horror flushed through me; I nearly put it down. But my curiosity was great and I had already come this far. I forced myself to focus. It started with Arin confessing that although she knew not to mention this, although we never, not once, acknowledged aloud the fact that she arrived by bus and not birth one June night, the truth was that she was a child abandoned—a revelation followed by an anecdote, a fragment of her life in Malaysia featuring brightly colored afternoons shimmering with noise and heat, before admitting that this was a fragment, that the memories of her life prior to her forcible transplanting were smudged. The feeling she often had, she wrote, was one of loss, yet it was a loss without origin, for with each passing day her life in Singapore grew in vibrance and layered over the remains of her childhood, like in this recurring dream of hers, where she was standing in the center of a small room, ripping the wallpaper off, trying to get at the concrete walls, only to discover the strips of gluey wallpaper were what held the room together, and now it was too late, too late . . . for without the clarity of memory, what did she have but the few objective facts of her birth and kin? And could she even trust that these facts, logged in her faulty memory, were real? And did it matter? Or was it enough to remember the atmosphere of childhood without being able to recall the circumstances that created them? Because before the splinter hadn't she felt safe, or was that another invention? Hadn't her other mother scared her into good behavior by threatening to give her away to the karang guni man? In fact, hadn't she known throughout childhood that it was but a matter of time before she was displaced? Arin's tone slipped effortlessly into plaintive, questioning prose, and despite myself, I was impressed. Moving on, she described the great pity she felt for her grandfather, quiet and kind (with a shock, I realized—*our* grandfather) as her mother harangued her father to harangue him, these indirect quarrels suffusing the air of their home that clearly, yet unspecifically, had to do with the conditions they lived in, with Arin's future hanging in the balance. He was her one great defender, this stubborn grandfather, who kept her safe, who refused to let them contact the other family across the border. And sure enough, after he died, they didn't even wait a week to get rid of her. Her mother didn't go with them to the bus station, she said she had too much work to do. Her father, on the bus, told her to scrub his name out of her mouth. Was this fact or memory? How much of it could she count on, how much was pickled and muddled by her confusion and fear? Yet she remembered the word he used— opportunity. This was the best thing they could do for her, going against her grandfather's last wishes to let the past die. Like this, Arin was abandoned, like this she was plonked in the lap of a strange family that clearly resented her presence. How many nights had she lain in this new and uncertain home, dumb with terror, how many days had she lived afraid of her own shadow, of being discarded again? I was nearing the end of the page, my hands gripping the paper so tight, some of the words near the edges were creased and I had to press the paper between my damp palms to iron it out. I continued reading. What opportunity, Arin thought, was this? Why did they have to dump her so far away, when there were plenty of perfectly good families in her town who might have considered themselves blessed to have a daughter? Did they want that desperately to be rid of her, to expunge her so completely that she might not even share a country code with them? Was she that dispensable, that troublesome? Who was she and what was she worth? And if you took these speculations away, stripped down these false memories, what would remain? Or were these questions all she had? For so long she clung to these questions like a crutch, afraid of asking, afraid. Yet only when she succumbed to the siren call of the school's computer lab, looking up transborder adoptions and their associated costs on the internet, did she finally understand how little she knew of her own life. All these years she thought herself unwanted, a sad balloon being batted from this side of the border to that, yet— and here we were on the last sentence—looking at that electronic figure on the screen, more than either family could comfortably begin to imagine, she understood that they had really given her the best they could, purchased with their dignity and integrity, this chance to deposit her on the shores of her grandfather's abandoned past, in a country just a couple of miles to the left of their own, this haven of potential, this land of opportunity, and now that she was here, it was up to her to figure it out, with not a single soul to guide her as she forged ahead blindly down this unmapped future, which stretched before her to infinity, or to take her hand and tell her that it was okay to be scared, that she was not alone.

23

The soft, feminine chatter of other girls in the restroom slowly reached me. I folded Arin's essay in half, flushed, slipped out, and rejoined the crowd in the school hall, where I was instantly spotted by her. She appeared beside me in a panic, her forehead bright with oil and reflected light.

"Can we go?" she whispered harshly.

I nodded. Then her eyes dropped to the essay in my hands.

Turning, I jammed it in my pocket, located my mother, and signaled that we were leaving. At the entrance of the hall, I stopped to face Arin.

Without saying a word, I removed the hairband from her head, smoothing her fringe back down. Some of it retained the shape of the band and bounced right back up, but otherwise she looked better, much less vulnerable. The whole time, I felt her gaze on me, but could not meet it. I was terribly afraid.

She moved to take my hand, and I let her, but did not twine my fingers in hers as I normally did. She held on to my palm like it was a dead fish. After a while of walking in silence, Arin let go, and I let my hand fall back against my side.

The essay exposed us all, and under its beam of light we squirmed. My mother ignored the contents of the essay and, to Arin's immense relief, treated it like the writing exercise it was, correcting it for grammar and syntax. My father became irrationally paranoid, convinced everyone had read this damning document confirming him as the son of a woman abandoned, but, arrested by the fundamental injustice of pinning his frustrations on a child, started escaping to the kopitiam to sulk into hot teas and Heinekens at night, sometimes missing our family dinners completely.

And me? I became cruel.

Secondary school was over. For the first time in my life, the conveyor belt of tests had spluttered to a halt, and until January arrived bearing my O-level results I was free to do as I liked. The day after the prize ceremony, I slipped out of the house and dialed Penelope on a public pay phone.

When she heard my voice, she cried: "I would have called first but I didn't have your handphone number."

"I don't have a handphone."

She sounded stumped. "How can you not have a handphone?"

I nearly laughed aloud. "I wouldn't expect a princess like you to get it." Then, boldly, I said: "I'll take that ice cream now."

I knew exactly what I was doing when I tugged on the string of Penelope's guilt. I knew she would leap at the offer of friendship, and I wanted, even for a brief moment, to be as opposite as possible to the life I'd known. I wanted to be the sort of person who could make Arin wonder; Arin, who had started to understand how furious I was, how hurt, even if she didn't have the language or audacity to articulate why. These thoughts pounded in my head as I sat across from Penelope, who watched in awe as I recklessly ordered three scoops of ice cream atop a fluffy golden waffle, then asked for extra sprinkles, chopped banana, and a Diet Coke.

"You won't be able to finish that," Penelope said, and I snapped: "Watch me."

I finished it, in fact, and an hour later Penelope was holding my hair out of my face as I threw up in the mall's restroom. Maybe she liked that I wasn't trying to impress her, or maybe she was still guilty, I don't know. After I wiped puke off the corner of my lip, throat burning and eyes watering from the vomit, she asked if I wanted to hang out again, in a couple of days. I said yes.

How the gallery of my life widened in just one week: each time we met, Penelope wielded her father's credit card and heaped favors on me. I was introduced to manicures; cafés; movies; shopping; neoprints; eyebrow shaping; poached eggs; aioli; cheese that came in hunks, not slices; lip gloss; log cakes. I visited her penthouse and wore her fluffy bedroom slippers, I let her paint my toenails and brush bright blue mascara on my eyes, I ran my fingers over her expensive art canvases and tried my hopeless hand at acrylic painting, an exercise that confirmed, interestingly, that for all of Penelope's affectations, she actually *was* visually talented. But I soon discovered that Penelope lived in fear that her family's wealth delegitimized her in some way. She paid for everything but was allergic to conversations around money. When I openly admired one of the Siamese figurines she'd made in Art Elective with plaster of Paris, she wrapped it in violet tissue paper and gave it to me immediately. Everything she offered I accepted with a vengeful wonder. More, I thought. More.

Arin lifted her head from the dining-room table and watched every time I left the house, a cloud of Sasa perfume pillowing around me. I felt a great and frightening joy in withholding parts of myself and seeing uncertainty reverberate in her. Go on, I thought, ask. Ask me where I'm going, what I'm doing. With a desperation so intense it sickened me, I thought: Please.

But she never did.

Until Christmas Eve. I woke to a hand towel, warmed in the microwave, against my cheek, and blinked at Arin standing above me. "So," she said, smiling tentatively, "another morning in the season of—"

It was seven. With neither the structure of school nor the demands of academia I'd begun sleeping in while Arin rose at daybreak to study. My heart turned over, seeing Arin's smile.

"Childish," I said, shuddering as the rapidly cooling water rolled off the side of my face in large drops, soaking into the pillow. She stuck out her tongue and giggled at my expression, long hair falling in front of her face. The soft, hopeful sound of her giggle made me want to cry.

"Jie Jie," she said. "It's Christmas Eve, let's go out."

We were like two actors colluding timidly in the farce of good temper. But on the train to Orchard Road, where we agreed to see the Christmas lights and soak in the festivities, I surprised myself by being the first to gingerly test the waters of conversation, desperate not to unleash the disastrous ripple that might ruin the day. From the other edge of this chasm Arin's eyes met mine, and we were both flooded with the inarticulate desperation for our old transparency, yet trapped by the path of stilted formality we'd already embarked upon.

In any case, Christmas Eve was the wrong time to come to Orchard Road. Crowds of harried last-minute shoppers surged between the gigantic conjoined shopping malls, hired choirs battled the looping Christmas carols blasting from the speakers; everywhere we turned, part-time promoters tried to press things into our hands: flyers, vouchers, hand cream, cookie samples. It was too much, too overwhelming. Flustered from the festive throng, our hands grasped for each other in the crowds, only to get knocked apart again and again. When a couple of shoppers started squabbling loudly, each accusing the other of shoving them in the mall's walkway, I produced a pair of movie passes from my pocket. They were a gift from Penelope, who seemed to have an unlimited supply of these coupons, a perk connected in some unclear way to her father's job. "Let's get out of here," I said. "People are getting crazy."

At the cinema, Arin studied the posters and scrutinized people in the popcorn queue, staring at the electronic board listing all the movies for so long the options were cycled through at least thrice.

"You pick," I said impatiently. "I've seen most of them already."

But she didn't want to. She hung back, nudging me ahead to the counter. I selected a movie I'd seen with Penelope, a romance obviously made for the festive season, and swapped the coupons for tickets. We went in.

The second time around, I already knew what was coming. I let my eyes follow along while my mind wandered. Beside me, Arin was leaning forward, completely absorbed in the film, her attentions in a different dimension. I recalled the first time I watched the movie and realized I'd glazed over half of it, passively watching the characters romp around, distracted by how good-looking the actors were. Not Arin. As the actors spoke, she mouthed along. Her face rearranged itself to mimic their expressions, painfully straining away from her physical body, trying to leave it behind for the world on-screen, me along with it.

How could she? The disappointment I'd been suppressing leaked through and stained everything it met with the preexisting sense of injustice that had been brewing in me for the past week. Was she that miserable here, what more did she want, what more could I have given her? "Land of Opportunity"; what opportunity was this—did she once stop to consider who was paying for it? I knew she hadn't intended for anyone to read the essay, I didn't blame her for its dissemination. The knife was in the actuality of her thoughts, her mind. For in this moving, award-winning piece Arin dashed out as a basic in-class exercise, which had been read by half the administration and presumably most of her cohort, in this narrative constituting the most significant moments of her life, where was I?

The lights came on, the movie was over. Arin shook her head several times, smiling to herself. Something had happened, she'd been transported, and now, floating back down to earth, I could see her trying desperately to hold on to the feeling of pure, good magic, conflating it with the dirt of our lives. She turned to me, face flushed, and laughed to see my cheeks wet, mistaking immediately a commonality of experience.

"Let's go," she said, her voice sated with relief, and I nodded yes.

24

The cloak of cinema that suffocated me had released her; Arin was practically skipping as we emerged into the dusky pink streets. The sun had set while we were indoors, and now thousands of hysterical birds descended upon the tree-lined pavements, making their daily ascension up their shrieking scales.

"That was wonderful, Jie," Arin said, laughing loudly as a little boy before us narrowly dodged a starling's shit, leaping to one side and setting off a swarm of pigeons that fluttered up and settled farther down the street. I'd never seen her laugh so openly in public; she hated the idea of anyone else noticing her crooked front teeth. "That was sublime."

I had taught her that word too. A memory swam up, unbidden, of my hand closed over hers, guiding her pen across a page of vocabulary exercises. Her biting down on my thumb in our private joke. She must have been seven then. With a sudden click, the whole belt of malls lit up in a crisscrossing web of silver lights, announcing the evening's arrival. The mannequins of tinsel and sequins mounted on every building glinted engagingly, and Arin clapped in delight.

"It's getting late," I said. "Let's go home."

"Look," she said, pulling me instead toward a yellow street cart. "It's the ice cream uncle. My treat."

She dug around in her pockets and counted out two dollars. As he wielded his large kitchen chopper, hacking out two blocks of chocolate mint ice cream and wedging them in between slices of rainbow bread, she chattered on, wanting to discuss the movie, eager to keep the good mood going. I listened darkly, and when the uncle handed us our ice cream sandwiches, muttered: "You didn't ask me what flavor I wanted."

Arin bumped my shoulder with hers. "As if you've ever picked anything but chocolate mint."

"And you, you don't want to try something else?"

"No," she said happily. "Whatever you choose, I'll choose too."

This was too much for me. I pulled my hand away and began chomping on my ice cream. The cold sugar caused spikes of pain to shoot into my gums, but I ignored it, trying to finish up my sandwich as quickly as possible.

Arin watched me in surprise. "What's wrong?"

But the thought of getting into it exhausted me. Suddenly I understood why my father chose not to challenge my mother's ambition, how he'd resigned himself to letting her be. I shook my head. "Nothing. Let's hurry up so you can get back to studying, we've already wasted a day."

"It's not wasted," she said. Tentatively, she ventured: "Jie Jie, what's the matter? You didn't like the movie?"

Closer, I thought. Closer.

"It was fine. Glad you liked it. If you want, I'll ask Penelope for more coupons and we can go again."

Arin recoiled. "The tickets were from her?" She shuddered delicately. "You should have said, I'd rather not have gone."

I blinked. This was unexpected. "What? Why?"

Arin looked at me, calculating. "Did you know," she said at last, "that Penelope's father owns Choann Cineplexes?"

I did not. "Penelope is a good person," I said, stung. "She was being generous."

"Generosity is cheap for someone like her. I can't stand how she moves through the world with no sense of consequence, wasn't she the one who—" Arin caught herself, then laughed uncomfortably. "Forget it, I have money now." She was talking about the cash prize that had come with her award, a hundred stunning dollars. All the moral outrage in the world wasn't enough to turn it down, yet when Arin kept the money, I remember feeling betrayed. "Next time we'll pay for it ourselves. How's the ice cream?"

I blinked away the sharp pain throbbing in my gums. "Money you made from airing our dirty laundry?"

Arin started. "What?"

I stood up and walked off. Even though the crowd closed in around me instantly, I could hear the distinctive patter of Arin's footsteps catching up. She grabbed on to my sleeve as I reached the MRT station and turned me around.

"Jie Jie, wait," she said, alarmed at the tears that had appeared in the seams of my lower lash line.

I turned my face away, humiliated by my body's betrayal, blinking furiously.

She continued speaking. "I know you're upset, but—"

I cut her off. "Why would I be upset? Because you advertised the trauma of living with us? Or because you wrote me out of your story?"

She blanched. "I didn't—"

"There's no me without you," I continued, my voice getting louder and more tremulous. "But it seems you were very happy to tell everyone that there is only *you* without me. I gave you everything and it's not enough. My God, just—just leave me alone."

Arin reached for my face, distraught, both thumbs out, ready to catch the tears as they fell from my eyes.

I stepped back.

We were standing by the gantries, commuters milling around us indifferently, pushing past us into the station. A whistling rush of air signaled a train's arrival, the announcer's voice booming for everyone to stand back, reminding them that food and drink weren't allowed on the trains and any breach was subject to a five-hundred-dollar fine.

"Don't call me Jie Jie," I said. "You don't mean it."

A hand on my shoulder. I turned. The stationmaster loomed above me, taking in my untidy face, my pomegranate cheeks. He wanted to know if everything was all right, if we needed help with the gantries. No, we were okay. Was I sure? Yes. The entire exchange took less than a minute, and when it was over, I turned back to Arin.

She was gone.

I saw her slight frame as it slipped away from me, melting into the crowds, leaving the station. She did not look back, and I, too, did not budge from where I stood. When I could no longer see her, I turned, tapped into the train station, and went home.

25

Dinner came and went, and Arin didn't reappear. Her chair remained empty, it was odd not to see her books spread across the dining table after we'd cleared the plates away. My mother discerned that we'd had a fight and was worried. So was I, but I pretended otherwise.

"She wanted to go off on her own."

"To where?"

"Who knows."

We were washing the dishes. My mother squinted at me, inched her hand forward, and touched my index finger with hers, but I shrugged and moved away.

I went to my father instead. He was lying on the couch in his threadbare polo tee, eyes open and staring at the ceiling fan. "Pa, what are you doing?"

"Digesting," he intoned, without looking at me. Once he could bring himself to sit up, he'd be off again, and if his lips touched a bottle of Heineken, I'd lose him for the night.

"If I want to go somewhere," I asked, "will you take me?"

"Where?" My mother was standing in the kitchen archway, drying a bowl. It was she who'd spoken.

"Nowhere, I was just wondering."

She came over and squatted before me. "Since when do you ask questions only for fun?" And when I didn't reply, she said: "Gen, where's Arin?"

We went out, my mother, father, and I, in his taxi. Back to Orchard, to Somerset. Nothing. The train station manager on duty was a different man from the one I'd spoken to that afternoon; it took twenty minutes to convince him to call the other manager. The entire time, he made irritated noises, as if we were wasting his time. See, he said, after hanging up, how are we supposed to remember one small girl, do you know how many people pass through here in a day. As for the CCTV footage, forget it. There were layers and layers of bureaucratic approval needed for that, it would take four working days to get clearance. By which time Arin should have returned.

Take it easy, he said, as we were leaving. There's no need to control every part of their lives, teenagers do what they want.

Traffic was bad. It took forty minutes to get back to Bedok. We drove round and round the neighborhood, stopping at all the usual places: the park connector, the longkang, our school, even McDonald's. My parents kept going over the same questions: who Arin's friends were, where she might have gone. Useless conversations—they both knew she didn't have friends. It was nearly two in the morning when we gave up and went home. I was sure Arin would be sitting cross-legged on the floor when we returned, freshly showered, waiting for us to walk through the door. I could see her, damp spot on her T-shirt spreading from her long, wet hair, head lolling against the arm of the couch as she dozed off. How could she think of sleeping at a time like this. Walking up the stairs, I began preparing for an argument. What kind of behavior is this, I would say, who just disappears like that, do you know what a scare you gave us. But my mother unlocked the door to an empty flat. Her shoulders sagged, and I realized she'd been hoping for the same thing.

"I'm sure she's fine," I said. Neither parent replied.

The next morning, Arin was still missing. I hadn't slept, but forced myself to maintain a stoic expression in front of my parents. Inside, I was churning. So she had decided to run away because of a few harsh words? How could she do this to me, to my mother? When my parents went out to look for her again, I refused to follow. When they returned that afternoon, my mother's eyes were wild. They darted to the couch where I was sitting, and I saw a flash of disappointment forcibly tempered. Although I had been sick with fear all afternoon, in that moment, rage lacerated the haze of my exhaustion.

"Su," my father said, breaking my train of thought. His chin was rough with uneven stubble. He dropped his keys on the dining table, then pulled a chair out and sat heavily. "It's time. We need to call the police."

26

The visit to the police station was a disaster. The policeman at the counter looked like he was barely out of school; he asked questions in the manner of someone reading off a checklist, speaking rapidly and impatiently in English. I attempted to translate for my father, who couldn't fully follow what was happening, but he brushed me off and tried to explain, in his slow, halting English, that we hadn't mistreated Arin, we didn't know why she had run away. This wasn't normal, we weren't the kind of family who raised delinquents. As he spoke, the policeman's face kept disappearing behind the large desktop monitor, clacking away occasionally at the keyboard, presumably generating a report. The more this went on, the worse my father's mood got.

On the other hand, my mother was strangely subdued. Only once did she venture: "Sir, is there anyone we can call?"

The policeman didn't respond. I leaned over the counter. He was sipping from an aluminum can of Coca-Cola and using his phone.

I rapped on the counter. "Are you listening?" I demanded. My mother's hands crept into my lap and squeezed my thigh in warning, but I ignored her.

He stood up, unruffled. "We'll call you if we find anything."

I didn't believe him. I snapped: "We've already looked everywhere, and we can't find her. Where are *you* going to look?"

I'd been trying to provoke the policeman with my imperious tone, but my father flinched. For a brief moment I must have appeared unrecognizable to him. I didn't like thinking of the ways he might have been subject to this tone under different circumstances, I felt ashamed. The policeman glanced between us, then addressed me with a surprising kindness he hadn't offered my parents. "Hospitals."

I blinked. "What?"

"We'll screen your description against our database."

My mother rose. "Thank you, thank you a lot, we appreciate it."

A dense rain had started up while we were inside. Wordlessly, my father grabbed a glossy magazine from the station's waiting area to cover his head and ran for the cab, returning with two umbrellas and handing me one. The black umbrella cleaved the downpour, enveloping me in a private curtain of despair as I stumbled after my parents into the parking lot.

I hadn't even considered the possibility that Arin's absence wasn't pure obstinance. But the second the policeman mentioned it, a multiverse of risk opened in my mind. And what description did the police have—a Chinese girl with dark brown eyes and blunt bangs? A million teenagers in Singapore fit that description. How could it possibly encompass her shy sideways gaze, or the way she opened her mouth a half second before speech arrived, moistening the air with a breath of hesitation? My imagination unraveled. A vision of Arin floated before me, pale and languishing in a hospital somewhere, having slipped in this storm and hit her head, dying alone, run over by a truck, or, worse, kidnapped, or, worse—

I stopped myself. As we reached the taxi, my father held the umbrella over the passenger door while my mother entered. I struggled slightly with closing my own umbrella, sprinkling myself and the backseat with rainwater. We sat in silence for a moment, shivering and trying to dry ourselves off with tissues. My father's right sleeve was soaked and my mother fiddled with the air-conditioning unit, trying to direct the cold air away from him. Then, she asked:

"Can you drop me at Bishan Gate?"

My father was incredulous. "At your parents'? When was the last time you spoke?"

Her voice wavered, but she didn't back down.

"You don't have to come up if you don't want to."

He shook his head and began driving. In the backseat, I blinked, my mind catching up to her words. As we turned into the glittering flyover that merged the expressways of Singapore, I realized, with a delayed shock, that I was going to see my maternal grandparents for the first time.

27

J ust one grandparent. Surprisingly beautiful, with a shock of silver hair twisted into a chignon. When she opened the door, she grimaced, and said: "You're lucky your father isn't home."

My mother and I had ridden the elevator up to the fourteenth floor in silence, my fear and apprehension doubling with every tick of the elevator panel. I started to feel as if I'd entered a different dimension, and when I caught sight of my mother in the tinted elevator mirrors, her throat was bobbing as though she were preparing to speak, to defend herself. I thought of the reason they were estranged. Was it worth it? My grandmother seemed to be thinking the same as she scrutinized me. Was I?

I don't know what she concluded, but she turned away and led us into the condominium unit, gesturing at a couch with surprisingly fat cushions. "So is this the Christmas the prodigal daughter is finally coming home?"

My mother said, point-blank: "I need your help."

Again she glanced at me. "What happened?"

I learned that my mother had scoured the neighborhood already, asking if any of the void deck aunties had seen Arin. No one had, but soon the entire neighborhood knew she was missing. Immediately, they drew upon their own stories: a boy who had been snatched off the streets in Thailand and sold for his kidneys, more and more girls inducted into local gangs. Arin might have fallen into bad company, perhaps she had a secret gangster boyfriend, or perhaps she'd been lured away by perverts. It was important to be careful these days, you never knew who was following you home, sick people were everywhere. Kidnapping, kidneys, perverts, boyfriends? What kind of kampung mentality was this? Although it's true that the aunties had a slightly different vision of Singapore from my mother, their irresponsible nattering drove her crazy. It was as if they had forgotten they were speaking of Arin, the book-ish girl who greeted them politely every day on her way home from school, and grasped at her absence to fuel their own suspicions and fears about the world.

My mother wouldn't have come if she'd had any other choice, but even the policeman had been no help. My grandmother was a school principal; did she know anything about situations like these, my mother asked, did she know if anything else could be done?

The entire time she spoke my grandmother stared impassively at her as if she were a child, raising a plucked eyebrow only at the mention of Arin, whose existence she hadn't even been aware of. I couldn't stand it, I looked away and studied the apartment. By the door there was a rectangular fish tank filled with angelfish and tetras, fish of choice for the solidly middle class, and beside that, an ornate walnut bookcase stretched across the length of a wall, stuffed with textbooks and thick biographies. It was the kind of bookcase with several small lights built into it, and under one of the lights sat a dusty terrarium with a large fingerprint on the glass bowl.

In fact the whole condo was like this, a little dirty. My surprise turned to anger. What were we doing in this careless house, in front of this arrogant old woman who despised my father and turned my mother out? Every additional second we stayed seemed like a betrayal of my father, but my grandmother's tremendous presence pinned me to the chair. I couldn't move, couldn't get up, couldn't leave.

She asked my mother a few pointed questions, then said: "I see a few cases like this a year. Unfortunately, there's not much you can do except wait."

"Wait?"

"I know it's hard." The words were sympathetic, her voice was not. She had heard my mother's dismay, too, the irrational hope she'd harbored, and calmly removed herself from it. Yet she spoke with such immense authority that I couldn't help blurting:

"Excuse me, ma'am, your missing students, were they all found?"

She noted my stumble over how to address her and seemed amused. "Eventually. Singapore is small, where are they going to hide?"

"None of them were kidnapped or killed?"

She moved to place a coaster under my water glass. "What kind of movies are you watching?"

But I was feeling fragile and couldn't take even this small bit of mockery. I burst into tears. She softened and handed me a box of tissues. To my mother, she conceded: "If you have a picture, I'll put a blast in my email chains. Sometimes word of mouth is the best way to go about this."

I asked: "So you don't think she's dead?"

My grandmother didn't laugh. "Thanks to your mother, I don't know anything about you or your sister. I can't say for sure what she is or isn't. But it's statistically unlikely."

"All right," my mother said. "You've made your point. We're leaving."

At the door, my grandmother put a hand on her daughter's shoulder. We were all surprised by the gesture, perhaps none more so than my grandmother herself. She removed her hand, coughed.

"Sue Li," she said stiffly. Her use of my mother's Chinese name, rather than the anglicized "Su" she preferred, jolted me. "It's good to see you again."

But my mother wasn't having it. "Is it? How is Pa?"

My grandmother looked away.

She continued. "He was the one who threw me out. And you didn't say anything. All those phone calls, unanswered. Good to see me? Shall I come back inside, wait for him to come home? Witness for myself if anything's changed?"

My grandmother's eyes darted to the clock: it was six. Her grip on the doorframe tightened. "Stop it. You know I can't afford for your pa to have a heart attack again."

My mother cried: "I was only a girl."

"Old enough to make your own choices."

My mother recoiled and drew me behind her. "You still defend what he did after all this time?"

But any softness my grandmother displayed earlier had vanished, like a trick of light. Impossible to say if it had ever been there.

"Between you and him?" My grandmother shrugged. "Yes."

28

My father was waiting in the taxi downstairs, engine off and staring into space, as if the last hour had turned him to stone. He didn't ask how the visit went, just silently started the car and began driving. We made a perfunctory loop around my grandmother's neighborhood, scanning the roads for Arin, but beyond the handful of hopeful teenagers braving the storm to gaze upon the mall's outdoor Christmas tree, no one was out. We went home.

I turned the day's events over in my head. In that monstrously pink high-rise condominium overlooking the MacRitchie Reservoir, my mother hadn't seemed at all out of place. Her voice had modulated itself to match my grandmother's clean Mandarin tones; she'd sunk deep into the belly of that great white couch, completely at home in the comforts of that apartment. When recounting the gossip of the void deck aunties to her mother, the frustration in her voice was a jarring slash against the grace she'd always espoused. The minute we left the house, though, this melted away. Watching her sit up front with my father, drained of energy, head leaning against the cab window, I got the feeling she'd regretted returning to her childhood home. That night, I crawled into bed beside her and nestled my head under her arm like an overgrown child.

My mother turned over and pulled me close, put her face to my scalp, and inhaled deeply. The tip of her nose was wet, she'd been crying.

"Your grandmother is a very cold person," she said, brushing the hair away from my face. She closed her eyes, hunkering through a fresh wave of pain. When they opened again, her eyes were bright, her voice urgent. "There's a reason I kept you away from them. You saw it, right? You can now understand why?"

I didn't know what to do. I nodded.

But I couldn't stop thinking about the complacency of that large fingerprint on my grandmother's dusty terrarium. How hard could it be to wipe it off, how could she live like this, didn't she care? How close I'd come to being raised with such moral turpitude—no. My bones rang as if I'd been slapped across the face. This, I realized, mind racing, *this fury* was the fundamental breach between me and girls like Penelope and Jia Min: I could not endure imperfection, and they could. It wasn't because I was better, or superior. It was simply because they could afford negligence. Had my ferocious discipline branded me with desperation the last four years, had my naïve perfectionism marked me for pity? Could *everyone* tell, except me? I thought of the world we'd just left behind, everything my mother had thrown away for the singular sake of pride.

Was it pride, though? Or was it the ultimate proof of her love for me?

The rain beat steadily against the windows.

"Mama," I said, aching for Arin, unable to make sense of the turbulent confusion in my mind, "I'm scared."

My mother sighed and pulled me in.

"Me too," she murmured into my hair. "Please let Arin come home safe."

I couldn't sleep that night either. In the morning, my eyes were swollen from crying, and the rain had stopped, yet: still no Arin. Instead, a small, black spider was crawling down the wall, extending a leg toward the cool landscape of her vacant pillow. I reached out and pressed the spider against the wall with my thumb, leaving behind a stain like a smear of jam. Then, staring at the trail of my own wickedness, I left my mother in bed and went into the living room.

Later, Arin told me that when I saw her, I didn't react. I just stood there, in the middle of the living room, dazed with exhaustion, looking right through her. I didn't move at my mother's yelp, or even when she frantically pushed past me, unlocking the gate. Only when my eyes lifted to examine the strangers huddling into the living room did I realize something was happening. Who were these people, well dressed but disheveled, suddenly standing in our home? The woman was very pretty, her sharp features set off by a dark purple headscarf, a thick layer of mascara leaving tiny black specks under her eyes whenever she blinked. The man's hair was all over the place, sticking out at weird angles, as if left to dry in odd, architectural shapes. He was wearing a black T-shirt with white rings of salt where his perspiration had soaked through and dried, and in front of him stood Arin, shaking not from emotion, but from the cold.

The cold? It was never cold in Singapore. I looked more carefully, taking in her hair, damp and sticking to her scalp, revealing the shape of her head, her ears. The shirt she'd worn to the movies, clinging to her skin. I blinked hard, the mirage didn't dissipate. It was Arin, alive.

According to Arin, I wiped my thumb against the side of my shorts, walked toward her, and put my hands on her face. My parents had rushed at the couple and were stitching together the sequence of events. For all her dismissal, my grandmother had forwarded Arin's picture to every organization she knew: the school principals' network, her neighborhood association, the Catholic church she attended only on Christmas and New Year's Eve, the Buddhist soup kitchen she donated to, her university's alumni association, several birdwatching forums, and a dementia watch group for missing elderly, which the young couple was a part of. They'd been on their morning walk when they spotted Arin, flailing off the shoreline of Woodlands Waterfront Park, clearly struggling, but not screaming. The man jumped into the water and pulled her out, pumping her stomach till she vomited a stream of seawater. Then he recognized her from the picture and called my grandmother. Hearing this, my mother burst into tears, both from the shock of my grandmother's effort, so incongruous with her cold demeanor, and from the knowledge that Arin had been that close to drowning. My father kept thanking the couple, he pulled out his wallet and tried to give them everything in it, fifty dollars, and when they said no and left, he turned to us, and for the first time, I don't remember any other, he shouted, not quite at Arin, but in her direction: It's too much, it's all too much.

I didn't register any of this. I had my hands on Arin's face and was examining her, making sure she was real. According to Arin, I just stood there, meticulously arranging her hair so it covered her high forehead, then, satisfied with my handiwork, I looked up at my parents, waited for my father to quieten down, and informed them that her skin was on fire.

29

The four days Arin took to bed with fever, I punished myself. I slept on the floor and woke up aching. I timed her antibiotics even though administering them wasn't my responsibility. I followed my mother to the kitchen at all kinds of odd hours, watching her retrieve the brown bottle of medicine, I hovered in the corner of the bedroom while she woke Arin and tipped a spoon of the syrupy pink liquid down her throat. I changed Arin's socks and held her feet, willing the fever to break. When that didn't work, I located the set of notes she had been making before our fight and read them aloud while she slept, hoping the information would osmose into her subconscious, hoping the fever wouldn't set her study schedule too far back. My father thought I was insane, pacing around the bed reciting chemistry formulas, but on the fourth night, when it was just us in that hot, swirling room, Arin whispered quietly: "Thank you."

A few people had seen her pacing the jetty, intermittently staring into the water and across the sea, but they'd dismissed her as just another moody teenager, until she heaved herself over the railings and fell in.

After they calmed down, my parents, the police, believed this to be a cry for attention, an attempt at self-harm, and the school would later mandate that Arin attend four sessions with the school counselor, sessions Arin would use to systematically decimate Mdm Rajah's behavior.

But they'd all gotten it wrong. I alone knew what it was.

"I thought I would go home."

It actually wasn't that far-fetched. Four years later, an escaped terrorist would harpoon the region's attention as he slithered through the prison's ventilation shaft and swam across the thirty-nine kilometers of sea separating Singapore and Malaysia, surviving on hoarded squares of foil-packed butter for months while evading capture. But I glared at Arin's underbaked lie, frustration cresting and breaking on my relief.

"You're bluffing," I said. "You can't even swim."

Arin smiled faintly at my tone, pressing her cheek against the hand I was using to brush away the sticky clumps of fringe poking into her eyes. She shifted, and I sat on the sheets beside her small body, radiating heat. "I would have found a way."

I stared furiously at Arin's sweat-slicked forehead, so pale even her acne seemed blanched of color. She'd made her way to the park, drenched from the Christmas storm, and hid out in one of the public restroom's cubicles to sleep, wringing her shirt and shorts out the best she could under the hand dryer. But her underwear remained damp; it was a miracle she hadn't gotten pneumonia and died. "But *why?*"

"Because there's no me without you either."

My breath failed. How plainly she spoke, as if flinging herself about on the seas of my temper were such a casual act. But her lips were blistered from the fever, the faintness of her breath alarmed me. I gathered myself again.

"Are you telling me," I demanded, "that you jumped into the sea because of one thing I said?" I thought of her shivering all night in that public restroom, waiting for the morning trickle of passersby to start up before leaping into the ocean. "What kind of crazy behavior is that?"

Her voice, though soft, was clear and untroubled: "You flushed Gong Gong down the toilet for me."

We held each other's gaze for a long time.

Then, I don't know who cracked first, but we burst out laughing. The laughter was wild and deranged with relief, it fed on itself and we couldn't stop. How stupid it sounded when put like that. What a couple of absolute idiots we were, raising dramatic gesture with dramatic gesture. Yet even as we doubled over, stitches shooting sharp pains into our sides, Arin's eyes didn't leave me. What was she watching for? Her chest heaved; an image of her rescuer pumping her soft, rounded stomach until she spewed seawater flashed in my mind. How long had she been flailing in the murky water, unable to gain traction, not understanding how to arrange her limbs or manage the silt and water that was all around her, over her head, going into her nose and burning her eyes? She could so easily have drowned. I felt her panic even now, in her gasps of relief. Five, ten minutes at most, before the man jumped in and dragged her to shore, as she must have known he would.

In that musty bedroom, as her laughter finally slowed, Arin shifted and the damp sheets fell to one side, exposing the light blue veins of her jugular. I reached out and curved my hand around the base of her neck, wiping away the clammy sweat that had accumulated there, continuing to dab the skin around her cheeks, her forehead. I felt as though someone had put a shell-less egg in my cupped hands, and I alone was holding it together. How daring her escalation, how efficiently her display of love checkmated and concluded our fight. Arin closed her eyes and hummed at the coolness of my touch. Her pulse, jumping feebly under my fingers, dampened the glow of reunion, the thrill that'd been building in my chest. She really could have died.

"Never do that again, Mei," I said, rising abruptly. "It's not funny. We're not children anymore."

30

As expected, I aced the O levels and had my pick of junior colleges. Penelope did not. She took herself out of the local equation and started at an International Baccalaureate program geared toward overseas study, regarding my selection dubiously.

"Are you sure? Han Zhong Junior College is known to be pretty cutthroat."

I was proud. "In my opinion it's the best possible runway to the university."

In fact it was not only the most brutal, but the most prestigious junior college among Singapore's top five. Not a single other classmate had made it in. On the first day of school, I donned my crisp new uniform, prominently adjusted the collar pin bearing the school's crest on my starched collar, and basked in the once-overs from other commuters as I strode onto the train. When I saw, carved roughly with a penknife into the side of my desk, *welcome to hell*, I felt thrilled this was a hell that admitted only a select few.

Hell indeed. Junior college was hard. Really hard. I hit my first roadblock remarkably quickly, but like an ostrich stupidly putting its head in the crumbling earth, I didn't know to be worried. Yet. Not wanting to look stupid before my new classmates, many of whom had come straight from a lifetime of academic enrichment programs, I feigned understanding and took my questions to my mother, whose academic bootlegging business had become the jewel of the void deck shops. She enthusiastically located the corresponding topic on binomial expansion in the photocopy shop's stacks and brought them home one night for us to pore over together.

For twenty minutes, she studied the notes, all her mental gears preparing to masticate the information and feed it to Arin and me as she used to do.

But a long time passed, and she was quiet. I read over the notes once, twice, then glanced at my mother, who hadn't moved, and ventured: "I can do it."

My mother returned to herself, shuddering. "No," she said and smiled, tapping her pencil on a rendering of Pascal's triangle. "It's fine. I think this equation involves a trinomial, so you can't apply this formula anyway."

She was wrong. I said carefully, "There are only two terms, so it's a binomial, but it's raised to the power of three. Is that what you meant?"

"Let me see that." She took a long time to understand what I was explaining and my panic began to grow. I looked at the clock again and again. A few times, I had to say, it's okay, let me move on. I need to move on.

Finally, slowly, and with great confusion, she said: "They've changed school." I stared at her. They? Who was they? Laughing, she continued: "It was different when I was in it. But math is its own language, how hard can it be? Explain it to me again."

"I can't, I don't have time."

She touched my index finger playfully. "I want to understand."

My patience only went so far. "Ma," I said, "you don't need to understand it to sell it, it's okay."

I saw her face; I regretted it immediately. But within a couple of days the wake of study closed over me and drowned out the guilt. I felt as if I'd missed a step I hadn't even known was there and was instantly being swept away in the undertow. And my old method of compensating for what I didn't understand by simply memorizing the formulas no longer worked. Before I knew it the first round of common tests arrived, and I, along with half my new class, failed. Most students picked themselves up, absorbing and tucking away their failure, calmly moving on.

Not me. I had never seen an F before, much less three—in H2 Mathematics, H2 Biology, and H1 Chemistry—and although I didn't tell a soul, the failures blazed brightly in my chest. For days I went around with my head down as if the grades were branded on my right cheek, so dazed I couldn't even cry.

From that point on I was plunged into a period of intellectual terror. Sometimes I would approach my teachers after class for advice, but found myself too ashamed to admit the extent of what I didn't understand, and often nodded congenially as if their off-hand remarks made complete sense. Sometimes I sat down with my textbooks, trying to read everything again from page 1, as if I could start over from scratch, falling further behind as the cogs of syllabus turned faster and faster. But more often than not I cut back on sleep, trying to plug the gaps in my knowledge with the pure volume of time spent staring at the words. A terrible cycle. The exhaustion made me careless, compounded my mistakes. At the end of my first year I was pulled to the side by a concerned teacher and given a form, printed on official-looking paper a sickly shade of green.

"Not everyone is suited for academia," the teacher said as I scanned the paper. It was a withdrawal form.

"But I am," I protested, citing all the A's that had characterized my schooling life thus far, only to be met with a look of incredulity. Was I really offering as my defense the petty achievements of a child?

"Just think about it," the teacher said. "Only three in ten students nationwide make it to the next stage, all the way to the university. You know you're graded against a bell curve for the A levels, which means you can't just be good, you have to be better than. And right now you're kibble for your peers."

"Are you expelling me?"

The teacher chose her words carefully. "No one can make you withdraw."

Finally, tears. I cried and cried on that walk home. I didn't want to confide in my mother, didn't want her useless noises of encouragement, and besides, I resented the fact that she'd stayed in contact with my grandmother since Arin's return, a relationship I secretly regarded as betrayal of my father and our family. But to Arin I recounted everything, my voice growing wild with panic.

"I can't give up now. But my brain hurts, I can't do anything right anymore. Help me, I've become stupid."

"You need to sleep," Arin said. She'd just completed her O levels and was dedicating most of her December holidays to napping with a vengeance. I had my head in her lap, and she was rubbing my shoulders, trying to calm me down. When she put her palm over my eyes, trying to coax me into some shuteye, I sat up.

"Not you too. Stop asking me to sleep, I don't have enough time, what sort of person can afford sleep."

No surprise, then, when Arin refused to even apply for my school—she considered their strategy of weeding out weaker students who might cause them to slip in the national JC rankings unethical, declaring herself allergic to that additional layer of pressure. When her O-level results came out, she went to a different junior college, not one of the top five but still a respectable enough school, and seemed happy there. Every morning, she donned her carefully pressed uniform, twisted her hair into one exacting braid, and approached school with the cold precision of a general going to battle.

Me, no. In 2006, my second year of junior college, I started applying myself liberally to friendship, thinking I could learn and replicate the formulas of success, if not from my teachers, then from my peers. But the more I learned, the more I panicked. It transpired that my classmates lived full, interesting lives, somehow running parallel to their academic achievements. A girl in my class had been actively volunteering with Lions Befrienders since 2001. The class president had written a play for the school's drama club. The students in said drama club had all gone on to win Gold with Honors in that year's Singapore Youth Festival. The school band had competed in Hiroshima, Japan, ranking third in the Young Adults category. A boy who sat behind me in Chemistry had collaborated with four other students to pilot a program helping first-generation hawkers transition from cash to card payments, demonstrating initiative. The vice-captain of the girls' soccer team had rallied her players to raise over four thousand dollars for that pilot program, demonstrating leadership skills. Another prominent student, who I'd assumed was merely contrarian for the sake of being interesting, represented the school on the national debate team. Even classmates who weren't actively involved in extracurricular activities had unique hobbies that could be crystallized into evidence of an all-rounded candidate for universities or internships—several students were revealed to be minor celebrities in internet communities like DeviantArt or the blogosphere.

Each new revelation horrified me. Surely there were other students like me, who had primarily done the thing we were called to do: be students. But no—even the most antisocial person I knew turned out to be a secret entrepreneur making bank through his online art commissions, charging fifty dollars a pop to illustrate clients as comic-book characters like Spider-Man or Iceman. As a last resort, I made an appointment that August with the school's career counselor, a perpetually sweaty man with a goatee.

He sensed immediately that I was there for reassurance and considered it his sacred duty to douse me in reality. Didn't my school name count for anything? No, he said, sighing, then proceeded to communicate two diametrically opposing truths: one, that in matters of university admissions and internships, perfect grades were the bare minimum, and two, that the polytechnics, long regarded as the less prestigious educational path, were churning out students trained in practical, technology-based skills, making them far more desirable to employers than we sheltered junior college kids. Get a job with just the A levels? Forget it. Junior college was but a stepping-stone; if I didn't make it to the university, my A-level certificate would be as useful as toilet paper. It was in my best interest to locate what made me special, immediately, and whittle it into a point so sharp it'd give my future a fighting chance.

I left his office in a hurry. I had to get home, right now, I had to pick up my books, I was losing time. At the bus stop, I paced up and down, jerking my head toward the street every few seconds to check for the bus's arrival. Then a classmate, who'd been eyeing my quiet mutters with increasing alarm, stood and approached me.

I glanced at him: Guo, Choir, Tenor One, subject combination Bio-Chemistry-Physics-Literature, straight A's. I'd asked him the week before if he'd be willing to share his revision strategies; now, as he pulled out the right side of his wired earphones, I perked up, thinking he might put me out of my misery.

Instead, he offered me the earbud that had just been wedged in his ear canal. I stared at it. There was a smudge of yellow earwax on the white plastic. I recognized the lead singer of F.T. Island trilling squeakily through the tiny speakers, midway through the opening track of a popular Korean drama. Around us, the mempat trees bloomed, a twice-yearly occurrence, and as we stood facing each other, a gust of wind dislodged a series of soft, pink petals, which swirled around us and onto the streets, plastering themselves against the windshields of passing cars.

Guo followed my gaze and murmured: "Don't they look like cherry blossoms?"

"Are you hitting on me?" I demanded.

The hand holding the earbud fell uncertainly to his side. "What?"

We were the only two people waiting for the bus, a fact that surely must have encouraged him. Guo paused the song playing on his iPod, pocketed it. "I was only going to ask if you wanted to study together sometime." Then, bravely, he continued: "I've always thought you were cute."

I was not. Late nights and desperation had drained my skin of color, and no matter how much water I drank my face remained puffy from exhaustion and water retention. Whenever I caught sight of myself I couldn't help but think of the squishy stress balls the school gave out around exam time, with their comically frazzled faces printed on the side.

I stared at Guo in hysterical despair.

"Are you prepared to marry me right now?"

He faltered. "Come again?"

"The average university graduate is twenty-three. Which means to qualify for HDB housing you have to be hitched by then; counting backward, factoring in an average two years of serious dating, most couples pair up at twenty or twenty-one," the words were spilling out faster and faster, "and any relationship that begins *now* is likely to end in failure, since eighty-five percent of JC couples break up when the boy goes for National Service or the girl starts university, so what are you doing asking me out, are you trying to sabotage me, are my grades a joke to you?"

I'm glad, too, that no one else was around to witness my meltdown. Guo took a step back, frightened.

"Okay," he said. "Message received."

Within a week, word had gotten around that I'd cracked. My JC schoolmates were less inclined to gossip than the girls in my secondary school, yet more than once I caught quizzical looks thrown in my direction, my display of cutthroat ambition misaligned with the reality of my mediocre grades.

Terrible, terrible times. One day, I stopped by the photocopy shop on my way home, said hello to the void deck aunties. I'd been coming less and less since junior college started, so they didn't know of my academic troubles. They spoke about me with the same glow of my secondary school years, and for a moment I found myself relaxing, comforted by their simple admiration.

But as I left the photocopy shop, the feeling faded. Replacing it was the realization that I hadn't felt this same calm confidence for a single second since entering junior college. Had I so quickly lost the image of myself I'd treasured, of a student so assured in her season of success, and if so, what was the alternative? To be like my mother, whose extravagant charisma burned bright and fast, but who had ultimately returned, subdued, to intermittent communication with my treacherous grandmother? Or to be like my father, who, when he wasn't dividing his time between taxi flag-downs and discreet, cash-only arrangements where he ferried office workers, grad students, and in one particularly ludicrous agreement, a bushel of Maltipoos, to and from their appointments, spent his time impotently on the couch, having developed a new and pointless hobby of devouring manhua comics on his cellphone?

Or, I wondered, was there a third choice, something I couldn't yet see?

31

In the middle of September I did something I'd have never considered before: I cut school.

It was a Tuesday. I woke at 5:30 a.m. as usual. Both parents long gone: my mother off to open the shop, my father all but living behind his taxi wheel. As Arin washed up, I prepared breakfast for us both—a cup of 3-in-1 Nestum Instant Cereal—and ran through my lines again. Arin emerged from the shower, dressed in her school uniform, settled into her chair, and hunched over her mug like a horse putting its face to water, slurping up the cereal without using a spoon.

Before leaving the house, she hugged me briefly, raised my index finger to her mouth, and bit down. "Good luck." And then: "Don't forget your promise."

"Yes, yes."

"If it doesn't work out you go straight back to studying."

"Don't nag me, I haven't stopped studying for a moment."

She looked at me ruefully. "Only you would think of something like this." In her voice was disapproval mixed with genuine admiration; it filled me with optimism.

Following a front-page feature in *The Straits Times* about the burgeoning internet video phenomenon, I'd written an impassioned email pleading my availability to every local YouTube channel I could find. Incredibly, one responded with details of an open call. They sent me a sample script and penciled me in for a screen test.

My pleas were audacious, but the second I received a response they began coalescing into a shimmering reality. The sample script was a monologue, less than a page long, detailing the amount of carbohydrates in a popular hawker dish, written in an exaggerated style of Singlish with Hokkien, Malay, and Cantonese words thrown in for local flavor. I read it aloud once, turned the printed sheet face down, and repeated it without looking at the paper again. I can scarcely describe the wonder I felt at discovering my old faculty for memorization intact, the rush of restoration that lit up my soul. From then on, every day leading up to the screen test—while showering, in between studying, before sleeping—I spoke the words aloud like a prayer, varying my tone, playing with emphasis, perfecting my routine down to the intonations of each linguistic interjection. Delight crept back into my mind, my manner; keeping one eye on the impending A levels and another on my revived motivation, Arin withheld her explicit disapproval and simply begged that no matter what happened with the audition I channel my excess energy into study after.

It was a promise easily given, I gave it.

After Arin left for school, I pulled on my best outside clothes, went through my mother's makeup, smeared some eyeshadow on my lids, and headed out. The screen test was in an industrial building in the armpit of Paya Lebar. When I alighted from the bus and located the squat concrete building, there was nothing in my brain except a humming anticipation, the sense that my life was about to begin.

I was prepared, I thought. I was ready.

Along the windowless corridor I passed a series of units wildly unrelated to show business—the stockroom for a paint company, a car-leasing company's office, a boutique advertising agency— scrutinizing the steel placards above each unit's doorbell till I came to the production company. I rang the bell. A short, brusque woman with shockingly turquoise hair opened the door and said: "You're late."

I was early actually, too early. The person scheduled to audition at that time appeared behind me, out of breath and apologizing. She was a skinny girl, very pretty in all the regular assembled ways, with large, gray contact lenses and rebonded brown hair.

"Wait outside," the woman said to me, and motioned for the girl to follow her in. I put my ear to the door but couldn't hear a thing. Ten minutes later it swung open again and I nearly fell into them both. I was embarrassed, but the woman didn't seem to care. She let go of the door and turned around. When I continued standing there, she said, "Well, hurry up."

Inside, four young people sat at computer stations, editing videos and replying to emails. The woman led me past them into a studio. When she closed the glass door and drew a thick curtain across the space, the sound of keyboards faded away. She introduced herself as the producer, writer, and casting director, then gestured for me to stand where an X had been marked on the floor with masking tape, in front of a tripod. The space was very small, the camera seemed too close.

"Introduce yourself to the camera first," the producer said. "On my cue."

"My name is Genevieve Yang," I said. "I'm eighteen this year." Then I launched into the script.

"Stop, stop!"

I broke off. "Am I speaking too fast?"

"The script we sent is only a sample, it's just for reference." She shook her head. "This is a screen test for presence. Just be yourself. No need to do a voice."

I stammered: "But what do you want me to say?"

The woman turned off the camera and snapped. "What is this, your first audition?"

"Yes."

She looked taken aback. I could see her evaluating whether I was worth her time. She stuck her head through the door—the next person wasn't here yet—and came back irritated. Then she gestured to the dusty-rose loveseat by the wall.

"Sit." I obeyed. "Look, we aren't casting for specific characters, this isn't a drama. We're seeking out personalities and building shows around them. Some YouTubers affect a persona"—she gave me a speculative look—"I thought that was what you might've been doing. No? Fine. Others have the pure force of charisma that makes them inherently watchable, even if they're talking about a doorstopper. Tell me," she said, leaning forward, "what are you interested in? What occupies your imagination, your mind?"

What? What was this, a personality test? I couldn't think of a single thing, my mouth opened and closed, Arin's anxious face floated before me, begging me not to forget my promise.

Impatience returned to the producer. She sighed, stood up, thanked me for my time.

I gripped the fabric of the loveseat and blurted: "Wait."

The producer glanced at my knuckles, sat back down.

"I was caught off guard, I can do it." Desperate to keep the producer there, I began speaking, slowly at first, saying whatever came to mind. I scrambled to assemble bits and pieces of the daydreams I'd disciplined myself against while growing up, I told her about my machinelike focus in school, about the panic that had plagued my junior college years, the belated realization of my peers' extra-curricular achievements, I mentioned the career counselor; I got angry. Why were we asked to be, basically, bullet points of interesting people? (Here, the producer chuckled, and encouraged, I spoke even louder and faster, inflamed.) What happened to good old-fashioned work ethic? And now I was asked to, what, *spontaneously sparkle*? I knew we were supposed to study, but nobody told me I was supposed to be interesting too. I nearly cursed, but sensed the producer's focus sharpening as if she had some kind of radar for disrespect; I remembered what she'd said about charisma, I remembered the courteous behaviors and lilting, self-deprecating jokes that had endeared me to the void deck aunties, I tried to calm down, to infuse my speech with a similar, understated charm. Look, I continued, attempting geniality, if there was one thing I had, it was moxie, if I'd known I needed a personality I would have gone out and gotten one before coming in today. I didn't know, that was my only fault, it was an accidental ignorance. But hadn't I been on time, didn't I display initiative and gumption? I could work hard at this, I could be the best host they'd ever seen. Please.

When I was done, the producer took off her glasses and rubbed at the dent it left on her nose bridge. I watched her, then, unable to bear the silence, said hopefully: "I heard you laugh."

"Did I?"

"Yes, thank you."

"Do you want me to be honest with you?" How was I supposed

to answer? I said yes. She sighed. She had been in the local media industry for a long time, and when she first leapt from the safety of television to the untested grounds of YouTube people thought she was crazy. But she had an eye for these things, a finger on the pulse of the attention economy, and in less than a year the channel's original skits and recurring talk shows had amassed an impressive subscriber and view count that continued multiplying quicker than bunnies. What the producer was looking for was someone with that special, compelling watchability only one in a million people had. It was hard to find, most people didn't even know they had it, and thank God because if they did they'd be even more difficult to work with. That's why she auditioned nobodies, random people off the streets or on the internet who responded to the open calls—she was doing as big a sweep as possible, all in hopes of finding that one gem. Most of the time it didn't happen, and she would have to work with someone halfway there, groom them toward the impression of charisma. See, now, you, she continued, putting her glasses back on and looking straight at me, lifting my hopes, causing me to nod obediently to signal that, yes, I was paying attention, I was eagerly soaking up every word—you're not bad, not superspecial, but not completely *un*interesting either. She had laughed—only once, she was quick to clarify—because the idea of monetizing stress was funny; but I, unfortunately, was not. The problem was, she said, I was too self-conscious, too desperate to be liked. It was obvious from the way I talked that I was mirroring behavior I'd seen before, preempting positive reactions. I spoke not like someone blurting spontaneous thoughts, but like someone imagining what a person resembling me would say. The hardest thing, she concluded, is to be authentically yourself. Even if the part is a skit, a caricature, the audience has to feel the force of personality behind it. Most people can't do it, they're held captive by an image of themselves they want people to believe in. That's fine if you're just living a normal life, but in front of the camera, no.

Humiliated, I asked: "So everyone in your videos, they're all a hundred percent like that in real life too?"

She paused. "No. But if you can't tell they're putting on a show, then I've done my job well." One of the video editors knocked on the door, popping his head in to announce the next person's arrival. The producer briskly stood. As she showed me out, she said: "Don't be too discouraged, girl. I'm doing you a favor by telling you this."

32

Arin came back that evening to a house with nothing on: no lights, no fan, not even the windows were opened to let fresh air in. She found me lying curled up on the bed, where I'd been pickling in disgrace for the last few hours, still in my outside clothes, and stared at me in alarm.

Without lifting my head I said in a small voice: "I know what I promised. But can we take a break, just for tonight?"

A long pause. Then she said: "On one condition."

"What is it?"

"Get up and take a shower."

It felt good to follow orders. I rose, shed my clothes, stepped into the bathroom, and began washing my hair.

Then the water turned ice-cold. Arin had switched the water heater off.

To this day I don't know what exactly was going through her mind, but its effect was immediate: it was as if a valve had been wrenched shut and the resulting pressure led to a small explosion. I shrieked, initially more out of shock than anything, then, mouth already open, kept going.

The bathroom door opened; ever since our grandmother died I didn't have the habit of locking it. Arin watched silently as I sobbed and raged, alternating between childishly stomping at the pooling water and recounting word for word the producer's cruelty, concluding that, despite what she claimed, YouTube was a pathetic shadow of the actual movie industry, all you needed was a digital camera and an attitude to call yourself a talent, what a joke. I wept savagely, mortification and frustration charging my voice, which was getting louder and more incoherent by the second. If they were real actresses, I demanded, real writers, real producers, why weren't they signed on to MediaCorp on Caldecott Hill? Under the icy

water my body pulsed, turning numb, as if tiny needles were prick-
ing me all over, leaking my shame. I experienced a loss of control
that terrified me, that I hope never to experience again; yet right
then, shivering under the unrelenting shower, an undeniable fact
emerged: I felt more awake than I had in years.

Some of the cold water bounced off my body and splattered on
Arin's cheeks, clothes. She didn't move, just stood there and took
it all in. Later she confessed that my words struck her profoundly.
She hadn't taken my plan that seriously before, dismissing the purported media company as the failing hobby of some rich person. Yet
listening to me recount so vehemently the words of the producer
changed her mind. Here was serious thought, intelligent design
behind a product that seemed so offhand, that compelled thousands of eyeballs. Clearly *not* everyone could walk in and do the
job, even though it seemed so easy. And perhaps that was the point,
the appearance of ease, every aspect and element of this endeavor
working in tandem to sell a viewer the perfect mix of relatability,
entertainment, and disgust, the delicious taste of moral superiority
that came with the viewer's assumption that they, too, could command this much attention. How sly, how canny. How effective. If it
truly were, as the producer said, down solely to spontaneity, a flow-
ering of original character, it wouldn't have snagged Arin's attention. But no, there was a blueprint for success, a calculated perimeter
within which a persona could be studied and formed.

When I turned the water off, Arin held out my towel. I wrapped
myself in it, feeling much better now that my anger was, at least
temporarily, milked dry.

"Now you go," I said, and Arin laughed.

"I'm not afraid of cold water." She washed up quickly, barely
flinching under the icy shower. After she toweled herself off, Arin
turned the kitchen lights on, saw that I'd calmed down, then asked:
"What do you want to do now?"

A little sheepishly, I said: "What else—let's study."

But instead of looking pleased, Arin frowned. "It's dinnertime."

"Fine, we'll eat, then we'll study."

"No," she said, pointing to the wall clock. It was eight. "Where
is everyone?"

33

We didn't have to go far to find my mother. She was sitting on the green playground slide, alone. Her hands in her face. Had she heard me screaming from the second-floor bathroom and stayed here, delaying her encounter with her increasingly deranged daughter?

"Ma," I said guiltily, and she looked up. "What are you doing here?"

"Just taking a rest."

Arin and I exchanged a glance. "We live right there."

She stood, offered no explanation, and walked toward our block. Arin and I followed mutely. I spotted the bakery auntie, who lived in the estate too, walking toward us from the opposite direction. But instead of their usual greeting, my mother froze as the bakery auntie hurried by. My own greeting died in my throat. The women blinked at each other as they passed, didn't say hi.

The second the bakery auntie vanished, Arin flung herself against my mother, hugging her from behind. I stared at them both, astonished. Arin was not one to give herself over to emotional bursts.

My mother softened instantly. In her old voice she asked: "Are you hungry?"

"Starving."

"Let's go upstairs, then."

"What is it?" I hissed to Arin, as we started walking again. "What's going on?"

She shook her head. "I don't know." But her face was pale, frightened. Our hands reached for each other behind my mother's back, fingers interlocking tightly as if we could form a protective net, though whether we were trying to shield her or ourselves in that moment, neither of us could say.

34

For weeks it was all the neighborhood could talk about. It was a tremendous scandal that unfurled like a banner over our household. If you lived in Bedok, if you'd ever had an interaction, even in passing, with any one of those void deck aunties, you would surely have heard a version of the afternoon's events, the cud of gossip being dissected and regurgitated. Its reach was such that I, who hadn't even been present, could piece things together, forming a picture so intense, so shameful, it took on the force of actual memory, becoming an incident I could relate as if I'd been standing right there, starting from the moment my grandmother materialized in the photocopy shop.

Seeing her there must have been a shock—not just to my mother, but to the void deck aunties whose only context for their beloved Su Yang was her generosity of spirit and attention, her successful production of two courteous, hardworking daughters, her business acumen. In the past year, her entrepreneurial hustle had really paid off—thanks to the increased demand for study guides from a new breed of schools that weren't exactly top-tier, but were well respected and rumored to have implemented a new kind of heuristic learning method, and guarded their secrets closely. Schools like Crescent Girls' School, Cedar Girls' School, Catholic High. Two years in a row, teachers from these schools had accurately predicted Cambridge's exam questions, bestowing an unthinkable advantage on their students.

After that the country was in a thirst for the internal practice papers those schools designed. It got to a point where students weren't allowed to take their own test papers out of the exam hall—they'd get their grades back on a separate printout, and teachers would go over the answers by copying the questions onto a transparency sheet and projecting them on the wall. Most students colluded in this secrecy—after all, national exams were graded on a bell curve. We no longer had the advantage, even, of using the grades of British schoolkids to prop ourselves up—Singapore had decided to isolate our marking pool from the rest of the world, so although the questions for the O and A levels came from and were marked at Cambridge, when it came to adjusting for the bell curve we were competing only with other Singaporeans.

But there were always a few students who needed the money. And who, if not my mother, could cultivate those relationships, coax them into coming to her before any of the other black market academic dealers? The void deck aunties, who initially thought my mother totally insane for, just this month, paying a hundred and twenty dollars for first look at a typed-up, pirated copy of an Anderson Junior College exam paper (questions memorized and regurgitated by a student the second she exited the exam hall), watched as the money tripled, then quadrupled in a matter of days, their disbelief ceding to glee as desperate cosmopolitan mothers humbled themselves before the photocopy shop, exchanging folded bills for copies of illegally gained intelligence. And nobody was prouder than the photocopy auntie, who behaved as if she alone had unearthed my mother from the pits of our neighborhood. From one end of the void deck shops to the other you could hear her bragging: how successful they were, how visionary.

They? Profits might have been shared but surely the success was my mother's alone. And although the void deck aunties' admiration was gratifying, they didn't fully appreciate the genius of her machinations. They'd have clapped the same if she'd started a business selling boiled eggs. Drunk on their praise yet lonely for true understanding, she must have boasted to her mother, the one person who'd always believed she could do better: See, I've made something of myself, look what I can do.

A mistake. When my grandmother barged into the photocopy shop that afternoon, silver hair gelled into place like a helmet, acid stink of her overripe perfume blown everywhere by the rotating table fan, did the void deck aunties look between them, did their first inklings of doubt take root?

My mother, still laughing, slipped off the high stool. "Ma, hello, what are you doing here?"

"Ensuring my school's papers aren't part of your little scheme. My teachers work hard."

My mother stopped laughing. She didn't say what everyone thought, which was that no one wanted practice papers from my grandmother's extremely mediocre school. "I already said, they aren't."

"I'll see for myself."

Her long fingers reached for the stack of stapled paper, and, unbelievably, audaciously, in front of everyone—my mother slapped her hand away.

"Stop that." How magnificent she must have seemed in that moment, matching her mother word for biting word, employing the same tone of authority. "You have no right."

But she had fatally miscalculated. My grandmother reeled back, drawing her hand to her chest, as if from an open flame. Her head whipped toward the watching women, then back to my mother.

"You would hit me?"

My mother shook her head, trying to salvage the situation. "I didn't hit you."

The public incursion was too great. My grandmother snapped. "You can lie to yourself all you like, Sue Li, but what you're doing is *theft*. This is what you left home for? To become someone who'd strike *your own mother*? Your girls have run away, your husband is unfaithful—"

My mother stilled instantly.

"—you lie and cheat and steal. What *happened* to you?" Abruptly, my grandmother broke off and looked around her. At the lizard shit on the ceiling of the photocopy shop, at the makeshift stacks of stolen exam papers, at the shell-shocked audience that had gathered around the two women. Her voice was swollen with grief. "You could have been so much more than this."

As the void deck aunties watched, my mother recovered, and spat: "Do you think *I* don't know that?"

How those minutes afterward stretched.

My grandmother put a hand on her heart, gripped the fabric of her blouse. When she let go, the nylon retained the crease of her fingers. "I'm going the same way as your father. I can't watch you do this to yourself."

People don't die of broken hearts, though relationships certainly do; my grandmother hardened herself, we never saw her again. Leaving my mother surrounded by the women who'd just heard her disavow them. She looked at each one of the aunties and saw their mute, hurt faces, already drawing back from her, closing ranks among themselves. Not one of them said a thing. My mother blinked wildly, then stumbled out of the shop.

No one stopped her. Who could stop her? My mother wasn't one of them, she had never been, and now the truth was drawn into stark existence. Already the aunties were turning to the next person to whisper their version of events, latching on to the most scandalous of details, their growing humiliation and anger accelerating the spread of gossip. My mother walked to the hawker center, smiled, made small talk with the chicken rice seller, bought some food, ate it. Painfully aware of the chatter fast seeping outward from the void deck shops. Soon the entire neighborhood would hear, repeated and distorted, my grandmother's shocking accusation: your husband is unfaithful. They would never ask her about it directly, and so she'd never have the chance to clarify the statement. Gossip would simply, per its slippery nature, swirl and accrete around our family. My mother kneaded her temples, breathing shallowly. How far back could her mistakes be traced? She recalled the sweet, singular moment of comfort she felt, when she, hurt by her husband's actions and seduced by the naïve possibility of rapprochement, confided in her mother.

She called my father.

35

Later I would learn that my father had, for the better part of a year, embarked on an ill-fated friendship with a woman called Lim Pei Wen. She lived in Pasir Ris and had a standing private arrangement with him; every Monday, Wednesday, and Friday, he ferried her through the seas of morning traffic to a private dialysis center in Ang Mo Kio, where she sat, for four hours each time, reading fresh pages of whatever manhua she was presently translating to her older sister, who had lost three ulcered toes to diabetes after years of stampeding the slimy channels of 628 Market in slippers. Thrice a week, my father's taxi became a companionable oasis of calm as Pei Wen, like some kind of Chinese Scheherazade, spoke softly about her translation work, told him about her sister, who relied heavily on the hemodialysis that washed her blood but left her in chronic pain, or simply climbed into the passenger seat beside him, leaned her head against the headrest, and closed her eyes for the duration of the drive.

It was, I believe now, the most important friendship of my father's life. He adored Pei Wen. Her presence became a salve to his soul, their conversations an escape from the increasing burdens of home, and he was able, by whatever private negotiations, to convince himself the necessary emotional boundaries were in place, even when Pei Wen introduced him to her toeless sister as her special friend. But my mother wasn't stupid. When she investigated, interrogated, confronted, and forgave his emotional infidelity early that September, my father amputated his friendship with Pei Wen, and for all intents and purposes, returned to mechanically enacting the gestures of living, though with a little less light.

That's all it was, technically—a friendship. Whether it disrespected their marriage or not was a matter of opinion. The understanding was that my parents were, no matter what indignities they endured, a unit.

How difficult, then, to sit in the hawker center and call my father.

"I told her," my mother said, when he picked up. "My mother." And, thinking it better to rip the Band-Aid off at once, she relayed what happened in the photocopy shop. My mother's voice cracked when she got to the part about the void deck aunties absorbing her insult, her immediate regret, the impossibility of taking it all back— the lightning strike of understanding that she'd wrecked everything with a single slip of the tongue. How awful their faces were afterward. How hurt. Other than that, she kept her voice steady. Not daring to articulate that bead of hope, that irrational yearning for an echo of comfort.

But my father could only manage: "Why did you tell *her*?"

She was so disappointed she nearly laughed. "Anyway, you know how people talk. Better you hear it from me."

Then she hung up, truly alone now, and stood, intending to go home, energy leaking from her body with every step, getting only as far as the playground before sinking onto the green slide where Arin and I found her.

The hurricane of judgment that engulfed my family in the weeks ensuing proved too much. My poor father, who couldn't catch a break, perpetually battered by life, now found himself publicly branded a philanderer. Old gossip got trotted out again: the way he'd deferred to his wife for years, handing her all his earnings, see, you can never tell, it's always the quiet ones. A smaller, traitorous faction whispered: But it can't have been easy living with a woman like Su. This is why one should beware marrying women who have big ideas, who think they're better than you, who think they're above us all. A man can only take so much. Though: Who knew he still had it in him? That quiet, taciturn man? *Really?* The gutter jokes wrote themselves, laughter abruptly muffled only when the children—that is, Arin and I—came within earshot. As a result, for a period, every time we left the house, pitying, prying eyes followed.

And perhaps if my father had been anything other than the son of a woman abandoned, things might have turned out differently. For the truth was: he *had* crossed a line. But was he a hypocrite or simply lonely? Was his friendship an emotional dalliance or a matter of survival? After a particularly mortifying incident where the drink stall auntie took my father's order sullenly, simmering with womanly judgment, my father hunkered down at home, flayed by humiliation, and stopped going to the kopitiam. Yet I wished our relationship had been permissive enough for me to just open my mouth and ask what all of this meant, for him, for us.

One night, I crept up to where my father had dozed off unshowered on the couch, squatted beside him, and slid his cellphone out from where it had fallen between the cushions. He was using a Motorola clamshell back then, and when I flipped the phone open, the latest chapter of the manhua Pei Wen translated was on the screen.

I looked up, my eyes met his. Not a muscle in his face moved, and if not for the very slight way his eyes flicked from my face to the phone screen, it would've been easy to mistake him as being still asleep. I closed the phone, replaced it on the couch, backed away. *Sorry,* I mouthed, but his eyes were closed again.

That was October 2006, a month before the most important national examination of my life. Shortly after that night, which I was too ashamed to speak of for years, not to Arin, not even to myself, my father packed the contents of his sad existence into a polyester duffel bag and left.

36

That A-level season, wildness saturated the air. A sleep-deprived PRC scholar mixed her schedules up and appeared outside the exam hall twenty-four hours after Chemistry Part B concluded, missing her exam and effectively obliterating her scholarship and visa; she was later hospitalized for a suicide attempt. Guo, who I'd dismissed as having no real mettle, had been stung on his forearm by a stray lesser-banded hornet midway into the Economics paper, but gripped his pen tighter and continued relentlessly formulating his arguments on allocative efficiency and monopsony until the invigilator called time and an ambulance.

As for me, the abrupt nature of my father's departure ripped open a vortex into which my anxieties, my awareness of my classmates, and my panic at my own ignorance vanished; without looking too closely at it, I turned back to my books as one would an oxygen line. It was like being drugged—I made more headway in that eleventh hour than through the panic of the last two years, and went into the A levels feeling not as if I were scrambling to prove myself but simply meeting my fate. In March, the results were released. Out of 375 students, there were 22 perfect scorers, and I wasn't one. I hadn't expected to be, but felt a little stab, mentally striking medicine, dentistry, and law from my future. Still, I thought. There was accounting. Business. Communications. A world of options yet. I sat cross-legged in the school hall waiting for my name to be called. Before me, the slim shoulders of a girl I'd occasionally lunched with started to shake. She hadn't gotten a perfect score either.

We were called by surnames, in alphabetical order, to receive our results. Ang, Budihardjo, Chen . . . the hall swelled, students clamoring and signaling to one another with a singular question in their eyes, aggregating the scores of their friends and peers, desperate to understand where they stood in the battle for the hallowed gates of university. Tengku, Wong, Shen . . . I noted with careful surprise that I was shaking. The prickling sense of blood awaking whispered through my body, my legs pulsing from cramp. Anything could happen. Anything could still happen. Yang. I pushed myself up, unsteadily, ignoring the scream of my calves, and walked to the front of the school hall to receive the blue folder containing my future.

So. I'd gotten B's and C's. And I'd failed H2 Mathematics. I didn't know you could fail math—it was formulaic, and I'd done the work. I stared at the E, uncomprehending.

The vortex returned.

I closed the blue folder, grades disappearing again. Someone was making her way toward me, the same teacher who'd nudged me toward dropping out. It was of utmost importance that she not reach me, that she not confirm her prior assessment. A shadow crossed her face as she registered my hostility; she faltered, and I vanished. Pushing my way past the warm, sticky bodies of people I'd once considered my peers, ignoring their questioning faces, I found a quiet alcove and leaned against the wall.

Again, as I had so many times in the last months, I pulled my father's contact up on my new phone.

He'd changed his number; texts I sent apologizing for going through his handphone had gone undelivered. Yet I pressed the call button and brought it to my face.

I waited till the end of the operator's recorded spiel informing me the number I'd dialed was not in service, gripping the phone and listening intently to the scuffling hum of static. It seemed to contain the abyss of alternate lives now lost to me, ballooning from the abscess of his absence. Still I listened and listened, waiting for his voice to emerge. Surely, I thought, this time would be different. Surely today, of all days, he would sense my anguish and pick up, revealing the operator's message to be an elaborate prank. He hadn't even said a word to me when he left. I hadn't been worth even that.

But the whispering static rolled on endlessly, like a suffocating fog. I saw myself, as if on the edge of a cliff, waiting futilely for absolution. There I would stay, forever, looking for a point in the past where a single choice made differently might absolve me of my present. With great difficulty I lowered the phone and stared at it, still sick with hope.

Then I hung up. Exhaustion rushed at me, I felt my body congealing into a shape I would live in from here on. This was who I was, this was the life I'd made. I said to myself: Good, I'm relieved.

37

For several months, since taking my A levels, I'd been working part-time in an ice cream shop near home while waiting for the results. It was new, one of several changes in the neighborhood that seemed to happen overnight—a childcare center sprouted a few blocks away, not far from the photocopy shop; a store selling truffle wonton noodles opened in the hawker center, drawing unprecedented queues; the ice cream shop was announced, triggering neighborhood speculation about the intelligence of the new tenants. It was opened by two university graduates and served only ice cream, waffle cones, and coffee, at café prices, as if this were the Central Business District. Did they know this was Bedok? Did they know the kind of people who lived here? What a strange and stupid decision. But I went straight there and offered my services to the young couple, joining the rotation of part-timers who scooped, served, and cajoled customers into sweet and temporary temptations.

Now it seemed like I would be here for much longer. The day after the results were released, two of the girls I worked with quit, devoting themselves fully to university and scholarship applications, leaving the owner (just the wife; the husband's role was primarily financing) and me to handle the influx of customers. She had a face like the moon and it was darkening with every second.

"I specifically asked," the owner said irritably, "for a six-month commitment. You girls are completely unreliable."

It was a particularly humid day, people kept coming into the air-conditioned shop to cool off under the pretense of surveying the flavors on display. An ogling child was pressing his face against the glass while his mother, visibly sticky and uncomfortable, half-heartedly patted his shoulder and told him to hurry up.

"I failed my A levels," I said. "I'm not going anywhere." I turned to the mother and caught pity flashing in her eyes. Blazing, I recommitted to my role as the genial shopkeeper, beamed at the sweaty child, and offered him a scrape of butterscotch ice cream off the side of a disposable spoon.

"Say thank you to the pretty Jie Jie."

"Tankyut."

The child announced his order imperiously. I glanced at the mother, waiting. I'd clocked her the second she walked in: her clothes were all slightly loose and she had the guilty look of a woman weathered by the constant battle with self-control. A bead of sweat rolled off the side of her chin and darkened the shirt under her collarbones. She put her hand out and the child deposited the spoon, licked completely clean, in her palm; her fingers closed around it, ignoring the tiny countertop bin. I could practically smell her hesitation, her consideration, but to ask explicitly would douse her in shame. Instead, I filled a plastic cup with cold tap water and handed it to her. The small kindness wobbled her, she succumbed. The mother paid for two ice creams and left.

I'd done this dance many times before, but now the owner considered me in a new light. At her evaluation, a slow, familiar excitement stirred.

In a deliberately cool voice, I said: "I've never taken a day off."

"Except yesterday."

"Every eighteen-year-old in Singapore took a day off yesterday."

Her eyes narrowed. "And you're not retaking the exams or going private? What do your parents think?"

All the air had gone out of my mother, who'd slumped against the dining-room chair. After my father left, she'd exiled herself and was the third and final resident behind that shoji screen, citing our burgeoning need for privacy, yet the short gulf between bedroom and screen had never felt as vast as it did that long, sleepless night. Arin recoiled as if she'd been slapped.

"Who has money for that kind of thing?" But my voice betrayed itself, it drew a line between the owner's life and my own. She softened at my bravado, became embarrassed, muttered something about checking with her husband, repeated her lament on reliability, caught herself, and told me I'd always been a good worker. Her praise concluded our tiny tussle; I'd won, but what had I won? I'd secured a place I hadn't known I was fighting for. By the end of that conversation she'd doubled my shifts, and in a couple of weeks when a new girl was hired, the owner referred to me as her supervisor. Soon, it was just me managing the ice cream shop—the owner spending more and more time teaching at a yoga studio in Kembangan, dropping in only occasionally to check on things.

I applied, privately and uselessly, to the local universities, was wait-listed, and prayed for the students with options to choose otherwise, though by July it was clear the available spots had been filled by the sea of candidates more intelligent or suitable than me. Penelope came by the ice cream shop a couple of times—we'd barely seen each other through the last two years of academic hell, but now that she was preparing to leave for her law degree in the UK she had nothing but free time. She kept an endless Rolodex of who ended up where and announced her findings constantly; perhaps she thought she was doing me a favor by keeping me in the loop. But the endless project of hope exhausted me, and I was tired of seeing the neighborhood's expressions of aggravated surprise and disappointment, that for all my potential I'd landed a mere stroll from the void deck shops. The day Penelope breathlessly informed me that Jia Min, my old academic nemesis, had rejected one of the courses I was wait-listed for in favor of a more prestigious university, I got fed up. I snapped at her to pay for her ice cream; she didn't come back again.

During this time it seemed as if the only person for whom the future remained in flux was Arin. But she had changed too. At first, the same A-level syllabus that suffocated me created a trellis around which her calm determination grew, but in her second year of junior college, that determination sharpened to the point of brittleness. Purplish rings appeared under both eyes, and Arin developed the bad habit of chewing her bottom lip while working, frequently breaking the skin and leading to ulcers. Had I looked this wretched when I was mired in study, or worse? Pity flooded me whenever I saw her lonely figure at the dining table, soaked in our gloomy ceiling light, though whether it was pity for Arin or for a version of myself, I couldn't say. I would go over and massage the hard knot between her shoulders, which had seized up from long hours hunched over her notes. She was so intensely focused her eyes wouldn't leave the page even as her muscles yielded and relaxed. At night, she slept curled like a shrimp beside me, though if I ever brushed against her, she'd spring straight up, raring to start a new day even if it were the dead of the night.

It took too long for me to realize she was terribly frightened by my failure. One night, she came into the bedroom still in the feverish haze of intellectual irritation and cast her eye on me. "You're eating ice cream in *bed*?"

Whenever she was studying, the living room transformed into a tense dome of concentration. My mother retreated behind the shoji screen most nights rather than sit on the couch and risk distracting Arin, and although I hated to admit it, once she rendered herself invisible behind the screen it was almost easy to forget she was there. And I hadn't wanted to stand like a fugitive caught in the cold refrigerator's light. "Are you done for the night? I'll finish this outside." I looked at her. "Or do you want some? It's lychee."

I felt her exasperation rise. "Do I want *ice cream*?"

"Look, are you upset about something?"

She stared at me, calculating, as if she'd been restraining herself for a long time. Then she blurted: "Are you going to work in the ice cream shop forever?"

I was stung. "Well—no. I'm still figuring out my next steps."

"It's not too late, why don't you sit for the A levels again?"

I burst out laughing. "The exams are in two months."

She slid into bed, turned her back to me, and refused to speak.

I stopped laughing. "Are you throwing a tantrum?" I asked, incredulous. I walked my fingers over to her side of the bed and up her spine, tapping her nape. When she didn't move, I put aside the ice cream and flipped her over.

Her cheeks were wet. Arin covered her face with both hands and mumbled: "Without you, I don't know what to do."

My annoyance evaporated. Did she feel like I had abandoned her? Hollowly, I said: "But you're doing well."

She dropped her hands. "Am I?"

"I know what it's like, but you have to keep going. Once you get there, you can start to breathe."

Her eyes narrowed, she came alive again. "There? Jie Jie, where is *there*? The university? And if I make it, then it's test after test, year after year, for four years, and then what? I get to compete some *more*, now with the rest of the country, to get and keep a shitty job?" Her voice was thin and wild. Gone was the kingdom of innocence we'd lived in, when we'd pronounced this our season of success. We were still so young, but already the endlessly repeating pattern of struggle seemed to unroll into our future. Yet what choice had she but to continue down this ever-narrowing path? A single false step and she'd be eating melted ice cream in bed like me. "I can't do it alone," she said. "I can't."

"You're not alone," I said uselessly. "I'm here."

She nodded.

Gradually I felt her shift into resignation, acceptance. There would be a new dawn, a new day. What was a small outburst here and there: the most important thing was that she regained her self-control and returned to her books.

"What are you thinking?" I asked, lightly. The lychee ice cream had melted into a pale pink mush. I picked it up and ladled some into the spoon for her. Her lips parted and she winced at the shock of sugar.

Wiping her mouth, Arin got up to close the bedroom door, returning to sit beside me on the bed. Then, as if she'd been mulling over this for a while and was relieved I'd finally brought it up, she spoke, so seriously that for a moment her skin lost its pallor and seemed to glow: "Do you think you'll ever audition to be a You-Tube personality again? And if not, can I?"

38

One afternoon in the middle of December, Arin swept into the ice cream shop, flung herself against the marbled counter, at the exact spot where the air-conditioning was the strongest, and beamed at Zahirah, the new part-timer.

"Hi, hi," she chirped. "It's hot out."

Zahirah blinked. "What can I get you?"

Arin leaned forward, scanning the flavors through the glass display, then, realizing she still had her giant plastic sunglasses on, took them off and perched them atop her head, inadvertently disturbing a few strands of her bangs, which now stuck out from under the sunglasses in small tufts. The inner corners of her eyes were shimmery with sweat. "What's popular?"

"Lemon, Rocky Road, Tiramisu . . ."

"But what do *you* like?"

Exuberance didn't suit her. It was like an artificially high note she was holding, which obliged the other person to stretch for. I didn't think much of Zahirah, the sixteen-year-old daughter of one of the owner's coworkers, who'd gotten into some trouble at school and was currently taking an extended gap year; I found her frivolous. But when she looked at me helplessly, I stepped forward.

"I like chocolate mint."

Instantly Arin relaxed into her usual seriousness. "The best people all do."

"So I'll ring you up for a scoop?"

Mischief crept into her voice. "From where? Are you moonlighting for another ice cream shop?" She drummed her forefinger on the glass display. "You don't sell that flavor here."

"Yes, but we have chocolate *and* mint."

Arin's laughter, threaded through with relief, rang through the shop like a bell. "What a salesman! Ring me up for two scoops."

It finally dawned on Zahirah that Arin wasn't just a random customer. She looked between us, trying to figure out if a joke was
being made at her expense, then gave up and carved out two perfect
balls of ice cream, wedging them on a waffle cone. A little grouch-
ily, she handed it to Arin, brightening only when I nodded my
approval.

Zahirah turned back to Arin and said, sternly: "Seven dollars."

Arin paid, aware now that the game was up yet still clinging
awkwardly to the vestiges of our charade. I could see her running
uncertainly through potential jokes, quips in her mind, before raising the ice cream cone and simply thanking us both. Then she
backed out of the shop, and Zahirah and I watched her go.

"So much," I told Arin that night, lying side by side in bed, our eyes
wide and staring at the ceiling, "for charisma."

"Jie, it was terrible."

"Painful."

"Agonizing."

"Excruciating."

"Terrible."

I elbowed her. "You already said that. Did your brain empty
itself of vocabulary the second you finished your A levels? It's barely
been a week."

"Are you a thesaurus?" But she turned her cheek slightly on the
pillow and threw me a brilliant sideways smile. Her ulcered lip had
healed over, and although her skin retained the ash of exhaustion,
Arin's overall demeanor had improved considerably since I vowed to
help her develop a personality so lovable it'd wrench attention from
the most skeptical of viewers, as soon as she finished her exams. But
the exercise in the ice cream shop revealed we had a long way to go.

"Well," I murmured comfortingly, "what did you do the rest of
the afternoon? Did you even finish the ice cream?"

"I couldn't. I split it with Auntie at the photocopy shop."

I grimaced. I hadn't told Arin, but my mother had obviously
overheard our bedroom conversation and had been showing up at
the ice cream shop uninvited, pestering me to return to school.

She'd become fixated on the idea of my applying for a private university, although a private education was far more expensive than attending a local institution; she swore she would find a way to finance it, no matter what it took. She often touched her finger to mine while saying this, a vision of perfect and immutable calm.

No, no, and no. The revival of her overbearing intimacy irritated me; I was starting to understand why my father sought refuge elsewhere. To live under the stink of her sacrifice was unbearable. I turned back to Arin.

"Next time," I said, "try playing off the other person. You gave poor Zahirah a fright, suddenly demanding her opinion."

But Arin surprised me.

"Sweet Zahirah," she mused obligingly. "Tell me: What *does* occupy her imagination, her mind?"

A moment of astonishment, then I burst out laughing. "Very good," I said, with admiration and a little jealousy. She'd shaken off the afternoon's embarrassment and dived right back into make-believe, this time more smoothly. I shook my head, pushed myself upright, and poked her arm. "All right, get up, let's practice. This might not be a lost cause after all."

New YouTube channels were popping up left and right. That December, we spread our net wide, lining up a ferocious string of auditions. In the weeks leading up to them, I studied customers at the ice cream shop, noting gestures, mimicking them to Arin at home. Arin got a holiday job distributing flyers for a teeth-whitening company near Raffles Place with a bevy of other teenagers caught in the post-A-level limbo, and spent her daylight hours charming harried office workers into accepting those neon advertisement slips from her and not others, each new day a fresh opportunity to put different aspects of her public-facing personality into practice. At night, when we reunited, we would exchange notes, parodying the more ludicrous behaviors—the gaudy parades of self-consciousness enacted by dieting women eyeing the ice cream flavors; the sly, kind confidence of the finance professional smoothly accepting a flyer without even slowing her walk; the transparently choreographed charm of that military recruit who paid for a girl's ice cream by proffering his debit card between his index and middle finger, as if holding a cigarette—often collapsing into fits of laughter.

It felt as if we were re-creating that binder of the neighborhood aunties all over again, except it was now a magnificent map of charm and charisma, a key that could be used to scrape away the rougher edges of Arin's personality or a guide with which we might layer the simplest of smiles with more texture. And in a matter of days, as we sculpted together the exact angle of her small, rueful frowns and calculated the most inviting tilt of her head, Arin's natural seriousness grew into a bedrock of quiet charm.

"Again," I'd say, as we distilled and practiced gestures, phrases before the kitchen mirror. "Again."

Yet the closer the audition dates drew, the more anxious Arin got. I had to remind her the screen tests were privately held; even if she embarrassed herself, no one outside that room had to know. But the night before her first audition, she paced the kitchen endlessly, thumb in her mouth. She didn't respond the first few times I asked her to rehearse; finally, I pinched her arm hard.

"Snap out of it," I scolded.

Arin looked surprised. She rolled her shoulders, drew herself up taller, and gratefully shot me one of her uncertain smiles. "Okay," she said. "Okay." It was a different smile from the sinuous smirks we'd rehearsed together, paired with a slight, kind crease of her eyes. Then she inhaled, refocusing herself, and the scales of her reticence fell away in layers.

Voilà—she was Arin, the personality, standing beside me, holding my gaze in the mirror, direct and amused.

"Tell me," I said, deepening my voice. "What are you interested in? What occupies your imagination, your mind?"

She tilted her head back, a clean ripple of unrestrained laughter unfurling from her throat. "Oh, that," she said, pulling a face. "Who has time for interests? All I do all day is study, it's *very* boring."

"No interests, no hobbies?"

"Show me one Singaporean teenager with a hobby," she smiled. "And I'll show you a rich girl." Words that bordered on resentful coming from me sounded merely bemused falling softly from her lips. Her tone shifted into one of straightforward sincerity. "Which I *desperately* want to be me someday. Quick"—and, I counted, right on time, a touch of playfulness entering her voice and spreading like ink—"hit Like, Share, and Subscribe."

She straightened, tore her gaze away from the mirror, and turned to me.

"How did I do?"

But we both already knew: her performance was impeccable. A shiver trembled through me.

"As always," I said, squeezing her arm, "very good. Very, very nicely done."

But no matter how much attention I devoted to helping Arin, it never quite distracted me fully from the problem of my mother harassing me to return to school. I don't know why I kept it a secret. Perhaps part of me didn't want to risk Arin taking her side, but perhaps another part of me was embarrassed by my mother's dogged devotion to my withered future. Besides, it was wishful thinking. The public universities were subsidized by the government, and only people with money could afford private degrees, which were far less prestigious and, in some cases, not even recognized locally. My mother was persuading me just to hear herself talk. So: let her. There wasn't much else for her to get excited over, life amid the void deck aunties must have been miserable. Still, when she sailed into the ice cream shop one morning carrying a stack of glossy brochures and prospectuses from private universities, online universities, part-time universities, I turned away, annoyed.

I busied myself with scooping cones and counting coins for the dribble of schoolkids sweltering for a midafternoon treat while my mother monologued, employing that same confident charm I'd once so loved, extolling the virtues of private education, putting all her strength into luring me back onto the right path with her long leash of love. But when I noticed the normally blasé Zahirah watching everything with wide, interested eyes, my irritation vanished. I heard the laughter of other people, I felt the great and tender urge to protect my mother from their curious gaze.

I waited for Zahirah to leave the shop for her break, then

touched my mother's forearm, and asked lightly, with the intention of putting a stop to this once and for all, why she thought we might, in any universe, be able to pay the fees for a private education.

It was the moment she'd been waiting for. She threw me the long-suffering smile of my childhood and revealed that she'd quit her job at the photocopy shop. Instead, she'd applied for work at the new neighborhood childcare center, which didn't pay much more but with which she could service a loan from the bank. No, not could. Had. She had already done it, she'd gone and applied for a loan, without even waiting for me to say yes.

I withdrew my hand.

"Absolutely not," I said pleasantly, trying to control the shake in my voice. "Go back to the bank and return them every single cent."

The glass door swung open, a little electronic chime rang out in the air. I transformed instantly into the pleasant shopkeeper, but it was only the owner, doing one of her random drop-ins. She looked bemused and slightly impatient as my mother introduced herself, then conferenced with me quickly about scheduling an electrician's visit. After the owner left, I turned back to my mother.

"Did you hear me?" I was still smiling, but my teeth chattered. "I don't want to go back to school. Thank you, but I said no. You should head back to the bank before it closes to tell them you've changed your mind. Okay? Go on, bye."

My mother didn't leave. She had one more card to play.

"If you go back to school," she said quietly, "I promise to put you in contact with your father."

39

I was furious, I accused her of being manipulative, I unequivocally rejected her offer. Pressuring me constantly, trying to wear me down, that wasn't enough? Now she had to bring my father into the picture too? Did she still think I was a child, whose feelings could be leveraged and bartered with so easily? Yes, I was: I suffered for days after that. I couldn't help remembering the way I had been: ambitious, delighted by my own intelligence, my future stretching into the horizon. But I was also scared. Deep in my heart was the inky suspicion that I'd never truly understood what I was learning, that it was a false intelligence I'd held dear, enabled only by a pig-headed capacity for memorization. What if going back to school confirmed I was stupid, that my failure had been well deserved? I wouldn't be able to bear it, I would rather die.

Then, in January, Arin successfully auditioned for a gaming YouTube channel despite knowing absolutely nothing about games. The channel was a newish one, with only ten thousand subscribers and nowhere the level of professionalization of the channel I'd auditioned for; their videos were filmed not in a studio but after hours in the back room of a guitar store, a space on loan from one of the producer's friends; they used a Handycam instead of a proper full-frame camera. They would pay her thirty dollars per episode to sit beside Lyla, a prominent LiveJournal blogger already locally beloved for her extravagantly online presence and maximalist approach to beauty, and figure out newly released games on-screen.

Thirty? Even her job giving out flyers paid sixty-five dollars a day. Arin's eyes scanned the talent agreement contract, initial excitement deflating. It was for ten episodes, renewal dependent upon performance. "Maybe I should give it up," she murmured.

I was strangely disappointed, too, but pretended otherwise. So this was what all our work came to: a small role, a grainy picture, a dirty room somewhere. I thought of my mother's insistence that I return to school, the dimming of alternative lives, and slipped Arin a pale blue envelope. "Don't say that. It's a start."

In it was three hundred and fifty dollars. The difference between her flyer job and a trial run of ten episodes. Look, I was saying. I believed in her, I was investing in her.

Arin was quiet for a long time, and I was afraid she was going to cry. "Come on," I said, finally. "I don't even need the money now. Pay me back when you get rich."

She nodded. "I will," she said, very seriously.

With the money she went to the old neighborhood barber and paid him ten dollars to trim her long hair in harsh, angular lines with his razor. She came out looking like a determined doll, thick black hair falling straight down to her waist, framing both sides of her face in a glossy slate, signature bangs receding up her forehead and showing off the elegant arch of her newly plucked brows. The rest of the money she used to buy a series of cheap black dresses with stiff white collars, from Bugis Street.

At home, in the mirror, she tilted her head right and left, brushing out her bangs with a fine-tooth comb. "Well," she said bravely, clipping a stray thread from her white collar with a nail scissor, "at least the low-resolution picture will be forgiving."

I felt a pang. How vulnerable she looked, how painfully our dreams had adjusted to accommodate reality.

"It's missing a little something," I said.

I went to the neighborhood Econ minimart, pushing past the rows of marmalade and potato chips and gachapon machines till I found the small rack of beauty accessories at the back of the store. I purchased a cluster of neon-colored hair ties for a dollar and braided Arin's long hair into two sleek ropes, the bottom of each braid bound with a small but violent dash of color.

"There," I said, tenderly brushing the end of her left braid with my thumb. "Now you're ready."

On the fifteenth of February at exactly 7:00 p.m., the first episode of her show was released. We didn't tell anyone, not even my mother;

that way it was easier, Arin reasoned, if the entire thing turned out to be a farce. We would watch it in secret, then decide.

At 6:30 we sat down to dinner as usual, my mother nattering about work with a forced cheeriness. She had left the photocopy shop for the childcare center after all, and now she spent all day negotiating with tiny terrorists, coaxing them into nap time, into wiping their buttocks after they took a shit, into sharing and caring, and as she spoke, despite the building impatience with every tick of the clock's second hand, I found myself overcome with the sudden desire to weep. What was worse: the solitude of being barely tolerated at the photocopy shop, or the profound loneliness of spending your waking hours with small children who couldn't understand you? Seven p.m. came and went. Arin, who was better at indulging my mother's rants, looked increasingly haggard with anticipation. I couldn't stand it: at 7:13 I stood up, leaving my bowl of picked-at food, went to my mother, and cut her off midsentence by wrapping my arms around her shoulders.

She stiffened. I hadn't told Arin about my mother's attempt at blackmail, but the strain in our relationship was obvious. No one said anything for a long while. When I let go she laughed, a lonely little sound, and said: "All right, all right. It's not that bad."

"Ma, go shower, we'll wash up."

Her eyes crinkled and I had to stop myself from reaching out to smooth the creases that had appeared in her skin. "Are you sure?"

"You should rest."

She got up, patted my arm, then brought her plate to the kitchen sink and tottered into the shower.

It was 7:30. Arin and I dove for the couch. She turned her netbook on and I squeezed her hand, trying to forget the way my mother's face lit up at what she must have perceived as our minor reconciliation. The page loaded: already two thousand people had viewed the episode. Arin drew a shuddery breath; we didn't even know two thousand people in real life. I nodded at her, she hit play, and we settled into the uncanny hypnosis of watching Arin's tiny, replicated figure immersed in gameplay.

At first I was proud. Hours of practice lay smoothly embedded in every gesture, every slide of her gaze. Here I am, I thought, watching Arin raise a finger and fit it unwittingly in the dent of her dimple as she puzzled over an instruction manual for a new racing video game, here I am again. The show's concept was simple: two pretty girls competing in video or board games, reviewing the material in layman's terms; an uncomplicated premise perfectly engineered for mass appeal. It became immediately obvious that the games weren't the point, but someone should have told Lyla. After winning the first round easily, Lyla turned to Arin and said in an astonished tone: *You really suck.* And Arin, brimming with delight, as if receiving the greatest compliment of her life, curtseyed: *I know.* This would become a problem—a few episodes in, Lyla would grab Arin by the elbow and demand an after-action review. *If you don't laugh when I make a joke, I'll look like a bully.* Arin shrugged: *I'll laugh.* But by then, their audience had already been swayed. This strange, self-deprecatory girl, with her large eyes and secret smiles that, when turned on the camera, made the viewer feel held, as if they, too, were in cahoots against the endlessly oppressive onward grind of modern life, as if they, too, could simultaneously raise an eyebrow and nod graciously at the world's critique of them being not fast enough, not smart enough, not hardworking enough, had sparked an enduring affection that spread through the hearts of exhausted Singaporeans like wildfire.

On-screen, Arin rose from her curtsey. Best of three: the girls began playing again. How striking her silences were against Lyla's showy confidence, how endearing her quiet, sincere smiles. How naturally her shyness glinted into a staggering self-possession, how intelligently she wielded it against Lyla's sharp wit and hot takes. Arin won the second round, but only barely, and Lyla, the originally intended star of the show, sped ahead to her doom, winning the third. I glanced at the view count: eight thousand since we'd started watching, by the end of the night it would be forty thousand. In a week, the episode would've been viewed two hundred and seventy-three thousand times. I would scour the comment section: not a single one of those viewers would pick out, as I did, the barely perceptible delay in Arin's thumb hitting the plastic controller's buttons, ensuring she was only very slightly ahead of Lyla in the second round, her small triumph rendering viewers breathless, their hearts beating for her as she steadily ceded the tiebreaker. They would only lean forward, drawing closer to their screens, struck dumb with the rare and grateful feeling of witnessing lightning form.

I turned to praise Arin; the compliment died on my lips.

The real Arin wasn't smiling. As Lyla narrated the outro, bursting with triumph, Arin studied herself, eyelashes trembling as her gaze flitted from herself to Lyla, back to herself, then up at me, checking my reaction to something funny on-screen. Then her eyes met mine again, and this time, something in that empty, fearful glance reflected back the gaze of thousands of anonymous Singaporeans who must have been critically assessing Arin at that same moment. I saw that Arin, who wore her childlike shyness like a lampshade, had not truly understood what it meant to voluntarily present herself to the world to be perceived until that very moment. And now it could not be contained.

The video stopped playing. Her entire body was rigid. "That was—"

I interrupted: "Perfect."

"Really?"

"Mei," I said, my own heart thumping unreasonably in my chest. I pulled my sleeve up to show her the length of my arm. "Look. All my hair is standing."

She emitted a strange, strangled sound, halfway between a yelp and a laugh. I reached for her hands, found them clammy, and rubbed the spot between her thumb and index finger to calm her down. Her fingers yielded slightly, her fear receding. In a very soft voice, she said: "It wasn't going to be a big deal."

I gave her a bright, confused grin. "Too late for that, Mei."

My mother emerged from the kitchen, freshly showered, and started at the sight of us, hands clasped on the couch.

Immediately Arin pulled her hands from mine.

She leapt up, cleaving to my mother. "Auntie," she said, and my skin prickled at an unfamiliar note in her voice, "I have something to tell you—"

I watched her disbelief grow as Arin explained, the puzzled way she glanced between us. Then Arin picked up her netbook and restarted the episode, and all of that melted away.

"Oh," my mother whispered, an arm wrapped around Arin's shoulders. She was pressed up so close that droplets from her damp hair dripped down the back of Arin's shirt. "Look at you."

Something happened on the screen, and my mother burst out laughing. Had anything been that funny? I tried to catch Arin's eye ironically, but she was trained on my mother, soaking up the singular light of her attention, aglow with happiness and relief.

Pride. The unfamiliar note in Arin's voice had been pride.

The episode ended again.

"I couldn't have done it without Jie," Arin said. My mother was still enraptured by the screen, already hitting replay, and didn't look up, but Arin turned to me and continued: "Right?"

It wasn't rhetorical. She was waiting for a response.

The seconds ticked by.

My face grew hot. Gestures, quirks? Hair ties? In the end, what were they but garnishes on the bed of her character. How foolish I'd been, how stupid my belief in my own equity. I thought of Arin's brilliant, private smile, on offer to the world. I thought of the world smiling back.

"Yes," I said quietly. "Yes, you could."

But Arin's eyes were already drifting back to the screen.

Then Lyla's stupid laugh crowed from the netbook speakers, and I saw Arin's watchful, waiting smile floating before me. How charming her patience was in the face of tiring personalities. A delayed sense of recognition, like a sharp and slim silver needle, pierced straight into my heart.

It had been like looking in a mirror. I *had* helped Arin, just not in the way I'd thought.

I had been training her for this my whole life.

Arin leaned against my mother, nuzzling into her shoulder. She didn't look at me again. As the episode played on, I didn't get up. I just continued sitting there, listening to Lyla's laugh reverberating through the room, smiling idiotically in case it occurred to either my mother or Arin to glance my way.

40

One evening in March, after the last customers had left, after Zahirah clocked out and the day's earnings were tallied, I wiped down the counter slowly, relishing my last moments alone. When I turned the lights off and Arin materialized, standing outside the glass doors like an apparition, lit by the dusty glow of the nearby shop lights, even as I started in shock another part of me thought: So, here we are.

It had been exactly a year since my own academic flame-out. Arin pushed the door open and stood before me.

I rearranged my face, I said: "Let's hear it."

But despite all my practice, my confidence faltered. I'd been dreading this day for so long. As the anniversary of my failure drew close it became harder and harder to pretend at normalcy; now it had arrived and there was nowhere to run. Arin looked at me, worried. "I got a perfect score."

Something small died, deep in my soul. "I knew it."

"I didn't."

Lies. We both knew she'd adapted better to junior college than I ever had, dodging the same pitfalls that felled me, learning from my mistakes. And now the world was hers for the plundering. Malice, bright and overly familiar, twisted in my gut. I gave her a tolerant smile, I asked: "Are you glad?"

"Are *you*?"

Her question slipped out. Immediately I saw that she was dismayed at having lost control, at not having been able to restrain the question that had been hovering on the tip of her terrified tongue. Then her face shifted with resignation, the bravado emerging. She'd already asked, might as well commit to it. So much useless courage in her wide brown eyes. My earlier bitterness flashed and faded, I felt cornered and stepped forward to pull her into a hug.

"Of course I am," I said. "This is really amazing, it's actually incredible. Do you know how many perfect scores your school produced this year? Or what the nation's percentage is?" I registered bleakly that I was blabbering, but couldn't make myself stop. How could I communicate that my own growing sense of inadequacy was separate from her success? How could I make it sound like the truth, even to myself? She had bested me in every way, and the only thing I could do was smile and smile and smile.

"Jie," she said, pulling away to check my expression, "stop. I know it's hard, but you can take the exams again, I'll help you this time—"

I covered her mouth with my palm. "Rubbish."

When I lifted my hand, she whispered: "But it's not fair."

As if I didn't know this. A helpless indignation trembled within me—what response could I give that would lift the tricky burden of shame from her triumph?

"Mei," I said firmly, "we're growing up, things are different now. You'll be offered nothing less than a full scholarship to the university, and you will go."

Her eyes were damp. "We were supposed to stay together."

How much easier it would've been if Arin were proud, or at least a little selfish.

I shook my head and tipped my chin backward, blinking rapidly, then steadied myself and reached out to catch a tear hanging on Arin's lower lid. God, I thought, how do I live like this, it's not possible. Can you blame me. Blame me for doing what it takes to survive. "Actually," I said, bracing myself, "I won't be too far off. I'm going to get my degree too."

A sharp, surprised inhale. "Really?"

"Really. I worked it out with Ma. It won't be the same as yours, obviously, it's a two-year part-time degree at a private university. And I'm only doing night classes, so I can keep working."

I saw Arin waver between consolation and comfort. Don't, I thought, don't pity me. I can't bear it. I took a deep breath and hugged her again, properly this time. Very quietly, into her hair, I said: "I'm proud of you. I really am." I didn't add: It's just hard being left behind. It's hard when so much demands happiness of you. "We should celebrate."

But when she finally spoke I was hurt by the palpable relief in her voice. "Can we?"

"Obviously. Go on home. I'll clean up and be right there."

I watched her go, walking at first, then picking up her pace, almost breaking into a skip, noting privately that it had been close to five hours since she'd gotten the results. I waited till she disappeared around the block and returned slowly to the counter.

How I would have liked for my heart to subside into its routine acceptance. But what did I have left that was purely my own? Only this: I had gone shamefully to my mother the week before; now, I looked at my phone, scrolling down to my father's old, out-of-service number, which I could not bring myself to delete.

Right below it was his new one.

I let the phone ring only once before hanging up. Then I tried again, two more times. Only on the fourth attempt did I let it ring through. The voice on the other end was already irritated. "What kind of prank is this?"

My voice faltered. I cleared my throat a few times, trying to speak, but it was enough. My father recognized my cough. "Gen?"

I closed my eyes at the sound of my name on his lips. It had been over a year since I'd last seen him. "Yes."

"Did something happen at home?"

I nearly hung up. What right did he have to concern? To irritation? Yet my traitorous heart was screaming, screaming. I could hear my own voice: thick and barely controlled. "Are you actually worried about—me?"

He repeated: "Did something happen?"

"Can we—" then I corrected myself, and spoke a little louder, a little more forcefully. "I want to meet."

My father sounded resigned, as if he'd been waiting without eagerness for this call to come. "All right," he said. "When?"

41

I arranged our meeting with such secrecy I didn't even ask for a day off, not wanting the owner to know I was doing something else. Instead, I threatened Zahirah unnecessarily, told her to watch the shop, said I had urgent business to attend to, changed my mind, said I had a stomachache, gave her the keys, warned her not to speak of my absence to anyone, smoothed my hair down, and at three in the afternoon rushed out of the shop.

I'd chosen a public place: somewhere nonintimidating, a short bus ride away. A Starbucks at Tampines East Community Center. I had a whole plan. I wanted to buy my father coffee, whatever he wanted, to say: Look, I'm successful, I can afford to pay eight dollars for a Frappuccino with cream and chocolate and not even blink, you better take me seriously. I'm not a child you can just leave behind anymore. What did I hope for—that he'd be so overcome by my newfound maturity he'd collapse into a heap of apologies and renew our relationship? That with one look at me, his deep and immense affections would come rushing back, all at once, that he'd be thunderstruck with guilt at having missed even a single second of my life, much less a year? That after I got everything off my chest—my disappointments, the betrayal and abandonment I'd felt, my subsequent spiral and failures—it would be *me* who would graciously forgive him and lead my father back to the family, restoring us to fullness and warmth once again? Or were my dreams smaller, did I just want to prove I could still exert some modicum of control, however humble, over my life? I stood in line, timing it so I'd reach the counter at exactly 3:30, which was when we agreed to meet, intending to casually call out as he walked in and add his order to mine.

But he was late. I requeued, but he did not arrive when I reached the counter for the second time. I went to the back of the line again.

Finally, to the amusement of the baristas, I ordered a small cup of water, which turned out to be free. I accepted the cup and located an empty seat, shaking so hard that the group of students at the adjacent table inched their chairs farther away.

My father walked in.

"Gen," he said. It was clear he wasn't sure what to do. He seemed thinner, his skin more drawn, yet his movements possessed a quietude I'd never seen before. As if I were looking at a man happier, more settled. He pulled out the chair across from me and sat down.

Reason deserted me. I didn't trust myself to speak, just stared at him.

Had he been this calm, this controlled, when he packed his life into a worn duffel bag and evaporated from our lives? When he terminated his handphone number? He wasn't tech savvy; he wouldn't have known how to do it online. He must have waited, in line, at Singtel, inserted an ejection pin into the SIM card tray, surrendered it; he must have voiced the words: I don't want this anymore.

Suddenly I wasn't sure why I had wanted so badly for us to meet.

"Sorry," I choked. "This was a mistake. I just wanted to see if you were well. We're all good, don't worry. Hope you're doing fine." I got up, I didn't wait to see if he had anything to say in response, and left.

42

Two weeks later, as I was timing a pour-over coffee with my back to the door, I heard the left-leaning gait of my father's shuffle entering the shop, and before I could turn, his slow, taxi-driver English demanded: "Three fifty for *one* scoop?"

Zahirah's hand was hovering over the cash register. "Yes, unless you want durian or hojicha, then it's *four* fifty." She looked over at me, as if to share in some private joke. But the look on my face must have startled her.

She stepped to the side: there he was, at the other end of the counter.

My father. Wearing a dark green T-shirt too big for him, hanging off his frame, in shorts that didn't match. The bright lights of the café seemed to hurt him, he shrank away from the yellow walls, and in the unassailing cheeriness of the ice cream shop his face appeared more lined.

"It's fine," I said automatically. "That's my dad, let me take his order." But Zahirah had already made herself scarce, furiously adjusting the knobs on the coffee machine, pretending not to pay attention to us both. I switched to Mandarin. "What ice cream do you want?"

"Which one is good?"

"I like the lemon."

"It's not too sour?"

"It is, but I like it." He nodded in assent. I said: "I can give it to you for free."

His voice cracked: "No, I want to pay."

Zahirah abandoned the coffee machine and stared at us, her eyes darting back and forth, trying to decipher our conversation. It was clear she was witnessing something exciting; she stepped forward and inserted herself between us, took the money from him, went to scoop the lemon sorbet. We were still talking in circles when she handed him the ice cream cup.

"Your ice cream is expensive for this neighborhood."

"The neighborhood is changing."

"Yes, I saw that the duck rice seller is no longer at Fengshan Market, it's a pasta stall now."

"The pasta is no good, it's dry."

"You're ordering pasta from the hawker center? You must be doing well."

Someone else came into the café, started looking over the flavors of ice cream. I glanced at Zahirah in desperation, and she, delighted to be included, leapt in. Go, go, she said in English, I've got this. It was the most emotion I'd ever seen from her. I left with my father.

It was one. I'd already eaten, but when he suggested we go for lunch, I said yes. Conscious of being spotted by the neighbors, he put up some window sunshades when we got to his cab. I slid into the seat beside him, overwhelmed by the familiar smell of the leather car seats mixed with Glade air freshener, and he started driving aimlessly, not even turning on the radio. His previous quietude had vanished, interrupted, probably, by my barging into his life: Good. Yet as we turned another corner into the far end of Bedok, weaving deeper into the maze of landed properties down Frankel Avenue, he barely spoke, preferring to respond only to my superficial comments. Despite my anger, I was terrified he'd disappear again if I ventured even one wrong word. Very carefully, I began talking about the weather, the surroundings, useless things that had changed in the year he'd been gone. The block of flats we lived in had been painted over from green and white to a bright blue. The government had ripped up the playground by our house to make way for an exercise corner and installed metal armrests in all the public benches so the wandering old men had nowhere to sleep. The prices of everything had gone up slightly, now the stalls at Fengshan Market charged for takeaway boxes even if you were all old friends. The FairPrice supermarket beside the hawker center was open twenty-four hours now. The Indian barber had had a stroke and his son could be seen lurking in the barbershop, sweeping up hair, belatedly trying to learn the trade from a perpetually exhausted man. The son of the mee pok sellers had broken up with yet another potential wife. New business had sprung up everywhere, too, I said: the childcare center, another nail salon, the ice cream shop.

My father interrupted. "You want to sell ice cream for a living? But you went all the way to junior college."

"I'm a manager."

"It's still working in the service line."

I blurted: "What do you care?"

The lemon sorbet sat melting in the cup holder between us. He hadn't taken more than a couple of bites; my father had never liked desserts.

The cab pulled into an empty parking lot.

"As you can see," I lied, "I'm doing well, I'm making more money than I've ever made, I'm the happiest person around." I lifted my chin and wore my hurt blatantly; now that I'd breached the dam of cordiality, I wanted to disturb, disrupt, destroy whatever peace he'd found alone; compel him to witness the cost of his quietude.

But the instant our eyes met I faltered. It was as if I were looking again at the father of my childhood, exerting himself greatly to maintain his composure; I saw, as I'd been blind to all these years, the blisslessness of this endeavor, each second of tolerance slowly extinguishing his spirit till he arrived at the tremulous moment of his departure.

Did he waver, on the doorstep, did the echo of his own father's silence ring loud in his heart? Would a single word, look, encounter right then, in the dead of the night, have felled his resolve? How life turns on the hair of a decision, then calcifies. With his first step out of the door it already seemed impossible that things might have gone any differently. And if I'd never contacted him, he would have continued on this resigned path, living alone, never looking back. I understood that now. Still, I presented myself, I let the tears gather. What was the point of pride? I had nothing left.

I watched his Adam's apple quiver.

Finally, he said: "You're right to be angry."

I was overcome, suddenly exhausted. I turned my face away, staring out the cab window at the unfamiliar houses. "I have to go back to work," I said. A lonely tear slipped down my cheek, I wiped at it with the back of my hand, sniffling a little. I couldn't keep the plaintiveness out of my voice. "Will you come to the ice cream shop again?"

In the window's reflection he nodded, once. "Next week."

43

Thus began a series of meetings that have since taken on a magical feel. They lasted over a year, and had no real consistency—sometimes we would meet every week; sometimes a month would pass without us seeing or speaking to each other. The meetings always took place over my lunch hour while Zahirah, whose gap year seemed to have settled into a permanent delinquency, covered for me. My father and I worked really hard at these meetings—he, out of a determination to set himself apart from his father, and me, hoping, somewhat embarrassingly, that in my weathered vision of self, we might now be friends.

But we failed each other in increasingly wretched ways. In the years since, I've deliberated the matter and thought that perhaps integral to all loving relationships is a necessary distance, not because of the old excuse of familiarity and contempt, but because it allows us to make sense of and articulate our stories in a manner that's essential to our survival, whereas when we push forward in pursuit of boundless intimacy, we provide the opportunity for the other person to perpetually puncture our sense of self, to, in moments of excitement or vindication, say, no, I remember it differently, that's not at all how it happened. And in doing so crush our self-regard in accidental, devastating ways. Certainly it became clear to me, almost from the outset, that my father considered his departure—that was the word he used, so mild and gentle, like a boat detaching from shore—radically different from the abandonment of his father and stepbrother.

I learned that after leaving home, he'd met my mother, just once. This was a month after they separated, and during this time he slept in his taxi, in various car parks around Singapore, often seeking out the open-air lots near the beach where he could shower in the public washing areas. He likened that period to sleepwalking, he was perpetually tired and never completely clean. His hands had taken on a tremor, probably due to the lack of rest. Whenever he tried to shut his eyes, barely two hours would pass before a policeman came knocking, telling him to get a move on. It was obvious this wasn't a long-term solution.

But he didn't want to commit to living anywhere else yet. He had started, he confessed, to wonder if he had overreacted, if the scandal of the neighborhood's judgment really was that annihilating.

Yet when he actually met with my mother, any thought of reunion vanished. His body reacted strongly, he felt nauseous. The more she extended benevolence, pushing her insistent forgiveness onto him, the more his shame compounded. He felt his chest twisting, trying to get away from her. He saw that I was dismayed and smiled sadly.

"She looked exactly like that."

"What?"

"You're like your mother, neither of you can hide your feelings. It's written all over your face."

"I'm like *you*," I protested, thinking of my mother's constant attempts to force her thwarted ambitions onto me, her oppressive cheerfulness in the face of crisis. "I know exactly what you mean. She's impossible, if I were you I'd have left her too."

But I'd miscalculated. My father wasn't looking for allies. "Enough," he said, his voice cracked through with pain, and I subsided. I didn't want to lose him again.

After that meeting he started searching for a rental place and ended up sharing a four-room HDB flat in Yishun with an Indonesian programmer his age and a young gay couple. The rent was cheap, everyone minded their own business. Their interactions consisted of only pleasantries and administrative exchanges, like negotiating each person's turn to use the washer. Nothing at all like our home, where you couldn't untangle one existence from another.

I couldn't help myself, I demanded proof of his new address, I wanted to know where he spent all his time, who his new friends, if any, were. My father understood: everything I asked, he provided.

"It's not like that," he said, when I asked if he still faithfully followed Pei Wen's weekly manhua release online. "I would never have left you for another family."

But he couldn't come home either. For years, he had been miserable, depressed; to return to that state would be akin to self-destruction. Leaving had granted him the peace essential to survival, edging him back from the brink of despair. Did I understand? He still loved me, in fact he felt better equipped to care for me now. It was the first time he'd used that word, love, and as he spoke I watched his hands. They were steady, his tremor vanquished. I knew then that he was never coming back.

Yet alongside my aching disappointment grew a parallel, pathetic joy that leapt forth whenever he reappeared at the ice cream shop bearing a red plastic bag in his left hand, Styrofoam food boxes poking through the translucent plastic. In them would be famous dishes from whatever neighborhood he'd been driving in that morning— Yio Chu Kang's kolo mee, Pasir Ris Drive 6's roasted chicken rice, Roxy Square's ban mian, Marine Terrace's lontong kering. In these boxes I saw treasured proof of my own residence in his heart and mind; I imagined him making inconvenient detours on his shifts, imagined him queueing, selecting, and paying for these dishes with a singular intimacy and care he'd not afforded me even as a very small child. Each time he appeared, I'd hand the shop's reins over to an enamored Zahirah, who considered my life her education in the ways of the world, walk with my father to the nearby parking lot, and get into the front seat of his taxi. It almost felt as if we were a normal father-daughter pair again, except he never took those window sunshades down, obscuring our meetings from the rest of the world.

I clung to these clandestine meetings especially in the wake of Arin's new absence at home. For all her talk of staying together, she had enrolled as a Sociology major in the top local university on a full, bond-free scholarship that came with a generous monthly stipend and a single room on campus, which she immediately rented out for $280 a month, $20 below market rate. The university was on the other end of Singapore. Without on-campus accommodations, she often woke at 5:00 a.m. in order to make the 8:30 lectures, and once she got to campus she stayed there till dinnertime, at which point she either made her way home or to the guitar shop where more episodes of her increasingly popular YouTube show were filmed.

Childish; did I think we'd remain joined at the hip? Life's acceleration wasn't her fault, but still I felt forsaken. And her absence intruded on me perpetually. One day, when I was having lunch with my father, Arin called.

I signaled for him to be quiet, then picked up. Without even waiting for my greeting, Arin said: "Jie, I have to go for class in a second, but I need help."

"What happened?"

"I have no idea, there's a deliveryman outside our home, he keeps calling me, he can't leave till he gets a signature."

I cut short my lunch, I ran home. The deliveryman was rude, he told me off for taking so long, didn't I know he had other deliveries to make. As if still playing the role of shopkeeper I apologized automatically, but became annoyed the second he left: Why did I apologize, who was he to tell me off, was he the only person in the world who had to work, and who on earth sent this large cardboard box?

It turned out to be a gift from a skincare brand. The YouTube channel had no fixed address at which to receive press packages, the guitar shop was already doing them a favor by letting them film there at night. So when PR companies inquired, the channel gave out Arin's home address; now, massive, extravagant packages started appearing at our doorstep, creating postal exigencies that had me rushing across the streets and up the stairs at all kinds of odd hours till I got fed up and told Arin to redirect any deliveries to the ice cream shop, where my presence was at least guaranteed.

She hesitated. "Are you sure?"

"Yes, yes, I'll carry them home, how hard can it be."

In fact it was a huge burden. Even more gifts came, knighting her with commercial approval, ferried by a nonstop rotation of DHL, UPS, and SingPost couriers traipsing into the ice cream shop and cluttering its walkway with increasingly ornate, eye-catching packages, the most memorable of which actually sang when you kicked it, like a musical greeting card. Soon our house was crowded with detritus Arin wasn't yet in a position to refuse for fear of being dismissed as a diva. We were bemused; what were these things—skincare, clothes, makeup, merchandise, some of which I recognized from Penelope's house—doing here? Were they really free, were they truly so easily distributed? To us, who from childhood diligently clipped our toenails so they wouldn't fray holes in our canvas shoes, who habitually wore our clothes till they fell apart, the sudden and exponential proliferation of pure and often impersonal *stuff* in our lives seemed vulgar.

Or perhaps it only seemed excessive to me. One night I came home to an unfamiliar fragrance: an expensive-looking candle burning on the dining table, saturating our home with the scent of orange and sandalwood. My mother and Arin were sitting on the couch, laughing together, Arin massaging hand cream into the creases of my mother's cracked skin. Several other tubes in various flavors scattered between them. As I walked in, Arin called, her voice ringing with generosity: "Jie, come take your pick."

The unwieldy star-shaped box lying beside her had arrived just as I was locking up the ice cream shop. Rushing home to deposit it, I'd missed my usual train and was late for my night classes, which were held in a nondescript room on the seventeenth floor of a bleak office building. And the week before, I'd mistaken a shipment of ice cream, which had come in a white Styrofoam cooler box, for another one of Arin's press packages, and left it sitting in the corner of the shop amid the rest of the deliveries. The ice cream had melted into an unsellable soup, the losses docked from my salary. What did Arin know of my struggles? Nothing. I didn't want to be the sort of person who said, look what I've done for you; like some beggar starved for affection, I kept all of it to myself.

"Maybe later," I said. "If I don't shower right now, I'll simply pass away."

My mother lifted her wrist to her nose, sniffing wondrously. Arin handed her the rest of the moisturizer, then followed me into the kitchen, where I was easing out of my pants. Oh, so she had come, surreptitiously, to thank me, I was pleased. But she switched to our private tone of conversation and asked: "Do me a favor?"

I stepped into the shower. "Another one?"

"I have a class barbeque next weekend, will you come with me?"

I didn't want to. "Won't it be weird for me to tag along?"

I thought she would spout some platitude about sticking together again, but to my surprise a shadow crossed her face. She hesitated, glanced at the kitchen doorway, then said: "My classmates scare me. They watch me nonstop; I feel like an animal."

I joked: "Did you or did you not sign up to work as a YouTuber?"

"I didn't think it'd be like this."

But what would my presence change? Or was she confessing that she'd survive the experience better with me there, her secret source of strength, the way my covert meetings with my father allowed me to better endure Arin's burgeoning success? At the thought of my father I felt guilty, I backtracked. "I'm only kidding," I said, already regretting it. "Of course I'll come."

She cheered up instantly, left me to shower. Later, when I emerged from the kitchen, my mother had retired for the night but Arin was sitting cross-legged on the couch, reading from a book. On her left knee balanced a tub of leftover ice cream I'd brought home from the shop, into which her metal teaspoon dipped, again and again.

44

On the day of the barbeque I was in an atrocious mood. I thought the collegiate obsession with barbecues stupid. Singapore was hot; why would you put your face to a fire on purpose. The pit Arin's classmates booked was a significant distance from the bus stop, and Arin and I were both perspiring as we approached. Then a petite, well-groomed girl spotted us from afar, rushed up to Arin, and said: "God, you're glowing, you really do have great skin."

Arin assumed a bemused tone. "It's sweat."

The other girl burst out laughing and put a proprietary hand on Arin's arm.

"Come on, have a hot dog." To the rest of the classmates, the girl announced: "The superstar is here."

But they'd already noticed her. Several girls had stiffened upon her arrival, adopting a falsely casual air, others turned toward us, their faces frank and friendly with hunger. Hi, hello. Surprised you're here, a slot opened up in the schedule? With practiced ease, Arin demurred and introduced me; for a few minutes I was politely passed between a few of her classmates like some kind of conversational beach ball. I was glad for their obvious disinterest, it made things easier for me. When the person I was talking to escaped in search of food, I stepped back and looked for Arin, but she was already chatting with someone else.

All night, I watched Arin flit among her classmates like a fairy, attention clotting around her. It was clear their fascination and animosity was tied up with the nature of YouTube; it would've been different if she were an athlete, or a violinist. Relatability wasn't as revered as pure talent was; in fact, I realized, it invited a special flavor of bitter jealousy, for if there was nothing obvious differentiating one person from the next, why was Arin elevated over everyone else? I heard the undercurrent of judgment in their tone, the way they condemned the commercialization of personality as an intellectual failing; I noted the transparent ways they tried pulling gossip from her, peppering Arin with overly offhand questions about what Lyla, or the other YouTubers contracted to the same channel, were like in real life.

But they were no match for her. Arin wasn't the prettiest or most well-dressed girl, but that night she effortlessly lit up with an aura that stupefied everyone present. I watched her dance down the tightrope of her classmates' questions, keenly attuned to the unspoken motivations behind each turn in the conversation; with great astonishment I saw her face shining with the enjoyment of a child called to play a game they were very good at. Even when a penguin-shaped boy said, in an accusatory tone: I game too, you girls dumb it down too much, she didn't show offense. She asked him what he played, enveloping him in her wonderful bubble of attention, and after listing a series of classic and newly released dual-player games, he wandered off, gratified.

By and large I was left alone. As expected. What could they say to me: So you're the sister, we heard you're very close, how nice. I hovered by the grill, picking at the burnt hot dogs. Then the same girl from before sidled over. I'd figured out that she was trying to weasel her way into YouTube and was hoping to get into Arin's good books. In the tone of someone talking to a younger sibling, or pet dog, she asked what my major was.

"I don't go to this school."

"Oh? Which one do you attend then?"

I told her.

Her eyes glazed over. In them I saw the contempt of those who believed the part-time degrees offered by overseas institutions useless, the knowing smile she would give to the graduates of those off-brand programs while she remained cloistered in the safety of her superior degree, a contempt I'd once shared. Remembering that naïve, arrogant version of myself, I felt a rousing desire to slap the girl, to say, who do you think you are, look at me. I turned away so as not to make a scene, accidentally caught Arin's eye.

She appeared beside me immediately.

"I was just asking your sister what she does," the girl said.

Arin slipped her sticky arm in mine, resting her chin on my shoulder. Her entire body radiated heat, but I didn't want to embarrass her by pulling away.

With evident affection, she said: "She's not like us, arguing over hypothetical worlds, she does real work, she's on her feet day to night. Of us two, she's the better one."

My face burned.

"That's right," I said, smiling brightly. "Move over, let me handle the grill, you're burning the meat. Don't any of you have real-world skills?"

Arin was in high spirits as we left the barbeque, still coming down from the adrenaline of performance. She breathlessly recounted conversations, the way she'd skillfully batted back conversational darts from this or that person, repeatedly analyzing compliments and scrutinizing them for sincerity. I'd never seen her this excited, it was like a dam had broken. The whole way home, she barely noticed my silence.

She kept going as I gathered my things and crossed from the bedroom to the shower. I pulled my shirt off; it stank of smoke. When I tried to close the bathroom door, she put a hand in the doorway and continued talking. Irritated, I said: "Let go. And don't ask me to go with you to these things anymore."

Arin stopped short. "Why not?"

I ignored her, pulled some hair to my face, sniffed. It smelled of charcoal too. Arin persisted: "Jie, why not?"

I spun around, snapped.

"Because, as you so beautifully said, I'm doing real work, in fact I have an actual job, plus I study, and on top of *that* I have to listen to your patronizing drivel and organize my life around you and your stupid deliveries, so I'm tired, will you let me be?"

I slammed the door in her crestfallen face.

Later, as always, I felt bad. But the moment for apology passed, and I became—I'm ashamed to say it—disloyal. I started bad-mouthing Arin to my father. My rationale was simple: they had never really liked each other, and now had no reason ever to meet again. Conversation with my father was a black hole where anything potentially libelous would never see the light of day. All I needed was for him to nod, even minutely, as I spoke, for my entire day to brighten.

But he resisted. I had not accounted for his mental nest of fragile moral logic that could not be disturbed. He kept urging me to take the higher ground, reminding me that one had to be accountable not only to others but to oneself, to guard against any possible deterioration of character.

I was incensed. Rich words, coming from him. "Did you live and let live?" I demanded. "You cobbled together some bullshit justification for abandoning—yes! abandoning—me with all your stupid leaps in logic when all you're doing is following in the exact same footsteps as your father and brother. Wake up, Pa! At least they came away with a family. You spent all this time mooning after some woman and you didn't even fuck? What was the point of it all?"

It was June 2009. I had, for the first time, truly lost it, I'd let slip my normally secret resentments and twisted the knife deep. In the driver's seat, he twitched once, then again.

"Let's head back," he said finally. He turned off the ignition and, without looking at me again, got out of the car.

That walk from the car park to the ice cream shop was the worst walk of my life. We proceeded in silence, neither of us even pretending at normalcy as we tossed the empty food containers in a nearby bin and followed the curve of the block back to the shop.

As we pushed open the glass doors, I felt certain I wouldn't see him again for a while, that he'd retreat to whatever dank hole he'd rented in Yishun, licking his psychic wounds. I was so preoccupied with my thoughts that I didn't notice Arin standing with her back to the door, making small talk with Zahirah, right until Zahirah's voice, lifting from excitement at my return, went: "Oh, here she comes. She was at lunch with your dad."

45

I froze.

Arin turned, slowly, her gaze gliding over my father and me, but all she said, very pleasantly, was: "Oh, there you are. Hello, Uncle. Long time no see."

Zahirah did a double take at her referring to my father as "Uncle." She looked at me, back at Arin, then at me again. Then, discerning that she'd fucked up beyond measure, Zahirah retreated into the tiny kitchen and stayed there.

My father recovered first. "Gen tells me you're doing very well."

"I'm just lucky."

"You look nice."

A flicker of amusement crossed Arin's face. "Yes, I suppose I grew up." She turned to me. "Ma's making dinner, are you coming home tonight?"

My father stiffened. It was the first time Arin had referred to my mother as her own and not "Auntie." She was drawing a line in the sand. On one side, our family. On the other side, my father. And me, where would I choose to stand?

I nodded, forced myself to speak. "You know I'm on term break."

Calmly, she said: "I don't know anything about your schedule." She turned to my father. "And, Uncle, are you coming too?"

"No, I have"—he made a vague gesture, and my heart stuttered; I wished he were not so old, not so helpless, in front of Arin— "dinner plans already." He winced. To me, he said: "I'll see you." Then he nodded at Arin, and left.

Her calmness dissolved instantly.

"I came to apologize about the barbeque." Arin turned on me, her voice trembling with anger. "But you've been out gallivanting with Uncle this whole time? In front of the whole neighborhood?

How long has this been going on—did you even stop to consider how Auntie would feel? Or how I would?"

"Arin—"

"Who *are* you?"

I flared at her accusatory tone. "I didn't think I had to report my comings and goings to you," I snapped. "Or did you think that now because the world bows to you, I should too?"

She went very still.

"No," she said quietly. "I don't think that at all. But if the situation were reversed, I would certainly have told you."

The door opened, a couple of girls walked in. One of them gasped with obvious delight, torn between the desire to embrace Arin and play it cool. The other flushed a deep, noiseless pink. With an unfamiliar recklessness, Arin glanced at me, then beamed at them, her mask of civility bright and brittle.

"Did you want an autograph," she asked, facing them, "or did you come in for ice cream?"

The girls couldn't speak, arrested like deer in headlights.

Arin laughed, releasing them. "I was only teasing." With her back still to me, she swept a hand in my direction. "That's the person to talk to, enjoy."

46

I closed the shop early and rushed home to find Arin sitting, half hidden, in the stair landing midway between the ground floor and our home.

"Mei—" I began, ready to apologize, but she interrupted.

"You're right. It's your life." I'd expected her to rage at me, or cry out with hurt, but there was a faint trace of irony in her tone. I faltered, I didn't know how to respond. Then she handed me a worn blue envelope.

"What's this?"

"The money I owed you."

Only then did I recognize it. She'd kept the envelope, back from when I first convinced her to accept the YouTube role. Heart thudding, I shook my head. "It was a gift."

Arin smiled. "I don't want to ask for too much." She left it in my hands and went up the stairs.

Arin maintained an artificial sunniness throughout dinner, trying to spare my mother from worry. Guiltily, I played along, feigning enthusiasm, pretending everything was okay. And whenever I managed to catch her eye, the smile she gave me ripped open a split second of possibility; it was a smile luminous with understanding, and I could feel my own heart lifting in response, as if pulled by a thin thread of hope, hope that my fears were overblown, that all we had to do was make it through this dinner, this moment, to collapse into an oasis of confession and forgiveness on the other side. I could have crawled into the delusion of her smile and lived there forever. But the moment would pass, and she would turn that same smile away, shining it onto my mother, leaving me cold. That night, I didn't get a single moment of privacy with Arin. After dinner, she remained in the living room, listening attentively to my mother tell a long, wet story involving three preschoolers and their diapers. I retreated to the bedroom, and while waiting for her, opened the envelope. It was then that I understood just how deeply I'd hurt her. After leaving the shop, she must have gone straight to the bank teller and withdrawn a stack of crisp, new notes. It was there, all three hundred and fifty dollars.

From that point on, Arin threw herself fully into school and work. Perhaps the fracture in our relationship was more tolerable to her than to me; each time I tried to broach the subject, she brushed it off, offering me only that same insincere smile: it's fine, everything's fine. But there were no more deliveries to the ice cream shop. When Zahirah commented on it, I snapped at her and treated her coldly for weeks.

As a result, some time at the start of 2010, Zahirah quit unexpectedly. Her parents, tired of her play at independence, had agreed to send her abroad if she promised to stay in line. She jumped at the opportunity, didn't say goodbye. But the university she had chosen, in Australia, was the same institution my part-time degree was attached to. This was the most unbearable part: it was proof she'd admired me. I joked with the owners—they shouldn't have hired an unreliable teenager—but when I asked if I should put up a sign advertising help needed, they said no. No? No. The ice cream shop was doing so well they'd decided to sell it off to new owners, who would bring in their own staff and grand plans for franchising. Consequently, they no longer needed me. To make things worse, on my last day, the owner said, in a disparaging tone: Don't forget to change your mailing address, this isn't your personal P.O. box. I was mortified, I hadn't realized she'd known about Arin's deliveries. Instantly I saw myself as she must have seen me: young, unprofessional. Instead of making a dignified exit, I mumbled an apology and fled, nearly in tears.

Without the neutral ground of the ice cream shop, my meetings with my father dwindled. We rode around in his taxi a few times, he asked if I wanted to come visit his room in Yishun. But he lived in a house full of men, it didn't seem convenient. I said, sure, let's make plans, but we didn't. I called him once or twice, but the phone stripped away all external stimulus, and neither of us had the conversational skills to carry on. By the time I was due to graduate in May, we were barely in touch.

Things got worse. I'd applied—listlessly at first, and then with increasing desperation—for a variety of entry-level jobs in advertising firms, banks, and government agencies, only to be either rejected or ignored. I didn't tell anyone of my job hunt, preferring to wait till I had some success, but one night as I was switching off the kitchen lights on my way to bed, I turned to find my mother in the living room, frozen uncertainly by the mouth of the shoji screen. Our eyes met; it became abruptly clear that she had been restraining herself from comment, aware I had no good news to share.

I held her gaze for two, three enormous seconds, then caved. "You okay?"

She caught herself, straightened. "About to sleep." The uncertain look returned. "And you?"

"Me too, sleep well."

She nodded gingerly and moved, blundering almost, behind the screen.

My despondency ballooned. I started to find it pointless to get out of bed and reenter the endless cycle of self-immolation, clicking through job descriptions I didn't qualify for, opening rejections, staring at the pending status of other applications, feeling shamed for my defiant hope that persisted no matter how lousy the odds were. My mother could never know what her choice had done to me. Yet even as she proclaimed the wonders of private education, hadn't I suspected the faulty confidence of her voice, hadn't I understood these were the false promises of a woman who hadn't graduated from any university herself, who had never stepped out of this country even once? Why, then, had I brushed aside my doubts, accepted her sacrifice, cleaved so easily to her unfounded authority? Had I just wanted to believe, in my heart of hearts, that she would always be right, that she would always have the answers? Oh, God. I felt so, so utterly alone.

May, June. The months progressed like this, horizontally, pointlessly. I humbled myself and reached out to old classmates and acquaintances, asking if anyone was available for lunch or coffee, transparently hoping for salvation. Yet nothing sets off alarm bells more quickly than the contagious stink of failure, and the pride with which I'd insulated myself now isolated me—no one loved me enough to see past my disenchanted life, there was no one out there who might brave the swamps of mediocrity to help me.

Day after day, the walls of silence grew, closing in around me. I would have given anything to go back in time and allow myself to succumb to the mild humiliations of friendship and love. Anything to escape the life I found myself in. It was this version of me Penelope discovered, when she finally replied to my series of increasingly deranged messages asking to catch up that July. She was back in town for the summer holidays and agreed to meet for lunch.

47

Y ou have the air," she said, when I sat down across from her, "of someone who's given up on life."

"Thank you."

She laughed. Penelope seemed different too. It wasn't just the touch of highlighter on her nose, or the sleek bob cut of her hair. To the perspiring waiter who'd led me to the table, she nodded at her water glass, indicating that she'd like a refill. We were in a new, alfresco-style café, situated on a large balcony jutting out from the second floor of a mall on Orchard Road—Penelope's choice—and as she gestured to the waiter again, communicating some invisible message about food, water, I don't know, I realized that although the gestures were the same as the ones she used to make, commanding and disbursing attention with each flick of the wrist, she had grown into her wealth like a well-fitted jacket, and in her behavior there was now no longer any hint of an apology.

"On the other hand," I said, "you look great. Thanks for making the time. How's Exeter? How's school? I can't believe you didn't end up doing art, you were actually quite good. I still have the plaster cat you made."

I was rambling. Penelope looked taken aback, then relaxed into a laugh. "Art? I was okay."

It was the only subject she'd gotten an A for. "The school obviously felt differently."

"They thought I would be an excellent arts administrator, more like. Why'd you think elite schools like ours were the only ones offering the Art Elective program? Because the real artists were hiding out amid us nerds?" She rolled her eyes. "Enough about me. What happened to *you*?"

I shrugged. "You know what it's like for people like me."

The waiter appeared and set down a bronzed birdcage with layers of tiny sandwiches, tarts, and pastries. Penelope waited till he left, then said: "People like me—elaborate."

I admired her crisp accent, her precise articulation. Her time abroad had really improved her; I made a note to say so later. "I don't have a safety net," I explained. "If I fuck up, that's it. Ever since I failed my A levels, things have pretty much gone to shit."

She assessed me with faint puzzlement while pulling apart an egg sandwich with her acrylic nails. "You've really lost faith in yourself." She sounded disappointed. "A person doesn't just become stupid. Intelligence doesn't go away, it's like energy, it can't be destroyed."

I began eating. "Thank God you're majoring in law, not physics."

Penelope smiled. "As you said. It's not hard to get into law school abroad."

"Did I say that?"

"That and a lot of things."

The air between us had shifted subtly. I sat up straighter. "I *am* stupid now," I said. "So please speak clearly."

She helped herself to a tiny pastry, piercing the yolk of a quail egg lying atop it. The yellow leaked out, soaking the dense dot of scone. "Do you want a coffee?" she asked. And when I didn't reply, she sighed. "Listen, I was happy to hear from you, I don't want you to think I came out to settle old scores or anything like that. But I did really admire you for your hunger and ambition, even if it was obvious you didn't take me seriously." She saw I was about to interrupt, and held up a finger. "Did you know how badly I used to want your approval? How jarring it is to meet again all these years later and see that you've simply given up."

I was stunned. "I never knew you felt that way."

"Yeah," she said, popping a fruit tart on my plate. "I know."

The waiter came and took away the carcasses of our meal, discreetly placing the bill on the table. I glanced down involuntarily and hesitated; it was slightly over eighty dollars. Without looking at it or me, Penelope slid a black credit card into the check book, closed it, and handed it to the waiter in one smooth motion. When I unzipped my purse, she shook her head.

"Don't be silly," she said, and when I insisted, her face flickered between frustration and amusement. "Gen, seriously. Let's not do the back-and-forth."

While waiting for the waiter to come back with her card, we returned to superficial conversation: who else she was seeing while back in town, what local foods she missed the most, how difficult it was to adjust back to Singapore's humidity. I could sense Penelope slipping away, filing this interaction as the natural close of a long and uneven friendship. The line between my derelict status and the resources at her disposal not even occurring to her. I hesitated. If I let things be, we'd part ways amiably and I'd remain in her memory as a person she was once close with. She would forever think of herself as someone with the benign capacity to befriend people from all walks of life, who was liked for herself and not what she could offer. But as we stood up to leave, I leaned forward and said plainly: "I'm sorry. Help me."

She paused. I could see the disappointment in her eyes, the echo of favors reducing her to that damning fund of generosity. Still, arrested by some lingering trace of affection, or pity, she asked: "How?"

I just repeated humbly: "Help me."

Her eyes raked over me, she pursed her lips. "Send me your CV. Let me see what I can do."

48

A couple of days later, Penelope shot back a scanned copy of my documents. The papers that represented my life were covered in impudent red ink. I flushed, I nearly deleted her email, but controlled myself and carefully looked through her changes. My phrasing was too unprofessional, I used too many exclamation marks, I emphasized all the wrong things. In an accompanying message, she suggested rephrasing certain lines, positioning them in terms of applicable skills. *I managed a small local business from its inception, I pride myself on the ability to adapt a business's voice to the community it's situated in.* My heart slowed, comforted by the immunizing distance of her sentences. I read them again and found that I was amazed. I gave her a call.

"It's no big deal," she said, amused by my wonder. "Everyone knows the most important language to be fluent in is corporate bullshit."

"Not me."

"Ha, well, listen. I have to go soon, but—" Penelope spoke honestly. With my part-time, private degree, don't be offended, she said, it was going to be hard. I'd lose out to the graduates from local universities like NTU or NUS, I'd even lose out to the private university candidates who had done a full-time course. "So there's only so much a well-phrased letter can do, don't get me wrong."

"I'm not offended."

She was cheerful: "Okay, then. Have you considered applying abroad? It'll still be hard, but hard is relative. Everyone likes hiring Singaporeans—we're famous for being insanely productive, as you know, and it's easy to get a visa with our passport—so companies overseas may not mind so much, about your qualifications."

I was floored. "Abroad? Me?"

"Why not?" And when I didn't respond, Penelope laughed. "You can take yourself out of the pool, Gen. I did. All right, I really have to go. Don't be a stranger, let's catch up again soon."

I found my voice and thanked her, then hung up, thunderstruck. Penelope's candid question ringing in my ear. Why not? Yes, why not me? It was like waking from a long, pointless slumber to find oneself ravenous. I revised my CV and cover letter and began devoting six or seven hours a day to applying for jobs, both locally and abroad. Penelope's narration of my life as one of determination, resilience, and ability injected fresh optimism into my days; frequently I found myself reading and rereading my new cover letter for strength. Finally, replies started trickling in. A Skype interview for an English teaching position in Cebu. An assistant managerial role in a resort in Lombok. Secretarial work at an architecture firm in Christchurch, New Zealand. Concierge agent in an airport in Krabi.

I conducted the interviews privately, while my mother was at work, and could not gauge how successful I was. For weeks after I was a wreck. That I might shed my life and start afresh—the idea had wormed deep into my soul and now I couldn't shake it. I moved through the days restless, waiting. Haunted by the knowledge that I would truly take any job offered, pride be damned, I would even drain the last of my ice cream shop savings to front the relocation costs, so long as I could escape into the anonymous life already building in my head. At night, I dreamed of a mirrorless existence free of the disappointing past, of my parents, of Arin, where I might exist unencumbered by expectation and association. Dreams so vivid I often jolted awake with the taste of salt and sea on my tongue.

But, silence.

Penelope wrote to me again, she wanted to know how my job search was going, I took longer and longer to reply. I felt tricked and ashamed: she'd led me to believe in a version of myself long expired, while she'd gone back to her perfect little life in England.

Finally, after far too long, I sent her a message: *Nothing.*

Her reply reeked of revenge.

Keep trying.

We both knew she would never have to cycle through the humiliating boroughs of LinkedIn.

Then, at the end of July, the resort in Lombok came back with an offer. No acknowledgment of the weeks that had passed since our last correspondence. They simply said: Start next week. I sat on it for a day. All right, I began to type, but then another email popped up. It was from someone called Damien, asking if I could get on a call. The email was vague, I checked the sender's address, and realized it was Damien Fifield, from Fifield & King, the architecture firm in New Zealand. I hadn't been interviewed by him, I'd been interviewed by a woman, but it didn't matter. Yes, I replied, when?

On the call, Damien apologized for the late response. They'd been restructuring, and the hiring process had been delayed. He wanted to make some things clear before a formal offer was issued. Yes, I said, sure, I understand. He continued. While the title was secretarial, the work was far more similar to that of a personal assistant. In fact, the workload was quite heavy. Fifield & King was expanding aggressively and could not afford to pay a premium, and that, combined with the relatively high cost of living in Christ-church, made the role hard to fill. But in the next couple of years, they had plans to open a branch in Asia, headquartered in Sin-gapore, the only predominantly English-speaking country in the region. That was why my application had stood out. It seemed use-ful to have someone from the country, who might be able to help with the transition when the time came. But all of that was further down the road. He needed me to be absolutely clear on the fact that at the current moment, the work was boring and the pay was low. Did I understand, did I still want to come?

Yes, yes, and yes. None of those things mattered to me. I spoke rapidly, not wanting to give him a chance to change his mind, I overinflated my abilities, how I was comfortable working in a team or independently, I situated the ice cream shop within the context of how I was used to working in fast-moving, rapidly expanding environments, and sure, it was only ice cream, not architecture, but parallels could be drawn. I spoke of my ability to multitask, of how I worked full-time while completing my degree.

Finally, Damien said, with an air of bemusement, that I seemed to really want this job. In which case—and the rest I didn't hear over the roar of relief, I was too happy.

49

Things moved quickly from that point, to everything I said yes, yes, yes, without allowing myself to reconsider a single decision. I no longer wanted to be burdened by the same pragmatic considerations that had slowed me down in every other aspect of life. Before we'd ventured one week into August, the paperwork was done, the company bought my flight tickets, I would depart on the eleventh of September, 2010. Accommodations had been arranged too—Damien, conscious of how my salary would barely cover the basic cost of living in Christchurch, had negotiated for me to rent a room at a significantly discounted rate from his sister, who also lived in Christchurch.

By the middle of August, everything was settled, it was happening, it would happen. For someone like me, who hadn't even left the country before, the idea of relocating across oceans seemed like a joke. I broke the news to my family only after everything was confirmed—it didn't feel real before that.

To my surprise, it was Arin who couldn't comprehend what I was saying. She cleaved from her practiced cheeriness and blinked, repeated what I'd said, blinked again.

"You're leaving us?"

"I'm moving for work."

"Forever?"

"No, they're opening a Singapore branch in a couple of years, that's when I'll come back."

"And this Damien, he's—"

"My boss."

I looked at my mother, who had nodded once, then subsided into silence, letting Arin take over. I couldn't help but think of the banter between them earlier, before I'd interrupted with my news, their gentle currents of gossip and tender exchange. Not for the first time I thought of how much happier they'd be if I left, how much more comfort Arin was able to provide my mother, when I, her firstborn and original daughter, must have represented only a lifetime's accumulation of disappointment.

Arin's alto voice was getting lower, compressing the way it did whenever she felt stressed. "And everything is signed?"

"Yes."

"Check if you can back out, what the terms are."

I was furious. "Why would I back out? Do you know how hard I worked to get this?"

Arin shot me a look of pure exasperation and turned to my mother. "Auntie, talk some sense into her."

But my mother's gaze darted around, not meeting my eyes. I realized she didn't know what to do. This was so far out of her realm of experience, she had no idea what option was best. I ignored Arin and appealed directly to her. "This is what I want, Ma," I said. "It's a really great opportunity for me."

Arin tried to interject, but my words reached her, their meaning diffusing like a glow across her face. In a soft, tentative voice, my mother said: "Go, go. I'm proud of you, you're doing so well."

50

That night, my mother begged away to bed early. Arin watched the shoji screen till the lonely dot of light indicating my mother's mindless cellphone scroll vanished, then grabbed my wrist and yanked me outdoors.

"Look," she said, before I could protest. "Don't go. You're being ridiculous, you can't just leave the country."

"Actually," I snapped, pulling my wrist out of her grasp, "I can. And what's the alternative, continue being unemployed?"

We came to the bottom of the stairs. Arin stopped and looked at me. "How is it possible that you couldn't get a job here?"

In her tone I heard echoes of her old, sincere belief in my abilities. But hearing it no longer gladdened me. "Must you make me say it?" I asked bitterly. It was our first real conversation in months, and already she was conveniently forgetting that it was she who'd gone ahead, she for whom the doors had opened, forgetting, as so many did, how difficult the journey was once they themselves had crossed its hurdles. "Our paths are very different. You have options, I don't."

She seized upon it. "But what if you do?" The gaming channel had blown up so much that they were moving out of the guitar shop and into a proper studio, they would need assistant producers, cameramen, editors. Arin, who'd rapidly become invaluable to the channel, had in fact already spoken to the producers; she would leverage her position to get me in. She spoke as if painting our futures through the force of pure will, as if her desires alone were enough to cancel out our history of hurt and manifest a life in which we continued powering on alongside each other.

No, I corrected myself mentally, not alongside.

I interrupted. "You've already asked them? Why didn't you tell me?"

Arin turned away. "It hasn't exactly been easy to talk to you lately."

She started walking, aimlessly, in a loop around our estate. The sad slope of her shoulders moved me. So even when we weren't speaking, she was thinking of me? I caught up to her, we walked side by side in silence. Then I said quietly: "I've missed you. Let's not do that again."

Arin mumbled: "I've missed you too." She brightened. "So there, it's settled, you don't have to go anymore."

Her abrupt turnabout amused me. "I'm not being impulsive, Mei. I really want this."

"But—"

I didn't feel like hearing her convince me of my own worth. I continued: "I'm not cut out for life here, I don't want it. You think too highly of me, but even in school, toward the end it was you who loved it, not me."

"And did you think that was a choice? If I didn't make myself love it, where would I be?"

You'd be like me, I thought, remembering Penelope's look of disdain. A jarring disappointment.

I saw the thought flit across Arin's face too. So she did understand. How could she expect me, then, to trail after her forever, alternately keeping pace with and nipping after her success? In a subdued voice, she said: "It's not a dead end yet, Jie Jie. Just try a little harder. Don't give up."

"I'm not giving up. You and I have different ideas about what it means to be successful; for me, it's not having to struggle to the death every day." I recalled how lost she looked after I failed, how unmoored, and felt myself soften. But I needed her to see that I was desperate too. After months of waste, this opportunity had appeared in my life like a miraculous ember, and I was dying to blow on it, to let this little thing flame. "I'm finally excited about something, Mei. Don't ruin it for me," I pleaded. "Please."

But Arin rummaged around in her dress pocket and pulled out a folded, worn piece of paper. It was the old childhood contract we'd signed by the silvery slice of moonlight years ago, the blood smeared under our signatures oxidized to a dirty rust. She held it out to me. "We promised to stay together," she said. "Remember?"

It took everything I had not to rip the contract out of her hands. So she'd rather I remain exactly where I was. She'd rather I choose her, rather I choose to stay, rather I condemn myself to a perpetual drowning.

I felt cold.

We'd made a loop and came to a stop outside our block. "It's not forever," I said, turning toward the stairwell. "Eventually, when they open the Singaporean headquarters, I'll be back."

51

I texted Penelope the news, but she didn't reply. So be it. The only other person I had left to tell was my father. It had been months since we last spoke. We met at a kopitiam; I broke the news. He seemed pleased, but I couldn't be sure. Like Arin, he had some trouble comprehending it initially. He didn't know anything about New Zealand, he got it confused with England. I had to pull up a map on my phone and show him that it was closer to Australia. There was no question of him coming to visit, it was far too expensive, but he seemed comforted by the idea that I would eventually be back. He complimented me, without real understanding, and said he was proud of me. Although in the past these would have been words I'd have given anything to hear, I cut him off.

"You aren't going to try and stop me?"

"I can't stop you if it's what you want to do."

"That's the same thing Ma said." I was being unfair, but I didn't care. "Neither of you even tried to convince me to stay."

He drove me home in the taxi, but declined when I offered for him to come upstairs. As I was leaving, he said: "Su didn't stop you because she doesn't want to be a burden to you."

"What do you mean?"

His voice was tender. "You've already gone to school, to university, now you're only twenty-two but you have the opportunity to work abroad. It's amazing, you've already surpassed her. The best thing she thinks she can do for you is get out of your way."

I left his cab without a word. From then on, I immersed myself fully in preparing for my move. I bought a piece of luggage from the market. It was a handsome navy blue and made of soft polyester; it cost forty dollars. In it, I rolled and stacked my best clothes, including a cheap black coat bought from the same market stand. The coat was old-fashioned, from a factory in Guangzhou, but after

I cut out the glass buttons and sewed on my own, more trendy ones, you couldn't tell. I collected my passport, visa approval stamped within. I checked my email neurotically, scrutinizing the offer letter, memorizing the flight details on my e-ticket, still trying to convince myself it was happening. But no matter how hard I attempted to forget my father's words, they curdled in me, staining with guilt moments that should have been happy. As September drew near, I felt less and less settled, even though I continually told myself: Here is my life, it is beginning.

Then, on the fourth of September, exactly one week before I was due to leave, the earth ruptured at 4:35 a.m., ten kilometers below ground. It ripped a seam in Greater Canterbury, forty kilometers west of Christchurch City, right by the town of Darfield. The whiplash of the Darfield earthquakes was felt through the South Island, rumbling people out of sleep, and when we all woke up in Singapore on Saturday morning, it was to the news that Christchurch had declared a state of emergency.

52

All morning, the air was pregnant with the obvious question. I emerged from the bedroom to Arin and my mother having breakfast at the dining table. They turned to me, hesitating. Arin's eyes flashed in triumph, I hardened. I ate my breakfast in silence and continued packing. The main door slammed: Arin had left, either for a shoot or for school; I was no longer privy to her schedule. I squatted on the floor, checked my email again, and read through the signed contract. Yes, the job was confirmed. Christchurch was working hard to resume regular operations and my flight, nearly a week away, wasn't canceled. I put my phone down, but instead of returning to packing, crawled into bed and curled up under the covers.

The bedroom door opened softly. I felt the mattress depress, my mother's body sliding in behind me. A hand on my back, rubbing gently. We both lay in silence, listening to the gradually slowing sounds of my breathing, inhaling the familiar cheap scent of vanilla body moisturizer. My mother was trying to figure out how best to stop me from flying headfirst into a disaster zone; I could hear the old gears ticking in her mind. But she knew she had to draw me out. She waited for me to speak.

"I'm scared," I admitted finally, studying the swirling patterns of concrete on the wall.

"They would understand if you said you couldn't go anymore," she said. "The government said it was an emergency. They would understand that it was mitigating circumstances."

An image of my mother flickered before me: bent over the ripped dictionary behind the shoji screen, picking her words carefully while I packed in the room. I closed my eyes. "I have to go."

"But why?"

My mother's hand was no longer rubbing my back. With her

index finger she was drawing patterns on my bare arm, my mind forming the shape of each letter of the alphabet as she moved. It was how she'd taught me to read as a child, the tactile knowledge of each word nestling its way into my brain silently, so as not to disturb my father's sleep.

"There's no space for us both here anymore," I said. "Why can't anyone see that? I can't keep living like this. I can't."

A long, preparatory silence, my mother cycling through the alphabet a second time. *G*, I thought. *H, I, J* . . .

"How can I stop you," my mother whispered, "when this is all my life is? I understand what you're saying, Gen, but forgive me, I still have to try." Her fingers continued moving: *Q, R, S* . . . "So what if you're not extraordinary to everybody else? Is it not enough," she asked, "to be special to me?"

When I think back on this period, this was the one moment I truly faltered. The reaction I had to her question was a visceral one; even now, remembering it, I feel a similar shudder of revelation. I snatched my arm away, broke our skin contact, not out of anger but because the sensation of my mother's whorled finger pads, ruined by bleach, overwhelmed me. I'd charged forward without pausing, traipsing down the chain of yes yes yeses, now, for the first time, I wondered: Did I truly have no choice, as I'd convinced myself, or was I inelegantly trying to restart my life the way one did a dead car engine, making the facts of my life interesting to myself again?

I recalled the comfort I felt, reading my rewritten cover letter, the way I'd lulled myself into believing it was an accurate representation of who I was—the same comfort I felt when reading Damien's offer letter, when looking over my flight details. I was deriving pleasure from the bullet points of my future, yet hadn't the most precious moments of my life resided in the unquantifiable spaces between these facts? Why was I amputating myself from my problems? Were these antagonisms really so insoluble, or was I simply running away because it was easier than the alternative? And wasn't an unextraordinary life, as my mother said, still a life worth living? Wasn't I the one person able to give my mother what she most needed? Here she was, letting herself be vulnerable, shedding the false charm of my childhood, putting herself, her needs, her desires, openly in my hands, willingly taking on the mantle of holding me back—could I really ignore all of it and leave? And Arin, hadn't she broken from her intellectual arguments to reveal the truth: that the actual thing that mattered to her was us staying together, neither leaving the other behind?

My mother drew her fingers back, left me to my ruminations. The door thudded shut, I could hear her moving around in the living room while I pressed my face into the pillow, trying to stave off the migraine of reasons whirling in my head. I truly believe, up till this day, that if my mother had left me be, if she'd said her piece and retreated, I would have changed my mind and stayed.

But she didn't. The next day, when I turned on my computer, intending to read through my employment contract again in order to better understand what my options were, to know whether I would have to pay any penalties if—*if*, I told myself I was merely gathering information—I decided to stay in Singapore, I found an email from Damien waiting at the top of my inbox.

It was a very short message, factual, devoid of emotion. *For your reference.* My reference? I scrolled down. After some lines denoting the chain of recipients the email had passed through before landing in Damien's lap, I reached the original email he was pointing me to. It was forwarded from a university email address, the one my mother had used years ago when she was working at the university library. I hadn't known it was still active. In language that laid plain a complete misunderstanding of how corporate authority operated, mixing both emotional appeal and inflated vocabulary, my mother cited safety concerns related to the earthquakes, made reference to my youth and worldly inexperience, and begged the company to release me from my contract.

For a second, I was paralyzed with shock, humiliation. The email I eventually sent back to Damien was full of flowery apologies, excuses he was uninterested in. He only wanted to know one thing. Was I still coming? Yes, there was never any doubt. I didn't say a word about the email, to Arin or to my mother, I was done wasting my breath. On the eleventh of September, I called a taxi, left for the airport, and boarded the flight for Christchurch, New Zealand.

2010

Christchurch, New Zealand

53

I lived, those first days in Christchurch, in a state of near violent joy.

It truly felt as if I'd entered a kind of second childhood, but one conjured by my imagination. Hard to believe Mother Nature, not the long arm of my daydreams, had sprinkled everywhere these linden trees harboring countless songbirds in their delicate fluffy plumes; had, like a maestro, collected the sun's diffuse violet glow each evening into creamy collisions of rose and apricot. I marveled at the pale concrete landscapes of pavement, split in the recent earthquakes and curling upward like corners of a worn storybook; the rows of comically short houses that looked like they'd been drawn by a child, with their triangular roofs and occasional chimneys. Fences I loved, and hedges, too, in their attentive rectangles! I saw my first cow, and live duck; I found the seagulls that swooped low in the air and waddled imperiously in tiny squads hilarious. And bunnies, which I'd only ever seen in cages or picture books, ran wild everywhere in the abandoned rubble and dusty fields, breaking at a second's notice from their frenetic copulation to sit on their haunches, tiny ears like twin flagpoles of felt quivering in the air, a breath shy of a beat, before hopping out of reach whenever I, in my wonder and curiosity, ventured a step too close.

For my living arrangements, Lorraine, my landlady—also a new concept—afforded me a choice. Staying with her in the Blue House, which had two large, empty rooms, or in the stand-alone studio (which lacked amenities but had the advantage of being separated from the Blue House by a small stretch of grass) out back. Even though I was tempted by the idea of living in one of these gable-roofed fairy-tale houses, I picked the studio. When I pulled the door shut and surveyed the space—full bed, a desk, and a tiny sink in the corner that, when prodded, released cold water after a two-second delay—joy spread within me like a rash.

No one else, not a single soul alive, would have described Christchurch as an Eden. But I was from Singapore.

"I haven't met any of *those* before," Lorraine grunted, amused. She ran a youth hostel across town, identical in style, furnishing, and condition, only multiplied three stories to the Blue House's one, and was accustomed to far more worldly visitors. "Where's that, somewhere in China?"

Even this thrilled me. I waited with interest, hoping she would say more, like shout nǐ hǎo at me, but she didn't. When I next spotted Lorraine in the garden hanging her laundry to dry, I rushed out from the studio to accost her, laptop balanced in hand. I showed Lorraine the concrete jungles of Singapore in pictures and on the map, trying my best to avoid looking at her great gray underpants, which ballooned like windsocks on the laundry line.

"That one's from Singapore," she announced, by way of introduction, at a potluck dinner that weekend. She held these often in the Blue House, a kind of social value-add for her hostel guests, and though this was never explicitly articulated, I sensed that my discounted rent obliged me to attend. At that first potluck were four European backpackers, two of whom were a couple. While everyone chattered excitedly about the recent earthquakes and their own experiences with disaster, one of the noncoupled figures broke away to start a conversation with me. They'd either been to or wanted to visit Singapore someday, I don't remember which. But before we could get very far, Lorraine clapped her hands loudly.

"Move along now," she said, indicating the mismatched pastel ottomans and stools we were perched on, "swap seats so you can talk to someone new."

We cut looks at one another. I frowned to indicate that I had only just arrived myself and had no intimation of this strange practice.

A lanky American youth with startled elbows emerged, mantislike, from the kitchen, where he'd been retrieving a casserole from the microwave.

"She'd like you all to get an equal chance to meet one another," he explained calmly. His eyes landed on me and widened a little, but he continued: "This will keep happening."

After three rounds of Lorraine's musical chairs, I found myself sitting with the first backpacker again. He was asking what language we spoke in Singapore when the American youth intercepted: "Singapore's main language is English."

He had just finished distributing mugs of strawberry ice cream and settled on the couch beside me. I was still jet-lagged and felt as if I were moving through a dream. The room filled with the xylophone-like tinkle of metal teaspoons hitting the edges of their porcelain cups, and I took the chance to close my eyes briefly, letting a pleasant wave of exhaustion wash over me.

"You're the new tenant, right? I'm Micah," the American said, turning his head as he spoke so his warm breath tickled my left ear. Startled, I leaned away slightly, and Micah immediately recalibrated, sitting up straight. "I work at the hostel."

I began to explain that most Singaporeans in my generation were bilingual, but the backpacker I'd been talking to erupted into a grin and said: "Micah's great."

Micah glanced at Lorraine. "Say it louder."

Peaceably, Lorraine announced: "I'm paying Micah very well." She was rocking slightly on a computer chair, knocking randomly at points on her knee with a plastic hammer.

"Food and board," Micah whispered theatrically, nudging me with his elbow, "and chump change."

Now the whole room was listening in. I felt a thrill at being singled out, but having discerned earlier that my rent arrangement was a reluctant favor extracted from an otherwise estranged relationship with her brother, my boss, I was wary of engaging further and giving Lorraine any reason to take offense. I crossed my ankles and changed the subject. "Have you been to our little island city?"

"God, no," he said, eagerly. His feathery dark hair fell into his eyes, as he spoke he swept it into a tiny, ridiculous bun with a red rubber band that had been circling his wrist. "But I really want to. I've watched all the documentaries and wrote a research paper on its economic policies in college. No crime, no natural disasters, clean, modern—it sounds like Disneyland."

This was such an unlikely image that I burst out laughing.

But I had set him off. Micah put aside his ice cream and started excitedly telling the European couple how if you peed in a public elevator, the urine detectors would catch you, you'd be punished. Everything was automated, he was saying. Robots were everywhere.

As he spoke, he kept looking over, throwing me slight half smiles. I realized he was waiting for me to confirm his statements, and thinking of the horde of rule-following classmates I'd grown up with, I agreed, modestly: "We do have a lot of robots."

Everyone in the room regarded me with such awe that I couldn't help but add: "And at ten years old you can join a Robotics club and start building little toy cars."

"They whipped an American in 1994," Micah interjected, "for vandalism. Even after Clinton personally appealed for leniency! And it's illegal"—here, he paused, reverentially—"to chew bubblegum."

I blinked. "That's neither here nor there."

But the spell of attention had broken, and the backpacker I'd been talking to started discussing travel plans with the couple, who were volunteering their own anecdotes of robot encounters in Tokyo. Micah turned to me again, voice dropping to a murmur. "It must be hard, adjusting to a new place. Things are a little unsettled now, so be careful."

I was thrown by his strange, sincere eyes, twin pools of olive and gray. We were sitting so close I could smell the melted strawberry ice cream smudged against the side of his lip and suppressed the urge to dab it away.

I broke eye contact first. "So far it's been fine."

His voice was kind. "Still, you're not in Kansas anymore."

"Who wants to go to *Kansas*?"

I took pleasure in Arin's incredulous tone, in the scrunch of her nose. International voice calls were expensive, and I'd been worried our conversations would distill to emails, if at all. But Arin walked me through installing Skype, WhatsApp, and other free communication apps on my phone and computer. We were talking regularly again, and I was glad of it.

"It's a reference to *The Wizard of Oz*," I reminded her. We'd read it together as kids, but from Arin's blank look I could tell she'd deleted the book from memory. "There's a movie too."

She perked up. "Any good?"

"Apparently."

"I'll watch it."

Arin was on a new mission to develop her artistic tastes. She devoured films I mentioned, watching them at 1.5x playback speeds between classes (or read the scripts if she lacked time for even that) and forced me to discuss them; she spent hours skimming internet forums to discover nonmainstream musicians; she flirted briefly with retro cameras before realizing how expensive repeatedly developing rolls would become. I knew she was trying to rapidly cultivate new footholds of personality, hyperaware of the fickle nature of public interest, but it sounded exhausting. And futile. It was impossible to please everyone. A classmate of Arin's had spotted her perusing the classic cinema archives at the library@esplanade, a social watering hole for artistic types, and mocked her online for being pretentious. Arin dismissed it, but I knew it bothered her.

"You don't have to watch *everything*, you know."

"All the world's a stage," she quipped, "and unprepared players call damnation upon themselves."

"How do you have time for *Shakespeare*, too?"

"Don't worry, Jie," she said, bemused. "I'm getting credit for the reading. I'm taking a literature class as a contrasting subject."

But I thought her fear of irrelevance overblown. Her show, two years and going strong, had more viewers than ever. Her producers constantly loaned her out to star in collaboration videos with other up-and-coming channels, and since CLEO included her in a roundup of the most popular local YouTubers, I'd been getting a steady stream of friend requests every time I plugged my computer in from people who wanted to claim adjacency to Arin.

I mentioned this, and Arin's face darkened.

"I'm just the newest flavor. No one takes me seriously."

Neutered by distance, I found it easy to placate Arin without jealousy or irritation. "By all measures, you're doing well, Mei."

She ignored me. "But they will."

I, on the other hand, had never been happier. As Damien warned, the secretarial work was tedious and boring but not difficult. I realized immediately that I was not only the youngest, but the only person in the office without a background in architecture or city planning. My presence heralded a positive shift in the company's direction, it was a test to see if they could justify expanding the head count to include assistants and secretaries. Perhaps this imbued my arrival with a sense of good fortune. My coworkers treated me well and were in equal parts shocked and amused by my youth, which plastered over my initial mistakes and cast me with a sort of affectionate unseriousness. In fact, they often expressed concern over the unfulfilling nature of my work, especially when it came out that I had neither plans nor money to explore the rest of New Zealand's South Island. This resulted in a harrowed Damien calling me into his office at the end of my first week to inform me that it was impossible to pay me more, but that he'd called up a childhood friend who owned a cinema and needed some part-time help. I was touched by the concern but found the charity unnecessary, and when I arrived at the address—an independent theater, Insomnia, owned by a married couple, Hannah and Lily—I was prepared to thank them for the opportunity and reject it.

Instead, I fell in love.

Novelty, Arin retorted, isn't the same as love. But she didn't see the theater, so different from the cineplex chains in Singapore, in the midst of being, inch by inch, tenderly upgraded, half the carpet new and the other half stained with all manner of filth from the last two decades. Nor did she understand my instant attachment to Hannah and Lily, who were nearly fifty but behaved like teenagers with each other. After my first day on the job, I gushed to Arin about Insomnia's plush seats of red velour; its two showing halls (endearingly called Midnight Rendezvous and No Sleep Club); the fact that it had an actual, illuminated marquee, not just an electronic billboard; and the marvelous intimacy of how Hannah, like a bubbly mother hen, knew the names of nearly every patron who swept through Insomnia's glass doors. But stress and exhaustion showed on Arin's face, and through the delayed crush of pixels I could see her losing interest, attention returning only when I switched to recommending films I heard about that day at the theater.

It didn't bother me. Very quickly, I began spending all my after-work hours at Insomnia, even when I wasn't scheduled for a shift, since the cinemas were rarely full and Hannah and Lily didn't mind letting me watch movies for free. Twice that first week, I fell asleep in the plush red seats and woke long after the movie ended to a fleece blanket draped around my shoulders. At first I thought Hannah was the one doing it, but the second time I woke to find Lily bending over me. Pragmatic, stern Lily, who looked like she'd just stepped out from a tintype picture and rarely smiled because she didn't like how it contorted her face. Immediately she turned to the door ("Good, you're up, we're closing soon"), but the warmth of that fleece blanket lingered on my skin for hours.

The sense of good fortune continued. The next day, a Saturday, I was sitting cross-legged between Insomnia's video rental shelves, still smiling to myself as I slid CDs into my laptop to check whether they worked and matched titles to their sleeves, when the solemn sounds of Lily at her keyboard stopped. My left ear tingled.

Hannah chirped: "She's back there."

I looked up at Micah peeking around the shelf as Hannah continued: "Genevieve, someone's here for you."

"I see him."

"It's Micah Miller," he introduced himself again, "from the potluck . . ."

Insomnia was small, his voice carried. Hannah, who had grown up neighbors with Damien and Lorraine, groaned dramatically. "Those potlucks are the only way Lorraine can convince otherwise intelligent people to spend time with her."

Lily chided: "Hannah."

"It's true. Those poor tourists don't know what they're getting themselves into, but I can't believe Damien put you in that house, Genevieve, it's unconscionable . . ."

Hannah did this a lot, affectionately using me as a pretext for any number of topics about which she held strong opinions. I blushed, then glanced quickly at Micah. "Outside?"

As we stepped into the dusty sunlight, Hannah's cheerful diatribe faded. I grinned at Micah and was surprised to see him wrangling with some private distress.

"I wanted to apologize," he confessed, pulling a small cardboard box out of his back pocket. "I got carried away the other night talking about Singapore, I was rude."

His formality threw me off. "Were you? It didn't bother me," I said, accepting the box. "What's this?"

"A peace offering." It was a keychain, with a toy robot in bright vermillion hanging off it. I pinched the robot's plastic arm between my thumb and forefinger, moving it up and down. It was the kind of thing I might have found in gachapon machines back home; he must have ordered it online.

"I really wasn't offended," I said, moved. "But thanks."

Micah glanced at his motorbike, parked against an unlit streetlamp, and said, reluctantly: "I have to get back to work, but it's really nice to have another young person around. Christchurch is full of old people, there's not a single person in their twenties, like us."

I slid my finger into the keyring and closed my palm around the robot, smiling at this show of presumptive familiarity. "Us?"

Micah frowned and explained: "You and me."

His literalness reminded me of Arin. I softened. "Yes, the city skews old. I've noticed."

"So—friends?" In the dilute sunlight, his freckled skin warmed to a rosy hue. I'd observed it back at the Blue House, too, but Micah was stooping a little, as if to minimize the height difference between us. His eyes tracked my free hand as I lifted it to my earlobe and scratched.

How earnestly he wore his feelings. I was amused, I nodded.

"Okay," he said, smiling shyly. "Bye, friend."

"Bye."

55

I hadn't spoken to my mother since leaving home and had no intention of doing so. The second I touched down in Christchurch, I
blocked her email and phone number on all my devices, creating a
private island of peace around which her attempts at justification
might silently flow. When Micah asked, over coffee, what my story
was, after blurting out the genealogy of his ancestors beginning
from Adam, I said: "All your research on Singapore and no one told
you we don't just go around regaling strangers with our life story?"

"Strangers?" he said, put out. "I thought we were friends."

His gaze skittered across the table, and I struggled to restrain
my mirth. Micah was two years older than I was but easily immo-
bilized by any sort of teasing. One time I joked, during another
potluck dinner—"I'm not a real person to Micah, he only cares that
I'm Singaporean"—and instead of laughing he stumbled on the
edge of Lorraine's peach-colored carpet and nearly sent a tureen of
cranberry sauce flying.

I found all of this endearing. Not Arin. "Oh my God," she said,
when I relayed this to her. "Is he touched in the head or are all
Americans like that?"

"With my sample size of one, I can confirm it's probably just
nerves."

Her eyes narrowed at my tone. "Are you going to start dating?"

Teasing her was fun too. "Why not? I don't have anything else
to do."

"Stupidity is contagious, you better be careful."

But she was confusing intellect with existential anxiety. Micah
could speak coherently and at length about topics familiar to him,
and over the course of knowing him I learned more than could
be considered reasonable about the process of making your own
peanut butter or brewing your own beer. In these moments he

radiated a puppyish excitement, and I, too, reveled in the simple joy of watching someone giddy in their own obscure passions. Yet any unexpected conversational turns left him stumped and unable to recover unaided. We'd caught a couple of movies together at Insomnia, and when I interrupted his soliloquy on the artistry of Wong Kar Wai to indicate my preference for pure entertainment, he seemed thrown.

"Like what?"

I thought about the films I'd seen with Penelope. "*Love Actually*?"

He started, then attempted a joke. "Cinema of the colonizers? How *dare*."

"Well," I said cheerfully, "they're *my* colonizers, so it's different." Then I took pity on him, so clearly struggling, and tugged on his sleeve. "Joking."

Four topics of conversation later, he concluded: "You're funny."

We'd moved on to cloud formations, yet another one of his interests, and I broke off in surprise. Was he still thinking about an appropriate response to my earlier quip? What must it have been like to live trapped in the amber of your own presumed social gaffes? He continued, with evident admiration, eyes roaming over my face: "I've never met anyone quite like you."

How rare it was not to suffer the joys of comparison. I held his gaze, smirking: "You've never met another Asian?" Anxiety infected his features, and I relented: "Come to Singapore."

I was always saying things like that now. Transposed across borders I'd become the unwitting ambassador of my country, and whenever office watercooler conversations became stale, all I had to do was throw out a beguiling fact about our food or cost of living for people to perk up into a reenergized dialogue.

Yet in my mind, nothing was further than the thought of returning. There was nothing special about those early days in Christchurch except that time passed in a way that flowed, not lurched, and even the simplest things, like rubbing my cheek against freshly washed sheets, filled me with tactile and depthless wonder. That the inside of life could be so vast, when unhooked from the expectant eyes of others, was a revelation: I existed peacefully alongside my coworkers, basked in Micah's admiration, and felt loved by Hannah and Lily. If I felt the sudden urge to stretch languorously while walking, I did so; I allowed myself the easy distractions of stopping to listen whenever the two-pitched call of a morepork rang out amid the trees, and experienced, as I never had before, a kind of complete and utter serenity.

I suppose these were all signs that I would never be anything but an interloper in Christchurch. No place can exist so unridged except in the imagination; it's the frictions of living that weave you to a place. And as expected, Arin wouldn't let me slip away without a fight. In all our conversations, she was determined to involve me in the life I'd left behind, insistently asking my opinion on games she had to review, updating me on developments at home. When she thought she could get away with it, her favorite subject was my mother, who was no longer working in the childcare center. They'd begun hiring only newly minted graduates with an early childhood education degree, so my mother had left before being fired and now worked in the grocery store. But I was serious about protecting my peace. Each time Arin went down this path, I would hit the mute button and nod along sympathetically. It was a peacekeeping strategy I found both elegant and innovative, until one time my phone buzzed while we were on a Skype call with a text from Arin asking me to unmute her immediately.

Our tug-of-war seemed more a benign game than any kind of actual quarrel, though I knew one of us would eventually have to give. I did not think it would be me. Yet for all my efforts to convince myself this newfound happiness was now my climate and not simply passing weather, I felt my conviction slip when, one afternoon at the end of October, after nearly two wonderful months in Christchurch, while I was in the office transcribing messages for Damien and letting my brain wander down fanciful pointless paths, a single email from Arin came in.

No subject line, no salutation, nothing.
Just one line:
Can we talk? Urgent.

The fantasy of independence evaporated instantly. I stared at the screen for a long time. It was my mother, she was sick. No, it was Arin, calamity had struck. No, it was my father, he had returned. My mind flipped through the possibilities rapidly, and a coworker, walking by my desk, paused.

"Are you okay? You look funny."

"I just—" I put the computer screen to sleep and stood, the swivel chair rolling backward and bumping against the wall. "I'm not feeling so good."

I excused myself and went into the hallway, made a sharp turn before reaching the restroom, and entered the stairwell. Sitting on the second-to-last step, I steadied myself, breathing in and out. Then I dialed.

Arin picked up on the first ring. "That was fast."

Her voice sounded dreamy; things must have been more serious than I'd expected. "What happened."

When she didn't say anything, my breath quickened.

"Just say it," I continued, my voice thin and scared. "Is it Ma?"

She made a small, gasping sound. "No."

"No?"

"No, it's nothing bad."

"At some point, anytime this year, can you elaborate, please."

I'd resumed the imperious tone of the older sister, and Arin inhaled deeply, arranging her words and thoughts properly. Still, they tumbled out of her mouth too quickly, stumbling on each syllable. "It's nothing bad, it's good. I've done it. I've been cast in a film. It's all happening so fast. We start filming end of November. Jie Jie, I can't believe it. You have your life, now mine is starting too."

Slowly, the details emerged. It was a local indie movie, she said, with a small budget. When she told me how much, I wanted to laugh. No, she insisted, three hundred and fifty thousand was very little, for a full-length feature. To make things worse, she was a last-minute addition. Apparently, filming had wrapped months ago when the director was seized with conviction that the material was lacking and decided, in the midst of postproduction, to complicate the story by writing in some additional scenes. And even though it was only a minor role, Arin's casting was controversial; she'd gone up against a veteran local actress and won. How? She wasn't that pretty; her acting subpar. Rumors swept the crew that she was a diversity hire, cast in hopes of bringing in a younger crowd, the sort the local media industry was afraid of losing to the likes of streaming and YouTube. Already local audiences were opting to illegally download Western films and Korean dramas, with their higher production values. The interest in locally created content, which had always been low, was dwindling. No one but Arin and the director, and now me, knew the other actress had turned the role down after hearing the pittance she'd be paid. Arin didn't mind, she confessed in a rush that she would've done it for free. Back at the YouTube company, too, there was trouble. The producers were happy, it was good publicity for the channel. The link to cinema artistically legitimized their short-form skits in a way they welcomed. But Lyla, jaundiced by jealousy, had completely iced her out, going around saying it was sad, really, how desperate Arin was for attention, auditioning for a different movie or TV show every week.

Arin was practically singing as she told me this. It was true, she said gaily, all true. She did audition nonstop, so what. She did want to be taken as an artiste, not just a YouTuber, she made that sentiment clear and it didn't sit well with some, so what. Any strong stance was bound to attract disagreement, any success bound to attract jealousy.

Her voice was loud and loose, her enthusiasm bordering on manic. I'd never heard her like this: I listened carefully and realized she'd been afraid. This unfettered happiness was unreeling from an undercurrent of immense relief. But I hadn't even known she'd been auditioning for movies. *Movies.* The prospect so large it threatened to capsize us both. She laughed, and I had to hold the phone away from my ear.

"Look at us," she was saying. "Aren't you proud of us, say you are. Look how far we've come."

"Yes."

"Once I've made a lot of money I'll come visit you. Better—I'll fly you home. First class."

I felt as if I were watching myself from a great distance. "Didn't you say they're not paying you much?"

She laughed, again. "This is just the first one, Jie. What about the next, and the next, and the next? Everything is riding on this first film. But you'll see. I'll show them, I've already shown them. This is it, Jie, our lives are going to change, you and me."

58

The call only lasted fifteen minutes, but when I stood up again, dusting my skirt off, I felt lightheaded and had to put a hand on the banister so as not to topple over.

Damien started when he saw my face. He had emerged from his office holding a sheaf of paper, presumably for me to proofread. "Are you all right, Genevieve?"

His voice was thick with concern, my eyes welled. I turned away, apologized softly. People glanced over, and Damien, noticing, ushered me into his private office, drew the blinds, and shut the door.

"Take all the time you need."

It only made me cry harder. He pushed a box of tissues toward me and waited. "Sorry," I choked. "I don't mean to be unprofessional. I just got some bad news from home."

"My condolences."

"It's okay, I'm okay now."

"Are you sure?"

His still, blue eyes were trained on me, so full of worry I was afraid I'd start crying again. I closed my eyes and felt, rather than saw, him leaning back into his chair, waiting for me to gather myself. When I felt ready, I opened my eyes and said: "Actually, would you mind if I took a half day?"

I left the office without much fuss; my coworkers averted their eyes so as to spare me from embarrassment. But once I was outside, I didn't know what to do. It was after lunch and the streets were empty. I considered going to Insomnia but withered from explaining my unexpected presence. So: home, then.

Fifield & King was a thirty-minute walk from the Blue House. As I made that trudge back, I tried to reconcile myself to the shock of having the ground beneath my feet rumbled, my carefully calibrated equilibrium disturbed by the unexpected threat of everything changing again. It was a Wednesday. Skies the color of cream and eggshell, air trembling with a crisp chill.

What even, I scolded myself, are you upset about? You said it yourself—your paths are different. Look around you, look at all you've fought to have.

Yet everywhere I looked, anxiety multiplied. So she was thriving. How clear it was, suddenly, that I'd been demoted not from associate to accessory, as I'd assumed, but to encumbrance: Had my absence unclipped her wings? How far would the shadow of her success spread? Would she not stop until she had the entire world in her thrall? Passing a lonely bus stop, I imagined movie posters bearing Arin's smile reaching me, across continents, across oceans, in this dusty city that, if I was honest with myself, I'd been drawn to precisely for its old-world charm, its sense of being stuck in the past, rooted in the natural world, away from the creeping fingers of the internet. Yet how naïve I'd been. Why had I eliminated the potholes and cracks from my radiant vision of Christchurch, why did I insist on training my gaze only on the glittering motes of dust swirling in the air, without acknowledging the constant grind of postquake repair that had kicked them up, making stardust of plain gray powder? What had my life come to, why had I fled so far from home only to find the same unrelentingly pathetic, jealous self waiting for me in this broken town?

I couldn't, as I normally might, stop myself from going down this rabbit hole; these poisonous thoughts fed on one another and bloomed in different corners of my brain. I told myself: Stop it, stop it, but nothing helped. I was still trying to get my mind under control when someone rode up to me on a bicycle and stopped.

59

It was a boy, a child on the cusp of manhood. No one else was on the streets; Christchurch really was a ghost town. I turned, stared hard, found nothing familiar about the generic teenage face, and continued walking. There was a slight scuffing sound of the bicycle pushing off again, and I became aware that the boy was now riding next to me, trying to catch my attention. Well, bad timing: I had none to give. We plodded on, side by side, until he couldn't take it anymore. In an impatient voice, he said: "Hey, lady. Do you have two dollars, could I have two dollars please."

I didn't stop. I'd heard of instances like these, Lorraine certainly complained about it a lot, as did my coworkers. Ever since the earthquake, you couldn't go anywhere without being accosted for coins and empathy. There were no jobs, and getting insurance to pay out for quake damage was a long and wearying campaign.

"Sorry," I said, without slowing down. "I don't have any money."

"How can you not have money," he called. The bicycle right beside me. "Aren't all you people rich."

"Not me," I snapped, then regretted it. I didn't want to be someone who squabbled with children in the streets. Where are your parents, I thought, picking up my pace. At fifteen I was barely leaving my desk. Why wasn't he in school?

"No?" he asked, punctuating my reverie. His voice was disaffected and lazy, it was almost in my ear. "What about something else then? What about a good time?"

I started, tripping on some rubble. On my left was a tall chain-link fence cordoning off a sandy area full of construction materials; my hand shot out and caught it, trying to steady myself. "What?"

The bicycle swerved and stopped before me.

Even though he was right in front of me, a boy of considerable heft, I didn't feel threatened. He was playing at manliness, making his voice rough on purpose, looking to intimidate someone on the streets so he could feel good about himself. The boy jerked his shoulder toward the chain-link fence. I followed his gaze to one of the colorful containers, used to store brick and sacks of cement. "How about a blow job?"

I wanted to laugh, but now that I'd stopped walking, my body unlocked itself from its temporary stasis and began to sweat. Lorraine had groused several times about my forgetting to wedge the bathroom window open after each shower, citing differences in climate that would lead to mold growing between the tiles; I made a mental note: shower, window, laundry, later. A line of perspiration soaked the underside of my bra, the cloth sticking to my clammy skin. I let go of the fence and made a movement intending to fan myself. The boy reached out as if to offer me a hand, then put his whole palm against my right shoulder and pushed.

He hadn't used that much force, but it caught me off balance. I toppled into the fence hard, the metal springing back against my weight and nearly causing me to fall forward onto the ground. I let out a surprised huff of air. In a dense patch of grass, a startled pair of rabbit ears materialized, twitching attentively, waiting. In one smooth, almost lackadaisical movement, the boy leaned forward again, one foot planted firmly on the ground, and roughly grabbed my left breast.

I looked down at the hand.

"Will you look at that," he said. His voice was measured and still. The hand squeezed, lightly at first, then harder, as if searching for something. It began to hurt. I blinked. The grass was just grass again.

He withdrew his hand.

"Sorry," he said, in that same treacly, heavy-lidded tone. It looked like he was falling asleep, even while standing right before me. His weight was fully back on the bicycle, the bicycle upright and facing forward, he was leaning away from, not toward me. Both hands were on the handlebars, which were now oriented toward the path. "Have a nice day."

He turned and rode away, pedaling hard. A couple of times, he glanced over his shoulder, then he reached a bend in the road and took it. I could still see him, hefting down that adjacent road, getting smaller and smaller, and finally I could not see him at all. I looked down, again. My shoes were covered in dust and a fine layer of sand, kicked up from the construction site behind me. There were stains on them too, but whether from that day or the day before, I could not remember.

60

I was early to work the next day and, by the time Damien arrived, had been at my desk for two hours. He paused by my chair. "How was your afternoon off?"

"Good," I said. "I've caught up with everything, sorry for the trouble—"

"Genevieve," he interrupted. Barely concealed horror in his voice. "Your hands."

I looked down. Smudges of dried blood circled each nail. "Oh," I said, moving my hands into my lap, under the desk. "Old eczema flare-up. Don't worry about it."

He nodded, but later I could see him looking over, conspicuously, through the glass windows of his office, as I shrieked with laughter at something a coworker said.

That day, for the first time, I followed a small cluster of office women out for lunch. They went to a French bistro, the kind that wrote its daily specials in chalk on the board.

"No packed lunch today?" one of my coworkers asked. I shrugged. Ordered the most expensive thing on the menu—a dense hunk of halibut and a fizzy drink with grapefruit syrup—but when I tried to pay, found that someone else had done so. We went back and forth for a bit, till my coworker said: "Genevieve, come on."

"I should be paying for my own food."

She checked at my tone. A pause, then: "Let's say you'll get the next one."

I could feel my coworkers eyeing me throughout lunch, making familiar, absent conversation about their families, homes, children, weekend trips, side projects. It turned out they all knew the owner of the French bistro, whose two kids helped out in the bistro from time to time.

My skin prickled. "Kids?" I asked.

Nine and fourteen, one of them told me. The sweetest girls you'd ever meet. Absolute angels.

A sharp, cold sting spread under my thumbnail. I looked down. I'd sunk my nails into the space where skin met nail, breaking the hyponychium. There were little crescent marks all over my palm, pressed in so deep that at some points the skin had turned a slightly darker plum.

"Cute," I said. And made a show of slicing and spearing my fish.

I had fallen asleep the night before, still drenched from my shower, naked but for the towel wrapped around my body. The bathwater had leaked into my sheets and returned to my bones with a metallic chill.

I think I'm catching a cold, I emailed Arin.

She replied immediately. *Why don't you take a half day? It's not like they can't function without you.*

An hour later, she followed up—*Want to Skype?*

No, I replied. *I'm catching a cold.*

I was running down the main street, pushing past confused, post-work officegoers. Halfway down the street my calves began to scream. What was it my P.E. teacher had said? Stretch before you run. Hey, I tried to shout, wait up. Stop.

The boy on the bicycle didn't turn around. He had zoomed by so quickly my mind stuttered for a precious second, struggling to connect the dots of coincidence. And now I was losing him. Again. I tried to gulp air and yell simultaneously; my eyes met a bald shopkeeper's, smoking by the pavement. A flash of understanding—

I stood above the tangle of bodies, the spinning bicycle wheels. A crowd had gathered, their curiosity snagged on the hangnail of public drama. The boy shoved the bald shopkeeper off him and blustered, at the exact same moment I realized I'd never seen him before, "Lady, what the fuck?"

. . .

The bald shopkeeper was angry. I'd turned him into an assailant, and he wanted answers. He reached for my arm and I careened backward, nearly crashing into an elderly woman.

"Leave her be," someone in the crowd chided. "Can't you see something's the matter with her?"

I looked down at my hands; they were patchy with blood. I'm fine, I told the crowd. The sky had erupted in its regular beauty, I was late—absent without cause, I amended—for my shift at Insomnia. Hannah and Lily would have been expecting me an hour ago.

I'm really fine. Look, I'm going now.

In the privacy of my studio, I tried to steady myself.

My phone buzzed with a concerned text from Hannah, and as I glazed over it, saw the crescent dents in my finger pads staining red. It dawned on me that something was probably very wrong. "Hmm," I said, aloud.

I swept away Hannah's text and dialed. On the third ring, the call went through.

The voice on the other end was curious and warm. "Gen?"

"I know this is out of the blue. But do you have a minute?"

61

Micah had been surprised to hear from me. I need a friend, I said.

This he knew how to do. Are you in the Blue House?

Yes.

I'll come get you.

Before we hung up, I asked for a favor: Please, no questions.

There'd been a long pause.

Yes, he said. Okay, sure.

"It's your favorite Singaporean," I said as he pulled up. I'd been waiting by the curb, impatient to escape before Lorraine came back. He smiled weakly at the joke. When we got to the youth hostel, he walked me up to the attic, where his room was, and left me there. No one will come in, he said, but you can lock the door if you want. I collapsed onto the single bed by the window and fell asleep immediately, I didn't even hear him leave.

I woke again close to midnight, in a dark room. The small night lamp next to the bed, which had been off before, was emitting a soft glow. But everything else was the same. I took a few crisp breaths and felt infinitely better. As I descended the hostel stairs, I saw Micah sitting alone on a perfect replica of the Blue House's couch, except this one was lilac. How easily consistency comes to some, I thought, watching Micah sway. He was struggling to stay awake; before him, the television was on.

"You should have woken me," I said finally, appearing beside him.

He started and wiped his mouth. "You seemed to really need the rest. Want to talk about it?"

I tensed. "Not really."

"Gotcha." He gestured at the TV. He'd been watching some

kind of family sitcom; it wasn't very interesting. Beggars can't be choosers, he explained. The hostel was only at half capacity, and most people were asleep already. There was nothing else to do. He missed the American television shows he grew up with, but they weren't available here, and the locally produced shows were boring. But even as he was saying this, something happened on the television, drawing his attention again, and we settled into silence, watching characters flit around the screen. We watched the show for, I don't know, twenty minutes. An episode ended, the credits rolled. A preview for the next episode started playing.

Quietly, I said: "I was assaulted. Yesterday."

Micah moved to turn the television off, but I held a hand out. "Don't."

He lowered the remote. Another show began, a police procedural. "Thanks for telling me." He paused, then added: "I'm sorry it happened."

I nodded, training my eyes on the television as the characters blurred, arguing in low, hushed tones. Some more time went by. I felt Micah's large hand on my back, patting me slowly, and realized I had bent over and was heaving into my knees.

I wanted my mother.

I wanted her bleach-ruined finger pad on my skin, drawing out letters of false and temporary assurance. This desire, so abrupt, skewered me, made me gasp with pain. But the thought was dangerous, it threatened to undam the flood of humiliation and rage I'd so painstakingly kept at bay. I allowed myself a second to indulge in the fleeting memory of her tactile comfort prior to her machinations of manipulation and sabotage, then severed the moment before it could evolve to its inevitable conclusion. I caught my breath, straightened, and returned to staring at the screen.

Micah retracted his hand. We sat, side by side, watching the drama on-screen play out.

When the show broke for advertisements, I cleared my throat: "Is it okay if we don't talk about this again?"

Micah turned to me, his eyes warm.

"Genevieve," he murmured. "Of course."

62

So often, during our Skype conversations, I imagined Arin's head tilted to the side, studying me.

See, I wanted to say. Who's the actress now.

In reality I said nothing while she prattled on about her new role. She was still waiting for the script but could already say with certainty that she preferred acting—cleaving to a director's vision, to her, was far easier and less exhausting than the perpetual project of self-presentation hosting required.

"No reason you can't do both," I said, when I needed to say anything at all. "Lyla must be spitting blood."

"Not yet," Arin said, preening. "Not yet."

New Zealand was becoming beautiful again. I asked Micah to take me out of Christchurch, and he rode slowly the entire way to a nearby beach town, New Brighton, stretching out the twenty-minute journey to an hour, attentively avoiding any abrupt accelerations or brakes that might slide my body down the motorbike seat and slam me into his sticky, sweaty back.

After he parked by a sandy bank, we strolled down the coast, amused at the sight of our hair being tossed about by the sharp, salty wind. I had never seen sea like this—by the time the ocean filtered through Singapore's neighboring coasts and reached us it was a gentle, roiling lick—and was arrested by this unfamiliar, muscular water, screaming, drawing back, and violently toppling the tiny figures wobbling on the white dash of surfboards that peppered the blue.

When we came across our fourth surf shack advertising beginner classes for forty dollars, I asked: "Shall we?"

Micah looked terrified. "If you want."

I laughed and laughed. We bought promising coffees from a cerulean food truck and settled on an empty spot of warmed sand, sipping the day away while watching overstimulated dogs lose themselves in the fantasy of sea spray.

Back in the office, much was made of the landing strip of sunburnt skin running across my nose and cheekbones.

"You should see my friend," I said, and when Micah materialized in the Fifield & King lobby radiating heat like a boiled crab, the giggle he was met with confused him.

As we walked to Insomnia, he said: "I don't think your coworkers like me much."

I was amused. "I don't think they think of you at all," I said. "Go on, I'll see you tonight."

Four hours later, Hannah looked up through Insomnia's glass doors and said: "Genevieve, your friend is here."

"I got you something," Micah said. "A present."

"Again?"

He waited patiently for me to stop chasing a spiraling blot of dust I'd mistaken for a ladybug before navigating himself back between the road and me, presenting me with a shiny blue plastic button you could clip on a bag and depress in case of emergency. "It's apparently," he said, as if delivering a compliment, "louder than a vuvuzela. And harder to lose."

The robot keychain still hung on my keys, but the week before he'd gifted me a dazzling red motorcycle helmet, which I'd worn exactly once. "Sorry about the helmet." I pulled a face. "I don't know where it could have gone."

"Don't mention it." He watched as I tossed the button into the depths of my bag, then started monologuing about his workday.

Micah was being the best friend ever. Someone he knew had been raped at a college party five years back, and he had therefore become unusually attuned to the dangers of everyday situations, aware the best thing he could do was proffer his large, male body as a barrier that women around him could use as protection. He'd related this anecdote in such a concertedly neutral tone that his pale, freckled face had turned pink with the effort. I'd watched him stammer it out, then suggested the day trip to New Brighton. Now if he blushed it was invisible against the sear of sunburn.

Other things he no longer mentioned: Peanut butter. Beer. Clouds. Cinema. Now, all my jokes were met by his round, soulful eyes.

We came to the Blue House. Micah stood a respectful distance from the gate, watching as I walked to the studio. When I reached, I turned, as I always did, to him waiting under the glow of a streetlamp, feeling the sting of guilt meet with my sharp flare of relief at his considerate consistency.

Bye, friend.

Bye.

He raised a hand, as did I.

63

In my studio, I examined the allegedly lost helmet more closely. It really was beautiful, it gleamed like an apple, and when I knocked on its side with my knuckles, the sound it produced was thick and pleasurable. I lifted it up and sniffed. There was an overwhelming smell of newness, which the fruity smell of my shampoo interfered with only slightly. Micah bought it after he'd started his daily practice of escorting me around, and it looked expensive. I'd accepted the helmet, thanked him, then destroyed the helmet's inner foam lining immediately with a pen knife.

I knew this resentment, which had taken root with a sudden and inconvenient intensity, surfacing every time I simpered some thanks to Micah, was senseless and my fault alone. The first time I felt it I was stunned by its strength. A couple of days after that night in the hostel, Micah had come by Fifield & King to take me to lunch at a café he'd preselected. As we approached an empty table by the wall, he leapt forward and pulled out the seat facing the door.

I felt my back brush the wall as I sat down, but the beginnings of gratitude swelling in me were annihilated the instant I met Micah's caring gaze. Heat flushed through every pore; I couldn't speak. My jaw was clenched so tight I had to massage it with my knuckles later to release the tension. "Thank you," I finally choked.

His eyes pooled in pity. "Of course."

I couldn't understand, at first, what was happening, I hoped it would resolve itself as time went on. But it only got worse. Every time I encountered Micah's cloying compassion, I felt a directionless violence bubble up. It extinguished our repartee, our jokes, reducing us to functional exchanges of concern. Even as I tried to discipline myself into courtesy, dole out the requisite thanks as he held doors open and walked me home, I wanted to dig my nails into his skin. The day he gave me the helmet, I came close. I reached out, took his forearm between my thumb and index finger, and pinched down hard.

There wasn't enough loose flesh for me to do much damage, but he was surprised. "Easy," he said.

Holding up the beautiful red helmet, I arranged my face into a smile: "Thanks."

It'd taken me a while to trace my muddle of fury to its roots. That night, in the hostel, I had used the generalized word—assault—then closed the door on any future conversation; without clarification, he'd assumed the worst. Predicated on this assumption, he treated me gently, the unspoken consideration of my presumed rape threaded into everything he did. Mocking me. For what other violation would trigger the severity of my collapse, my complete and utter fragility, my dislodged sense of self? I had trapped myself in a deception I could see no way out of, and now his kindness had me pinned like a moth.

Stop it, I told myself. You're being unfair.

On the table, my phone lit up with a text from Arin. I felt the wave of nobility rise as I prepared to confront yet another piece of good news, but as I reached for the phone my hand cuffed the reflective visor's edge. My distorted face in the iridescent glass roused me—the tender strip of reddish skin bending with the visor's curve, the reflection's low angle enlarging my nostrils and shoulders. I drew back, holding the four fingers of my right hand with my left, to prevent myself from digging my nails into my palm again. In the reflection, my nose twitched, the sanitized stink of antiseptic creams mixing stickily with the stench of my sweat, which no matter how I scrubbed, I could not rid my sheets of.

The phone buzzed again. I remembered the way Micah had insisted, gently, that I disinfect my wounds after each meal. Each time, I composed myself into a portrait of gratitude, but inside I was seething. What was the point, why not just let me bleed.

The phone buzzed one last time.

In a fit of irritation, I grabbed the helmet and shoved it under the bed, where my luggage was stored. It rolled around noisily, thudded into the luggage, and came to a standstill.

64

Another one of Lorraine's potlucks arrived and with it an uncertain resolve. I'd been acting out, and each tiny burst of cruelty drew such bewildered looks from poor Micah that I could no longer live with his acts of consideration. Although the prospect of him withdrawing his care terrified me, I decided after much consultation with my conscience to be honest with him. I caught him alone in the late afternoon when he brought the hostel guests over and whispered: "Can you stay—later? We need to talk."

He was surprised I was there at all. I'd been missing the potlucks ever since picking up weekend shifts at Insomnia, something Lorraine never ceased making passive-aggressive comments about. Was the relief in his eyes from burden absolved or something else? I forced myself not to dwell on it. He said: "Of course."

After everyone left, he cleaned up and looked at me expectantly.

"Micah," I said slowly, "there's been a misunderstanding." He started to say something, I held my hand up. "Wait. Hear me out."

I had prepared in great detail the contents of my confession, down to its delivery, but when I started to speak everything went to shit. I couldn't stop digging into my palms while I spoke, raising a crop of new red welts against the forest of purple bruises, and Micah finally intercepted, grabbing both my hands in an unprecedented show of personality.

"Shh," he said, "it's fine, forget it, that's enough now."

But I wouldn't be derailed.

"Do you understand what I'm saying?" I demanded. "It was just a touch. Barely even. It's no big deal. I hadn't intended to lead you on."

I felt him spread my left palm out, very gently, felt the cool sensation of an ice cube against my skin. Slowly, I calmed down.

"Gen," he said. "Thank you for sharing this with me."

The thickness of his voice made me look up. "You're not mad?"

Micah looked like he was about to cry. "Look. I'm just really, really glad nothing worse happened to you."

I pulled my hand away. He glanced at the melting ice cube in his palm, then ventured, for the first time, a comment on my shredded skin. "Why don't you trim your nails?" At my look, his voice trailed off: "It might help . . ."

"Let me go get my medication."

Micah had never seen the inside of my studio before. He followed me across the garden and hovered in the doorway as I riffled through the closet. I wanted to laugh.

"You can come in," I said. "Just sit on the chair. But take your shoes off first."

He perched gingerly on the chair's edge, watching as I wiped antiseptic balm down the underside of my nails and over the broad curve of my palm, wincing.

"That looks really bad."

"Everyone needs a hobby."

But he didn't even register my joke. "Don't you want to talk to someone about it? Professionally?"

"No."

"Do you want me to accompany you to the police station?"

"Just because I clarified my position doesn't mean all of a sudden I want to have a heart-to-heart." My vehemence shocked us both; I restrained myself. "Sorry."

Compassion saturated his stupid face. "No, it's my fault for being obtuse. Do you want a drink—water, tea?"

I nodded. He leapt up, eager to be of use, and tripped. The sharp sound of his inhale recalled me.

He was holding the red motorcycle helmet in his hands.

"I thought you lost it," he said quietly.

A profound boredom settled over me. "Obviously, I lied." Again: "Sorry."

But he didn't demur. "It was actually quite expensive. If you didn't want it, you should have said. I could have returned it."

"I said sorry."

He turned the helmet over, wiping its surface with a thumb. A layer of fine dust came away; his breath hitched at the sight of its decimated interior. I could feel his mind working overtime to stitch together its scarf of oppressive understanding, I saw Micah resist it for one tremendous second, then soften: "It's fine."

How disappointing. I drawled sarcastically: "Is it?"

A flint of irritation crossed his face, sparking a thirst in me, for, I don't know, combat. "Yes, of course."

I chased it—"Really? Totally fine? You're not pissed at all?" I was goading him, I knew, but I couldn't stop. I had smelled blood and could not let it go. "Because if you're pissed you should say it, Micah. Are you angry? Are you?"

Without warning he roared: "Stop it."

He turned on me, and I flinched.

It registered on his face, shock spreading. Abruptly, he deflated. "I wasn't going to hit you." He sat heavily on the corner of my bed. "Did you think I was going to hit you?" I shook my head, but he continued, voice bare with awe. "You looked so scared."

He let go of the motorcycle helmet, it thumped to the floor. He put his face in his hands and was quiet for a long time.

Just as quickly as it'd materialized, my bloodlust evaporated. I'd gone too far, now I didn't know what to do. "Hey. I didn't think that," I said, sitting down by him. I put a tentative hand on his shoulder; he didn't respond. "Micah?"

He was mumbling something unintelligible. I put my face closer to hear. What am I doing, he was saying, over and over again. What am I doing. I wouldn't have hit you. But the look on your face.

"I didn't think that," I repeated. "Please. Micah. I'm sorry. I really didn't." I shook his shoulder, lightly at first, then with more urgency. "Please don't be angry."

Finally he raised his head. The shock of having seen himself the way I might've perceived him was so great it emptied all intelligence from his eyes. He stared at me blankly. The blankness, more than anything, scared me; this was it, I understood, the obligation had drained away, I'd finally provoked him into detachment, I'd proved myself ineligible for care. I started talking, rapidly, blabbering. I was sorry, I said, again and again, I'd lost my head for a second there, I didn't know what was happening to me, why violence had bloomed like desire, why I couldn't stop enacting this gleeful cruelty, where this impulse to ruin every good thing I touched originated—please, I needed him to understand, I *was* grateful, so grateful for his presence, for his care and consideration, for his goodness, I didn't want to push him away, please. With increasing wretchedness I insisted: It was me, did he understand? Me who was the problem. Me who was the evil child.

We were sitting very close together, wrapped in the haze of that sickening medicated cream. My chin dropped, tears falling fast into my lap. A moment later, I felt a soft bump. Micah had come to rest his forehead against mine. Relief poured through the small puncture of his kindness, and I sobbed freely. Micah was breathing heavily, trying not to cry; I repeated, over and over again: Sorry. But as his hand touched my face and tilted it toward him, I saw, immediately, that I'd gotten it all wrong.

"It's okay," he murmured soothingly. "It's okay. Don't cry."

He pressed his lips against mine, at first searchingly, then with a slightly firmer insistence. My stillness encouraged him. He put his other hand on my face, too, cupping my cheeks like he was cradling something precious, he pulled away and stared at me. I couldn't bear it, I closed my eyes. *I didn't think you were going to hit me*, I repeated, but only in my mind. *I didn't.* He burped softly, the warm, distorted smell of dinner emerged, he moved through it and toward me, repeating the same things as before: don't cry, it's okay, don't cry—but now the shape of words had changed, it's okay, he was saying, you're okay, you're fine. Micah's fingers trailed lightly down the side of my arms, raising goose bumps, then traced a path up my back, under the damp cotton of my shirt, pausing, lingering, with a show of courtesy, under the catch of my bra. My nails, rusted with blood, bit into the skin of my palm, catching and tearing at the scabs that had only just begun to form, I held myself very still, waiting, it must be clear, for the choice to be made for me, for culpability to slip from my shoulders. And was it fair for me to hold it against Micah, the ways in which he was educated in the language of consideration, the sticky heat of his breath against my ear as he waited, thumb brushing over clasp, for my nod? And did I nod? I must have. Or must have given some sign that predicated the medicated balm mixing with the scent of apology as he clung to me; the restrained care with which he finally proceeded to breach the distance between us, giving way to the precision of recycled script. The unfamiliar assuredness of his movements struck me with shame—how childish my surges of pleasure at ribbing poor, helpless, plain Micah seemed now, so incongruous with this dark-haired figure toiling above me, easing me onto my back, continually uttering a stream of useless questions—is this okay, is this okay—as if the act of articulation fulfilled both call and response. If I had ever conceptualized the act of sex it would not have resembled this blur of movement, this lack of perspective, the prodding of his fingers not quite aligned with the visual information of sweat dripping off his nose, the crepe-like texture of his sunburned shoulders, which, at such close proximity, looked dehydrated and flaky. And I don't think I ever even saw it, the purported penis, though I understood that it existed, that it was somewhere in the company of my thighs. An understanding jolted by the slippery flinch of his fingers, at which my mind balked, simultaneously staving off the reality of the moment and screaming at me to understand that this was no flight of imagination, no escape of fantasy, that this was real and actually happening. My consciousness bucked, my body twisting in a sharp, disoriented panic, but again, I'd miscalculated. It was a reaction that roused enthusiasm in the person before me, dissolving the veneer of courtesy in a painful collision. I thought, again: How little I know.

The breath in my ear turned humid, dampening my terror with its delicate, private rhythms. Then, without cue or reason, it retreated, and with a feeble bleat fell forward into my hair, uttering murmurs I had to strain to understand. You're okay, you're safe, it's okay.

Micah rolled off me, grabbing my fingers, kissing them softly, sucking each one clean. There was blood on the sheets too. We'll wash them tomorrow, he said, already fading. His voice was so tender. We lay there, swaddled in the sheets, and even in this half-slumberous state he curled his body protectively around mine, pulling my head tight against his chest. After a while, it got too hot, and he turned away sleepily, taking the sheets with him. Even though we were no longer touching, I could feel his snores, rumbling through the mattress, and lodging deep in my body, again and again.

It was close to three in the morning when I slipped out of bed. Micah was still concussed, but I moved in jerky, frozen increments, afraid to wake him. My head was thick with pain; in the dim moonlight I could see the dried snail trail of male fluids streaking down my thigh and belly. The Blue House was dark. Behind me, Micah stirred, then snorted, in his sleep. For days my bladder would whine consistently with tiny dribbles of pee, my irritated urethra smarting each time I sat on the toilet. I dressed, pulled the door shut, careful not to let it creak, and stood shivering from the night chill. Then I crept around the side of the studio, leaned against the wall beside the laundry lines, and closed my eyes.

I was so tired. If I stayed here all night, would they find me the next morning, frozen over? No—it was only 8 degrees Celsius. Not cold enough to die, only to suffer. An irresistible confusion spread—what was I doing here, where was I? Even with my bare toes wedged in the tufts of grass I could not believe that if I turned there would not be that shoji screen, that musty couch, the nest of books everywhere, and in the middle of it all, Arin, reading quietly with my mother.

Where was I, what was I doing. I unlocked my phone and dialed.

"Don't tell me—you've spent so much time in Insomnia that you've finally become a bat. Isn't it some unholy hour for you over there?"

The rich timbre of her alto was so clear that for a second my mind stuttered. I drew a jagged breath and sensed the live wire of Arin's attention snapping.

"Arin," I gasped. "Something's happened. I was attacked."

"What do you mean, attacked?"

I told her.

She was quiet for a long time. Then she said: "Send me your address. I'm coming."

65

Arin arrived three days later and stayed for ten. At such short notice, tickets were exorbitant, but she brushed it off with one line, *I'm working now.* She came alone, with one giant hard-shell case, which she'd purchased specially for the trip. In it were clothes, shoes, jackets, most of which were unfamiliar, and half the bag was filled with dried foods from home. Instant noodles, miso packets, sauces, snacks. Her plane had landed in the middle of the afternoon. I took the day off to wait for her, but told nobody about her arrival, disbelieving up till the very last minute that she would come. Even when the taxi pulled up outside the Blue House, I didn't believe it. Arin emerged violently, in a flamingo-colored sweater, her suspicious eyes scanning the exterior of the Blue House until I drew back from the curtains and opened the front door. I called out to her, and for a very slight moment, I was afraid. But she left the taxi door hanging, let the driver wait, flung herself into my arms and didn't let go.

Later, she said: "Jie, this isn't a studio. It's a shed."

I'd managed to get rid of Micah for the day. He'd become extremely attached and had basically lived in the studio in the days leading up to Arin's arrival. I didn't know how to broach the topic without hurting his feelings, so I waited till he left for the hostel then texted asking for some alone time. He replied immediately, apologizing for not proactively realizing I might need privacy, et cetera, et cetera. I didn't respond, and spent all morning cleaning the studio. But no matter how much I tidied, signs of him remained littered all over the room. His toothpicks, in the bin. Small black hairs, lodged in the side of the mattress. The lingering oaky smell of cologne. I watched Arin take it in. The studio suddenly seemed very small.

There was no space for her suitcase in the studio so we opened it in the garden, unpacked her immediate necessities, then stored it in the Blue House behind the couch. She slipped her hand in mine, checked at the scars, and said: "You need to get out."

We went to a quiet café on Queen Street, which served imported coffees and bottled beers.

"It's a bit of a tourist trap," I whispered, but she rolled her eyes.

"I don't see any tourists."

"Well, it's the middle of the workday."

"Jie, it's Christchurch."

The café was empty. Arin spit the bubblegum she'd bought at the airport out into a piece of tissue paper, pocketed it, then selected a couple of pastries. She'd become leaner in the couple of months since my departure, and moved with such sophisticated certainty it made me a little sad. How grown-up she seemed. How different we were now. Had I become someone she had to look out for, was she suppressing her inevitable disappointment, as I once had with my mother, at the smallness of my life? When she turned and gave me a thumbs-up, I said quietly: "I've missed you."

She smelled of baby powder and stale airplane sweat. "Come home, then," she murmured into my shoulder. The familiarity of her retort made my heart turn over.

We stayed in that café for hours. Arin chose a leather couch at the far end so we'd be obscured by a pillar and the soft sounds of background piano. As if knowing I needed to hear her prattle, she went first. Things were, she confirmed, more or less good. As she'd suspected, once her casting was publicly announced the attitudes of her classmates drastically shifted from condescension to admiration, something Arin relayed with triumph, though I detected an unexpected mournfulness in her tone. On the other hand, everyone at the YouTube company was mad at Arin—the producers, because they wanted a clearer performance of gratitude for having discovered her; Lyla and the other YouTubers indignant at the comparison she'd unwittingly cast on them. As a result, they'd taken to resentfully scrutinizing her every action, waiting to pounce whenever she messed up a line.

"That's good?" I asked.

"It's hell. Look." She held out her wrist, and I was surprised to see a silver charm bracelet from Pandora hanging off it, the kind girls gave one another on their twenty-first birthday, more branding than metal. Arin and I had mocked it, and the girls who wore them, as sheep, yet now as I looked curiously at the bracelet, touched it, I wondered aloud. Had she given in, what else had changed? She shook her head. "It's a gift." Pandora, yes, Pandora itself, had sent it over as congratulations when she'd been cast. She took a small white box out of her bag and adjusted an identical bracelet on my wrist.

"I asked for one more, for you too."

"You can do that?"

"No. I said the first one never arrived." She flashed me one of her secret exuberant smiles. "Since my mediocre acting is apparently going to humiliate me nationally, don't you think I should be fairly compensated for putting myself on the line?"

I admired the bracelet, and said: "And the movie?"

At this, her voice dropped. "It's fine."

"Just fine?"

Yes, just fine. Her mouth was drawn into a tight line as she explained—and I could see it pained her deeply to admit this—the bottleneck was her. What her haters said was true, she wasn't experienced. And Arin's role, while only a supporting one, was challenging. When I asked why, she clammed up and wouldn't say.

The conversation turned to me. We were sitting, on that couch, with our bodies tilted toward each other, knees touching, and as I started talking, not of the shattered weeks past but of the mundane march of secretarial work, I watched the flicker of confusion in Arin's gaze grow, saw her temper, forcibly, her curiosity, her questions, and I wished, with an unreasonable desire, for her to reach into my mind and pull from it the events I could not find words to articulate. Yet I did not want to be one of those people who hinted darkly at affliction, whose wounded demeanor demanded empathy without recourse. And she had come all this way. She sensed my struggle, she volunteered, hesitantly: "Jie . . ."

It was enough. Midsentence, I broke off, I said, in a weak show of bravado: "As you can see, I've come undone."

She nodded for me to proceed, waited as I braced myself. In a jagged, disjointed manner, I began to circle the afternoon without directly addressing it: I spoke of everything else—my attacking a stranger on a bicycle, the furious bald shopkeeper, proffering Micah's body as a scaffold to regrettable ends—in precise, factual terms, before finally alighting on the moment of fracture, when a boy looked into my eyes and understood how I saw him as nothing, how my mind drifted even then into the chores that would follow the minor inconvenience of this encounter, and how he put fear in me, with one savage assertion. I used the objective words: grope, breast, my voice sounded cold, medical, I wanted to leave no space for misinterpretation, and waited for the doomed relief that would flood Arin's face the instant she grasped the glancing nature of my assault, preparing myself for sounds of comfort.

But none came.

I watched Arin take everything in, accumulating and carrying the weight of my words, fright flashing frequently across her face, and understood that she had not demanded this explanation, that I was giving it freely. And I understood that once started, I could not stop, could not halt the words flowing out of my mouth nor the fluent tears streaking down my face.

When I was done speaking, it was late, the sky outside turned to dusk. I felt emptied, reduced again to frailty. The café owner had come over twice to tell us he was clearing up, but the second time he approached Arin flung him a glare so intense that he backed off, hands up. As we were leaving, I blew my nose with the free napkins, whispered my apologies to him, and left, led out of the café by hand.

Under the streetlamps, Arin raised my hand, turned it over to examine my palm, then brought her fingertips to mine, lightly.

"You can't stop?"

I shook my head. "I don't even know I'm doing it."

"Why didn't you call me earlier?"

Yes, why? While speaking, I had been ashamed, or perhaps protective, of my envy; I kept the dates loose. I did not want to forge the link between her success and my stumbling out into the dusty streets. Now, floundering for the truth, I murmured: "I didn't want to be a burden."

"Jie," she said. She wrapped both my hands in hers, then leaned forward, forehead resting on my shoulder. We were in the middle of the street, but she didn't seem bothered by the occasional passerby staring. "I'm here now."

66

Lorraine was waiting in the living room when we got back. "What's this?" she demanded, referring to Arin's luggage. "And who are you?"

I introduced Arin, explained that she would be staying in the studio with me, apologized for not giving her a heads-up. Lorraine clearly would have preferred for Arin to rent one of the spare rooms in the Blue House, and as I spoke, it looked like she was going to kick up a fuss. But then Arin's face changed. She moved forward, pulling Lorraine into a hug, and when she stepped back, her eyes were compelling and teasing. She thanked Lorraine for putting up with me: they'd been worried about me back home, but now that Arin was here, she felt at ease, what a wonderful place, how lucky I was to be living here. As she spoke, she touched Lorraine frequently, resting a hand on her shoulder, squeezing her arm.

Incredibly, Lorraine responded in kind. She defrosted, waved away the issue of the luggage, even smiled at me, saying, yes, it's been nice to have company, it'd been great having me around. What a lie. I cut my gaze to Arin, but she didn't flicker once. By the end of that conversation, Lorraine was enamored. Arin could stay with me for no extra cost, there was no need to worry about the luggage, please let her know if we needed anything. I couldn't believe it. Once we were back in the studio, I said, incredulous: "She loves you."

Arin shrugged, grabbed my hands, folding her fingers over mine. "All she needed was a bit of attention," she said. "She was screaming for it. Couldn't you tell?"

"No."

"Well."

The next day, at Arin's request, I spoke to Damien about taking some time off. My sister had unexpectedly showed up, I started to explain, but Damien immediately agreed without hearing the rest. He seemed relieved. They couldn't afford for me to disappear completely for the ten full days of her visit, but a couple of days were fine, and if I wanted to work from home for part of the rest, that was fine too. Arin was pleased, she teased me afterward.

"What sort of secretary works from home?"

"I told you, they don't really need me after all." I'd been feeling this way for a while. It was obvious that Fifield & King was operating at a loss, especially since most projects were on hold while the city remedied earthquake damages. And Damien was dispensing more favors than they could afford. When a tree in Hannah and Lily's backyard tumbled into their roof, he devoted months to fortifying their house's frame for almost nothing. I was lucky to have signed my employment contract right before the quake, but suspected that my hire originated from the same brand of glass-half-full delusion. "If not for the severance pay and effort they put into hiring and bringing me here, I think they'd have let me go by now."

"Great," she said easily, "then you can come home."

In those ten days, Arin and I did more than I had the entire time I'd lived in Christchurch. She was stunned to hear that the only time I'd ventured out of the city was to the beach with Micah, and immediately set about planning a formidable expedition. She called up bus companies, booked accommodations, charted and compared different routes and options. Neither of us could drive, or Arin would have rented a car: she did the math and was amazed. For the rest of the trip she couldn't stop talking about how cheap cars were in New Zealand. I saw—despite her protests that the only purpose of knowledge was its yield, despite all her dismissal of Christchurch—the immense pleasure that met each new discovery, each fresh encounter with something yet unknown, and felt a shudder of pride at being the vector for her excitement. As we left Christchurch on a four-hour bus ride to Lake Tekapo, I could see her wrestling with distraction as we spoke, eyes darting away from my face and over my shoulder to the South Island unfolding beyond the window.

Yes, I recalled, I had been like this too. We'd lived so much of our lives cloistered in academic focus that neither of us had had much experience in the real world, in the ways it could scald or stupefy. I patted her hand to release her from the conversation, and Arin turned instantly, plastering her face to the glass pane.

"Told you," I murmured, as an expanse of water large as the ocean rippled serenely into the horizon.

She had no smart retort for once. Tears were sliding down her cheeks.

I entwined my hand in hers and squeezed.

When the bus pulled up, it was late afternoon. We checked into the bed-and-breakfast, showered, changed, and, stumbling over ourselves, raced down to the lake. It was peak lupin season. Pink, lavender, and yellow stalks swayed in the wind, syrupy in the thick gold light. Arin collapsed in the middle of the lupin field, exhaling loudly.

"Okay," she said, ruefully, gazing up into the sky. "Fine. Now I get it."

Sprawled on the ground, her entire body was relaxed. I lowered myself beside her tentatively, pushing the stalks aside, and joked: "All it took was a flower field?"

"Lupins aren't flowers," Arin said, surprising me. "They're an invasive, nonnative species, an environmental threat. But look," she continued, tugging on a stalk, which bent, then snapped. She held the pealike leaf toward me, and I became aware of how florid the deep purple plant was, how intricate its dense spires were. "How beautiful it is. And how far people like us travel to see it."

I was caught off guard. "I thought you traveled all this way to see me."

She laughed, flipping a switch. "I traveled all this way to show you that beauty is nothing compared to coming home."

"You can be like this with others," I said, turning away. "But don't be glib with me. It doesn't suit you."

"Am I being glib?" she countered. "Or are you being avoidant?" She laughed at my expression and pushed herself upright. "Come, Jie. I packed us dinner."

We sat by the lake, chewing on the sandwiches, my head in her lap. The sunlight warmed us gradually, and my breathing slowed.

We stayed like this for over an hour, until the sinking sun gave way to cold night air.

As we walked back to the bed-and-breakfast, hand in hand, I spoke.

"Thank you, Mei," I said quietly, "for being here. I know how much it's costing you not to be back home, rehearsing, but I'm really glad you came."

We were almost at the bed-and-breakfast when Arin turned to me, holding up her hand in mine. I was shocked to realize I hadn't picked at my skin all day.

"Worth it," she said.

We traveled from Lake Tekapo to Arrowtown, Wanaka, spent a night in Queenstown; we queued for famous burgers, we kayaked, we were rendered speechless by the ice-capped mountains cutting lines against the sky, we marveled at the absolute clarity of the waters, the way the sun glinted off their surface, transforming it into a perfect mirror of the world. Arin was particularly enchanted by the colors of foliage turning—it took her a while to understand the red of the leaves was because of the season and not because she was staring at a new type of unfamiliar tree.

I was charmed to see the replay of my own early wonder in her astonishment, in the spontaneous bubbling of her stunned laughter as she put her hand out to touch the leaves, then checked her own fingertips, as if half suspecting a trick, as if someone had come by just a second ago and dipped the leaves in shades of vermillion and gold so the pigment might come away with her touch. We'd known only hypothetically of the seasons, and all Arin's research couldn't prepare her for how the chilled air might feel whistling against her cheeks; for the incomprehensible vibrance of a dying leaf. In her childlike delight, she began collecting them, pressing the leaves between pages of her notebook, trying to preserve them against decay.

Each night, while I slept, she stayed up late reading her script, which she still wouldn't talk about, citing both the NDA and her fear of jinxing things. I would hear her while half asleep, though only indistinctly, trying out different tones and inflections, repeating certain words in different ways, and feel myself being lulled deeper into slumber, comforted by the old familiarity of our physical proximity. And each morning I was similarly eased back into the waking world. The soft sounds of Arin up and about, reading emails, or having just returned from a morning run, would gradually enter my consciousness, room filling with the enticing aroma of freshly brewed coffee while she held a warmed towel against my cheek. I began sleeping deeper and longer, rising later each day, till one morning I woke to her gently massaging my palm with her thumbs.

For a split second it felt like our childhood positions were reversed, as if she were the older one cradling me in her care. Drowsily, I wrapped my fingers around her thumb, trapping it, and Arin giggled. "Hi," she said. Seeing that I was about to drift off again, she pulled her hand away and tapped my nose. "Breakfast's ready."

I groaned. "Don't you ever rest?"

I was only teasing, but she said, seriously: "No. Why would I?" Then she laughed.

Frequently, when she sensed I was amenable to it, Arin would draw me into conversational potholes that I assiduously avoided otherwise. We might be admiring a particularly beautiful sunset, for example, or dipping in the lakes, or simply walking down a dirt path, when she'd turn to me and plunge straight back into the conversation that had begun in that dirty café and seeped, no matter how I resisted it, into the dreadful underbelly of our days. And while I shrank from it, Arin met it head-on. She would ask me to recount even the things she'd heard before: the mental fracture of assault, the terror of sex with Micah, the disaster of dissonance that bloomed between cognitively understanding what I'd allowed to happen and the physical realization that it was too late.

It was like applying salt to an ulcer. Each time Arin led me through these interior turns, holding both my hands tight and preventing them from wandering, sensitive to every twitch and flinch, I'd weep, anguish drawn away from my skin and into the light. In those isolated landscapes of soil and fauna I wept; how I wept. It exploded out of me and left me depleted and dazed. And yet underneath all this was a growing sense of shame at the extravagance of my pain, and it was this shame I fled from with the opposite and equal force of my hunger for Arin's tremendous attention, which wrapped around me like a dense blanket. One day, I wiped my eyes and said, finally, with a pathetic attempt at dignity: Yes, it's something that happened to me—it happens to a lot of women—and by and by it seems I've gotten off lightly. You're here on vacation, we don't have to talk about it anymore.

Arin just stared at me. I squirmed for a minute, then laughed. What?

She threaded her fingers through mine, brushing one of the welts with her thumb. But, Jie, she said, what happened with the boy *was* scary. It was terrifying.

I blinked rapidly. What?

Of course you're shaken, you still are.

How staggering that statement was. How it rinsed shame from me to see things as they were. How free it left me to lift my eyes to follow the brilliance of a fuzzy bumblebee humming between the low blades of grass; to say, ah, that's all in the past now. It matters less, and it will keep mattering less, now that we are here together. All that matters is the absolute present. Look, a swan swanning.

Look, this is a lake, that is a tree.

Look how the lupins are blooming.

Look.

When the time came for us to return to Christchurch, it felt as if we'd been on a long journey, yet one that'd lasted only a few seconds. Arin had booked us seats on a coach that would take us directly from Queenstown to Christchurch, and as usual she'd paid for it all, waving off my attempts to reimburse her. *If you think this is good*, she laughed, when I objected, *just wait, life will be better for us, I promise.* Yet, after uttering these words, she turned pensive. On the coach, she was quieter than usual, weighing her confidence, no doubt thinking of the role she had ahead of her, upon which everything depended.

When we were about halfway through the journey, she turned to me and said, mournfully, that she didn't want to return to Christchurch, she was grieving the end of our time together.

I got upset. "It's not the end. You're still here for another week."

"Less than a week."

We watched the parabolic arc of a single black-billed gull cut through the air.

"Four days," I said.

She reached for my hand, brought it to her mouth, and bit down. "A whole lifetime."

67

It was important to me that Arin meet Hannah and Lily, so the night we returned to Christchurch I called ahead to let Hannah know I'd be bringing my sister to Insomnia the next evening. She was pleased; she commented that the short getaway had obviously done me a world of good.

"How can you tell?"

"Your voice, Gen," she said, "your voice." Then she paused, and in her pause, I felt it—the slight shift in the dead air of the phone line, the contemplation.

"Yes?"

"Gen . . ." She paused again, and I smiled at Arin, who was crossing back to the studio after a shower in the Blue House. "Your friend came around a few times. You didn't tell him you were going away?"

Micah. For the past few days, I hadn't thought about Micah, the person, only Micah the event. Immediately, guilt flushed through me, chased by irritation: he could have texted, or called, but no, he'd gone to my workplace and probably asked after my where-abouts with Lorraine too. I thanked Hannah and hung up. Now I'd have to introduce Arin to Micah. I could see it already, Arin's gaze raking over Micah's pale skin, dark hair, his self-conscious gait and unfunny jokes, his puppyish eagerness to please. I looked up at the real Arin, perched on the corner of the bed, twisting her wet hair through a clean towel. She had her back to me and was flip-ping through her script while chewing furiously on a new stick of bubblegum. Without turning, she said: "Go shower."

I put my phone on the table and picked up my bath caddy. As I moved toward the door, she added: "Your hands look a lot better, they're not bleeding anymore."

. . .

As expected, Hannah and Lily took to Arin immediately. Curiously, it was Arin who seemed nervous to meet them. She'd put in a real effort to dress up, even though she hadn't indicated any interest in my part-time job beyond commenting in a mildly frustrated fashion that I'd crossed oceans to perform the exact same labor the ice cream shop had demanded of me. As far as I could tell, she hadn't registered anything I said about Hannah and Lily, even when I expressed my gratefulness that they'd basically adopted me. But when I introduced her to them, I noticed the foundation she'd worn caking slightly around the crease of her lips, and the careful swipe of her eyeliner. When she said she was an actress, she seemed genuinely ashamed to reveal that she'd not yet appeared in any actual movies, that her repertoire had only extended to short internet skits thus far.

Hannah, picking up on Arin's discomfort, tried to be her usual effervescent self. "Anything we might have seen?"

It was the worst thing she could have asked. "No," Arin said, her face falling further. "Our viewers are mainly regional."

"That's all right, what's the channel called? We'll watch it right now."

Lily stepped in. "Stop embarrassing the girl," she said sternly, putting a hand on Hannah's shoulder. To me: "You look wonderful, I'm glad you finally got out of town. Genevieve was basically living here at one point."

That last part was addressed to Arin. Embarrassed, I said: "I wasn't here that much."

Lily let it slide, but Arin spoke up with a tentativeness that surprised me. "I would too, if I lived in Christchurch."

Hannah's face was pink with pleasure. "You like the theater?"

She nodded seriously. "I love it."

They went off together, Hannah pointing out the cream-colored fixtures that laced the ceiling's edges, the vintage art-house posters plastering the walls, the range of DVDs they had, the weekly flyers I designed, advertising each week's Throwback Thursday screenings. Lily and I stayed by the counter. She repeated that she was glad I'd stepped out of my comfort zone, then with nothing else to add, returned to her computer and started printing out pre-reserved tickets for the night's showings.

Hannah returned in a state of excitement. She was holding on to Arin's wrist, Arin lagging slightly behind. "Lil," she was saying, "she's in a movie, it's coming out soon."

Arin was clearly uncomfortable. "I haven't even started filming."

"Let go of her," Lily said, voice warm again. "Sorry, Arin. She can be a bit much when she gets excited."

Hannah let go of Arin's hand, but didn't stop talking. She'd actually heard of the independent director attached to this project—a queer prodigy who'd made waves with a low-budget psychological horror shot on a Handycam, which swept a short-film festival two years ago. Arin's film was an expansion on the short, and Hannah already knew about the director halting postproduction to rewrite a whole subplot despite it putting them in the red. Rumor was he'd bet the film's success on the additional scenes, even coughing up his own cash for the supplementary days of shooting, an ingenious PR move that focused the media's attention—and pressure—on this yet unveiled work of genius. And now Arin had no choice but to perform.

I looked at Hannah in surprise. "That's more than she's told me."

Lily groaned. "You see what I mean?"

Arin mumbled: "He's a genius, it's true, but don't get excited, no one knows yet how it's going to go."

Her dejection was so overt that Hannah's mouth formed a little O. "Lovey," she said, "you'll be great."

I saw, reflected in Arin's face, my own thoughts: Hannah didn't even know her. Didn't understand the pressure she was under, didn't understand the scale of her humiliation, should she tumble before the eyes of the world. People did this, said things without knowing what they meant, they were irresponsible with their words. Even if they were well meaning.

Arin struggled, I stepped in.

"What's genius," I said, rolling my eyes, "but humanity obscured? Don't let the director intimidate you, Mei. Remember how you tried to swim across a literal ocean? You're deranged, I know you have what it takes."

"What it takes," Arin repeated.

"Yes," I said, and I was certain as I spoke. To the rest I said: "The real genius is here." I smiled. "Who would know it better than me?"

After that, Arin relaxed. She became more chatty, less jumpy, and over the rest of the evening engaged in long and witty conversation with Lily about the rankings of cult film classics. When customers started streaming in for the evening shows, she watched intently as Hannah set up the theater, stamped tickets, and after both cinema doors were shut, she had questions about everything she'd just observed. This wasn't like the motivated charm she applied to Lorraine, this was all her—the bright-eyed interest of our girlhood, keen to grasp everything, drinking in the pleasure of knowledge for its own sake. I remembered the first time this side of Arin had emerged clearly, the widening delight in her eyes as I pinched an ixora stem to reveal the drop of hidden nectar at its center, and saw, even now, her secret satisfaction as she worked through the sticks of gum she got at each convenience store, determined to master blowing the perfect pink bubble despite knowing this to be nothing more than a temporary hobby that would come to a legal halt once she headed home. Useless pockets of effort, useless but for the pleasure they conferred. So much of our relationship followed in this same vein. Why had I allowed jealousy to disrupt me, why had I succumbed to pettiness, when so much goodness was here for me to partake in, if only I set myself aside and allowed it to? I let myself sink into an uncomplicated happiness at Arin's success, contentment diffusing through me with a warm sigh. Arin, still deep in conversation with Hannah, cocked her head at me, gaze questioning. I smiled at her, she squeezed my hand, then turned back to Hannah and said: "Are you serious?"

She was excited about something. I forced myself to pay attention again.

"Yes, of course. Anything for Gen." Hannah was beside me now, putting an arm around my shoulder, and I responded to the comforting touch without any real comprehension of what was going on. Lily, perceiving that I hadn't been following the conversation, spoke up.

"We'll show Arin's movie here, when it comes out."

I was amazed. "You can do that?"

Arin laughed. They'd gone over this just a second ago, obviously I'd been daydreaming. Yes, they could. It wasn't as complicated to negotiate screening rights for independent films, especially since smaller studios appreciated any chance to have their film travel. Hannah would get the producer's contact from Arin, they'd sort it out. Arin wasn't sure exactly when the film would be done, it depended on how quickly things could come together, but it would definitely be early in the new year. The director was ambitious, he wanted to make the film festival circuit. Like a shark circling closer and closer to its goal, he'd already identified key decision-makers for each festival's selection committee and pulled every string available to broker introductions to them.

At my marveling face, Arin smiled. "We're not in Kansas anymore, Jie," she said. I started, but there was no intimation of a joke in her gaze.

Hannah chuckled in delight. "We'll even throw a party. A premiere screening party."

Lily's voice was full of reproach. "Let Gen get a word in edgewise, would you?"

They all turned to me. Arin's face trembled with a fleeting moment of tension, torn between hope and restraint.

"Yes," I said, beaming at her, watching her spirits lift. "Let's do it, it'll be fun."

We stayed in Insomnia way past closing time, after all the lingering customers had left. Even Lily, normally reticent, chatted unreservedly with Arin; by the end of the night they'd bonded over the emotional complications of striking out on their own. After that, Hannah insisted we take a group photo, so Arin would remember them when she was famous. Hannah said this as if it were a fact, as if there were no possibility that this radiant girl before her might not succeed. She brought her digital camera out and balanced it on the counter, playing with the lobby lights until she was satisfied that our faces could all be seen clearly. We huddled together, the flash went off.

By the time we left Insomnia it was close to two in the morning. We were all yawning continuously, but none of us were willing to break the happy spell of conversation, and even though we kept saying, it's late, it's late, no one got up until it was apparent that Hannah could barely keep her eyes open. Still, Arin was reluctant to leave. She hugged them repeatedly, she promised to drop by again if she could. When Hannah whispered to me—*be safe as you walk back*—Arin laughed and said we'd take a cab, brushing off my protests at the expense. In her good mood, Arin was more careless with money than usual; it was as if she'd seen far into her future and assumed the financial security that would come with her success. But when we stepped out of Insomnia looking to flag a cab, it became clear there was no need to.

Micah was standing under a streetlamp, leaning against his parked motorbike, waiting for us.

68

Instantly, my good mood dissolved. Arin made the connection, her smile tightened, she stepped between us.

"You must be Micah," she said smoothly. "Why didn't you come in and say hi?"

"I didn't want to intrude."

Arin's presence didn't surprise him. So he already knew about her arrival, so he'd already asked around. I interrupted. "So you just stood out here for hours?"

"It wasn't that long."

"How long?"

His shift had ended at eleven. It had been three hours, we both knew it. He wouldn't meet my eye. "I just got here. I thought you might want supper."

"Nothing's open."

"I can whip something up." A lock of dark hair fell into his eyes, and I felt the tug of familiar affection mixed with irritation.

I looked at Arin. I wasn't hungry, and it was late. But this new turn of events had rejuvenated her. In her posture, I sensed a whiff of hunger as she sized him up.

"Sure," she said, smiling easily. "I'd love a bite."

We couldn't both fit on the back of his motorbike, so Micah pushed it while we strolled beside him. It was heavy, not meant for pushing over long distances, and halfway through he began to tire. But still Arin proceeded leisurely, dictating the pace of our progress. By the time we reached the Blue House, he was perspiring mightily. Arin plopped down on the couch while he moved around in the kitchen, whipping eggs and toasting leftover bread slices. We could both hear the clink of ice cubes as he filled a cup, gasped, and guzzled the cold water. Arin widened her eyes slightly at me, and I resisted the urge to giggle.

"Breakfast?" she observed, as Micah brought out three plates of toast, scrambled eggs, and jam. "Is everything upside down in this country, then?"

He was unable to meet her wit, he floundered.

I cut in. "I haven't done groceries in a while."

Arin paused, recalibrating. "It smells great."

We ate around the low coffee table, sitting on the couch. Arin leaned back, relaxed, balancing her plate on her slim knees, but Micah had his on the table and hunched over it, bending down every time he had to take a bite. I felt like snapping at him to sit straight, but I felt so much pity for him that I couldn't bring myself to speak. He was trying, without much success, to strike up a conversation with Arin, whose high spirits had receded into a compact elegance.

"How long are you in town for?"

"Not sure I'd call Christchurch a town."

"A city . . ."

"I'm only joking, I'm here till Wednesday."

"That's so soon—I thought we'd have more time to hang out."

She looked deeply amused. "We're hanging out now, yes?"

I couldn't bear to watch this. "We can have lunch tomorrow," I interrupted, "or the day after. My break is at noon."

Arin held my gaze, assessing the situation. Then she broke off, exhaled, and said: "All right, whatever you want, Jie."

She got up, brought her empty plate to the kitchen, left it in the sink. The restroom door clicked shut, and Micah exhaled. "You guys are very similar," he said, and I let out a surprised laugh.

"Not at all. But we used to be."

He reached out and touched my forearm questioningly, retracting his hand when I involuntarily stiffened. I opened my mouth to apologize, but Arin reappeared and resumed her place on the couch.

"I should get going," Micah said, then looked unsure when neither of us contradicted him. "See you girls tomorrow."

"See ya," Arin called.

. . .

Once we were in the studio, she burst out laughing. "I have never seen such a dull boy in my entire life. The look he gives you, my God."

She was still employing the elevated charm of her public persona. I waited for her to calm down. Her manner with Micah had disturbed me. "He's a good person."

"Have you realized," Arin continued, in the high wattage of entertainment, "you always say that as if it's an excuse?" She imitated Micah's voice, replicating his cadence so precisely that I got a shock. "I didn't want to intrude," she quoted, pulling a hangdog face. Then her voice reverted to its regular tones, she laughed again.

This time I gave in. The memory of Micah skulking around under that streetlamp suddenly seemed ridiculous. Before long we were both cackling in bed like old ladies.

"You're too much," I said when we finally caught our breath.

She shot back: "And you're too kind. Volunteer at an old folks' home if you feel the need to do charity."

This sobered me. "I'm not kind." Arin quietened, watching as I spoke. I wanted to be fair, I said: "He was there for me, you know. When."

"Aren't *I* here for you now?"

Ah. We'd been winding down, Arin lying with her back to the windows. She shifted slightly and the dimpled dent of her frown emerged from the shadowy gauze of moonlight. In an instant I realized: all the jealousy I'd felt growing up, which plowed through reason and sprouted spontaneous acts of cruelty, Arin shared, too. Lightly, I said: "There's no comparison."

"Good," she said, a little huffily. "Because it's so obvious—you don't even *like* him."

Hearing her state it so plainly threw me. I murmured: "It's not so bad having him around." I shifted so my cheek would be on the pillows facing her and raised an eyebrow. "With the number of questions you've asked, one would think you're keen to try it yourself."

"Try what?" Then: "Oh, I see. No," she said slowly. "No, I don't think so. I only care inasmuch as it involves you."

"Eventually it'll happen. You can't just live life by proxy."

She shuddered delicately. "The thought of being so accountable to another person makes me sick, if I'm being honest."

Responsibility echoed in me. "Mei, that's love."

"Is that the only kind of love that counts, then? Is sex the epitome of a relationship?"

I was taken aback. Once again she had escalated the conversation so rapidly that all I could do was concede. "That's not at all what I meant."

She turned away from me and lay on her back so I could see the sharp valleys of her nose and lip glinting in the moonlight. "In that case," she asked, "why compromise? You have friends, you have family. You're worth too much to be giving someone you don't care for so much of your time, Jie."

In this moment she was all ambition. There was no room to volunteer a different opinion, and, I reasoned, no immediate need. Gently, I said, "You think too highly of me, as always."

"Someone has to. In any case, I have all the love I need." Her lips curved, to show that she was half teasing. "If only she would come home."

69

Arin left Christchurch in the very early hours of November 24. We stayed up all night talking, but when I wanted to follow her to the airport, she shook her head.

"That image of you sitting alone on the bus ride home is too sad," she said. "I can't let you do it."

"I'll take a cab."

She laughed. "No you won't."

We slipped into the Blue House through the kitchen door to retrieve Arin's luggage, trying to be as quiet as possible, but immediately the lights in Lorraine's bedroom came on. Even though it was 4:00 a.m., Lorraine emerged in her sack of a nightgown, following us to the side of the road to wait for Arin's prebooked taxi. Despite my hints and growing sullenness, she stayed put, chatting pleasantly with Arin, who raised her eyebrows at me, glancing suggestively at the dark outlines of Lorraine's braless nipples pushing through the nightgown.

I didn't respond; I was upset. I didn't like that I would be saying goodbye to this version of her, the public-facing, effusive Arin, but short of telling Lorraine to go away, there was nothing I could do. The only moment we had alone was at 4:30, when the taxi pulled up. Arin came over and gave me a tight hug, I wrapped my arms around her and kissed the side of her forehead. Then her expression slipped and I saw that she was as upset as I was.

"Stop being stubborn," she whispered, as we separated. I looked around for Lorraine, who was negotiating a discount with the cabbie. She must have truly adored Arin. "We really miss you. Come home."

We. Arin and I had been careful to tiptoe around the subject of my mother till now. I chewed on my lower lip and asked: "How is she?"

Arin gave me a rueful, protective look. "Oh, Jie," she said, without elaborating. Then Lorraine came around the side of the cab to announce that the luggage was loaded. The muscles in Arin's face and posture shifted infinitesimally, but before she could revert to her charming self, I pulled her in for another hug.

"Soon," I whispered in her ear, and she exhaled.

"Promise?"

"Promise."

Lorraine and I stood side by side on that pavement till the smell of the cab's exhaust dissipated. Then without saying a thing, we both turned and went back into the Blue House.

My days took on a muted quality after Arin left. She landed in Singapore safely and was immediately absorbed into her filming schedule; in those days we spoke infrequently, and when we did, she sounded overworked and stressed. On the other hand, I woke up, I went to the office, I went to Insomnia, I went home. I avoided the main street where I'd attacked the wrong boy and made detours around the street where I'd been assaulted. I also forced myself to admit that there was no purpose to my prolonged dalliance with Micah. When I broke things off, I was surprised at my own indifference.

He reacted to our breakup with a look of immense hurt. He didn't understand, he tried to protest. He started listing all these things he admired about me, which was fine, but then he started talking about my soul and how luminous it was. When he told me he loved me, I felt impatient.

"How is that possible," I said. "We met three months ago."

"It's true, I care for you deeply, you just can't see it."

"You care for everything," I said kindly. "That doesn't mean you're in love."

He came around the Blue House on several different occasions to try to strike things up with me again. I didn't feel upset then either. Christchurch really was boring, it must have given him something to do. The only time I lost my cool was when he said: "It doesn't matter to me."

Already, I felt my skin tingling, but I asked: "What doesn't?"

"I love you"—he'd gotten into a habit of repeating this—"what happened with the boy, it doesn't matter."

"I told you. It was—"

"It doesn't matter to me."

His voice was charged with sincerity. I felt the last of my affection toward him drain away.

"Micah," I said, and hope flared in his eyes. "Fuck off."

I was honest with Lorraine, I told her Micah and I had fallen out and I wouldn't be attending any more potluck dinners. She'd expected it, the only thing she wanted to know was whether "falling out" was a euphemism. I shrugged and made it a point to confirm my shifts at Insomnia whenever Lorraine had another potluck in the Blue House. Christmas came and went. A couple of interchangeable guests stayed in the Blue House over the year-end, and I even had dinner with one of them, a girl from Malaysia. She'd brought laksa paste and whipped up a pot of it. The minute Lorraine saw her pour coconut milk into the pot, she excused herself, and the Malaysian girl and I chatted about nothing of importance into the night. A few days later, she was gone, off exploring the Franz Josef Glacier. I was sorry, but not too sorry, to see her go.

Once Arin's filming wrapped, we resumed our regular correspondence. I went through my phone logs later, my emails. In all our conversations she seemed happy, and I was happy for her. I double-checked this, over and over—the frequency of our calls, the imperturbable tone of our texts. I hadn't misremembered: nothing but bliss.

Over the new year, I called Arin. She was on the way home from a YouTube party. I was surprised: it was four in the morning for me, the first of January, which meant it was still 2010 in Singapore.

"You didn't stay for the countdown?"

"I didn't want Auntie to be alone. And you, not sleeping again?"

I closed my eyes briefly at the mention of my mother, skin prickling from the ghost of her finger tracing its slow patterns down my arm, then opened them again and scoffed: "Sleep?" I could feel Arin smiling at my old playfulness. "Who needs it."

I continued, honestly: "You're really a better daughter than I am. She's lucky to have you."

Arin sighed. "I'm not her daughter, you are. Come home."

It was no longer a question of if, but when. I knew I'd have to revisit the ever-narrowing possibility of Fifield & King opening in Asia at some point. Even more absurd was the thought that I, who'd been making increasingly sloppy mistakes, might be the one to lead this charge. It felt like an adorable fantasy. But still, one I found hard to let go of.

"I'm figuring it out," I told Arin. "I really am."

Weeks passed, then it was February, and Arin's movie was done. It was from Hannah that I heard this, not Arin. The postproduction process, though rushed, had wrapped far ahead of schedule, thanks to an extra round of funding by a Singaporean investor. The cash injection had reinvigorated the editing process, oiled the administrative hurdles that had to be conquered for a limited theatrical release.

According to Hannah, this had generated significant buzz: it was thought impossible to complete a feature on that budget and timeline, even if the majority of the film had already been shot earlier, but the young director was not only supremely talented but an outrageous hustler. Clipping together a reel of his work, teaser scenes from the movie, and a primer on himself, he pitched not the film but his actual *person* to an angel investor, laying out the reasons he was guaranteed success in the current global market. He was asking the investor not to buy into the film, but into him, the genius. This audacious invitation, to purchase for an undisclosed amount a 1 percent stake in all the director's ventures, current and future, was so unheard-of that it had the entire film world transfixed. The exact sum the investor bet on the director's future wasn't disclosed, but the story whipped up a hurricane of interest in the film before even a single frame had been publicly released.

And now it was ready. The film would be out end of February or early March, barely making the deadlines for the Cannes festival circuit. "The axis of the world is shifting," Hannah said. There was a note in her voice I couldn't quite decipher.

"What do you mean?"

"Do you know how much money it takes for something like that to happen?"

When she told me who the last-minute investors were, I was stunned silent.

Choann Cineplexes. The last-minute angel investor was Penelope's father. A milky vapor of disgust bubbled up; Arin's voice from years past, saying, *Generosity is cheap for someone like her.* I recalled the tilt of Arin's forehead as I told her how Penelope and I had left things off, the unspoken *I told you so.* How Arin would hate being indebted to the same source of wealth Penelope drank from. How insulted she would be. Yet how helpless we were to resist.

70

Hannah called it a premiere, but it was more like a housewarming party. She wouldn't let me get involved in the preparation, but whenever I showed up at Insomnia, something else would've changed—a new poster, a freshly steamed carpet, the popcorn machine finally rinsed out and sent for maintenance. In the middle of February, she handed me the invitation, a physically printed flyer on glossy paper. When she held it out, rusty perm wound tight around her face, I had the dizzying sense that it was my mother standing before me, slipping me one of her many folded notes. I blinked, it was Hannah again.

INSOMNIA PRESENTS

The local premiere of *The Lecturer*

Featuring our very own Arin Yang, part of the Insomnia family

February 21, 2011

7:00 p.m.

Guest of Honor: Genevieve Yang

"Look," she said, too excited to wait for me to notice. "The letters are embossed in gold foil."

"I see it."

"Hen," Lily called, from behind the counter, "you're embarrassing her."

Everyone I knew was invited, along with plenty of people I didn't know. On Monday, the twenty-first, when I showed up at Insomnia after work, the party was already in full swing, even though there was over an hour till the screening began. Lily had assembled platters of mini sandwiches and cocktail sausages, which she handed out on patterned paper plates; Hannah was busy socializing. Streamers made of crepe paper, red and yellow like bougainvillea leaves, were taped to the ceiling and draped festively over every surface; copies of the movie poster plastered the walls; and a blown-up print of the photo we'd taken together, Arin, Hannah, Lily, and I, was framed and propped up on the counter. I smiled a private smile, thinking of the childhood confetti Arin had made with my mother's stolen paper puncher, wishing I had some. No one had noticed me yet, and I took the chance to examine the photo.

Then Hannah spotted me. "The guest of honor," she cried, and a few people turned and smiled. I raised my hand, gratified but a little shy, no longer used to being the center of attention, and noted Micah's absence with relief. I didn't want to do the dance of manners around Micah, who now tended to lurk around the Blue House with an aggrieved look that made me want to punch him.

I spotted a couple of my coworkers in the crowd, including Damien and his wife, who had a toddler strapped to her hip, and waved at them. Then 7:30 came, and it was time to usher people into the halls. I tried to help, but Hannah waved me away, and I ended up standing at the entrance of one of the screening rooms, nodding and thanking people for coming, like I was at a wedding or funeral. More familiar faces flitted by: the barista from that tourist trap on Queen Street; Lorraine; the owners of the French bistro and their children. After the lobby emptied, I felt my heartbeat slow—there'd been no unpleasant shocks in the crowd.

Finally, I went in. A dot of light from a cellphone flashed in my face: Hannah had saved me a seat. I made my way over and sat down.

Thank you, I whispered, and she shushed me. The lights dimmed, the movie began.

71

Arin wasn't lying about playing a small role—she didn't appear till a quarter of the way into the film and only had a couple of scenes. I looked it up later: of the 137-minute total run time Arin appeared in 17. The film was, largely, about a soggy middle-aged man struggling to live with OCD and frequent attacks of intrusive thoughts. *Variety* would call it a timely and tender look at mental health, and IGN would praise the aesthetic decision to render each depiction of an intrusive thought with a slowed frame rate. *The Mary Sue* would protest that this was an excuse to drag out gratuitous violence—who needed to see the Lecturer slamming his beloved wife's skull into the wall or running his own hand through open flames?—but admit the brilliant depiction of deflated modern masculinity that apparently plagued men everywhere. Bitch Media would question the film's very premise of the eponymous Lecturer being a genius—one who forced himself into camouflage among the mediocre minds of lower education, remaining a low-profile math lecturer at a small secondary school while his wife ascended the ranks as research assistant to a prominent economic adviser. But all media coverage concurred that the most moving scenes involved private moments of genuine struggle, where the Lecturer wept, battered by his own mind, desperate not to be a burden and liability to the wife he so loved as she climbed in the public eye. Every morning, he decorated his face with a smile, kissed his wife full on the lips, then braced himself to face down a bunch of lippy fifteen-year-olds as they debated him on binomials. And in that class was Kimmy.

It was Kimmy, no doubt, that we were watching, not Arin. The transformation was so complete that I experienced a slight dissonance looking at her face, fair and blown up on the screen. Arin's features, Arin's slightly too widely spaced eyes, Arin's mildly crooked teeth, but Kimmy's snark, Kimmy's arrogance, Kimmy's tendency to people please. (*The New York Times:* How much of another person's interior struggles can we know? How much excuses it?) Sinking into a world of make-believe, I watch as Kimmy's hand waves in the air, pointing out every tiny mistake the Lecturer makes in class, correcting his grammar, gaze darting to check the reactions of her classmates, seeing if they are amused by her cheek, seeing if they approve.

Guardian: How often will a woman's intellect prove fatal?

In a slowed flight of imagination, the Lecturer visualizes his house exploding, disintegrating the couple, when his wife is selected to give the opening address at a United Nations convention on state welfare. In the film's reality, he congratulates his wife with an elaborate home-cooked meal salted with tears. The next day in school, students do a bad job of pretending not to see his puffy lids, the gray landscapes of skin under his eyes. He falls asleep at his desk after the classrooms empty and is woken, hours later, by Kimmy at the door. She is smirking as he starts and wipes the drool from his mouth. Innocently, Kimmy ventures: she wants to ask about a discrepancy in a worksheet he's given out—is it a mistake, a typo, is she missing something?

He's comforted to find the mistake early in her calculations, the reason she can't tally her equations. See, Kimmy, he says, relief oiling his words and making him bold. You should have double-checked your work with more care. It's arrogance to think you can bully a teacher. You think you know all that, but you really don't.

Oh, Kimmy says, her pride stung, her claws coming out. Don't I?

After all, she's young. She has her whole life ahead of her. In ten years, the Lecturer will still be here, teaching fifteen-year-old kids who would rather be elsewhere. In ten years, who knows where she'll be—she puts her face very close to his—maybe an economist, giving speeches to the world?

Wired: The director certainly checks all his boxes, the rumors of an Oscar-hungry Asian sensation are certainly true. Yet how much of this is hot air?

Kimmy's face is still large on the screen, this suggestion of a future, this flickering possibility staring him down.

As the frame rate slows, his hand shoots out. An anonymous Twitter user bemoans: So, because it's not real we're supposed to find this okay? I'm so done with violence narratives . . .

His hand grabs Kimmy's face, it looks like he might hit her.

The fear that flashes across Kimmy's face is so real, so raw, that he feels his blood rise. It's the first moment of uncertainty he's witnessed in her face, the moment where he shifts, in her eyes, from a dreary middle-aged teacher to a man. She struggles, ineffectively, trying to slip out of his grip. Let me go, I'll report you, how dare you touch me. How dare you? He wants to laugh. Hey, are you deaf? What's wrong with you? She is afraid, now, and opens her mouth again to scream. The Lecturer reacts, slamming his other hand down on her mouth, and she bites him, like a cat, now she is really asking for it, now he is really mad. (*Metacritic*: Despite incredible performances from newcomer and veteran actors alike, one can't help but feel manipulated by the material.) As he paws at her schoolgirl skirt, he decides that he would put it in her, this fear, this knowledge of the world, what it is really like. You can't just go around living your life like there are no stakes. There are consequences to every choice, or don't you know that, Kimmy?

The camera pulls close on Kimmy's face, as her body is shaken, time and time again, as the Lecturer holds her, penetrates her, pours his rage into her. Oh, it is very tastefully done. All the sound effects, jump cuts, close-ups. The gradual, blank stare of Kimmy's eyes, the dead look of resignation and knowledge. The slight gap of her lips, as they fall open in a slight O, the exhales that come surprised and quick with each movement, as if she is a doll, simply being carried along a greater tide, as if despite the knowledge that she cannot fight what is happening, she is still surprised to find herself in this situation. (*Gawker*: A technical marvel, but the escape into cinematic imagination raises questions of artistic accountability. More to the point: Did we need two whole minutes of this? Did we *really*?) And just before it gets to be too much, the camera drifts downward onto her clenched fist, the sinking of her nails into the space between skin and nail, carving out crescents of blood, breaking the hyponychium, tearing her nail.

Ambushed by horror, I can't move. I'm still trying to tally the shifting plates beneath my feet, I recall, suddenly, with revised understanding, the steel in Arin's voice, steel I'd mistaken as anger as she asked, *What do you mean, attacked?* The way she'd leapt to be by my side, her unblinking gaze as she drank in whatever poured forth from my lips, steady in the eye of adrenaline. *Worth it,* she had said. Worth it. Beside me, people are sobbing, crying. I can hear sniffles echoing throughout the theater, a collective holding, and exhaling, of breath. When the camera cuts back to another close-up of Kimmy's head, fallen to one side, turned to look straight into the camera, I start. Both realities crash into each other, extinguishing the last vestiges of dissonance, of doubt, and for the first time I see things exactly as they are. Kimmy's gone. It's Arin looking back at me, drawing me out, questioning me. Arin holding my hand, coaxing me, studying me, doing her research, and then lovingly taking it all for her own.

72

I ran out of Insomnia and into the streets, squatting on the pavement. Retched and retched. Nothing came out.

Hannah appeared beside me momentarily, she wanted to know what was wrong. I claimed food poisoning, but when she asked if I thought it was the cocktail sausages or the sandwiches, I said I wasn't sure, please, Hannah, leave me alone.

She was taken aback. Are you sure, she asked. Yes, yes. Yes. She lingered for a second more, then said, well, that was intense. She's very good, your sister. And left.

The rest of the night proceeded on autopilot. I made it back to Insomnia somehow, I mingled, smiled, nodded, praised Arin's acting. Everyone concurred: even though she wasn't the main character, even though she had the least on-screen time, my God, she seized control of every scene she was in, didn't she? Didn't the camera just love her? They looked at me curiously, a little awed, as if her brilliance could not possibly have fallen from the same tree. Comparing us, sizing me up. Had I known? Had she always been this talented?

Yes, I had. Yes, there was never any question about her brilliance. Yes, she'd always had the steel needed to get the job done. Yes. Yes. Yes. Thank you, Hannah, thank you, Lily. I couldn't ask for more. Did I like everything? Yes. Everything—the premiere, the embossed invitations, the sandwiches and cocktail sausages, all of it. Arin would've loved it, she would've loved to be here. I would send their love to her. I would.

Later I sat, unshowered, in the center of my bed. No. *The* bed. The bed we'd shared. Not mine. Not ever again. Every nerve shrilled with the memory of Arin curved over my body, watching me sleep.

Coaxing me awake. Fingertip to fingertip. Wound to skin. Measuring her handspan against mine, then slipping and entwining our fingers together in a charade of our childhood. I would have to move. Perhaps to one of the empty rooms in the Blue House. But—there, also. Lorraine. Lorraine, melting in the puddle of Arin's sticky, warm affection. Arin, eternally perched on that couch; Arin, drinking from my cup, eating off my spoon. No. Moving wouldn't bleach her betrayal from my life. Had I brought this upon myself, by making a sister of her so many years ago? Drawing her a map of the neighborhood, meticulously marking out the path of my life? What a fool I was to think I could've escaped simply by trading one dim room for another. Everywhere I turned would be a place scoured by Arin. There was nowhere she wouldn't have passed through, dragging her fingers and greedy gaze over, like a trawler's net.

And I would have continued letting her. But for this. This.

My phone lit up, buzzed, went dark. I'd sent Arin just one text, hours ago, after leaving Insomnia.

How could you. I hope it was worth it.

Arin had been calling ever since. But I didn't want to listen to her collect her arguments in that placid, tranquil tone of reason. Hearing her voice would ruin me. Even now, skin scratched raw, I could feel myself itching toward capitulation. Enough. I was done.

I didn't go to work the next day, I didn't send my apologies either. All morning my mind pulsed with electricity, flitting from memory to memory, rinsing it through with the clarity of hindsight. News of the premiere had already begun flooding the internet and my inbox. On Facebook, Penelope had reshared a glowing review—I can't remember from which outlet, *Variety* or *Vogue*—appending a spinning pink heart emoji to her caption. *Hometown hero, so proud of my girl!!* When I saw it I froze. Penelope, too? I did not think it was possible to be stunned further, yet I was. Then my naïveté seared me with shame. Of course Arin had initiated contact with Penelope, of course Penelope had, in her eager, affected way, leapt to broker introduction between director and father. How much had Arin hidden from me, even while biting down on my index finger, recalling a private childhood world inhabited only by us both? Was it not enough for her to have taken over my life, my mother, my future? How much more would she plunder?

The phone was still ringing. I could have turned it off, severed the line, but I didn't. It would have been too definite an answer. Let her wait. Let her suffer.

When the battery died, I shut my phone in the bottom drawer of my desk and left the studio, taking a bus to the city center, then turning on my heel and pacing back in the direction of the Blue House. I thought: Everywhere the light falls, Arin's fingerprints have been also. The sky was as clear as water, the streets scattered with office workers milling about leisurely as they headed back to work postlunch. I stepped around them, phasing through the city like a feral ghost, retracing my steps in a tightening loop.

All of this I had offered up to Arin. All of this she could claim as hers too. The sunlight glinted off the rocks, I ran my fingers along the chain-link fence and stopped.

Everything but this.

Here.

The square of dusty concrete I stood on was indistinguishable from the pavement two steps down, but this was where it had happened. I knew, even though there was absolutely no way of proving it, that in this exact spot I'd been pushed, calmly and carelessly, against the fence. I hadn't been back since the assault, not even with Arin. To her, I'd described the disassociated fog of shock I'd been operating in, the blurring of comprehension, and at the time I truly believed I couldn't have identified the street even if I tried. But my body had brought me back. My fingers closed around the fence, metal cold even after hours in the sun. The wildness quietened. Here was the only thing I had left that was purely my own. The carnal knowledge of fracture's coordinates.

I let go and leaned against the fence, drained of all energy. I sank into a squat, put my face between my knees, and felt the blood rush to my head. I would stay here, I thought. I would never move again.

"Miss?"

I didn't stir.

"Hello, Miss, are you okay?"

The voice was getting louder and louder, like a honk, becoming impossible to ignore. I lifted my head, saw motherly concern scrawled over a stranger's face, and dropped my head again, willing her to vanish.

But she wouldn't let me be. The woman tapped my shoulder.

"Do you need me to call someone?"

She wasn't going to leave me alone. I exhaled, tried to stand, began to say, yes, I'm okay, it's all fine. I'm just tired. But my head was light, I lost my balance and fell over. Sorry, I wanted to say. I don't know what happened there. The woman's hand was still extended toward me, but the look on her face had twisted into horror, and I felt the old urge to reassure her, to tell her I hadn't slept, it wasn't anything serious. She opened her mouth, leaning over me, but I couldn't hear what she was saying. For a second, I couldn't make sense of what was happening, it was incredibly noisy, as if the ocean were screaming. The ocean? My mind caught up, the woman was shouting.

QUAKE.

Quake? Quake. Run. The woman had her hand on my arm, tugging, pulling, then she gave up and I didn't see her go. The street, I didn't see it go either. A building in the distance was on the floor. My eyes were stinging, a thick wall of ash roiled toward me; I scrambled backward on all fours and almost crashed into a jogger, who leapt out of the way, and leapt again, like a gazelle, as a piece of debris appeared in the spot he'd just been in. The cars parallel parked along the street shuddered and wailed, disjointed alarms clashing at one another. My mouth was open, I tasted dryness on my tongue as I ran, tripped, ran, crawled.

The city groaned. And then, for a long time, nothing.

73

That winter, the worst snowstorm in seventy years hit Christ-church. It started in the North Island, where it never snows, and spread to the South, covering everything in a dense, heavy blanket. When I heard the news, I was already back in Singapore. I scrolled through the news coverage, stopping to look at each photo, admiring the halation around each traffic light, the glitter-ing expanse of unbroken white powder that looked so much like a fairy-tale winter. In one picture, the snow was almost bluish gold, scooped up in the mittens of a child holding it up to the camera at sunset. How easy it is to find anything beautiful, I thought. How easy to dispose of crisis in the face of such beauty.

It felt like hours, that afternoon, hours and hours of rolling chaos and panic. Any other city would have been flattened, but Christ-church's stringent building codes limited the disaster. The street I was on was badly hit. The building I'd seen had completely crum-bled, only one person survived. I have no idea what happened to the woman who helped me, or the jogger.

In reality, the earthquake lasted ten seconds. From those ten seconds, one hundred and eighty-five people died. It seemed mirac-ulous that I didn't know any of the dead, only the injured. Lor-raine suffered PTSD and anxiety attacks for nights; eventually she reunited with Damien, even moving in with him and his wife for a while. Micah went home to Philadelphia, cutting his stay short. The boy who'd attacked me, I don't know. Some things you'll never get answers to, but I don't wish him ill. I don't wish him anything at all.

What of Hannah and Lily? I didn't go back to the studio that afternoon, or to Fifield & King. I went to Insomnia. It wasn't a con-scious decision, but once I could move, I stumbled back toward the city, flinching every time the low houses bucked or the pavement boiled. I did not know it then, but as I pushed past the neon-vested firefighters shouting into piles of rubble, people around me were crushed unseen and slowly dying. For days after that, they would continue to die. When I found myself a few streets from the theater, I started running.

They were shaken, they were safe. Hannah and Lily were standing outside Insomnia, arms wrapped around each other, tear tracks streaking through the dust on their cheeks. Initially, I thought it was from the shock, I was crying too. But then I saw the building, the side of which had fallen in.

"Hannah—"

They both turned at the same time. Hannah's eyes, swollen and red, were blank. They searched the air before me, unseeing. Her mouth opened, she laughed.

"It's over," she said. "We aren't going to recover from this. First the house, then Insomnia." Her voice snagged on the theater's name, it broke. She spoke to Lily now in a voice that was thin and wanting. How had I not seen before that Lily, quiet, reticent Lily, was the pillar in their relationship? Yet Lily was crumbling too.

"The contractor was going to come tomorrow, to put in the new shelves."

"That's right, what time tomorrow?"

"Two."

I took a step forward, I said: "Guys—"

They turned to me again, and it abruptly occurred to me that they were in their late forties. They'd already restarted once. Their home had been wrecked in the September quakes, the renovation wasn't even done, and now their life's work was gone. And they would have to keep going. They had no choice. The years stretched out before them, they'd have to sift through the wreckage and rebuild their lives again. I reached out, I wanted to touch them, their arms, their faces, pull them into a hug, convey through touch that which I could not find words to articulate.

Instead, Lily drew back as I approached.

I paused, unsure.

"What do you want, Genevieve?"

"I came to see if you were all right—"

Lily registered the flicker of warmth in Hannah's face, the preparation of cheer. Readying herself to offer me assurance she herself lacked. Hannah had always been unusually generous with me, I realized, yet I'd never stopped to consider its source. Lily's arms, wrapped around Hannah, tightened. "If we're all right? What do you think?"

"I—"

She shook her head. "Go home, Genevieve." Her voice faltered slightly. With her thumb, she brushed some of Hannah's hair out of her eye. Hannah blinked, hard. "Haven't we done enough for you? Go home."

Arin tried all means and ways to reach me. My phone being off, she assumed the worst. She found the Fifield & King office number but the building was abandoned, the Central Business District cordoned off. She reached out to Micah on Facebook, but he hadn't heard from me. The hostel's line wasn't working, and she didn't have Lorraine's personal number. She'd dialed Insomnia too. No dice. In the end, she extracted Lorraine's cell from Micah, then berated him for not volunteering it earlier. Look, he snapped, finally, everyone's going through shit, okay? I'm not a customer service officer. You, your sister. You two should learn some manners.

The Blue House and studio weren't affected structurally, but new cracks spiderwebbed the walls, and the wooden fence had split in places. The worst of it was over, but how was I to know? I was terrified, I wouldn't go back into the studio all afternoon, I paced the tiny patch of garden for hours, eyeing the ground suspiciously. Every muscle tensed in anticipation of another split. But adrenaline eventually gave way to exhaustion. When the world started blurring, I went into the studio, curled up on the floor, and slept badly.

I woke to Lorraine knocking on the door, phone in hand.

"Holy shit," Arin said, her voice burrowing deep in my cranium. "You're alive."

I held the phone away from my ear, stared at it. I hung up.

Lorraine wouldn't take the phone from me. It started ringing in my hand. I stared at it blankly, brought it to my face again. "Hello?"

"Jie, what—did you just hang up on me? Do you know how worried Auntie—"

I hung up.

The phone buzzed once more. This time I flinched, then hit the red button without picking up. Was there no ocean I could swim across to escape her? "Here," I said, "take it."

Lorraine's face was a flat line.

"She called to know I'm safe, now she knows."

I saw in Lorraine's eyes the decision not to get involved. She pocketed her phone. Before leaving, she said: "At least you have a home to go back to."

74

Electricity returned after a day. I felt curiously detached as I retrieved my phone from the bottom drawer and plugged it in to charge. When it came back to life, I had three hundred and two missed calls and messages, from Arin, from Micah, from work. Some from acquaintances I hadn't spoken to in years, their memory of me drawn sharply back into existence by the irresistible lure of disaster.

I scrolled to the first message, sent right around the time of the earthquake, and began reading. Texts of concern, relaying the news as if I might have somehow missed it, texts demanding confirmation of status: alive, not alive. Texts from the Singapore Embassy asking me to mark myself as safe in the earthquakes—vaguely, I noted that someone must have previously registered me for consular services, since I'd forgotten to do it myself, and just as quickly I understood—my mother. Later, much later, when I unblocked her number from my phone, months of lost messages would tumble in, dating all the way back from when I first moved. The last one, sent without hope in the aftermath of the quakes, simply read: Is anyone there?

Reading it right then would have felled me. But in that room, on the other side of disaster, watching the missives pile up, watching Arin's panic unravel, all I felt was a mounting clarity. Here I was, sitting cross-legged on my bed. And what did I have, a skinned knee. A ringing ankle, rolled from skidding over and around acres of destruction. I really could have died.

Please mark yourself as safe in the Christchurch earthquakes. Please.

From Micah: Your sister is looking for you. Again. Are you all right. And then: I hope you're okay. Really. I do.

And through it all, a barrage of messages from Arin. Pick up. Oh God, pick up. If anyone is seeing this, pick up. The news carried stories of aftershocks, disaster after disaster rolling in, and with each update, her insistent texts, calls. Jie. I know you're there. Don't hang up. Are you seriously choosing this moment to throw a tantrum, are you fucking kidding me, Jie, do you have any sense of proportion at all.

I let the messages spill forth, amass, build. In the absence of my answers, Arin began reasoning with herself. I would have told you. I wanted to. The minute we wrapped that scene, I was going to call. But I stopped myself. It might not even look like anything in the final cut. I didn't want to dredge up old wounds. Retraumatize you. Look. We reshot it many times. It's a complicated sequence, it demands a lot. And yes, where the fund of experience stops an actor must reach for stories, for emotional attention and information, and yes, I'd take it back if I could. In fact. I did try. The director promised. He promised he wouldn't use that particular take. But. It was the best take. But. I have no control over the edit. But. Actors have no creative jurisdiction. You know that. You know. Besides. Is it that bad. So bad that you have to do this.

Every hour more deaths were reported, someone had collapsed of an aftershock-induced heart attack. My mother was glued to the news, close to catatonic.

Please mark yourself as safe in the Christchurch earthquakes.

It's bad, Arin texted. Her tone pleading now. Really bad. Jie. I've never seen Auntie like this. I'll do anything. Please. What will it take. Just call her.

I forced my hand to stay. More, I thought to myself, just a little more. Nearly there.

A message, so transparently calculated it turned my stomach: You're killing your mother.

I kept reading till I reached the end. There was a gap of a couple of hours between the last message she sent me and the one before it. Arin's tone had cooled significantly; the last message was formal and straightforward.

Genevieve. I am booking a flight to Christchurch for your mother and myself. We will see you in a day.

The message had come in less than five minutes ago. The pot had simmered and boiled over. It was time. I swiped the message away, pulled up the keypad, and dialed.

75

Arin picked up before the first ring finished its trill. As expected, she'd been calling my bluff. Nothing had been booked, but her voice was hoarse from crying.

"Jie Jie," she rasped. "Thank God."

"Hey." My voice was controlled and steady. "Good show. You're going to be very successful, I'm proud of you."

"What?"

I repeated: "I'm happy for you."

She sounded confused. "Are you safe? Are you coming home?" When I replied in the negative, she asked, almost childishly: "But why? If it's about the movie, I'm sorry, come back and we can talk about it properly."

"What do you mean, why? I live here."

She expected anger, maybe accusation, she wasn't prepared to deal with this strange calmness. "In the middle of a disaster zone?" she asked, then laughed once. An uncertain sound. "Jie, you don't live there, you just work there. It sounds like things are really bad, stop playing."

"I'm not coming back."

"Why?"

"Because I don't want to see you or live with you anymore."

So: we'd breached the grounds of our actual conversation. The parameters defined, the shape of the problem presenting itself to be systematically tackled. I felt Arin clicking into a different gear, her mind darting this way and that, weighing her options. "What exactly are you angry about?"

I thought of Arin, beside me in those lupin fields, grabbing my hand and holding it up.

"Worth it," I quoted.

"All right, Jie," Arin said, relaxing into reason, "I was wrong, I should have told you about that scene before you saw it, but I wasn't trying to hurt you."

"It's not about that."

"Okay, then what's it about?"

She was being so sensible that I could feel the membrane between us quiver. How impossible it was to articulate her violation. Two throwaway minutes in a character's imagination, barely skimming even the film's own reality. For an exhilarating second I was tempted to fall into her version of events. But the memory of Arin coaxing me into confidence intruded, real concern underlined with a calculating curiosity, questions framed and filed away in her mind for future reference. I remembered the ways she deflected my questions about the film, the ways she sat, angled away from me, whenever she flipped through the script.

The script. Did she realize as soon as I called that she would need this part of my experience to fulfill her role?

I thought of the three days between my call and her arrival. A slim, desperate thread of hope flowered. I asked: "How long?"

"How long what?"

"When did you get the script? Before or after I called?"

In her silence it withered away.

I thought I'd prepared sufficiently for this conversation, but the confirmation left me breathless. So what I had taken for love, she'd meant as strategy. The entire ten days we'd spent together in Christchurch, days which had been so precious to me, she had been duplicitous, and here she was asking me to let it go.

Me, who had nothing. Me, a bank she had drawn on, again and again. How had it taken me this long to see it? I was back in the theater of my humiliation, watching Arin step cleanly into the scene of assault, my pain draped around her like a cape.

"Do you know," I said, shaking, "how much it meant to me when you came? And do you know what it was like to realize: every second we were together, you were just doing *research*?"

"I *was* there for you."

"Don't." I interrupted. I stood abruptly, my face burning. "Don't be glib with me. You knew what you needed from the *second* I called, and you made a calculated decision. How very many chances you had to bring it up. Ten whole days."

From the window I watched Lorraine leave the Blue House, wandering aimlessly down the main road, touching the gates separating each house. Across the street, a neighbor emerged, trying to lead her back. She nodded, then shook her head, dazed. The phone was slippery against my cheek, my right arm ached from gripping it so tight.

I continued: "You know what the worst part was?"

Arin was quiet. No doubt waiting for me to lay all my cards on the table, waiting to know the extent of damage control required.

"I would have given you everything, Mei. I always have. If you had just told me what you needed, I would have excavated my whole soul for you. You didn't have to lie."

My cheeks hurt. I realized I was grinning widely, lips drawn over my teeth, as if Arin could see me, as if I needed to pantomime courage even now. "So I'm done, actually. I'm not coming back."

Immediately, she said: "I'll fly over."

I'd been prepared for this too, for her to deploy money as needed. "I won't be here. I'll take a nothing job somewhere, doing nothing work." I felt her flinch. But I was a daughter of wasted potential. I didn't need a career. I could give everything up if it meant being free.

Almost everything.

I continued: "I won't be the first person in our family to vanish."

A sharp intake of breath. Just as I knew she would, Arin demanded: "You'd do that to Auntie?"

"You choose."

"What?"

I'd left once. My mistake was being sentimental, not cauterizing the wound. Letting it fester. "You want my life, take it. But I won't be there by your side."

"You'll break her heart."

I steeled myself. "Yes."

She balked at the certainty in my voice. "Jie Jie. You know I can't let you do that."

I pinched my thigh, very hard. "Then leave. Go be successful. I meant what I said: you really were very good. Your career is just starting, you don't need me anymore. You've taken everything."

"It's not a matter of needing you." Her voice trembled, I imagined her offering me a crooked smile. "I want to be with you. Isn't that enough?"

But she was wrong to think I'd concede this time. It was Arin who'd taught me that stakes were everything. "Whichever way you choose, I'll take the other path."

Arin began crying. Her voice was shaking so hard it was barely audible, yet no matter how hard I listened, I couldn't tell if grief was all it was, or if there was an element of calculation in her performance.

"Don't be like this, Jie," she pleaded, and I realized: I would never again be able to tell. I would always hold a part of myself back, always wonder at the glaze of every heartfelt sentiment. My knees nearly buckled; I leaned against the wall and closed my eyes. "We're family," she said.

"We were. We don't have to be."

"But we promised."

At her bewilderment I finally cracked. How naïve we had been to chain ourselves to a promise, as if a couple of childish words solemnly uttered one moonlit night would spare us from subsequent years of hurt. Even now, as Arin's soft, suffocating pleas covered me like a draught, I nearly yielded. But then I opened my eyes and saw my reflection in the window staring back at me with a terrible, cruel gaze. I hated her, hated how unrecognizable she was. Who was I, what had I become. How far I had come to meet myself at the end of the line.

I felt horribly cold as I turned away.

"No, Arin," I said, and I knew she'd gone stock-still at the great and awful calm in my voice. "I'm begging you. Give me my life back. I don't want this anymore."

A stunned exhale. "You don't?"

I repeated: "I don't."

Arin was quiet for a long time.

When she spoke, I heard realization coalescing in her voice.

"When I couldn't reach you," she said slowly, "I thought you'd died. You *let* me think you died."

Love is an action word, I thought. It can be committed, like a crime. "That's correct."

Her voice was thick with grief. "Fine. If this is what it's come to, I'll go."

I wanted to be absolutely clear. "If I ever hear from you, I'll leave again, this time forever."

Another long pause.

"Yes," she said. She'd finally composed herself, her voice was hard. "I understood you the first time."

A week after that, I confirmed that the Asian expansion plans were dead in the water, sent my notice in to Damien, paid Lorraine the penalty for the early termination of the lease, booked a flight, and flew back to Singapore, to that dinky, one-bedroom flat deep in the heart of Bedok.

....

June 2015

Singapore

76

From the outside, how might our lives have appeared to strangers? I say *our,* which in June 2015 meant my mother and me, but I could just as easily have been referring to any number of the interchangeable bodies that populated our corner of Bedok. We still lived in the same house I grew up in, but you didn't actually have to see it to know how it looked, nor to understand the number of steps needed to cross from the bed to the bathroom—after all, it was the same prefabricated apartment everyone else lived in, too, organized and replicated within the thousands of high-rise concrete slabs across the country. If you came closer, small things might start to distinguish this neighborhood from the next—you might notice the exercise corner outfitted with new, granulated rubber flooring that stunk under the noonday sun, or realize the HDB flats had gone from blue to beige in the latest five-year paint cycle. But no matter how individual elements blinked in and out of existence, the overall physical character of the neighborhood stayed the same.

In the afternoons, the streets would flood with students released from nearby schools, rushing to various enrichment centers or back to their homes and desks, weaving in their oblivious, rowdy manner around the implements of the neighborhood, among which I counted myself. Perhaps their pace picked up a little as they hurried past me, but they never looked up and into my face. I didn't mind. It had taken me a long time to get to this point, to be able to exist unscrutinized and uninterfered with. To lift the lid of the neighborhood and look more closely at the ordinary lives swarming the earth like ants, to come close to the churning infernos of their minds, would be to realize that the nutty auntie squatting by the drain and tenderly shampooing the roots of a plant she was propagating remained constantly surprised to find herself aged, would be to realize that within the humming fish ball uncle lived the suppressed spirit of an operatic tenor weeping for the stage. How vast the legion of unrealized, contradictory, impractical ghosts crammed within each mortal body was. How it scalded one to look so closely. It was too much. Just thinking about it was enough to make me cry.

I had returned, four years ago, from Christchurch to a mother much diminished. Arin had kept her word and vanished a day before my return. To my mother she'd begged away: the press tour really couldn't be delayed any longer, the film was outperforming every indicator, they had to capitalize on the momentum of its success.

It wasn't hard to infer that we'd had a catastrophic fight, though I doubt my mother knew the exact terms of our separation. But Arin's abrupt decision to leave right before I returned must have made it obvious—for her to beseech Arin to stay would be to forgo me. Yet Arin's disingenuous excuse, leveraging that old metric of our childhood—success—shamed her deeply. She knew my mother couldn't argue against it, she was offering her an easy way out. And my mother took it. (*Go, go, I'm proud of you, you're doing so well.* How disappointed Arin must have been, how she must have hoped beyond hope for a different outcome.)

Did my mother suspect, even as Arin tossed disparate scraps of her existence into that hard-shell suitcase, the nature of Arin's departure? Possibly. Likely. When I appeared on the threshold of our apartment, less than twenty-four hours after Arin left, my mother rushed up to me violently and grabbed the meat of my left forearm. I was taller than she was, and could see the flecks of dandruff peppering her unwashed crown as she pressed her fingers into my skin, ascertaining the physical reality of my return. Then she flung the arm back at me, turned away, and broke down.

I looked around the flat, breathed in its warm air. Later, going through the house, I would find the logic of what Arin took and left incomprehensible—a gel mask in the refrigerator, half her clothes still in our shared closet; yet she'd scooped up every last sock, even the ones with holes in them. But that was later. Standing in the doorway, only one difference impressed itself upon me. The shoji screen was folded and leaning against the wall, its rectangle of floor given over to an unfamiliar tall bookcase stuffed with cooking pots, folded grocery bags, and old newspapers. From the second I left, my mother must have returned to the bedroom, shared a bed with her other daughter. I recalled the protective tone in Arin's voice when I asked after my mother that last night in Christchurch, realized she had been trying to protect my mother from me.

Me, who had always proved so willing to be careless and cruel with my mother's heart. I swayed on my feet; I started laughing.

The thin, lonely sound of my laughter bounced around the house, accumulated. I couldn't stop, not till my mother took her face out of her hands and shot me a frightened look. I saw at once that the six months I'd vanished, the decisive way I'd excised her from my life, the death scare, had robbed her of something, unraveled some fundamental confidence of hers. I'd become the wild daughter she'd mortgaged every last thing to hold on to. Her first and original daughter, born of a sacrifice when she herself was barely twenty, a choice that, once made, was condemned to repeat itself and devour the future. How much more would she sacrifice for me? Some questions are too terrible to be asked. But I knew it, she knew it, worst of all: Arin knew it.

I sobered up.

"Ma," I said, reaching for her, "Ma, I'm sorry. I'm back now, I'm here."

I found work as a roadshow promoter for a local telecommunications firm. Four days a week and on every alternate weekend, I pulled on a Dri-Fit red polo shirt and stationed myself outside malls, waving with an enthusiasm I did not feel at strangers, trying to trap them in conversations about various phone plans. It was naïve to assume I could do this and not run into acquaintances in a country as small as Singapore, but the personality of a salesgirl was its own disguise, and in fact for months not a single face distinguished itself as I touted family and home internet bundle deals. Then, one humid afternoon in October, sweating outside a mall in Ang Mo Kio, I locked eyes with my old academic nemesis, Jia Min.

She was pushing a stroller, and when our eyes met, the years melted away and a wicked pleasure transformed her wearied face as she deliberately glazed over and pretended not to recognize me.

Then the baby wailed, the harried look returned. She maneuvered the stroller past the roadshow stand and into the jaws of the air-conditioned mall behind me.

After that I couldn't stop running into people. Teachers from school, old classmates, faces I thought I recognized from my time at the ice cream shop. Most of them ignored me, some struggled to place me, only a couple of times did they stop, out of some misguided social courtesy. One of these people was Guo. Once so relentlessly ambitious he didn't flinch in the middle of a national exam even after being stung by a bee, he'd become convivial, the type of person who liked small talk and laughed a lot. He spotted me first.

Hey, he quipped, remember how you asked me to marry you?

Panicked, I glanced at his wife. But she was smiling broadly too. She set her large, tinted aviators on top of her head, looked seriously over my pamphlets, asked me intelligent questions, and signed up for a home broadband and cable plan. Slowly, I relaxed, pushing my hair out of my face. I even allowed myself to joke a little as I packed up their new internet modem. As they were leaving, Guo told me about an upcoming class reunion. You should come, he said, pulling out a name card, scribbling details on the back, and underlining the words Class Reunion twice. I studied the card. He was a software engineer now.

Yeah, I said. Sure. Maybe.

I looked again at his wife, who seemed determined to hold my gaze. There was no hint of jealousy in her manner; in fact, as a second passed, two seconds, three, I felt increasingly unsettled by her piercing, interested eye contact. Then it hit me: she reminded me of the type of woman who'd unfailingly thank bellboys for doing their job. I felt myself recoiling into invisibility, hardening once again into the guise of a salesgirl. Some perspiration dripped into my eye and stung. I folded their receipt in half, shoved it at her.

If you have any questions about the bundle, I said, you can call the hotline printed on the side of your modem.

On the way home, I stopped by the grocery store and watched my mother from afar.

I did this often, without her knowledge. We'd grown polite with each other, our conversations mainly comprised of functional exchanges, yet in moments of silence I sensed her eyeing me with the sad and suspicious betrayal of dogs watching doors. At first I thought she was doing this on purpose, parading her hurt in order to choke me with guilt. I couldn't stand it, I wanted to shout at her to straighten her back, to stop slinking around. But then I realized she behaved like this outside the house too. I watched, stricken, as she bagged and rang up items for strangers at the grocery store, enduring their abuse whenever she moved a little too slowly. Never retaliating, either in anger or consolation. Simply continuing with her work, moving at the exact same pace.

I forced myself to keep watching until my agitation subsided, then went home and tossed Guo's name card in the kitchen bin. It reappeared on the dresser, details of the class reunion facing up. I tossed it in the bin again. A couple of days later, my mother emptied the bin, and it was gone.

Arin's film won no awards, but it catapulted her and the director into the global spotlight. For a period it was impossible to go anywhere without being confronted with posters bearing her face, and press gifts materialized constantly at our doorstep, congratulating her on the film even though it had made headlines that she was in residence at Awantas, filming a series of commercials as their new ambassador. My mother and I waded, for months, through impractical vases of flowers wilting under the equatorial heat, their floral stink wafting faintly through the house.

Then the wolves came. It started right before the one-year anniversary of the film's premiere, with an emotionally raw essay by a sexual assault survivor, condemning the director's infamous choice to add the scenes of assault later, almost as garnish, for narrative and commercial gain. The essay went viral, it caused a lot of trouble for the director. The story behind the film, once deployed so effectively to captivate the world's attention, now turned viewers against him. Then, reports of grueling on-set conditions emerged, scandalizing a public unversed in the realities of production and labor.

Why should a cameraman, a grip, an art director, suffer seventeen-hour days in service of one man's ambition? And what an ambition. Old interviews resurfaced, critics tearing into the director with an uncomfortable glee. A particularly cruel media outlet created a trauma bingo card for the film, while another buzzy website, hiding behind the excuse of satire, published a recipe for critical success with ingredients consisting of various identity markers the director had claimed in his early bid for investors, comparing the film's initial acclaim to the emperor's new clothes. The actor who played the eponymous Lecturer came out in defense of the director, protesting the absurd standards he was being held to, but when public distaste extended to him, he renounced complicity as an actor bound to cleave to a director's vision.

And in this storm of scrutiny, Arin's silence was resounding.

My mother and I followed each development separately and with an anxious impotence. She was terrified that each new lash of the critics' whip might clip Arin. I knew she ached at the thought of Arin bearing this alone. My own fear was less precise. It had been easy to choose me when I was the only daughter in crisis, but now? One night, as my mother slept, I crept out of bed, heart pounding, unplugged her phone from its charger, turned the volume down to zero, and set a random song to play on repeat. The whole operation took less than five minutes, my mother barely stirred.

By dawn, the phone's battery was flat. She frowned, plugged it back in, then headed to work.

I left the house with her, doubled back once we parted ways. Read through the messages spanning a year. There weren't many. Arin was based in Taiwan now, trying to break into the Chinese drama market; this much I knew from the news. The messages from my mother were infrequent, cautious not to presume. How are you? Are you healthy? What should I do with these deliveries for you? And Arin, her devoted and outstanding daughter, replied promptly each time with variations on the same theme. Things couldn't possibly be better. Success upon success. Not to worry. Keep the gifts if you want them, otherwise, throw them away. Short, declarative statements, never instigating or encouraging further conversation.

Each unfailingly cheery response a blade, slowly prying my mother's despairing fingers from her life.

How familiar this slow accretion of insularity, this shimmering dread of yet another loved one pulling away. How disastrously her attempts at corralling it backfired over the years. Still, my mother tried. When the media frenzy peaked, she must have broken from her titanic restraint, picked up her phone, and reached out one last time: *Mei, is everything okay?*

I'm doing really well, Auntie!

After that, nothing. I turned my mother's phone off, replaced it on the nightstand. I'd been afraid, initially, that I'd find evidence of her drawing Arin back, tempting her, in the face of all this trouble, to seek refuge with us. But Arin's pleasant messages couldn't be clearer: my mother had made her choice. Besides, even if Arin needed help, it wasn't the kind we could give her. Anyone who's ever had the slightest brush with fame understands that it's like contagion. Once you've let your image out you can't sweep it back into a jar, the only way forward is through. Arin had to find her own way.

And she did. Not a single announcement was made, yet somehow the news that Arin had donated her entire salary from the film to a mental health nonprofit was leaked. Who on this sad earth knew how much she was paid—two hundred dollars per day— besides Arin and me? When pressed for comment, Arin demurred, protesting gratitude for a mere novice having been given an opportunity at all. It really was fucking charming: a move that cemented the director's downfall while evading culpability.

I watched the strokes of her strategy unfold with admiration and fury, the way she managed the press, my mother. The way she had tried to manage me. I savored my anger, let it blot out my relief. That February, the shortest month in the year, I accosted so many people on the streets, and with such vigor, that I made more on commission than I did my entire time as a telecommunications promoter.

Throughout this, my mother was saving the front page, movie page, and any feature or write-up concerning Arin from our papers.

She did this so steadily, so surreptitiously, waiting a day or two to retrieve the newspapers from the trash and cut out the relevant articles, that I didn't realize what she was doing until much later.

But then I discovered she'd been hoarding everything.

I had been searching for something else when I saw the corner of the photo album peeking out from behind several large bottles of liquid detergent, tucked away under the kitchen sink. My hand stilled. Then I retrieved the album slowly, flipped through its pages. On the very first page, pasted next to selected school report cards, was the CORAL award certificate for Arin's old essay, "Land of Opportunity." Then: reviews, fashion features, op-eds. Headlines about the film premiering at Cannes, about Arin's nomination for several awards, news of her being cast in another, then another, then another film, regionally, then internationally. A glossy magazine page with one of Arin's rare interviews, given after her third film was announced, where in response to an interviewer's question on dealing with success so young, Arin proffered the cliché of leaning on her supportive family, recalling images of the grateful child, the filial daughter. A cliché so broad she could disappear into it completely. I imagined her visualizing me, at that very moment, scanning her mocking words, daring me to say a single contrary thing. Who would I say it to? Who would believe me?

I threw out the whole album.

The day my mother realized what I'd done was the only time we addressed our separation directly. She straightened, spine cracking from bending under the sink, a crumpling sheet of newspaper in hand, then turned, startled by my presence. I saw a flash of her old personality on her face as she stuck out a hand, as if I might produce the massive floral album from my back pocket.

"Give it back."

"It's gone."

Her eyes dropped to my fists, balled tight at my sides. I knew she'd seen the scars on my palms, I knew she'd tiptoed around me the past two years. I thought she'd back down now too. But then she said: "I've seen you."

"What?"

"I've seen you, late at night, under the blankets with your phone, when you think I'm asleep. Watching her movies, crying."

She was wrong. There was only one thing of Arin's I ever watched and rewatched compulsively. I told myself to stop, I torrented the movie file illegally and deleted it off my phone hundreds of times, but always, always, I succumbed.

She continued, in a familiar, pleading tone: "Gen—"

Was I a fool to have believed my shame private? Blinded by humiliation, I turned, stumbling.

"Where are you going?" she cried.

The pure, devastating panic in her voice arrested me. "Nowhere," I said finally. "I have nowhere to go." I dropped to the couch, shaking. After a long moment, she came and sat beside me. We didn't speak. Our bodies heaved, trying to steady ourselves. Although not a single part of our skin touched, I felt like we were falling endlessly, from a great height, our desperate arms locked around each other, both snare and salvation.

After that, I started sneaking out of the house in the middle of the night.

I knew my mother woke to my absences; I knew what they did to her. Yet these nighttime expeditions were my one, cruel, private joy, and I couldn't bring myself to stop. I wandered aimlessly down the humid streets, occasionally riding the night bus alone, looping between home and the interchange. Mostly I just walked. I didn't need to wake for those twelve-hour roadshow shifts as often anymore, so I stayed out late, pushing myself to the brink of exhaustion. Times had changed. I'd started seeing ads on Instagram for the same phone plans I promoted under the sweltering sun and knew I would have to find new work soon. But I made no move to better my situation, I wanted calamity to meet me where I was.

I lived in this pale shadow of freedom for weeks. But one night, as I was sitting alone in a red plastic booth, my mother's tired face materialized beyond the glass. I started. It was 3:00 a.m. As her eyes met mine, I realized she'd known where I'd been all along.

She pushed through the doors, entered. This wasn't the same McDonald's of my childhood, which had been demolished. It was a different one, by the sports complex, with a stylish, upgraded design, murals of Ronald McDonald and his friends replaced with modern, color-blocked walls. But as she slid into the seat across from me, the smell of salt swirled in the air, and for a surreal second it felt like I was a child again.

Silently, I pushed my tray toward her. She picked up a fry as if it were a matchstick, bit its tip off, and peeked back up at me.

I cleared my throat, embarrassed. "I found a fourth way."

"Yes?"

"To eat a fry. Look." I jabbed a golden fry into the side of my melting vanilla cone, pulled it out, offered it to her. My mother glanced at the holes in the soft serve, as if the ice cream had been eaten through by worms, and smiled.

"It's good. Sweet."

"Better when the fries are hot. They're soggy now." I started to stand, I said: "I'll get a fresh batch," but she shook her head and I sat back down.

"This is fine."

We smiled at each other tentatively, and I felt my spirits lift. The fries disappeared, slowly at first, then more and more quickly as we locked eyes and scarfed them down in unspoken competition. When we were down to the last two, I stifled a laugh. I distributed the remaining fries: one for her, one for me.

"I didn't mean to worry you," I said quietly. There was no ice cream left, just a sticky white puddle that had seeped into the tray paper. My face was warm; I shook my head and pressed the back of my hand to my cheek to calm myself. Then I saw her expression. "What is it?"

She raised her fry to mine, and when I didn't move, she looked at it, put it back down on the tray. I watched her straighten, dredge up the old charm of my childhood, and cock her head to a side. My heart stuttered at the sight of her unpainted lips curling into a rueful, determined smile.

Then in a calm, almost cheerful manner, she told me that she'd been feeling a lump in her breast, a lump as hard as the tip of her nose, and that it'd been there for a while now.

. . .

The months following her diagnosis were the worst of my life, made hell by the constant well-meaning refrain from doctors, neighbors, aunties, and my mother, that breast cancer was the easiest of cancers to resolve. I drained my MediSave and battled the paperwork required for hospital subsidies, I fought with everyone—lashing out at my father, who seemed befuddled by the monstrous daughter who'd returned from New Zealand; snapping at my mother, who acted like the diagnosis was a magical portal back into the early years of my childhood. After the mastectomy, she'd quit her job at the grocery store and returned to the photocopy shop, boisterously buddying up with the photocopy auntie again, as if time had erased all grudges and rendered her gossiping hand in my father's abandonment a speed bump rather than a break in their friendship. My mother signed up for a library card, too, and carried thick, optimistic volumes into the hospital's waiting room, only to abandon them once she got home in favor of tending to a potted sansevieria one of the void deck aunties gave her, which often meant long stretches of blowing exhaled carbon dioxide at it to make it grow.

Absurd, childish actions. This reversal in personality terrified me. I had heard of the massive energy burst that came just before death, and became convinced she was losing her mind. Everything put her in a good mood, even my irritation, and whenever she caught me crying she'd yank me into her skinny arms and draw whirling patterns on my skin, laughing as I pulled away. Even when the worst had passed, even when the chemotherapy course was nearly over, I couldn't relax.

My mother found my jumpiness hilarious.

"Look at me," she hooted, when the last of her eyebrows fell out of her sore, irradiated skin. "I'm an alien."

"Stop it."

She pulled her singlet up, over her chest, to show me the tattooed dots on her abdomen used to align the radiation machine. "These are my landing coordinates," she announced, and laughed some more.

Yet it was all bravado. When Dana, her new oncologist, praised my mother for how well she was taking to the medication, my mother lifted her hand in a girlish gesture, as if to brush an imaginary fringe from her eyes. The week after, I dropped my mother off for her radiotherapy session, then, instead of waiting outside the treatment room, boarded the hospital shuttle to the train station, intending to sell my hair to a wig shop in Fortune Center in exchange for money to purchase her a hairpiece.

I knew Arin was in town for a press tour, I knew the Ritz was putting her up. Arin's assistant was sloppy with Instagram, and a picture of the iconic hexagonal bathroom windows overlooking the Singapore River had appeared on her feed for two hours before being taken down. Tracking Arin, who didn't have social media, through fan accounts and the posts of people in her orbit had become second nature, my ability to gauge the distance between us directly correlational to peace of mind. It helped that Arin was famously prolific and had worked nonstop since leaving home— never dropping the ball on the public's attention, staying in the news just often enough to give her fans a constant stream of tidbits to chew on and dissect online. I told no one this, and back when I was still regularly working shifts as a roadshow promoter would often call in sick if she was in Singapore. But in that sleep-deprived, panicked period, my mind failed to knit these realities together until I was passing through Bugis Mall to get to Fortune Center. I pushed my way out of the train exit, through the mall, emerged into the harsh sunlight, and found myself face-to-face with a gigantic outdoor stage advertising a meet-and-greet with the cast of Arin's latest movie.

I froze, my body leaking iron and sweat, I fled. I'm pretty sure I knocked over a couple of unleashed toddlers as I grasped for the closest bathroom and locked myself in a cubicle. How could I have been so careless. Breathe, I told myself, breathe. My heaves echoed in the empty bathroom, my hair plastered itself to my scalp; later I would find a long line of red rashes along the underwire of my bra, from heat and irritation. I leaned my head against the pristine mauve walls of the stall and forced myself to calm down.

The door opened.

A distinctive patter muffled by the elevation of a stiletto heel. The smell of honey and apples, and underneath that, the faint tinge of gasoline. I knew. I knew. I knew. There was no way to know for sure, but I knew. I drew my feet up onto the toilet seat so my sandals wouldn't show in the gap beneath the cubicle door, imagined her flinging the door open anyway, barging back into my life. The tap was running, the click of a lipstick case being twisted and extended. The hand dryer roared. A pause. Awareness prickling. There was a slight inhale, a beat of hesitation moistening the air.

Then: an explosion of giggles, as a scream of schoolgirls whirled into the bathroom, a series of gasps interrupting the rush of gossip. When I finally emerged from the cubicle, I didn't recognize a single face in the mirror. Not even mine.

I was late picking my mother up that day. She tactfully avoided the blistered lower lip I'd bit down on in my panic, the bad body odor the wig shop nearly turned me away for, and complimented my newly shorn hair, enthusiastic over the return to my childhood bob. But she didn't want the wig I bought. She insisted that she'd always wanted to shave her head.

"I look great," she said, running a hand over her prickly scalp.

"The wig was expensive."

"Get a refund."

Her ebullience ached me. For the past months, every time my mother fell quiet, I'd tense, afraid she was weighing her words, preparing to ask for Arin. Yet I remembered the naked fear in her voice each time I turned away from her, demanding to know where I was going, the way her eyes sought me out each morning to confirm my presence. I thought of the last exchange between my mother and Arin. What was I doing. I put the wig back in its box, closed my eyes, then said quietly: "She's in town. You should go see her, if you want."

For a moment, I trembled, imagining my mother brightening, gathering all her unreasonable energy and bounding toward the door.

But she just smiled. "And burden her now? Forget it. Troubles are all we can offer her. In any case, daughters always leave."

"I came back," I said.

Even then I couldn't help myself, I wanted absolution.

My mother reached out and pushed a lock of hair behind my left ear. "You did."

. . .

To the doctors, to Dana, my mother acted as if she had only one daughter. Even when the churn of gossip made plain our relationship to Arin, my mother never mentioned her. And restrained by professional courtesy, the doctors never referenced Arin either, though when my mother's hormone-suppression medication raised concerns over osteoporosis, they began floating newer treatments, more comfortable ones, that might be available to us for a price. My mother refused it all.

I'd barely paid off the debt from my degree, and now to make each medical payment I took on more work. In addition to the dwindling roadshow shifts, I started a job marking papers at a tuition center, I went to people's homes, cleaned, ironed, watched their children. It wasn't enough. The various specialists would order further scans and tests during my mother's quarterly follow-up consultations, constantly scribbling down recommendations for bone-strengthening treatments or private physiotherapist sessions, oblivious to the accumulating costs.

Dana tried her best. She asked around and got information on different plans, drugs, schemes, trials, all of which were heavily subsidized, but—since my parents had never legally separated and still had the house under their name, signaling some kind of means— not free. If I could get a regular job, perhaps we could get a loan, but it wasn't a guarantee, and besides, what starting pay with my skill set would match the cumulative income of my many different part-time jobs? Dana didn't understand. Emboldened by her friendship with my mother, she perpetually floated new solutions and ideas, explaining that this wasn't a cost worth scrimping on.

I'm well, aren't I? my mother replied, each time Dana dropped by the photocopy shop, bearing gifts of vitamins and supplements. And when Dana offered to take my mother out for a nice dinner to celebrate the cancer being in remission, my mother shook her sparkling, shaved head.

Save your money, she said, exuberant again, *I have everything I need.*

. . .

I worked harder than ever, keeping a wary eye on my mother, who, against all odds, had begun looking increasingly rejuvenated, like a dying plant suddenly nourished by sunlight and water. Her infectious energy spread through the neighborhood as she gleefully slid back into the flock of void deck aunties. A month went by, then another. Then another. Slowly, despite my fears, I started to admit that each day, my mother continued not dying. Each new dawn brought her a step further into the firm embrace of life. For the first time in a long while, I felt peace. My irritation at her childish manner became routine, dulled at the edges, mixing with the relief I felt watching her chomp down her medications with the meals I bought. Whenever she caught me staring, my mother would make a show of finishing every last grain of rice, smacking her lips and presenting me with her empty bowl. I didn't show it but I was proud. Proud as if I had licked the bowl clean myself. Late at night, I'd lie awake counting each of her progressively deeper, clearer breaths. I could see it: glimmers of a future where all this would remain a distant, bad memory. It was so close I could taste it in the air.

Until the leptomeningeal disease. Terminal: a word I did and didn't understand. Couldn't. Call her, my mother said, for the first time in four years. I never ask anything of you. Just call her.

I was eight again, surrendering my life to Arin. Watching my mother claim her in the mall.

Yes, I said, I'm trying. But I wasn't.

Ever since her latest diagnosis my sleep had been intermittent and disturbed. The second my mother shifted in bed, my eyes would jump open, body jerking as if someone had pressed an exposed wire to my skin. My heart would thump, my forehead becoming clammy. And I would turn to look at my mother, whose eyes would already be open, full of mirth.

The last regular day we had together, at the start of June 2015, was no different. I jolted awake to my mother already in the process of sitting up. She'd lost even more weight. Her skin clung to her bones, as if it were simply a damp cloth sticking to the cage of her skeleton. Instead of covering this up, she embraced it. With a pair of kitchen scissors she cut the sleeves off her T-shirts, widened the holes of her singlets. Now, she lived in these handmade muscle tees, and whenever she bent over just slightly, you could see her chest through the armholes, the raised, pink-brown keratin of scar tissue, the paperlike texture of her skin as it pressed against her ribs. Her hair had started to grow out and she hadn't the energy to keep shearing it, so it resembled a short buzz cut. She looked like an emancipated sailor, or an army boy.

It was six. "Where are you going?"

"Work."

This again. I closed my eyes briefly, then sat up. It'd been a month since the initial diagnosis. Four out of the promised six weeks had passed. My mother no longer pretended to keep her regular working schedule, she headed to the photocopying shop as and when she felt up to it. Otherwise, she wandered around the house and neighborhood, then teased me when I got annoyed at her lack of accountability.

"The shop doesn't even open till eight."

"So I should stay in bed till seven forty-five?"

I scowled, and a smile broke out on her face. She had an unreasonable amount of energy for someone supposedly on her deathbed.

I closed my eyes again, took stock of the day. I needed to go to the tuition center to return my papers and pick up another set to mark. A cleaning job had canceled for the week, the family away on holiday somewhere in Japan, so I had extra time—perhaps I'd see if I could get additional papers. Otherwise, I'd offer my services to the perpetually understaffed value dollar shop that had replaced the bakery after the bakery auntie's daughter struck it rich and sent her off on early retirement cruises around the world. My mother had brought up the issue of my getting a proper job more than once, but in this hammock of time where she teetered on the precipice of life, it seemed stupid to take on full-time employment. After, I almost said. I caught myself in time. But she'd seen the thought cross my face, and smirked.

Despite her snark, she moved slowly, lowering herself off her side of the bed. Then she was off. I could hear her pottering about in the kitchen, pouring herself some cereal. She'd become addicted to sugar, our house was full of generic grocery store breakfast cereals, covered in frosted sugar icing and saturated with food coloring. Some even had little marshmallows that melted when you stirred them into milk. I'd objected to that too—cancer cells snacked on sugar—but she'd dramatically clutched her chest and asked me to let her live her last days in peace.

She was impossible. I could hear her moving around again; I got up and left the bedroom.

On the dining table she'd set out warm water in our cups. Before her was a bowl of cereal and two plates with fried eggs on them. She was lowering herself gingerly onto one of the dining chairs, and when I emerged, her face turned upward to me, bright with hope. My chest ached. What was it Dana had said? We were rapidly approaching the edge of a cliff. But she didn't live with my mother, didn't know how stubborn she could be. Look at her now, popping candy like a child. I could see her prancing around like this, teasing and goading me, for as long as it took for me to cave and call Arin. I pushed the thought out of my head, pulled the chair out, and sat down.

"How do you feel?" I asked, then, before she could answer, continued: "You look better today."

"Better?" She was smiling again, and with some relief, I felt the annoyance return. I looked at the eggs.

"If you wanted eggs, you should have said. I could have done that."

She tapped the side of her cereal bowl with her spoon. "Let's eat."

The eggs were undercooked. When my fork pierced the egg white, a transparent liquid wobbled and spilt over onto the plate. I looked up quickly, her face fell.

"I'll do it," I said. "Eat your cereal." She looked down at her bowl obediently, I took both plates to the kitchen. The stove was a mess, eggshell bits near the knob, and on the floor I could see a gleaming smear, telltale signs of a broken egg, badly cleaned up. I turned on the fire, tipped our eggs back into the pan, and waited till they were cooked through. Then I brought them out again. The cereal was barely touched, but a few drops of milk decorated the table. I pretended not to notice and put her plate down.

"Eat." My voice was gruff, and I felt my face get warm.

Her teasing manner returned. "Eat?"

"Eat, Ma."

It was 7:30 when she left the house. Once alone, I wiped up the milk, cleaned the kitchen, scrubbed the floor—it was stickier than I'd realized, she must have dropped more than one egg—and studied the contents of our fridge. I'd have to do groceries later. In the day, she could have all the sugar she wanted, but the compromise was that we would eat a proper meal at night together. On my way out, I took the usual detour and stopped by the photocopying shop to make sure she was actually there, that she hadn't invented the day's itinerary and gone wandering off elsewhere instead. As I approached the row of shops, I saw her tired figure moving very slowly, bent over the copy machine, light spilling out of the copier as it scanned whatever it held. Her bright orange singlet, embarrassingly loud, calling attention to her skinny frame. She looked up before I could walk away, and delight flashed across her face.

"It's worse than having a boyfriend," she commented, and the photocopying auntie laughed loudly.

"I'm going to work now," I said.

"Okay," she replied, rolling her eyes dramatically at the photocopying auntie. The photocopying auntie grinned back, the two of them like kids indulging in this brief jape: How silly our children are, they're the old people, they're the nagging ones. "Bye."

I could still hear her raspy laugh as I walked away.

The bus ride, the train ride, the tuition center, all of it was unremarkable. The twenty-five-year-old running the center barely glanced up as she passed me the next stack of essays. I took a seat in one of the empty classrooms and started on the pile. Most of it was unreadable. I went over the essays as my mother had once upon a time, picking out spelling and grammatical errors, circling mixed metaphors and scribbling vocabulary suggestions in the margins. It took half an hour per piece. Occasionally, I'd draw a little smiley face on an essay that was particularly well done, that is to say, attempted with care. You could really tell which students were trying and which ones were forced to take these extra enrichment classes by their parents to maintain a competitive edge. I used to resent these kids, oblivious to the advantages their parents bestowed upon them, but not anymore. Who was I to say anything when I, too, had become a cog in the production line of academic success? I trudged through the dense pages of prose, struck out lines, flipped the papers, continued.

I was about halfway through the stack when my phone rang.

I registered the tone of voice before understanding what was being said, it was frenetic and high-pitched, a warble I took a while to place: the voice of the photocopy auntie. You have to come now, she was saying, not to the shop, no, to the hospital. She gave me the address, repeated herself. Hello, are you there, are you still listening? Your mother collapsed, she wasn't doing anything, she was just trying to get off a chair and attend to a customer when she toppled right off and hit the floor. She hasn't opened her eyes since. Do you understand, are you still there?

I pulled the phone away from my ear, staring at it. The teeny electronic voice continued vibrating, frantic, through the earpiece. Hello, hello, are you there.

Yes, I said, finally, bringing the phone back to my face. Yes, I'm here, I'm coming now.

Did I have insurance? No. Medical plans? No. How much was there in my mother's MediSave? Nothing, it was all used up thanks to the previous hospitalizations and operations. All right, how about using mine? But I didn't have a proper job, the type with employer contributions toward my CPF, so there was barely anything in my MediSave. The nurse made a note in her computer. Her lack of surprise wounded me. I wanted to defend myself, but couldn't find the words. She waved her hand at me: all right then, go on in.

There were twelve beds crammed close together in the ward, with only a small sliver of space between each one, where a foldable chair could fit. I blinked. It wasn't the same ward my mother had stayed in two years back, but the clinical stagnancy in the air, the smell of bleach and urine, all of it was exactly the same. I understood at once that the suffocating dread that had characterized my every waking moment over the course of my mother's breast cancer treatment had never truly dissipated, only retreated to a consistent, dangerous undertow, biding its time. Panic gurgled in my chest. I sensed a presence near me and turned helplessly to my left, half expecting to see Dana standing there. A fat nurse, different from the one at the reception desk, pushed past me, dragging along a mop bucket on wheels, heading straight toward an oatmeal-colored splatter at the end of the ward. Ah, who was this nurse, I didn't know her. The unfamiliarity jolted me, triggering a temporary relief. That's right, my mother was in remission, we'd had both her breasts lopped off, one after the other. She had been laughing and joking with the photocopying auntie this morning, likening me to a boyfriend. But as quickly as relief sparked, the dread insisted: yes, all that was true, and then. And then. I looked around, and there it was, her orange shirt hanging off the end of a bedpost, like a flag.

Someone had changed my mother out of the morning's clothes and into the pale blue hospital gown. She was between two older women, one of whom was rambling deliriously in Cantonese, the other knocked out and smelling like shit. A patient two beds over was pulling on a cord, trying to get the fat nurse's attention: She's done it again, she's shit herself, this is no way to live. The fat nurse was almost done wiping up whatever that spill was, she was saying, patiently, kindly, wait, I'll be with you in a moment. But the patient wouldn't stop. She could still assert herself, she was not that sick, look at how loud her voice was, how strong. And in the middle of all that chaos—my mother curled up on the mattress, her body barely taking up half the bed.

The photocopying auntie was seated beside her, she got up as I approached. I could see her mouth moving, making sounds. I forced myself to focus.

"She wasn't doing anything out of the ordinary, she fell over, just like that."

It was the same thing she'd said earlier, but she was repeating it, with urgency. She needed me to understand that it wasn't her fault.

My mother hadn't even really been working, the photocopying auntie said, they didn't let her do much when she was at the shop, they understood that she just wanted to be around friends, to maintain a semblance of normalcy, and they were happy to maintain the illusion for as long as she continued to show up. Apparently, she'd been perched on a high stool while gossiping about a recurring customer who flirted outrageously with the ten-dollar barber, leading the entire row of shop aunties to speculate on the state of that customer's marriage. Apparently, as they were all cackling, a schoolboy had walked up, clutching a binder, needing thirty-two copies of the notes for the rest of his class. Apparently, my mother had raised a finger as he approached, put her other hand on the edge of the stool, lowered herself onto the floor successfully and rather smoothly, then, turning toward the boy, took one step, let out a surprised gasp of air, and toppled over onto the floor.

The photocopying auntie was in tears, she was shaking. I told her to go home, I'd take over from here. She wrestled briefly between disapproval and relief at how calm my voice was, but when I put my hand on her shoulder, she seemed comforted.

"I'll be back tomorrow."

"No need," I said, but when I turned to look, she was already gone. I found myself staring into the eyes of the geriatric patient who'd been asleep seconds prior. The smell of shit wafted toward me. She smiled.

Dana wasn't on shift that day, but she showed up as visiting hours were about to end. I unknotted myself from the chair, ignoring the screaming pins and needles in my calves. I hadn't realized it until that moment, but I'd been holding out for Dana. I felt better the minute I saw her. Even though it was close to eight, she looked fresh, her hair scraped back into a glossy, competent ponytail, the lines around her eyes taut but attentive. She was already filled in on the situation. A nurse trailed behind her, nodding. Yes, Dr. Ng, No, Dr. Ng, Right away, Dr. Ng. Dana put a hand on the nurse's sleeve, thanking her. The nurse backed out of the room, gratified. Then she turned to me and my brief prickle of comfort dissolved.

I spoke loudly. "She hasn't woken up at all. You said six weeks."

Dana didn't say a word.

"It's only been four weeks. Not six."

Her voice was surprisingly gentle. "That was an approximation, Genevieve. Not a guarantee."

"You didn't say that." But it was a desperate comment. She acknowledged it with a tilt of her head, and not much else.

"You should call your family," she said quietly. Dana raised a hand and I flinched, thinking she was going to touch me, squeeze my arm, offer some false comfort. But she just gestured to the drip cord plugged into my mother's skinny arm. "She's not in pain, Genevieve. We've done all we can to make her comfortable. She's on a lot of morphine right now."

All we can. I looked at her, I said: "Why are you here?"

Dana sat by my mother's side and touched her head gently, running her hand over the soft fuzz of her shaved scalp. "It's not good to be alone, at the end."

I shook my head. "I'm here."

"No," she said, finally looking up at me. "I was referring to you."

77

My father arrived late that night, long past visiting hours. Dana had arranged for an exception to be made, and when he entered, a couple of the other patients grumbled. He ignored them and came straight to us. I had seen him fewer than ten times since my return to Singapore, not out of any residual animosity, but because of a lack of necessity. He seemed to have shrunk too. His spine was curved and compressed from living in the front seat of his cab, and his gait was crooked, leaning more heavily on his left. But his hair was freshly trimmed, close to his head. He didn't cry when he saw my mother. Instead, he let out a long, tired sigh.

My mother had been drifting in and out of consciousness, we weren't sure if she understood where she was. Whenever I spoke to her, or touched her, she only smiled dreamily in response. At my father's sigh, though, her eyes fluttered open, then widened a notch, in surprise.

"Hi," she said softly. It was the first clear thing that had emerged from her lips the entire day.

"Hi." He shook his head, offering her a lopsided smile. "Long time no see."

Her brows spasmed, she was trying to roll her eyes. They'd met for lunch barely a month ago, when she'd told him about the terminal diagnosis, but as far as I knew they hadn't stayed in contact outside of that. I was hurt: I'd been here, I'd been by her side all day. But her consciousness surfaced only for him.

"Ma," I said, stepping forward. Her eyes drifted to me. They were bright, and clear, and I felt hope stutter. "It's me. How are you feeling."

She took a long time to respond. Her voice kept catching, she dropped the ends of each word multiple times.

"You can finally get a job," she said.

"Ma, seriously."

Her frame shook with soundless laughter, reveling in the delight of having successfully goaded me. Then she said, "I'm tired." And closed her eyes again.

My father stood by her side, watching till he was sure she was sound asleep. When the sandpaper rasp of her breathing steadied, he gestured at the corridor. I followed him into the hallway.

"Where's your sister?"

I'd expected the question, but still, I felt the old echoes of anger awaken. He didn't get to make demands when he was the one who'd abandoned us. He understood, and leaned heavily against the wall.

"Do you remember," he said, changing tacks, "the year you were eighteen?"

"The year you left."

"Yes."

"Are you going to say you regretted it? It's too late for that."

He shook his head. "I know."

I latched on to the anger. "Don't you dare apologize now." I wanted his temper to meet mine, for us to relocate to the familiar ground of conflict.

But he didn't retaliate. He gestured helplessly, arms flopping back down by his side. In the harsh fluorescent light, I saw that he was old, and very, very tired. "Gen," he said, "how long are you going to keep punishing your mother?"

I faltered. "What?"

He closed his eyes briefly; when he opened them again, they were glistening with pain. "Why do you think she hasn't reached out to Arin herself? Why do you think she waited for you?"

Because, I wanted to say, she wanted to torture me. She could have called Arin, it wasn't as if they hadn't corresponded. Forcing *me* to do it was a childish, vindictive move, once again she was behaving as she'd liked, gleeful at the thought of me handcuffed by her schemes. Besides, what did my father know? Hadn't I cared for her these past years? Didn't I know better than anyone how she'd been doing? The way she would, any time now, bounce back up to bargain with me, employing that inexhaustible, taunting energy?

So what was she doing, lying in bed? But as my father held my gaze, I found myself unable to articulate any of this.

My father straightened his back, pulling himself to his full height. He no longer towered above me, we stood at eye level. His tone shifted; he was trying to draw on his authority as my father, tug on the thread of owed respect. "You've made it so no one can say a thing to you, Gen." He saw that I was about to interrupt and continued bravely. "But they deserve to see each other one last time. If you wait till you're ready to forgive Arin it'll be too late. Don't be like me." Then his shoulders slumped, and he deflated again. "I miss your mother."

I turned around and went back into the ward, leaving him alone in the corridor. When I came back out, he was gone.

78

My mother was awake and clear-eyed when I woke the next morning, with a neck cramp from my pretzeled position.

"How did you sleep?" she asked.

"I should be asking you that." I stretched, cracked my neck, and studied her. She smiled at me, and I could suddenly see how much it cost to maintain her fragile charm. I got up and moved toward her, putting my hand on her forehead, her cheek, coming to rest on her arm. While I did this, she stayed quiet. I surprised us both by bending over and squeezing her in a small hug. There was so little of her. When I pulled away, my eyes were damp.

Her left wrist spasmed, she was trying to form a talking head. I closed my hand around hers, lowering it back down onto the bed.

"Gen," she whispered, "will you do something for me?"

Here it was. I braced myself for the inevitable, I said: "Yes."

But the effort of speech had tired her. In a soft voice she mumbled something, and I could only catch a couple of words. Water.

"You want water?"

I poured some out into a cup, but she shook her head. I put my face close to her lips, then realized she was asking me to water her sansevieria.

"You must be better," I told her, feeling a ridiculous rush of disappointment, "if you're worrying about your houseplants. Hurry up and get well then, so we can go home."

She smiled briefly, hand relaxing in mine. I fed her some water anyway, watched her throat bob obediently. Her eyes sparkled, her old mischief returning. "Don't get your hopes up, I'm still dying."

Was this what death looked like? How was it possible? I sat in the bedside chair, maintaining our eye contact, afraid that if I looked away she'd slip back into sleep.

Some time passed. I could see the exhaustion seeping back into her gaze, her energy clouding. "Ma," I said, hesitating. "Why did you want *me* to call Arin?"

She didn't respond. I tried again, differently.

"Do you still want me to call her?"

She was fading. "It's up to you."

Was it? Why *had* she left it up to me?

"Hey," I rolled her skin in between my thumb and forefinger, pinching it lightly. "Don't sleep. Stay with me."

"You're so clingy," she whispered.

The woman next to us started crying, she had soiled herself again. I endured it for as long as possible, but my mother's brow furrowed, obviously disturbed by the smell. I patted my mother's hand and her lips lifted in a small smile, yes, yes, I'm here. I got up, pulled the cord for the nurse. But the smell had reached the old woman on my mother's other side, she woke and started wailing loudly too. The nurses rushed in, too late, trying to placate one and clean the other. In the opposite row of beds, a young boy who'd been wheeled in the night before, postoperation, grimaced in pain. When things settled down, I turned back to my mother and was dismayed to find that she'd dozed off, a little bit of drool coming down the side of her lips. I wiped it with a napkin, and she shuddered, but didn't wake.

Things continued like this for the next few hours. I kept waiting for her to wake again, but she didn't. When a nurse came in to announce the end of visiting hours, I touched my mother's cheek. She didn't stir. I went home.

Dana caught me the next morning as I was arguing with the hospital's registration desk. It was seven, an hour before official visitation hours, and I'd been fighting with the nurse for twenty minutes. When Dana appeared, hurrying over, the nurse threw her a grateful glance and practically shoved me in her direction.

Dana looked over my hair, my bloodshot eyes, and I flinched, feeling the twinges of embarrassment for the first time that day. "Come on," she said finally. "I'll bring you in."

Early that morning, unable to sleep, I'd carried my mother's sansevieria to the kitchen, intending to water it, then leave it near the window. But the pot was heavy, my hand slipped. It hit the floor at an angle and cracked. As I lifted the plant, loose dirt sprinkling all over the floor, something white peeked out from the soil.

Teeth.

I rushed into the bedroom, rummaged through my mother's underwear drawer. Throughout childhood, my mother had disinfected and hoarded all of Arin's and my fallen milk teeth in a coin box, like a sentimental magpie, something I'd forgotten about till now, but as I flipped through her clothes I realized the coin box was gone, had been gone for God knows how long. Back in the kitchen I dug my horrified fingers into the soil, ignoring the tangle of roots, landing on another, and another, and another white nub.

Dana had barely let me into the ward when I took off, making for my mother's bed. I grabbed her arm, my fingers leaving brown streaks on her skin. "Wake up," I hissed. "Wake up."

I felt Dana's hand on my shoulder. A warning. But I couldn't stop. I shook my mother a few more times, then stuck a hand into my pocket and pulled forth a handful of dirt. "Look." I showed it to Dana. Bits of the soil fell through my fingers and onto the white bedsheets, onto the floor. In my palm lay two tiny, angular teeth. Arin's, or mine? Impossible to tell. Was this yet another one of her sly gestures, meant to prod and provoke? Dana stared at the teeth in my hand, confused. I turned back to my mother. "What's the meaning of this? What kind of fucked-up game are you playing?"

But even as I asked, I knew. She hadn't intended for me to find them. Ever. I had a bad personality, I would have reacted exactly like this; I would have interpreted it as my mother forcing Arin on me through guilt or manipulation, and my resentment would've been renewed. She missed Arin; of course she did. Yet all she could enact were these useless, impotent gestures, burying the teeth to hide them from me, afraid that in my rage I'd toss them out if I came across them, like I did the photo album. Was that why she so desperately insisted that *I* be the one to call Arin, that *I* take the first step toward reunion? Because she rightly feared that summoning Arin herself would shatter any chance of our reconciliation? And were her attempts to ensure that I wouldn't be alone after she passed worth sacrificing even her own well-being and desires to see her other daughter? *How long are you going to keep punishing your mother?* I thought of her brooding over the sansevieria, exhaling softly. Before me, my mother stirred, mouth falling open in a dense, tortured gasp.

A nurse appeared by my mother's side, increased her painkillers.

"Genevieve," Dana said, glancing at the other patients in the ward. The boy in the bed across from us was watching warily. Had I been shouting? My head hurt. I quietened, drawing a couple of ragged breaths. Then I followed Dana out of the ward and into one of the bathrooms, where she left me to wash up.

When I reemerged, Dana and my father were standing together, shaking hands. Her face revealed no surprise as she introduced herself to this crumpled man who was very clearly not a church deacon; immediately I realized that Dana had known my mother was lying all along. As I approached, my father nodded distractedly and handed me a Styrofoam box bearing food, as if there'd been no hitch in our relationship, my anger from before already forgotten. Back in the ward, someone had changed my mother into a clean hospital gown, mopped the floor. There was a yellowing bruise on my mother's forearm where I'd gripped her, and my father dropped into the chair, slowly massaging her skin in a gentle circular motion. I stared at the bruise in horror, feeling castigated by Dana's silence.

As she turned to leave, I caught her elbow. "You're not going to say anything about this morning?"

I expected her to reprimand me. Instead, I was surprised to see her eyes wet. "I know it's not my place," Dana said. "But I don't think your mother is playing a game with you."

It stung to hear my words repeated back at me.

She quietly added: "She gave you something, you give her something."

"What's that supposed to mean?"

"Only that you won't have this chance forever."

On the bed, my mother smiled and writhed.

79

I'd anticipated difficulties in reaching Arin. It had been four years since we last spoke, and I wasn't even sure she'd kept her number. The last correspondence any of us had had with her was those sad messages between Arin and my mother, a year after her debut. So much could have happened between then and now. So much had. It was 5:00 a.m. in Germany, where she'd been spotted on set for a new, untitled project two days ago. I pressed my back against the walls of the hospital corridor to stop myself from pacing and focused on the odd, slightly off-kilter ring of an international call being routed, heart punching in my chest.

I have no idea how long I waited. When the ringing stopped, I thought, for a very brief moment, that the call had been dropped, I thought, wildly, that at least I had tried. But then her voice floated, cold and amused, in my ear.

"Look who it is at last," Arin said. "To what do I owe the honor?"

Her voice slammed me back into my body. For a brief moment, I was paralyzed by the irrational urge to hang up, to protect her from what was to come. She had no idea. I had jealously guarded everything: the trials, the cancer, the diagnosis, thinking I could handle it all. I'd kept everything to myself.

"Well, *Genevieve*," she said, as the silence stretched, "if you're calling just to breathe down the line, some of us actually have lives to lead—"

"Arin," I said, interrupting. "It's Ma."

Things moved very quickly after that. In the seventeen hours between my phone call and Arin's arrival, her manager patched ahead, making arrangements for my mother to be transferred into a private, Class A ward. Arin had insisted. She was already unhappy that Dana had blocked her attempts to move my mother to a different, better hospital across town, citing that it wasn't wise to move her this late, and there'd been a fight on the phone I wasn't privy to. The compromise was the private ward within the same hospital, which wasn't easy to get at such short notice either. But Arin's money could, apparently, make anything happen.

Arin stayed in contact with the hospital the entire time she was in the air, flying business class from Berlin to Singapore. She wanted to know if there were any updates. There were none. My mother hadn't registered the move beyond a continuous spasm of her fingers, which they later identified as a mini-stroke. To make things worse, the nurses assured us that it was normal, that my mother had probably been having little strokes this entire time.

Normal, they had said. Strokes. We'd reached the point where these words were used in the same sentence. My surprise sneaking up on me like a spy.

I heard Arin before I saw her: the flurry of nurses, the gasps and double takes that preceded the urgent click-click of her heels. Accelerating with each step, a timer spending itself down. A second of silence, tending to infinity.

The door opened.

After staring at Arin in print and on-screen for so long, seeing her in the flesh was a shock. Her hair, now a deep auburn, was put up in a rumpled bun with strands falling messily around her face, likely untouched since disembarking from the airplane; her skin was makeup-free and supple from stardom; her high forehead, which she was once so ashamed of, shone proudly with matted oil. And she seemed shorter than I'd remembered, somehow. Our eyes met, our hearts staggered in unison. Her jaw was tight, but her fury briefly splintered into shock, as she took in my appearance.

Then she turned away and laid eyes on my mother. Arin's right knee wobbled, and suddenly I saw my mother, not as the frail body I'd become habituated to over the past few years, but as Arin must have seen her, grotesquely reduced. Arin drew in a long, shuddering breath, a sound so raw everyone in the room flinched.

She went to my mother's side, bent over, and whispered, "Auntie. Auntie, I'm here."

My mother didn't move.

She composed herself and nodded at the nurse, who stepped forward and provided an update, with an air of deference that was never offered to me. My mother hadn't been lucid since they moved her to the new room, but on this amount of morphine, that was expected. Also, they'd stopped administering fluids, since she'd rejected all treatment at the start of her diagnosis. Any fluids or antibiotics were counterintuitive to the death sentence of the disease; they would only prolong her suffering. She was very dehydrated, she was in the process of dying. She might resurface for a second or two, but it wasn't guaranteed. The nurse trailed off.

Arin couldn't accept this. "What treatments are available at this stage?"

"The patient indicated—"

Arin curled her lip in irritation and the nurse fell silent. I recalled Arin's face plastering the outside of every MRT train a year back, her brilliant, blown-up smile sailing along the overground train tracks crisscrossing the country during her ambassadorship for Invisalign Asia, but seeing her impeccably straight teeth in real life stunned me. How easily had she made that decision; had she felt anything at all when she bit down on her own thumb and saw, for the first time, the little goblin face erased? Or had she truly severed the past from her life, a goblin unstitching its shadow from its heel? She spoke, her alto voice clipped, each syllable articulated precisely. "I said, what's available?"

The nurse didn't know what to do, she looked like she might cry. I stepped in, heart pounding. "It's not what Ma would want."

Arin didn't even look at me. She turned back to the bed.

For the next forty-eight hours, Arin didn't move. She didn't leave my mother's side, she didn't eat, she didn't raise her head even to greet my father when he appeared again. She kept her eyes trained on my mother. Every so often, she'd whisper, intensely, "Auntie, I'm here."

It was as if I didn't exist. When I stepped forward to touch my mother's head, or wipe the spittle that formed in little bubbles by her mouth, Arin didn't move. She kept clinging to my mother's hand, not acknowledging my presence. Her face, when I studied it, maintained an expression of determination, the same strong-willed focus of our childhood. She was, I knew, willing my mother to wake up, even simply for a second.

It didn't work.

Arin's manager came and went, liaising with the doctors, arranging for the room temperature to be modulated every few hours, harassing the nurses for solutions that didn't exist. Her job seemed primarily to consist of asking the same questions over and over until someone gave up and provided the miracle answer we had all been waiting for. She brought food for us, packed an overnight bag, which neither Arin nor I touched, and tried, one time, to get an answer from Arin about some work-related commitment that had popped up. She just needed a yes or no answer, but Arin ignored her. Then the manager went back to harassing the nurses, even haranguing Dana, who eventually said: "Ma'am, this is a public hospital."

For two days, my mother lay there, on the hospital bed, in that private ward, the drip pumping morphine and comfort into her blood, breath whistling through her gaping lips. She didn't move, didn't flinch, didn't struggle. She could have been back in the Class C ward for all the difference the upgrade made. But on the third day after Arin's arrival, my mother stirred.

Everyone—my father, leaning against the wall; me, standing behind Arin; the manager, working on her laptop in a corner—snapped to attention. The manager went off to call for the nurses, Arin leaned in closer, and said: "Auntie, I'm here. Auntie."

Dana appeared, panting, but hovered by the door without entering.

My mother's breathing got raspier, louder. Her lids flickered rapidly, her fingers twitched. I looked from her to Dana, and back again—she was having a stroke, was she having a stroke? Dana didn't move, just kept her eyes on my mother, her face unreadable.

My mother's eyes opened slowly.

"Auntie."

But she didn't give any sign of having heard Arin. Her eyes stayed fixed straight ahead, at the ceiling. Arin's grip on my mother's hand tightened. My mother's wrist blanched from the pressure, and I had to stop myself from stepping forward. Arin tried again, her voice desperately controlled.

"Auntie, it's Arin." Then, irrationally, she broke from the same words she'd been repeating over the last two days, and continued, muttering urgently: "I'm sorry I took so long, but I'm here now. I don't blame you. For anything, for all of it. Can you hear me? I don't." She rubbed my mother's arm, caressing it jerkily. "Please. I need you to know."

My mother's eyes flickered some more, not registering her voice. Then, they closed again, and did not reopen.

"Arin," I said, after it became clear that my mother had gone back to sleep. It was the first I'd spoken directly to her since she'd arrived.

Arin didn't look at me. Her entire body was taut, every muscle held in place. I put a hand out, brushing her sleeve lightly. It was like an electric current had shocked her, her body tensed and jolted; finally, she turned.

Her eyes were bloodshot, her skin sallow from lack of sleep. One of her lash extensions had become dislodged and hung off the cliff of her left cheekbone like a feather. The tiny indentations of acne scars had been erased from her forehead, but the smatter of sunspots on her cheeks remained; I noted with mild disappointment how the canvas of her face succumbed to its selected history. Yet she looked so lost that I suppressed it all; I wanted to take her face in my hands and wipe away her tears with my thumb.

She recoiled from my touch. "Why? Why didn't you tell me?"

Maligned, I said: "You know why."

My father left the room, the nurses with him. Neither of us turned to watch him go. I felt the air shift, as Dana closed the door behind her, leaving just Arin and me in the room.

"Besides," I continued, "don't put this all on me. I saw your messages. You pushed her away too—"

I broke off. Arin's body had twisted in a single, violent convulsion, and I thought she might hit me. "Does it make you happy to believe that?" she spat. "Are you glad that with your stupid, small life you've done this to us?"

Arin looked at me, at my stunned expression, then made a sound that was a mix between a sob and a laugh.

"You shit," she said. She covered my mother's small ears, and repeated: "You absolute shit." But the energy had gone out of her, the insult fell flat.

She turned away and buried her face in my mother's side, the way she did when we were kids. Her hair was still in its airplane bun, the roots along her hairline grimy from days-old sweat and emitting the warm odor of our childhood, of salt and gasoline. For a split second I imagined my mother stirring, responding to her presence. Turning her wrist to stroke Arin's cheek. The image so vivid, the shock of relief flooded my veins momentarily. But no—she remained immobile on the bed. "Arin—"

She looked up, eyes wild.

"Do you understand," she mumbled, "what you've done. Do you understand that she was my mother too."

The body registers before the heart understands. I blinked, then blinked again. My mother was dying. Arin slowly started to sob, her shoulders heaving. She made a low, keening sound, and I felt myself moving automatically, reaching for her. But before I could touch Arin, comfort her, she slapped my hand away.

80

My father found me standing at the end of the hospital corridor, forehead pressed against the windowpane. Children were running around the hospital courtyard, unaware of their adjacency to death. A little girl was squatting near a bush next to the drain, plucking at the deep red ixora clusters, pulling the stem from the center of each bloom and placing it on her tongue to taste the nectar. I continued watching her, not moving even when my father came to stand beside me. Only when the little girl got up and left, called away by someone I couldn't see, did I raise my head and look at my father, leaving an oily smudge on the glass.

"It's been so long since I've seen a kid eat an ixora flower," I said. "I actually don't remember the last time I've seen an ixora bush."

"That's because you two devoured every ixora bush in Bedok," he replied. "You plucked them to extinction."

I turned away from the window. "Is she awake?"

"She's the same." It was the best we could hope for.

We were both making an effort not to look at the private ward's door. He asked, "Are you going to stay out here?"

I glanced toward the window again. As long as I stood by this window, I thought, things would stay exactly the same inside the ward. My mother would hover, suspended, in this thin state between life and death; Arin would remain by her side. It was the same magical thinking, I realized, that I'd operated on these last years. Believing my mother would stubbornly hold on till Arin appeared. A sudden, wild panic swirled up: had I triggered the beginning of the end, by calling Arin? No. Hubris, even now, to assume I might affect the flow of time. All I'd done was force everyone around me to bear the cost of my pride.

My father, seeing that I wasn't going to respond, left me there and shuffled back slowly toward the ward. I watched him through the window's reflection, leaning heavily on his left side.

"Pa," I called, and he paused before the door. "I left it too late, didn't I?"

His fingers twitched, and I suddenly saw them as I did in my childhood, trying to close around a pair of phantom car keys, itching to leave. But he held his hand out to me. "Come, Gen," he said. "Let's go in."

81

My mother hung on for another two days, but never regained consciousness. When her blood pressure started dropping, there was none of the frenzied hospital action I'd come to expect. The path forward was clear, nothing could be done. We gathered around her bedside, Arin, my father, and I. Dana hung back slightly, giving us privacy, but watching, still. Arin's small, pale hand dangled by her side, and I began to reach out, from pure habit, but stopped myself in time. Arin shifted, her hand moved away. *Ma, I thought recklessly, can you hear us? We're both here for you to reprimand, so stop playing, open your eyes.* But my pleas rang false even to myself. Once you're ejected from the Eden of imagination, you can't claw your way back in. The clarity of grief was unbearable. My mother was dying. Yet, still I tried. *Just one last time. Let this be another joke of yours. Ma, please.* But this was no trick, it was happening, it was here. In between each breath my mother drew, awful silence. The anticipation and dread that stretched between each rasp acute to the point of pain. For once in my lousy life, there was nowhere to hide. The ruthless seconds continued to tick. The gaps between each breath extended, lengthened, and finally, settled into permanence. There was no death rattle, no final exhale. Only a long silence, broken by Dana, quietly, from behind us, calling time.

82

Did it rain? Did the sun continue to blister? Did even a single ixora flower hide, unplucked, in the garden beyond? I must have made calls, or someone else must have. There were things to be signed. Yet in those unending hours afterward, nothing was certain except the fact of my mother's unextraordinary body, slowly stiffening on the bed. That morning she was first diagnosed, even as she pulled on a fresh set of clean clothes and bounded off into the neighborhood, did this same certainty descend upon her too? How rare it is to be offered foresight into one's future. How foolish the daughters who squander it. At some point I touched her index finger with mine and knew that she was gone.

83

We didn't have a funeral. My mother wasn't religious or superstitious, she didn't believe in the afterlife, not the Christian or the Taoist one, so there was no point. The three of us stood in Mandai Crematorium, watching through the glass windows as the staff, dressed in black, long-sleeved shirts, slowly pushed the teak coffin across the viewing gallery and into the next room, where the cremation would take place. My father wept, but quietly, in a self-contained way. Beside me, Arin held herself deathly still. We were standing so close my skin trembled every time she drew a breath, but throughout the ceremony not a single thread of our clothing touched.

Afterward, as we were leaving the viewing gallery, my father pushed ahead, almost blindly, through the tinted swinging doors. Sunlight came in like a slice. The abrupt presence of the steel threshold between this room and the unreasonable world beyond, emptied of my mother, made me stumble; Arin's hand instinctively shot out and caught me before I fell. I steadied myself, she retracted her arm. My father glanced back unseeingly at the both of us. He nodded, unable to speak, and left in his taxi.

Arin's manager had arranged for a car to come for her. We hadn't exchanged any words since the hospital, but standing together in the driveway, she opened her mouth and spoke first.

"What will you do now?"

Even though she'd cleaned up, the dark circles under her eyes and the slight puffiness around her cheeks were obvious. She didn't hide them under sunglasses, as I'd expected, but wore her grief with dignity. Other cremations were happening, cars and hired coaches kept pulling up to the driveway, unloading clusters of weeping families and relatives, who paused briefly at the sight of Arin. A teenager looked as if she might have approached Arin to ask for a photo, but her mother restrained her. They moved on, and entered one of the other viewing galleries. I waited for the people to pass. "I don't know."

She nodded, as if the answer was what she'd expected. In her demeanor, I no longer sensed any hostility, only a drained detachment.

"What about you?"

Arin pulled a slim metal case of cigarettes out of her bag, lit one, and offered it to me. I hadn't known she smoked. When I didn't take it, she shrugged, raised it to her lips, and took a thick drag.

"I'm leaving tonight." She didn't offer more information, or where she was going.

"Back to work?" I already knew she was in the middle of a new project, working with the same American director who'd hired her for the superhero film that was coming out soon.

She inclined her head slightly. A sleek, black car pulled up before us. She stayed there, not acknowledging the car, taking her time to finish the cigarette. In a minute, she would be done. And this moment, however we chose to spend it, would pass.

"Arin," I said humbly. "You're right. I should have told you." She tensed, and I continued, finally voicing the words I'd been so terrified of: "Also, the other thing—I've let it go."

"Have you?"

Without my anger, what did I have left? Nothing. But it was a mistake to have clung to it for as long as I did, seeking refuge in its eclipse. An existence animated by anger wasn't the same thing as a life. And I had gone too far. I knew that now. I bit my lip. "That's all I wanted to say. That—and that I'm sorry. I really am."

She acknowledged this with a nod, staring intently at the slim cigarette pinched between her thumb and index finger. I saw her come to a decision.

"I'm going to say just one thing," she said. "And I don't want you interrupting till I'm done." She gave me a hard look. "Can you do that?"

I nodded.

She took a deep breath. "Back then, it's not like I didn't know I fucked up. But I guess, a part of me just wanted to see. See if you couldn't forgive me this one thing. After all, Genevieve, my whole life I chose you. I would have thrown myself into the sea a thousand times if it only made you happy. So when the time came, why couldn't you, you who had all the love in the world, choose *me*?" She looked into my face and smiled bitterly. It was the smile of someone who'd been running for a long time, only to realize they'd been running away from, not toward, the unutterable truth. "Don't answer that. I don't think there is an answer in the world you could give. And perhaps some questions shouldn't be asked, regardless. That's on me."

She finished her cigarette, threw it on the ground, and stomped it out with her dreadful heel.

"I don't know what I expected when you called," she said, "but it wasn't this. God, how I wish it wasn't this."

Her face was transparent with grief. Never in all our years together had I heard her voice sound so utterly lonesome. She had waited and waited for me to call, only understanding too late that as time went by, staying away had been her choice too.

"Arin," I said, finding my voice at last, "if I ever—"

"Stop," she interrupted. "I don't want to hear it. If you have a conscience, Jie. If you still care for me, even a little. Don't."

It was her calling me Jie that stopped me. Older sister. I don't think she even realized it herself. Her eyes burned, she turned her face from me and stared straight ahead, into the sky. She wouldn't look at me; afraid, perhaps, that after all this time I'd crumble her with some belated gesture of care, some useless protest of love.

How could I tell her that I understood? That in this hell of our own choices, the same anger that sealed us off could be a life raft too? I began to cry, but fought to get it under control. I owed her that much, at least. We stood side by side, me swallowing my sobs, Arin trembling with grim determination.

"Thank you," she said, when I had stopped, "for letting me go." Her voice was calm again, and steady. "Take care of yourself, Gen."

Arin took a step forward, reaching for the car door.

I couldn't help myself, I cried: "Will we see each other again?"

She froze. What wouldn't I have given, in that moment, to see her face? By the time she turned, her expression was cool. She held my gaze. Then, as if flicking a switch, her eyes warmed, slowly and deliberately, creasing at the edges, and a dimple appeared in her cheek. "Who knows," she said, and slipped into the backseat of the car. She didn't say goodbye. Only after the car rolled out of the driveway silently, leaving me standing there, did I realize the version of Arin she'd left me with, my last image of her, would be that of the same charm shared with the rest of the world.

I stayed in that driveway for a long time. And then, slowly, painfully, I turn and make my way home.

84

I haven't been back in a week, but the apartment is exactly as I'd left it. The shoji screen, torn and dirty, folded against the wall. The brown bead curtain, with its gaps and missing strands. The smell of albumen. Smatterings of dirt on the floor. The hum of the empty fridge, the flattened cushions, the books, yellowed and moth-bitten. The worn *Oxford English Dictionary*, lying face down on the couch. I close the gate behind me, then shut the door. The windows are sealed, the air still. I breathe in, deeply, but nothing of my mother remains—not her vanilla body cream, not the metallic tang of her vomit, not even the horse oil she used, toward the end, to moisturize her cheeks and neck. If there is anything of my mother left, it is hiding from me. I run my fingers down the fine layer of dust that has accumulated on the dining table in the short time I've been away, pinch it between my fingers, bring it to my nose. Nothing.

Things, how quickly they shift, how drastically. Once upon a time, I'd believed that no matter how we fought, no matter what happened, how far apart we were, Arin and I would in some ineffable sense stay entwined, trapped by our twin minds. I thought I'd live forever with a sense of Arin, looking over my shoulder, silently evaluating every action and choice I made. Now that sense is gone. Along with her suffocating absence—gone. I pick up the dictionary with its old, ripped cover, which my mother read in the last year of her life from front to back, like a storybook. Will things change again a year, five years into the future? Impossible to say. Who knows, Arin had said. I nod, put the dictionary down, and say, aloud, "Who knows." I'm shocked to hear my voice, thin and echoing around the apartment, alone.

I'm in the bedroom now, the bedroom of our childhood, where Arin, my mother, my father, and I had lived once, intertwined physically, aching constantly. The bedsheets are smooth, they do not bear the indentations of our last movements. There is no evidence that anything momentous has transpired in the last week of my mother's life.

And yet I am here and she is not.

I sink to my knees, reaching under the bed.

The Milo tin is still there. Who knows how long I stay like this, slumped on the floor, the lid pried off with a spoon, reading and rereading my old report cards stuffed with praise and promise, a printed photo of Arin at her award ceremony, glaring at the camera, her crumpled essay, "Land of Opportunity." Little trinkets I bought with my ice cream store money, useless things. I read through the folded notes my mother left me over the years, coming to rest on the last one—in her loopy chicken scratch, the ink of her handwriting already fading slightly, inscribed one April morning in the shadowy hours of predawn. It's the only handwriting of hers I have. I inhale deeply, willing the memory to surface, and for a split second it does. The metallic scent of blue pen ink swims on my tongue, the faint, ghostly impression of her hand dashing the letters off. I gasp, gratefully, breathing in its faint scent again and again. Then, before it settles into memory, it dissipates, and I'm back on the floor. A mirage.

I read through the binder, too, musing over our childish expressions of confidence, our analysis of human behavior. I'm struck by our simplistic belief that people and reality could be empirically qualified and thus understood, when it's the inexplicable surplus that makes us who we are. How naïve Arin and I were. Yet how precious it is now, to be able to hold in both hands evidence of the way our minds once worked. I take my time with it, lingering over each page.

Then, when it's done, I put the binder aside and grope around under the bed until I find it. The blue biscuit tin, with a painted print of a vaguely Scottish landscape, buried deep under the bed, covered in spiderwebs and dust. I wipe it down with the edge of my shirt and marvel at how cheap it looks, when once upon a time, we'd regarded it as a tin of treasures. I exert pressure on the lid. It pops open.

In it, the notes, essays, trinkets from Arin's childhood, the entrails of her life regurgitated in a strange, distorted mirror image of my own. Scrap paper, photos, report cards. I sift through them slowly. Here, the movie ticket stub from the show we'd watched together, after my O levels. Here, the first report card she'd gotten, the teacher's handwriting in black ink, commending her efforts but warning Arin's guardian about her reticence in class. Here, the certificate from the school, for the essay competition she'd won, ink from our principal's signature faded but still visible. Here, the Air New Zealand ticket, for November 2010. Here, one of her square, ringed notebooks from her visit, full of drawings, notes, impressions of sights and smells, pressed leaves of red and yellow. Here— and I'm surprised to see—a small, worn rectangle of card paper, one of my name cards from my time in Christchurch. Genevieve Yang, Secretary, Fifield & King. I hadn't known she had my name card, I'd never given it to her. She must have taken it from my stash, without my knowledge.

There is nothing left in the biscuit tin. I go through it one more time, turning each trinket from her life over in my hands, feeling her absence keenly, unsettled without knowing exactly why. Then it hits me. I sort through her things again, and again. It isn't there. I go back to my Milo tin, empty it out onto the floor, and search through everything. By the time I've gone through the contents of both tins several times, I'm just going through the motions, but I already know.

Everything from our lives, accumulated in those snappy, pathetic pieces of paper, souvenirs of a childhood, is untouched, save for our childhood contract, hastily but seriously drawn up and signed by us both. Till death do us part. I see, in my mind, Arin's tiny figure standing by the kitchen window the night of my grandmother's funeral, trembling, sliding the kitchen knife under the skin of her thumb. Her eyes on me as I press my fingers to the paper, the serious way she imitates me, as if promising that no matter where I go, she'd follow. The way she draws that same paper out of her dress pocket, under a naked streetlight, offering it to me. A promise. You promised. Remember? And her pause as she waits for my answer. As if I might, by taking or leaving the contract, irrevocably rend the fabric of our family. How young we were, how ignorant.

I go through the tins again. Just one last time, I tell myself, my hands moving desperately with a life of their own, touching each object, feeling for something long expired. Over and over and over again. It's just a piece of paper, a promise between children. It doesn't mean anything, it's not important. Yet still I search, and search.

Did Arin take it with her when she first left or did she return for it? Is she unlatching the door for a new way forward or pulling it shut behind her? I consult the echo of my heart and find it silent. All that remains are her last words to me.

Who knows.

Here I am with all this freedom; a life, finally, of my own, released of the responsibilities and humiliations of love, yet as I scramble to my feet, whipping around the room, feeling under the elastic of the bedsheets and tearing through the closets, why is it that the only feeling I'm left with is the doomed sense of it being too late?

I'm panting now, pushing my hair out of my face, standing in the center of this room, shirt sticking to my back, my chest. Settle down, a voice in me cries, yet I sway on my feet. Settle down. What voice is this, who is speaking? What a fool I've been, how much time I've wasted. How various our excuses, as we flail about in our attempts to avoid facing the shame of wanting love. And how inefficient love is, trapping and interrupting us, patiently delaying us until our brittle spirits thirst again for repair. Did you already know this, Ma, as you watched me stumble, as you held back for once in your disastrous, sparkling life? How much longer will you wait for me to realize that so long as we live and breathe, so long as our voices still tremble for each other, no separation is final? How long will I be doomed to stand in my own way?

Our lives stretch ahead of us in an unsigned promise. How young we still are, Arin, how careless we've been. Stay your heart, wait for me. Let us fail again. With the back of my hand I wipe the sweat from my brow, force myself to breathe. I'm still standing. I feel the old hesitation of pride, a second of resistance, then I take a step toward the door and allow myself to hope.

Acknowledgments

This book took nearly a decade to write, and I feel sick with love for the people who've buoyed me with their encouragement and belief through the long, long years. It would be impossible to list everyone I'm thankful for, but I'm going to try.

My immense gratitude to my incandescent agent, Jackie Ko, whose wisdom, clarity, and heart have irretrievably changed my life, along with the rest of the incredible team at The Wylie Agency, especially Jessica Bullock and Thomas Wee. To my glorious editor Lee Boudreaux at Doubleday Books for our many wonderful phone and office conversations about writing, for always being so down to get deep into the weeds with me, for loving Arin, Gen, and Su so profoundly, and for being the book's best champion. All my life I've dreamed of an editorial relationship like this. Thank you for making my dreams come true. Thank you to the dynamite Double-day team, especially Maya Pasic, Elena Hershey, Jess Deitcher, and Julie Ertl, who I've watched, awestruck, as they worked tirelessly on shepherding this book into the world, plus the incredible PRH sales reps and indie booksellers for their early fervor. Thank you to Jane Cavolina for her careful copyedits. And thank you to my ingenious UK editor Alexa von Hirschberg for her brilliant, astute notes, and the rest of the Weidenfeld & Nicolson team for their immense enthusiasm and for bringing *The Original Daughter* across the Commonwealth and, most important, home, to Singapore.

To my Pansing team in Singapore and Malaysia, especially David Tay, Samantha Teo, Regina Quek, and Cheryl Goh, and the larger TIMES team, thank you for being my cheerleaders (and my book dealers!) all the way from when I was a reader to now, as an author.

To Gillian Tan from Clicknetwork TV and Munkysuperstar Pictures, where I was trained, mentored, and cared for—thank you for seeing me through the sweat and chaos and taking a chance on me. To my Clicknetwork TV crew, especially Vera Ang and Daniel Koh, thank you for always looking out for me. To my onscreen and real-life soul sister, Roz Pho, thanks for the adventures of a lifetime.

Various fellowships, scholarships, and grants gave me the time and space needed to develop this book fully, and boy, did I need a lot of time! I am especially grateful to Singapore's National Arts Council, Nanyang Technological University, Bread Loaf Writers' Conference, Sewanee Writers' Conference, Columbia University, Stanford University, and Writers in Paradise for cash and institutional support.

I wrote a lot of this novel in the coworking space The Hive Singapore, in Jewel Changi Airport's Starbucks, in the lobby of lower Manhattan's Ace Hotel, and in various rented apartments. Thank you to the Hive team, especially Yun Quek, Ryan Warner, Dayana Khafiz, and Iffa Khalissa, and my Starbuddies, Cheyenne Ng, Steph Loi, and Tan Li Lan, for your generous support as I overcaffeinated and wrote and wrote and wrote.

For sharing their medical expertise, thank you, Doctor Kay Ng, Doctor Gene Tan, and Elissa Wong. For answering my myriad questions on geography and Singapore's housing policies, thank you, Edwin Sia (realtor extraordinaire!!), Dr. Chih Hoong Sin, and Jasmine Tan from Singapore's Housing Development Board. And special thanks to my mother, Wendy Wei, for her unwavering help with my research on adoption, Singapore's developing years, and economic whiplash, and irresistible gossip (!!!) by tapping into her network of friends and aunties, who were immensely generous with their anecdotes, stories, and experiences. Being able to pick up the phone and call her, no matter where I was in the world, with questions and for the tea, has been one of the great joys of revising this book.

To my first reader, Heng Xiao Qi, who for over a decade has

endured my impossible attempts at prose and poetry, and read all my stories, emails, thought salads. To my tribe of hearts on whom my character was cut: Georgina Pang, Frederick Sia, Jenna Lim Ying, Emmanuel Goh, Martin Hong, Elissa Wong, Roz Pho, Yohei Ueno, Lexy Leong, Muhammed Shazwan, Edwin Sia, Amanda Wong, Marcus Tan, Tan Li Lan, Candice Choo, Seth Koh, Hansheng Tan, Ian Kong, Joshua Conceicao, Dafril Phua. It feels illegal, how we found one another so early in life, how much love this village has. Thank you for showing up for me at every stage in life, for early conversations about life, books, and character—I am so grateful for you all.

I moved to New York in search of a writer's life and she more than answered. Thank you to Grace Shuyi Liew—I can't believe we wrote our debuts side by side; it feels like we truly grew up together as writers. To Vanessa Chan and Gina Chung, what a writing life we've found together. There's no one else I'd rather write, weep, strive, and karaoke with.

For couch space and being my home away from home, Jackson Liang and Kate Pang. For found family across the world, Isabel Tan.

Thank you, thank you, thank you.

The Stegner has truly been a land of enchantment, fueled by so many flights of conviction. Rabia Saeed, Ashley Hand, Yohanca Delgado, Jonathan Escoffery, Francisco Gonzales, Faith Merino, Rose Himber Howse, Zach Williams, and Kyle Edwards—thank you for being the first people to read an early draft of this novel in full, and for holding her so carefully. Thank you, Adam Johnson, Elizabeth Tallent, and Chang-Rae Lee, for your mentorship and guidance, and for two years of pure magic. And thank you, Nicholas Jenkins, Christina Ablaza, Danielle Huliganga, and Mailan Smith, for making it all possible. I could not have written this book without the Stegner, and am forever grateful for the Californian life we built together: our many precious conversations on writing, our Tuesday Good News Train, our hype crew, and for always staying way past closing time.

Gratitude to my 2015–2016 Nanyang Technological University CW workshop, 2022 Bread Loaf cohort, 2023 Sewanee gang, 2019–2022 Columbia MFA mates for community in the most fragmented times, especially to Jami Nakamura Lin, Cindy Juyoung Ok, Marcela Fuentes, Jesse Ren Marshall, Marcus Tan, Connie Chen, Gauraa Shekhar, Elliot Alpern, Theo Spielberg, Nathaniel Berry, Liza Stewart, Melita Granger, Kim Hew-Low, Jinwoo Chong, Alex Burchfield, and Ronald Lee Robertson Jr. To Qian Julie Wang, Rachel Heng, Jeremy Tiang, Rozz Lee, Morgan Talty, Sterling HolyWhiteMountain, Katie Devine, Kate Tooley, R.O. Kwon, Vanessa Hua, Kirstin Chen, and Ingrid Rojas Contreras, a million hugs and thanks for welcoming me so warmly into your cities and lives, and for the various ways you've been a part of this journey.

To Tash Aw, to whom I owe my writing life. To Divya Victor, Jing-Jing Lee, Keri Bertino, Barrie Sherwood, Amy Grace Loyd, Joshua Furst, Monique Truong, Maurice Carlos Ruffin, Cara Blue Adams, Nicholas Christopher, BK Fischer, Rivka Galchen, Corinna Barsan, and Lara Vapnyar, for belief and encouragement. To Binnie Kirshenbaum, for tears and chairs. To Elizabeth Tallent, for seeing not just the work, but me, clearly. To Paul Beatty, for reminding me to make the work sing. An eternal debt of gratitude to you all.

Thank you to my parents, En Yi and Wendy Wei, for whom I would actually excavate my whole heart. My sisters, Keziah and Keran, for being my chosen, as well as blood, family. Thank you, Cheng Hong, Jamie, and Shaun Lim, for enfolding me so readily into your home and family.

How much love can a person hold? Thank you to my husband, Shane Lim, whose love renews me every day. Who has read everything I've written, spent hours talking through stories and syntax with me, designed writing prompts and character art, and literally moved across the world for me and my writing. My partner in life, mind, faith, and heart. I can't believe you exist.

Finally: thank you to the present tense for encompassing possibility and hope. To semicolons for weighing and joining. Love, I'm grateful for love.

ABOUT THE AUTHOR

Jemimah Wei was born and raised in Singapore; she is now based between Singapore and the United States. She was a Wallace Stegner Fellow at Stanford University and a Felipe P. De Alba Fellow at Columbia University, where she earned her MFA. A recipient of awards and fellowships from Singapore's National Arts Council, Sewanee Writers' Conference, Bread Loaf Writers' Conference, and Writers in Paradise, she was named one of *Narrative*'s "30 Below 30" writers and is a Francine Ringold Award for New Writers honoree. Her fiction has won the William Van Dyke Short Story Prize and appears in *Guernica*, *Narrative*, and *Nimrod*, among other publications. For close to a decade, Wei was a host for various broadcast and digital channels, and has written and produced short films and travel guides for Laneige, Airbnb, and Nikon. This is her first novel.

Credits